SAND RIVER

SAND RIVER

James Osbon

Library of Congress Control Number: 2013903351
ISBN: Hardcover   978-1-4797-9990-9
               Softcover   978-1-4797-9989-3
               Ebook   978-1-4797-9991-6

This is a work of fiction. Names, characters, places and incidents either are the product of the author's imagination or are used fictitiously, and any resemblance to any actual persons, living or dead, events, or locales is entirely coincidental.

This book was printed in the United States of America.

Rev. date: 03/27/2013

To order additional copies of this book, contact:
Xlibris Corporation
1-888-795-4274
www.Xlibris.com
Orders@Xlibris.com
129245

Contents

To every native Aiken resident who loves his hometown.

To every ex-Aiken resident who longs to move back.

To every Aiken transplant who never wants to leave.

To every new citizen who finally finds home.

PREFACE

Can I admit to a small amount of embarrassment when I tell you that I love Aiken—or at least I think I do?

I mean, I love it almost like you would love a woman; that's why it is embarrassing to admit. So what would be more natural than to write a story based there? That's partially what *Sand River* is all about.

I left Aiken to go to college when I was eighteen, in 1956. At the time, I didn't have any mature appreciation for the good fortune I had fallen into by being born there and living those first years there. If you had asked me at eighteen, I would have probably told you that I thought I was from a backwater well-off-the-beaten-path obscure little town called Aiken. In college, at times I was guilty of joking about Aiken—not in a mean, callous way—by answering the question "Exactly where is Aiken?" by telling the person that it was midway between Vaucluse and Montmorenci. Then I would walk away with no further explanation. It was like saying Washington DC was between Annandale and Chevy Chase.

I don't remember when I finally grew up, gained a better perspective, and could answer with pride about Aiken, but it did not come to me fast and did not jump off the page as my strongest suit. But it did happen, and this book is an attempt to correct an error and wallow in true regret about how I slighted it.

Most of the population of Aiken is made up of people who were born there, went to schools there, and ultimately lived their lives there. But the main people in this story came to Aiken from somewhere else, and the events in Aiken happened to them and permanently re-formed their characters in the story. Aiken stamped its brand on them, and they were forever changed.

The narrative starts in 1948 and continues to the present. A ten-year-old boy, Casey Gannon, is forced to relocate from out West to Aiken because of the unexpected death of his mother. By happenstance, his only relatives lived in Aiken, but he is not warmly welcomed by them at first. He is savvy enough to realize that any chance of a happy life will have to happen for him in Aiken, and he makes this discovery early enough to use the friendliness of the town to help in his development toward becoming a contributing adult.

You will see that I have come to my own conclusions that Aiken is unique and the story tries to make that point. The origin of the book germinated in my head when a midwestern-based Woodside newcomer met me, realized that I was a native, and said, "Jim, we really love your hometown, but we can't figure out what it is that has grabbed us so firmly. You're a native. What is it?"

It is my greatest desire for this book to answer that question.

ADAPTING

Chapter 1

As the train inched into the station, ten-year-old Casey Gannon's somber face was pressed against the glass of his dingy railcar to get a brief look at this new hometown that he had neither asked for nor wanted. The sign mounted on the roof simply read "Aiken." It was August 1948, and he was now somewhere in the back country of South Carolina and a long way from Butte, Montana.

The aging black conductor helped him down the challenging steep steps to a faded concrete platform. "Sonny, is somebody goin' to meet you here?"

Casey answered in his weakest voice, "I don't know. Somebody s'pose to. I don't care if they don't. Won't bother me none. And don't call me Sonny." He half pleaded and tried to stare down his helper. He struggled some with the small attaché case he was carrying.

The rumpled Casey had been riding trains for three days, and he was tired of it and needed this one-way trip to be finished to get off this damn train. The kindly conductor ignored the admonition and added, "I'll make sure your trunk gets off, but you have to find it by yourself when they put it inside."

"Thank you," Casey grunted halfheartedly, remembering that he had been taught some manners as he went into the Aiken passenger depot as the sole rider who got off.

He dragged his small duffel bag and his mother's attaché case to a bench and sat down. A few people were milling around outside, but he was the lone person in the waiting room. A single ticket agent stood behind the counter. After a few minutes, the agent came over to him and asked, "Sonny, would you be Casey Gannon?"

"Yes, sir, but I ain't no Sonny," he answered.

"I just got a call from your aunt and uncle. She told me that they will be here to fetch you in about ten minutes."

"Okay," replied Casey more meekly than he intended in a faint voice. His confidence was low.

He had thought for days that this was not a good idea, and he imagined that it wasn't going well already. *Maybe they're as sour about me coming here as I am about being here*, he thought. *For sure, they don't want me.*

The endless rocking railroad tracks and faceless cities and towns of the past three days still rumbled through his small body. Like a man at sea for several days, the earth seemed to be moving slightly from the incessant swaying back and forth and the clicking and clacking of the joints of the tracks. The blurred snippets he saw of Cheyenne, Omaha, Kansas City, and Nashville would be in his head for a while. He had bisected wheat fields, swaying cornstalks as far as one could see, treeless plains, woodsy landscapes and mountains, and the filthy back streets of city slums, all piled up in a telescopic period. It had all been just outside the window. It took all of his restraint to not take off and run away in Kansas City, but to where? How could a ten-year-old survive out there?

Then his mind jumped back to why he was here. His dear mother had just died tragically, and he had no one in Butte who was close enough to take care of him. No relatives, no family, nothing. If a person needed proof that life wasn't fair, Casey was today's poster boy. His father was dead, a victim of the Battle of the Bulge four years ago, so that was no option. And now his mother, too, was gone. He felt as if the very legs had been cut out from under him by a life he had taken for granted and had been enjoying.

A ten-year-old boy couldn't live by himself, they all said. He had to find some relatives who would agree to take him in. He had heard the sheriff of Silver Bow County say it himself. And he heard those social workers say it too. The problem was that there was only one set of relatives who could even be asked—and they lived in some godforsaken place called Aiken, South Carolina.

So after a long talk with Mr. Grover—his mother's boss and store owner in Butte—he understood that as much as he was liked in Montana, there was no one there whom he could live with. Casey pleaded, but to no avail. Nobody would agree to take him. The tragic circumstances led Mr. Grover to have a meeting with the sheriff and some county workers in order to pool their information about the late Sgt. George Gray Gannon, his daddy, and his now-deceased mama, Vera Dudley Gannon, so that they could decide the best course for the son, Casey.

A swarm of phone calls and telegrams ricocheted back and forth between Montana and South Carolina, and now he was being unflinchingly uprooted. He stood up and shuffled around the lobby of the depot, finally venturing outside for a closer look at this foreign place. He heard the old conductor announce, "All aboard for Trenton and Edgefield. Trenton and Edgefield, next stop."

He thought it was hot and sticky. It didn't look or feel like Montana. He saw street signs at the corner that said Union Street on one and Park Avenue on the other. The railroad track curved gently as it crossed Park Avenue. He watched as the train incrementally crept away from the Aiken station, on its way north.

He went back inside to cool off and wait, stopping at the water fountain to taste a sip of cold water. In two more minutes, a woman walked in and smiled broadly at him as she approached.

"You have to be Casey Gannon, right?" she said and focused in on the saddest face she thought she had ever seen. She sat next to him and added, "Where are your bags? Do you have any more luggage?"

He told her that he thought his trunk was in the baggage room. She talked to the agent, and in a minute or two, it was all outside being loaded into the rear of a 1939 Hudson idling at the curb. The middle-aged man sitting behind the wheel impatiently said, "C'mon, let's hurry up. I got to get back to work." The woman gave him such a scathing frown that if it were a blowtorch, blisters would have formed on his face.

Casey got in the backseat, and she sat in front. "Casey, this is your uncle, Jake Gannon. I'm your aunt. My name is Anne Gannon. Welcome to Aiken."

Jake shifted the car into gear and drove off, saying impatiently, "Y'all can visit all afternoon. I had to take off from work to pick you up, boy, and I got to get back." She gave him that searing look again.

Jake drove down Park Avenue, turned right on Laurens Street, and puttered briefly through a small business district to the north. At the top of a slight hill, the car turned left onto Edgefield and drove past the standpipe.

"What's that?" Casey asked, pointing at the green structure.

"That's our standpipe," Anne Gannon answered. "It's where our water supply comes from. It's full of water."

The car turned right on Pendleton Street and soon parked in front of a tiny one-story gray bungalow. "This is where we live, Casey. We're home," Anne said.

Jake left the car running while he unloaded everything to the small front porch. "I'm gone. Got to go earn some money. Be home at six thirty," he said brusquely. Then he drove off. Casey felt himself sag a little bit as the car disappeared.

Without explanation or apology, Anne showed Casey the entire small house. It was basic and served the needs of two people. She knew it would be crowded and uncomfortable trying to absorb another person. He finally said, "I'm so tired. I've been riding trains for three days and sleeping sitting up. Can you let me sleep for a little while?"

She immediately responded, "Yes, of course. Just take off your shoes and lie down on this couch." And he did.

She found a light blanket and covered him, again taking in the lines of sadness in his face. "I'll be in the back of the house. We'll talk when you wake up," she added. She turned on an oscillating fan on the mantel and left the room, quietly closing the door behind her. He was asleep in less than a minute.

Casey's father, George Gannon, had been born in Augusta, Georgia, in 1917, seven years after his older brother, Jake. It was fewer than twenty miles from Aiken. He had attended schools there and graduated in 1934 from Richmond Academy, an ROTC-type of public high school.

The Gannon family was known in the area as operating the best hardware store for a hundred miles around. It did pretty well even in the teeth of the Great Depression. George had planned for his whole life to work in the family business after high school. However, he had a wild side and an impulsive temperament that created ongoing friction with his far older parents. A few months after graduation, he had a big fight with his father over business decisions. George was so mad that when he departed, his comment was, "I swear to you, I will never be back here. You will never see me again." He left that day and started hitchhiking to California.

George's older brother, Jacob, also had his plans set for a lifetime of working in the family's hardware store. Jake was very different from George and more driven by what a handful of dollars would buy. But even Jake had big issues with trying to get along in the family. He partied and drank too much, could be generally disagreeable, and hung around with too many of the wrong element, as his parents put it. They were aging quickly and had always privately counted on George, not the older Jake, to be the son who would take over the business. They felt that Jake's demeanor was not suited to management and ownership. After George abruptly left, they decided to sell the operation to people outside the family. Within a few months, they did that quietly and retired to Sea Island. Jake was crushed and complained bitterly to them as he resigned. He left Augusta in a huff, moving to Aiken in 1938.

For as long as the younger brother George lived in California, he spent all of his time in Monterey, Salinas, and Carmel. On the Monterey Peninsula, he partied, sunned, drank, swam, and met a lot of attractive girls. One of these was eighteen-year-old Vera Dudley. She was the only child of a ranching couple in the Carmel Valley outside of Monterey.

About the time George and Vera began to date each other exclusively, her parents concluded that her future was about to be settled and decided to sell their ranch so that they could move into town. Poor health had forced them to want to be nearer good health facilities.

So George and Vera married in Carmel in early 1937. He was only twenty, and she was a younger nineteen. They lived in an apartment in Monterey, and he worked for a while on a fishing boat.

Within the next year, both of Vera's elderly parents died within a few months of each other and left her a modest amount of money. George and Vera needed it because she discovered she was pregnant. With that news, they decided to make a break away from California. George had heard of great jobs in copper mining in Butte, Montana, and they decided to settle there before their baby was born.

George was quickly hired by Anaconda Copper Mining, and the couple rented a small house. His job went well, and his manager doted on him as an example of how to be successful at Anaconda. Within a year, he had advanced in his job and saved enough money to pay for the baby and to buy a used 1931 Ford Model A, which George taught Vera to drive.

Vera stayed home to raise their baby, Casey Carter Gannon. Life was good, and they were thriving.

Then the United States was bombed at Pearl Harbor, Hawaii, on December 7, 1941. A mammoth wave of patriotism swept over the country. This led George and a great many other American men to join the armed forces. As soon as he was off in army training, Vera decided to get a part-time job at a general store, Grover Mercantile, in Butte. A friendly neighbor volunteered to tend to three-and-a-half-year-old Casey because she had a son about the same age.

In December 1944, Vera was officially notified that her husband had been killed in action in Belgium and was being awarded the Silver Star for bravery in combat. She and Casey were devastated but vowed to keep on moving forward. She asked Mr. Grover if she could go to full-time employment, and he agreed to it. During the next four years, both Vera and Casey matured very fast and became extremely close.

It was after four o'clock in the afternoon when Casey woke up from a deep nap. He wandered farther into the small structure where he found Anne in the kitchen listening quietly to the radio. *Ma Perkins* was on.

"You want something to drink, maybe some iced tea, honey?" she asked him.

"Yes'm, I'm pretty thirsty," he replied.

After he finished his drink, she said, "Let's go out on the back porch to talk some. It's a lot cooler out there." The backyard had a mature sycamore tree standing majestically right in the middle, which provided total shade from the hot August sun.

For the first time, he had a good chance to look at her and size her up. She looked to him to be about midthirties and pretty. She had a warm way about her as well. When they sat down, he said right away, "Mrs. Gannon, I have to ask you something."

She laughed lightly and said, "Casey sweetie, I can't let you call me Mrs. Gannon. I'm your aunt. You need to call me Aunt Anne, or Aunt Annie, or Aunt Annie Lou, but Mrs. Gannon just won't work."

He reddened from the embarrassment of having to be corrected. "I'm sorry. I never had a real aunt myself before. If I call you Aunt Annie Lou, is that okay?"

"That'll be just fine. And I want you to remember to call Jake Uncle Jake. His real name is Jacob, but nobody calls him that. Now, what did you want to ask me?"

He squirmed a bit and looked at the floor, but finally blurted out his question, "Do y'all want me here? I sure as hell don't want to be here."

Bam! What a question out of the mouth of a ten-year-old! She and Jake had been arguing and fighting hard for two weeks over that very question. And it was obvious from Jake's actions in the car that Casey's presence in Aiken was not popular with him. Casey surely had seen that.

Jake had previously explained his position very clearly. "Annie, we don't have room or the money for another person to live in this house. And we've never had any kids in our home in ten years of marriage. I'm not used to them. They're trouble. I don't want to change my life to cater to a damn ten-year-old boy. Let him go live with somebody else." And he was usually quick to explain that these were his true feelings and had been for a long time. He had never pictured himself as the father of small children. It seemed to be financially beyond them too. He saw everything in selfish adult terms and how it was going to affect him.

To counter his opinion, Anne had explained her own stance this way. "I think I would make a fine mother of a ten-year-old boy. He doesn't have anybody else but us. This is your brother's child. He is your nephew, for God's sake, your own blood! He will bring a different mood into our home, and I'll work hard to make sure it is a positive change. As far as this house and the money are concerned, somehow we'll make it work. If you give it a chance, your life might even get better."

Anne Gannon had secretly wanted to have children for most of her adult life. When they married, her unspoken plan was to eventually, gradually persuade Jake to get her pregnant so that they could be parents like almost everybody else their age. She had not succeeded with this and saw the arrival of Casey as a possible miracle from the heavens, a chance to raise a child even if it wasn't hers.

It was time to give Casey an answer to the question. "Casey, as you might know, we have never had children in our home, even though we've been married for ten years. We are going to work very hard, particularly me, to make sure that all three of us are happy with living together. I'm eager to give you a good home and to learn to love you as my own. Jake is not convinced that I am right about this. He doesn't think this house can hold another person. He's worried about the money it might take. He's got some other problems, and you'll probably see them soon enough. He drinks too hard and gambles too much. He thinks only of himself sometimes. He's pretty disagreeable sometimes. He'll need some time to adjust to having another man in the house. You understand? It would be best if, especially at the beginning, you take care to be on your very best behavior. We don't need to give him any reasons to dislike the arrangement or to blow up at you over some little thing. And I don't like hearing the word *hell* come out of the mouth of a ten-year-old. No cussing in this house."

"Okay," he said at last. "But I don't want to be here. I'm real worried about y'all. I could tell he doesn't like me much. But I remember what Mr. Grover told me out in Butte, 'Casey, you don't have anybody else but these people.' I told him that I had never even met you before. He said that he knew that and that maybe in time everything would be all right."

"And I know that, Casey," she said. "We are all going to work hard to make this situation work out for the best. I'll try to get Jake to be more agreeable and to accept this situation. But you have to try too. You have to give it a real chance."

She thought for a few seconds and then started to talk. "You don't know much of anything about us or about Aiken, so I need to tell you about your new life here. Let me start with me. Before I married Jake, my name was Anne Louise Harper. I was born and raised on a farm out in the middle of Georgia, about eighty miles from here. I was one of seven children. We grew all kinds of things and raised animals. By the time I was your age, I had milked cows, plowed fields behind a mule, killed chickens to eat, and cooked big meals for the whole family.

"Then my mama died of rheumatic fever when I was thirteen. My daddy said, 'Annie Lou, you are now this family's cook and caretaker. It's your job to feed us each day and get these younger children and yourself off to school every day.' I tell you, Casey, I was overwhelmed."

"You knew how to milk cows? And kill things to eat? Did you ever ride horses too?" Casey asked.

"Yes, I did all of that," she admitted. "I won't tell you I always enjoyed it, but I did it."

"I've rode horses some too," Casey countered.

Anne nodded and continued. "We had a family habit of going into town every month or so to shop for clothes, buy a few groceries, and go to a picture show. On one of these weekends—in 1935—I met Jake Gannon at a church social. They were having dinner on the ground at his church on the 'Hill' in Augusta. He was twenty-five and I was nineteen. We started dating on and off and we finally got married in 1938. I can tell you I was ready to leave farm life and live in town for a while. I was tired. My brothers and sisters did the same thing. None of them farm anymore. They are spread out from New Orleans to Atlanta to Tampa, and all of them live in town.

"At first, Jake and I lived in a rented apartment in Augusta while he worked for his daddy in their hardware store. Then they had a big fight over money and how to run the business and so Jake quit. He had been learning the hardware business and already knew a lot.

"Jake drove over here to Aiken and got a job in one of the hardware stores here as a salesclerk. That's when we moved to Aiken and rented this house. That was about six years ago, right during the middle of the war. We've been here ever since, but Jake has changed jobs a few times. He's good at what he does, but sometimes he's hard to get along with and his behavior gets him in trouble. It's lucky for us that a lot of hardware stores operate in Aiken."

Casey asked, "Do you work too?"

"No, not really. Oh, I have a sometimes part-time job, I guess, during the school year. My biggest hobby is history, all kinds of history. Since high school, I have read all kinds of American history books, Georgia history books, and a few about South Carolina. Sometimes, Aiken Grammar School lets me substitute for the history teacher in one of the grades. I always enjoy that. And I do get paid a little bit for it.

"One of my good friends in Aiken works at the county library. She feeds me new books about South Carolina and even about Aiken as soon as she gets them. Casey, you are going to like Aiken, I think. It has an interesting past and is pretty interesting right now. I can't wait to show you this sweet little town. Most people who live here really like it, and I know you will too."

He answered, "I don't know. I hope so. I already miss Butte and miss Mama even more."

"You poor child. You haven't even had a decent time to grieve for the loss of your mama. Of course, you miss her! I will pay more attention to that." With that comment, she decided to change the subject.

"Do you feel like a little walk around the neighborhood just to get a better idea of where you live? I'll go with you, of course."

"Yes'm, I feel like a little walk. Are we far from that standpipe we rode by this morning?"

She responded, "No, it's not far at all, just two or three blocks from here. We can walk over there and back."

When they left the bungalow, they walked toward Bethany Cemetery. She talked as they walked. "Just about everybody who dies gets buried over there," she pointed out. "Our house here is at the edge of what is known as Toole Hill."

"Why's it called that?" asked Casey.

"Well, most of the land in this area of town used to be owned by a lawyer named Mr. Toole, and he just sold it off gradually for these houses. And you can see, it is on a little bit of a hill."

They walked on the edge of Hampton Avenue to its intersection with Laurens Street, the same street on which the standpipe stood. They turned right at a small grocery store

and walked down a slight hill and then back up another hill
to the structure itself.

Anne was thinking about some of the things she had
learned in her first years here—that Aiken's streets are very
wide and unusual compared to most small towns, that there
are approximately one hundred blocks of these very wide
streets. For the busiest of them, public travel evolved so that
on one side, cars had adequate space to travel south, for
example, and the other side had enough space to travel north.
Sometimes, a grassy median stood between the two sides.

Laurens Street was Aiken's best known downtown street
because it traveled directly through the main business district.
Sometimes, people just called it Main Street. The southbound
lanes were just paved for the first time last summer. The
standpipe was located only two blocks from the center of
downtown. It was erected in 1893 and was one of two in the
town. She spoke of these things to Casey as they walked slowly.

When Casey arrived at the tall green standpipe, he was
able to walk up to it and rap his knuckles against the metal

plates, making him smile. Several large water mains were attached to the base at equidistant points around it. He sat on one of these mains and pretended he was riding a horse. The circular standpipe, which projected upward well over a hundred feet, was sitting in the middle of Edgefield Avenue just a mere fifty feet from the edge of Laurens. "This is pretty special," he said. "This whole street is nice. Do you know what makes it special for me? It's the trees. In Butte, there ain't many trees to look at. Here, there's trees everywhere you look."

"*Aren't*," she corrected, "not *ain't*. I ain't a-gonna let you say ain't," she said in a mocking singsong voice. "I plan to correct you every time." He finally loosened up and smiled when she sang it to him in the cadenced way she did. *Oh my God, he can smile*, she thought.

"And look at that pretty house right over there," he said, pointing at a large two-story Victorian home with large wraparound porches. "That almost looks like a Butte house. It's nice."

"Yes, it is," she said. "That's where the Marvin family lives. Been there a long time.

"Let's head back home. I've got to start on supper. Jake will be home before long and he likes to eat on time." She added as they walked, "Jake works only three blocks from here, so he's always pretty close by. Some days, I make him a sandwich for lunch and walk it down to him. He always drives the car because I can't drive. He promises to teach me how, but we haven't done it yet. Once you've driven a mule or a buckboard, a car doesn't look too hard to me.

"Tomorrow, if you'd like, we'll go for a walk all over the downtown part of Aiken. We can do that in two hours, and you'll get to see more of this pretty town."

Casey answered her, "I'd like to look around some. It don't look too hard to do. I mean, the hills are just little ones."

As he said he would, Jake walked in the front door at six thirty. He made a little nod in Casey's direction as he went through the living room, but said nothing. Anne led him immediately to their bedroom and closed the door for a brief talk about being nicer to Casey. He couldn't make out the words, but he could tell that they were heated comments. Within five minutes, the three of them were seated at the table in the kitchen area, and Anne asked Casey if he could say grace over the meal. He repeated the simple prayer his mother had taught him, and they started to eat, very quietly at first.

On his first bite, Casey started to discover that his aunt Annie Lou was a terrific cook. They were having fried chicken, mashed potatoes with gravy, corn sticks, and butterbeans. At the end was a fresh peach cobbler. Casey ate ravenously. Jake noticed and said, "Yeah, you get it. Her food tastes pretty good, don't it, buster? I agree with you. She knows her way around a streak o'lean." Casey just nodded as if he knew what that was.

Toward the end of dessert, Jake said, "When we finish here, I want to talk to you on the back porch. There are some things I need to say before any more time goes by."

"Yes, sir," Casey muttered nervously.

Anne asked, "Jake, can I sit in on what y'all talk about? I have to know what goes on here too."

"Yeah," Jake grunted. "You need to be there too."

When the dishes were washed, dried, and put away, the three of them went to the small screened back porch. There were only two chairs there, so Casey sat on the floor looking up at them.

Jake had some papers in his hand. He laid them down and lit up a Camel. "Boy, I guess you know this had to be a big surprise to Annie and me. As far as we cared, you and your mama were total strangers who lived in another state and that we were probably never goin' to meet. Y'all had your lives, and we had ours. Then all of a sudden, she's dead and you've got no place to live. You can look around in this house and see that there's not enough room for you to live here. Except for the couch, there's no place for you to sleep."

He continued. "I realize your daddy has been dead since you were six years old, and he was gone from home for a while before that. You might not even remember him, is that about right?"

"Just barely," Casey said.

"Well, I hadn't seen him for a long time either. I was seven years older than George, so we didn't exactly run around in the same herd when we were living at home in Augusta. But here we are years later and you got no place to live, I guess, and it seems like it falls on us, me and Annie. You ought to realize though that it's as much a shock to us as it is to you. Not the best news in the world to hear Vera's dead and you have to come here to live with us. Truth be told, I'd just as soon you went back to Montana.

"I've never been a daddy before and haven't been around young'ns much. When being a parent is just forced on you, you have to try hard to adjust to it. If you're gonna be here, we're gonna have some rules and you're gonna have to follow them, or we're gonna have a lot of damn trouble, you and me. I expect you to obey me and Annie when we tell you to do something. I expect you to say 'yes sir' to me and 'yes ma'am' to her. I expect you to be one hundred percent honest with us and never tell us a lie. I expect you to behave so that you bring credit to this family name and not make us ashamed to be Gannons.

"You'll find out soon enough, I guess, that I know some important people in Aiken, just from working in hardware stores for a few years. I know the police chief, Mr. George. I know Sheriff Fallaw. I know Odell Weeks, the mayor. I even met the governor, Mr. Thurmond, a few times. He's around here some when he's not in Columbia or when he's not running for president. I don't want to have to ever, ever have to explain to those people about your bad behavior. I expect solid passing grades in school. I don't expect to have to give you money just so you can go have yourself a good time. You can pay for your good times yourself, not me. We'll pay for the food and the clothes somehow. If you need more than that, you better think about finding some little jobs around here."

Anne cut in. "Jake, don't be so mean to him. He's only ten years old. Who would hire a ten-year-old boy?"

"Oh, I'm not being mean. There's all kinds of things he can do. Pick up trash for people, take drink bottles back to the store, sell newspapers, cut grass, rake yards, paint fences. He's got to be thinking about how to earn some money. We won't be supporting him forever. You understand what I'm tellin' you, boy?"

"Yes, sir, I get it. Do you mind if I say something and ask a question?"

"What is it?" Jake asked.

Casey answered, "I'll try to do those things, and I promise to say 'yes sir' and I promise to call you Uncle Jake, but I want you to promise to call me Casey and not 'boy,' okay? I heard you say you don't really want me here. I'll tell you something too. I don't want to live here with you either."

Jake sat back, chuckled, and said, "You got some gumption, don't cha? Okay, I guess you got yourself a deal. No more 'boy' if I can help it. And I heard you say you'd rather be anywhere but here. I got that too."

Then Jake picked up the loose papers he brought to the porch. "We got two letters from Montana while you were riding here on the train. I want to read both of them to you. Pay attention now. Only gonna read'm once."

He lit another Camel and continued. "This first letter is from Mr. Willus Grover, the owner of Grover Mercantile, of Butte, Montana."

Dear Mr. Gannon,

It was sad to have to talk to you on the telephone several days ago to tell you the awful news about Mrs. Vera Gannon's untimely death. As I said to you then, it was just a fluke that she had listed you as a relative on one of our employment forms. Without that piece of information, our job in finding you would have been more difficult.

I want to give you a full account in writing of her death so that your family will have all the answers as to what happened here in Butte.

On Friday evening, I had asked her to work on Saturday and for her to meet me at my Mercantile store at 8:00 a.m. She said she could do it because her son, Casey, was spending the night on a campout with the Cub Scouts. She must have misunderstood the time because the evidence now shows that she arrived at 7:00 a.m. and the door was locked, preventing her from getting into the store. It was unusually cold that morning, so she got back in the car and started the engine in order to run the car's heater.

The car is a 1931 Ford, not in good repair. I arrived around eight o'clock as I had planned and saw her car running in its usual parking space very near mine. I knocked on the window because she was still in the driver's seat. When she did not respond, I got a tire iron and forced open her door, turned off the engine, and opened all of the windows. Then I went inside the store and called an ambulance.

When they arrived ten minutes later, they started emergency treatment immediately and took off for the hospital. They could not revive her. She was already dead. A mechanic has looked at the car since then and found a rusted floorboard, which let in carbon monoxide.

I know that she had a small life insurance policy because we discussed that subject more than once, so you should be hearing from them soon. I told them where Casey would be located in the future. I am planning to sell the car and send the proceeds to you as soon as all investigations are finished.

There is a small amount of talk about this death being a suicide, but only because a few desperate people have used this method to end their lives. I knew Vera well and I can assure you and Casey that *this was an unfortunate accident, pure and simple, not a suicide.*

Casey stayed with my family after his mother died, right up until we put him on the train to go to the east. He is a nice boy and I know he would have loved to stay here with us indefinitely. But we have four children already, a fifth on the way, and a house busting at the seams. We could not have done justice to raising him properly.

Warm regards to you and to Casey,

Willus Grover

Jake folded the letter and put it back in the envelope and asked Casey, "Do you have any questions about the letter and what he had to say?"

During the reading, Casey had gotten very quiet and attentive and may have sniffled once or twice while reliving the past two weeks in memory. He finally said in a whisper, "No, sir."

"Then let's get on to the second letter. It's from the insurance company that Mr. Grover talked about. Here's what it says."

Dear Mr. Gannon,

I represent the Iron Mountain Insurance Company in the matter of the death of our insured, Vera Dudley Gannon. We understand that you will be the legal guardian of the lone beneficiary, Casey Carter Gannon.

Mrs. Gannon had a whole life policy with us in case of her death. She purchased the double indemnity policy option, which would pay out a doubled amount in the event of an accidental death.

We are prepared to settle the first part of the case and pay the proceeds to Casey Gannon, with you named as his guardian. Please tell us where to send the proceeds of the policy and we will send it forthwith.

As to the accidental death provision, we are not ready to make a final decision on that matter. Our company is conducting an investigation and will make a determination within the next year.

We look forward to hearing from you.

"And now that's the second letter. Do you want to ask about that?" Jake asked.

Again, Casey's answer was, "No, sir."

"The letter doesn't say how much money the policy was for. It probably won't be much. When it comes, Casey, we've got to make some decisions about what to do with it, how to handle it, and how to manage it. I can tell you that we are not rich people and raising you here will be a burden on my paycheck. But we'll just face that when the insurance money gets here." Figuring that he was done, Jake abruptly left the room.

Anne spoke up. "I want to talk about school, Casey. What grade will you be in this year and what are the things you've already learned so that we can place you in the right grade at Aiken Grammar School?"

Casey said, "I just finished the fourth grade in Butte, so I'm supposed to be in the fifth grade this year."

"What kinds of things do you already know? States? Capitals? Multiplication tables? Give me a hint," Anne asked.

"Well, I get pretty good grades, mostly As and Bs. I know all forty-eight states, and sometimes I get all of the capitals right, except I always have trouble with Kentucky and New Jersey. I know multiplication tables up to twelve. I can divide. In my mama's briefcase, I brought all of my old report cards and a birth certificate, and Mama's New Testament, and pictures of my mama and daddy. Oh, and I've got my daddy's Silver Star medal and a picture of his grave in some place in Europe, Belgium maybe. I can read and spell and I know nouns and verbs. I do okay in school."

She answered, "That's good. I've got to make some calls in the next few days to make sure we get you into school. It starts in less than two weeks."

For the rest of the evening, Jake listened to his floor model Zenith radio in the living room. He never missed *Inner Sanctum* and *Mr. and Mrs. North.*

Casey eventually started to get ready for bed on the living room sofa. He mumbled a quiet "good night" and quietly went into the living room. He opened up his trunk again to check on everything he had brought with him from Montana to make sure he still had it. All of it was there. It was sad, but everything he owned was right there in the trunk or in the briefcase.

He digested his new situation as well as he could, but that first night, a lonely, scared ten-year-old boy quietly cried himself to sleep. He missed his mama and his familiar surroundings so much. His last thought was, just how in the hell is this going to work out?

Chapter 2

The next morning, one of the first things Casey noticed again was that they lived in a small house without any noticeable soundproofing. When Jake and Anne woke up and began stirring, every sound carried. When Jake went out the door to fetch the newspaper, he had to come through the living room. Casey was aware of each bit of progress and each footstep. He pretended to be asleep as long as he could.

In time, the smells of coffee and the aromas of breakfast caused him to abandon his bed. The house had only one bathroom, and luckily, it was empty when he finally stumbled to his feet and visited it.

Afterward, upon entering the kitchen, he was greeted by the cheery Anne. "Well, sunshine, you finally decided to get up, did you?"

He didn't know if she expected an answer, but he managed to say, "I was really tired from all that riding on the train."

Anne asked him to sit down for his breakfast, and she proceeded to load his plate with scrambled eggs, two sausage patties, a generous serving of grits, and two homemade biscuits. Besides that, he had a large glass of fresh milk to wash it all down. He had awakened hungry and dived into his plate with relish.

"Aunt Annie Lou, you really are a good cook. This tastes really, really good." As much as he missed his mama and her cooking, he already knew that this lady's food tasted better than any he'd ever had.

Jake was already finishing up when he said, "You better watch out, Casey, if you tell her how good she is too much, she'll never stop feeding you and you'll look like a big fat sloppy Georgia hog in no time at all." Jake laughed hard at his own comment.

Casey just winced and kept on eating. He wondered when and if he could ever relax around Uncle Jake.

Anne spoke up and said, "Jake, Casey and I will be walking around downtown today and we might stop by to say hey to you. Casey, did you remember that we were going to take a closer look at Aiken today?"

"Yes, ma'am," he muttered while swallowing.

Jake left the table, visited the bathroom quickly, and then kissed Anne goodbye as he breezed out by the table and out the back door. His Hudson was parked in a little driveway on the right side of the house. They both sat at the table and watched him start the car and leave for work.

"Okay, big boy," Anne said, "I'll clean up these dishes and we need to head out in about thirty minutes. Can you make it?"

Casey nodded and went to get dressed.

A few minutes before ten o'clock, they were ready to walk out the door. She looked askance at Casey because he was barefooted. "Where are your shoes, young fellow?" Anne asked.

"I was hoping you would let me go like this," he responded. "I like to go barefooted. Out in Butte, my mama let me do it all the time in the summer. I'm used to it."

"Very well," she answered. "This time I'll let you do it, but I need to teach you about sandspurs. Some people call them 'stickers.' They're all over Aiken, and they love it when they find a tender bare foot. And where the sun hits, the ground will be hot as the blazes for your feet. Suit yourself this time, I guess. You'll learn."

There was no need to lock the door, so she just pulled it closed. They started walking toward downtown on their street, Pendleton. It was typical of most of the other streets near downtown Aiken. It was wide, with the shrubbery growing randomly in the middle and the travel ruts from cars and vegetable wagons meandering in ways to miss the growing trees and bushes. The entire width of 150 feet was unpaved and existed only as a sandy right-of-way.

In a few minutes, they were on Laurens Street walking toward the shopping area. Anne spoke up. "You've come here at a good time, Casey, because things are changing pretty fast. This street here on our left—can you see that it's fresh tar and gravel?—was not paved until last summer. Before that it was just a dirt road. Oh, the other side of Laurens was already paved and all of the traffic used that side. This near side was just a dirt road. It was that way all the way from the cemetery to downtown."

Soon, they were at the standpipe at Laurens and Edgefield. Just like he did yesterday, Casey ran ahead, rapped his knuckles against the green steel plates, and jumped on one of the feeder pipes to ride it. She walked on past him, knowing that he would catch up since he had no idea where he was going.

He was beside her again as they entered a new block with a large three-story building on her right and magnolia trees in every direction. "This, my friend, is where you will go to high school in a few years. This is Aiken High School." In the middle of August, of course, no school activities were being held.

The brick building on their right was a large structure with three distinct wings, fronted by a set of granite steps going into each wing. On the far right was the gymnasium. Its three levels of windows belied the fact that once inside it, there was only one large open space, with spectator stands on the left side.

The center wing contained three stories of academic classrooms and administrative offices. The principal's office was just inside the doors to the right.

The left wing contained the auditorium, with its overflow balcony and generous stage. Seating capacity was for several hundred people. Aiken High School occupied the entire block between Henderson Street and Barnwell Avenue and between Laurens and Pendleton Streets.

The next block started the downtown shopping area. On the nearest corner, they passed a new grocery store, Eden's, which she had not even tried yet. She wondered aloud why she hadn't even tried it even though she had to walk right by it to get to her regular store. As they walked further, Anne waved to a man who was standing in an alley, engaged in conversation. He quickly waved back.

"Who's that?" asked Casey.

"Oh, that's Mr. Efron," she said. "He's the owner of a few businesses here. This is his taxi and rent-a-car place, and his family also has a big grocery store over on Park Avenue, near the passenger depot where you came in yesterday. They're a nice family."

They took a few more steps and she stopped. "Wait just a minute, Casey, I want to point out something on the other side of the street. See that tallest building straight across the street from us?"

"You mean the one that says 'Patricia' on the sign?" he asked.

"Yes, that one," she answered. "That's the place where we go to picture shows in Aiken. That's the Patricia movie theater."

"Why does it have a name like that? It's just a girl's name," Casey observed.

Anne said, "There's a man in Aiken who owns a lot of property, and his name is Bert Ram. Mr. Ram likes to name things after his children. He has two daughters, Patricia and Rosemary. We have a Patricia Theater and a Patricia Apartments. I suppose one day we might have something named after Rosemary, but I think she's still pretty young."

They continued to the end of the block, where Richland Avenue crossed Laurens Street. There was a stop sign and a blinking red light on a post to help manage the sparse traffic. Casey had seen the highway sign that said U.S. 1 printed in the middle of a shield. "What's that sign with a '1' on it mean?" he asked.

"It means that we are at Highway 1. Jake told me that there is a national highway that starts way down in Key West, Florida, and goes all the way to the top of the state of Maine, and it's called U.S. Highway 1. I've never driven on it because I can't drive. It just happens to go right through the middle of Aiken. Our little town gets a lot of travelers who are driving from the north to the south and the other way around. On Richland Avenue, we have some tourist homes where these people can stay the night in the family's spare room for two or three dollars a night."

As they crossed the street, Casey's attention was drawn to a large water trough in the median, under the magnolia and pine trees. Two saddled horses were tied up to a post and drinking from the trough, enjoying their temporary break in the shade.

When they stopped on the other side of the street, Anne felt the need to say, "Casey, if there is a center of Aiken, I would say that this is it. On this corner is a fancy grocery store, Hahn's. We don't buy our groceries there because they carry brands we don't know anything about. And most of the items are more expensive than I like to pay."

"Who buys their stuff then?" Casey asked.

"The quick answer is, 'the rich people.' But there's a better answer. Aiken has several thousand people who come here every October from the North and leave again in March and April. Most of them come by train into the passenger station where you came in yesterday. Many of the families have their own custom-made train cars though, and those cars just sit on a siding until the family leaves again in the spring. They have big houses here, and they bring horses and maids and fancy cars. We call them the Winter Colony. They like to shop in the fancier stores. The reason they come here is for the mild weather during the winter. They are horsey people who play polo, ride horses, and hunt foxes in the woods on horseback. Aiken has a slew of shops and tradesmen and butchers and blacksmiths just to serve the Winter Colony. They are nice people, and they add a lot to this town. You'll learn a lot more about them in time. I can fill you in later."

Anne walked to the second store in the block, motioned for Casey to follow her, and walked in. It had the name McCreary's on the door. From the merchandise display, it was clear that this was a clothing store mostly for women. When a salesclerk came over to her, Anne smiled and spoke up, saying, "Can you show me that long skirt that was in your ad in yesterday's paper?"

The clerk led them over to a rack near the front window where Anne was able to see that they had her size. "Would you hold this for me for a few hours? I'm showing my nephew around town. I can stop by and try it on later." A man in the back of the store waved to Anne, and she waved back. She whispered to Casey, "That's Mr. Ernest McCreary. He owns the store."

When they walked out to the sidewalk again, Casey immediately glued his eyes to something across Laurens Street. "Is that a dime store over there? I really like dime stores," he said excitedly.

"Then you're in a lot of luck," she answered. "Aiken has two of them—Mack's and McCrory's. We don't have time to go in them right now, but maybe later today, we will." That last comment perked Casey up considerably.

Anne continued. "If you look right next door to the dime store, you see the Rogers Grocery. That's where I shop because their meats are really good and priced fairly for everybody. The only thing I don't like is the sawdust on the floor. I don't know why they do that and I wish they'd stop it. Some days, I even track it all the way home on my shoes."

They continued south on Laurens, crossing Curve Street in the middle of the block until they reached the corner of Laurens and Park Avenue. On the way, she pointed out Buddy Platt's Rexall Drugs, B. C. Moore Department Store, and Julia's Dress Shop. Stopping at the corner, she pointed at the unusual-looking building on the far corner and said, "There you have our post office. It's in a very pretty building. We'll go in there sometime, but not today. Let's turn left here and walk along Park Avenue toward the courthouse.

"Somebody told me something interesting recently about Park Avenue," Anne continued talking as they walked. "They said that Park is fifty feet wider than all of the other streets. The reason, they said, is that since the county courthouse and the federal courthouse are both on Park Avenue, it would have more traffic than the others. I suppose that makes some sense. But until a few years ago, there used to be a trolley line that ran the whole length of Park Avenue and all the way to Augusta. It stopped running years ago, and they just recently covered up the track. In Aiken's early days, this street was called Railroad Avenue, not Park."

In the middle of the block, she stopped and pointed to the nearest building. "As you can see from what's inside, this is the Aiken Fire Department. It only has this one truck and a volunteer fire crew. This whole building is called the Municipal Building. Mayor Weeks also has an office in there, and on the back end of it, the Aiken Police Department has its offices, and its door faces the other way on an alley. A long time ago, this place used to be the location of Patricia Theater. Before that, it was called the Opera House. But a fire burned it down, making the Patricia Theater operation move over to Laurens Street, and the city took over this spot.

"Casey, look out at that park between the streets. I think this is Aiken's prettiest one. Magnolias, deodoras, pines, azaleas, this one's got it all. That pretty house you see way over there is George Funeral Home. By the way, the other side of the street was just paved this summer. Before that, all of the real traffic was two-way on this side. When the paving was finished a few weeks ago, Park Avenue became one-way on each side for the first time ever and started to look like a real boulevard."

As they walked on toward the east, Anne pointed out Johnnie Eubanks's yellow house with a green roof and said, "He is a popular math teacher at the high school and is supposed to be really good. He's got the cutest 1926 black Buick you ever saw and he keeps it looking brand-new."

They crossed Newberry Street. On down Park, she made him take notice of Aiken Book Store. "I love this store. Not only is it the best bookstore in town, most people think it's the best gift shop as well. Every time I have to buy a birthday present, I walk right down here to buy something." Further on, they passed the new A&P store, which she also hadn't tried yet. It was just too far from home.

When they reached Chesterfield Street, Casey noticed the county courthouse for the first time. "So this is the courthouse, huh?" he asked. "I was expecting a bigger building, I guess."

County Courthouse

Anne decided to make Casey focus on another topic. "Let's talk about school for a minute. You have to start classes in a little over two weeks, you know. We are only a long block from Aiken Grammar School, where you will be going. Would you like to at least see it today?"

"Yes, ma'am, let's go. Which way do I go?"

Anne pointed to the south and led them across all the lanes and median of Park Avenue. Now they were walking on

Chesterfield Street. Directly in front of the courthouse, if a person proceeded north directly away from it, Chesterfield had the traditional wide street design. But beside the courthouse and leading behind it and away from it heading south, Chesterfield changed to a normal narrower two-lane road with two-way traffic. This was their direction of travel today, staying on the sidewalk.

Soon, they got to a bridge that spanned over a railroad track. "Wow," exclaimed Casey as he looked over the concrete rail straight down. "Look how deep that hole is."

Anne laughed. "Casey, what you just called a hole is known to everybody else around here as the 'railroad cut.' I think it's about forty feet deep right here."

"What's it for?" Casey asked. "Why is it so deep?"

Anne smiled at him and said, "Oh, you just ask me all the right questions! There's a good historical answer, and that's the one you're going to get out of me.

"That railroad track right under you was at one time a part of the longest railroad in the United States. In 1833, 115 years ago, it ran from Hamburg, SC, just outside of Augusta, to Charleston. It was all of 136 miles long. Aiken wasn't even a town with a name yet, but before it was ever built, the railroad company had a plan for this track to be thirteen miles south of here, about where Ellenton is today.

"Well, the main railroad route planner, a man named Alfred Dexter, came to this area to plan out the track, and he fell in love with a girl he met named Sara Williams. Her daddy was a wealthy man named W. W. Williams, who had a very large cotton plantation here. He wanted the railroad to run close to his plantation so he could ship his cotton to the market and not have it down there by Ellenton. Everybody assumes he put pressure on Alfred Dexter to reroute the railroad track. It *was* rerouted to here, and it made his future father-in-law happy. He must have given his blessing because the couple got married in January 1834.

"But there was a new problem they had to solve. The locomotives of that time were not powerful enough to easily climb the four-hundred-foot change in elevation from Hamburg to Aiken. There was always a big strain in climbing that slope. By 1869, the railroad had gouged out this deep cut for the track so that the incline would be lower and the trip would be easier."

"I get it," said Casey. "One day, I want to walk down in that railroad cut. It looks like it would be fun."

A few steps further along Chesterfield and they were standing at the corner of Colleton Avenue. A huge clump of mature nandina bushes occupied the entire corner. They walked around it. Anne said, "Well, Casey, there's your school, Aiken Grammar School."

Grammar School

"It looks pretty old," said Casey.

"I suppose that to somebody ten years old, it looks ancient," she responded. "It was built in 1891, or that's what my history-teacher friend told me. At first, this building was called Aiken Institute. Later, it became Aiken High School and eventually the Institute ceased operating. Then Aiken High moved out in the mid-1930s when their building on Laurens Street was finished. This has been the only white elementary school in town since about 1935."

They walked up on to the school grounds to try the doorknob to see if anyone was there. It was locked up tight with nobody present. They walked through a side gate and on to the playground; Casey gave a nod of approval to the equipment there after two trips down the steel sliding board.

"Let's walk back to downtown a different way," Anne said.

"Okay."

They maneuvered themselves back to the corner with the nandina clump and crossed Chesterfield, staying on the sand-covered Colleton Avenue going west. In a few seconds, Casey was staring at the beautiful, but rundown Willcox Hotel. "Wow, what is this place? It really looks special."

"Yes, it is," Anne answered, and she explained what she knew about the Willcox. It was all involved with horses and the Winter Colony. They continued on and turned right at the corner, which was Newberry Street again. They crossed back over the railroad cut but on a different bridge, this one wooden. Casey lingered and looked up and down the track, hoping to see a train. He spit over the side to see how far the track was below him. Newberry, too, was a pretty sand street until it crossed Park Avenue, then became sand again on the far side. A log cabin identified the location of the Chamber of Commerce, and just beyond that, in the middle of Newberry, was Aiken's only public swimming pool.

Casey got excited when he saw it. "I'd like to go swimming, but I don't know how to swim. Nobody ever taught me yet."

Anne laughed at him again. "Casey, you sound like me. I'd like to go driving, but nobody ever taught me yet. I'd like to fly airplanes, but nobody ever taught me yet."

It was Casey's turn to laugh. It was the first time Anne had seen his face when he looked like life was fun. She got some encouragement from that.

Anne kept walking and turned into the alley that was the termination point of Curve Street. Soon, they were standing in an unsightly alley in front of a gate that said Police Department. "This is where Chief Jesse George has his office. Down that alley on the side, you can walk to Park Avenue and to the front of the Fire Department. I'm saying all of this to you so you can get it all straight in your head. This is probably the ugliest, crudest-looking part of downtown Aiken right here. I wish somebody would come in here and clean it up.

"Casey, we're finished with the tour for today. Let's go find your uncle Jake to see if he can take us to lunch."

Post Office

"I know you told me that Uncle Jake works at a hardware store," Casey said. "I was looking around all over while we walked and I saw a lot of hardware stores. Where does Uncle Jake work? Which one?"

Anne laughed at Casey's comments again. "You are so right. Aiken does have a lot of hardware stores—most of them are within two blocks of here. There's Powell, Holley, Wise, Franzblau, and Laurel. He has worked for a few of them, one of them twice. And I might be missing one or two. I know where to find Jake."

When they entered the store, it was already close to one o'clock. She didn't see Jake, but the clerk on duty told them that he was at lunch and was probably eating at the lunch counter of the drugstore. Anne thanked him and they left, but not before Casey had a drink from a water fountain that said "Whites Only." He noticed a smaller fountain with throwaway paper cups that simply said, "Colored."

On the way to Blake's Drugs, he asked her, "What do the signs on the fountains mean? Why are there two of them? I saw the same thing yesterday in the train station."

"I'll try to answer that for you back at home," she said. "Let's go in here for a sandwich." They were at the corner of Laurens and Richland.

The double doors into Blake's Drugs were glass inward-swinging doors, set on a forty-five-degree angle. Once inside, Casey immediately saw the small hexagonal white tiles set in the floor. Along the right wall was an eating counter with eight to ten stools facing a soda fountain and short-order cook's work space. The pharmacy was in the back, even farther back than the side door onto Richland Avenue. Two Southern Bell telephone booths were just inside that door, and both were in use. Jake was seated at the stool farthest from the front door. He saw them and frowned in their direction.

"I'm sorry, but I'm just finishing up and have to get back to work," he offered. "Y'all's downtown tour took too long, I guess." His intention was to be friendlier, but he also showed his abruptness at the same time. He looked down at Casey's bare feet, frowned again, and continued. "Ya'll figured out how to get you and your stuff in that little house of ours?"

Anne answered him, saying, "We've had a good time this morning, Jake. It just took a long time. And we'll get him to fit in the house somehow."

"Okay," he said. "See y'all later. I'm gone."

Anne and Casey took the two end stools and looked through the menu. When the cook stood there with his pad, she ordered a tuna fish sandwich and Casey got a grilled cheese. While they were waiting for their food, she made sure Casey looked toward the drug counter in back to see Dr. Herman Blake, the pharmacist. "We get almost all of our prescriptions here. Dr. Blake is friendly, knows everybody in town, and gives good service. He's been here a long time at this store. Also, some people refer to this corner as the Commercial Hotel. After we go back outside, you'll notice that the drugstore is in a larger building that includes a hotel that faces Richland Avenue."

During the meal, Casey asked his aunt, "Does Uncle Jake really know all those people in Aiken, you know, the police chief and the mayor?"

She cocked her head a bit, interested that he was perceptive enough to question Jake's claim, and answered, "Yes, I'm sure they've met Jake and know his name. Now if you ask me how much they respect him and seek his advice, I won't swear to that." Casey liked the answer. It told him quite a lot about Jake and how Anne saw him.

While they were eating, Anne reminded him that he could go in the Mack's Five and Dime while she was across the street in McCreary's. He agreed. Within a few more minutes, she paid their bill and they were out the door.

On the street, she gave him a 50¢ piece and said to him, "Jake had a point last night. We aren't used to paying the expenses for a third person, but I'll try to adjust to it. You might be asked to do some chores or find a way around town to earn some of your own money. In the meantime, have fun with this half-dollar and meet me in front of McCreary's in thirty minutes."

In Mack's, Casey roamed every aisle, even the ones with sewing notions, bobby pins, candy corn, and wrapping paper. He bought a paddleball toy, the kind that has a wood paddle and a rubber ball attached to it with a long rubber band. When she saw it, Anne smiled and asked, "What'd you give for that?"

He got a quizzical look and said, "Ma'am?"

She said, "How much money did that cost you?"

"Oh, twenty-nine cents." He gave his aunt the twenty-one cents in change and immediately began practicing with it. Within a minute, he was hitting the ball with every stroke. A minute after that, he was able to hit a shot or two between his legs.

Annie Lou was astonished. "Have you ever used one of those toys before? I think the first time I ever used one, it took me half a day to hit the ball regularly. How do you do that?"

"I don't know," Casey answered. "I never had one before now. There's nothing hard about it. It's just watching the ball and swinging my hand at the right time, I guess."

"Well, you're mighty good at it," she exclaimed.

"Thanks," was Casey's only remark.

Within ten minutes, they were walking into their yard on Pendleton when Casey encountered his first South Carolina sandspur. "Yow, ow, ow," was all he could manage to say as he hopped on one leg to sit down on the front steps. Anne placed him on the top one and showed him how to extract it. Her only comment, delivered with a smile, was, "Going barefooted sometimes has its own disadvantages, and it's very educational."

After she rejuvenated them both with glasses of lemonade, they sat on the screened porch in back, enjoying the shady environment. She asked him, "Do you want me to talk about those water fountains? You know, the 'Whites Only' signs and the 'Colored' signs?"

"Yes'm," he said. "I can't see what it's for."

She thought for a few seconds about where to start her explanation. "Have you ever seen colored people before you came to Aiken yesterday?"

"Yes, ma'am, I had seen one of two of them in Montana, but I don't think very many live there," he answered. "And I saw some on the train."

"Well, you need to understand that parts of the South are just about half white people and half colored people. And that's because of slavery in the early history of our country. Almost all of the plantations where slaves worked were in the South, and when they were freed from slavery in 1865, it was easier for them to just stay where they were living rather than to move to somewhere else. So places like Aiken have a lot of colored people who live in them.

"Don't misunderstand me—freeing the slaves didn't magically make whites and coloreds have equality the next day, but it did force the white people in charge of everything to make some things available to coloreds that weren't available before. A water fountain is like that. In the old days, a colored man would have to take his drink of water with him in a jar when he left his cabin to work for his master. Once slavery was made illegal, colored people wanted to have access to drinking water when they were away from home, but white people didn't want them drinking out of the same fountains or same pumps as whites. So they changed the system so that each race would have its own fountain. The signs are there to tell you which fountain to use."

Casey looked a bit puzzled. He asked, "Are colored people okay? I mean, am I s'posed to stay away from them?"

Anne laughed and said, "No, sweetie, you don't have to stay away from them. They are just like people everywhere. You will meet nice, kind ones, and you will meet unfriendly ones. You have to decide on each one after you meet them. It's just like with white people. Judge them by how they treat people, not by what color they are. Do you have any other questions after our long walk this morning?"

"Yes, ma'am, just one more. All of the street names here sound really strange. In Butte, we had Main Street and streets with numbers and streets named after trees and mountains. What do things like Laurens and Pendleton mean?"

She sat up and said, "That's a really good question, and it has a simple answer. South Carolina has forty-seven counties, including Aiken County. About thirty streets in Aiken are named after other South Carolina counties. Laurens is a county, Newberry is a county, Richland is a county, and Edgefield is a county just north of Aiken. As you learn the streets here, you'll be learning a lot of the county names at the same time."

He was happy with her explanation and went into the front yard to play with his new paddleball toy, this time with his shoes on.

Chapter 3

The next day was Saturday, and it was Casey's first weekend in Aiken. Jake would be working all day downtown because Saturday was always the busiest day in the hardware business. After breakfast, Casey and Anne were talking when she suddenly said to him, "Run outside and stop Clarence, quick!"

Casey stood up and answered her, "Who is Clarence? Who am I suppose to stop?"

She jumped up and said, "He's the vegetable man. Go stop him. I'll be right there."

So Casey ran outside, letting the screen door slam with a noise that only a screen door can make. He was unsure as to what his role was now. Running off the porch, he saw a horse-drawn four-wheel wagon being driven by an old black man. "Wait, wait, my aunt Annie Lou wants you to wait."

"Whoa, whoa, Bubba!" said the man quickly. The old horse pulled up and stopped. The driver smiled at Casey and asked, "Jus' who are you, young man?"

"I'm Casey. I live here now, I guess. My aunt Annie Lou wants to talk to you."

"I 'spect she wants to buy some vegetables," he said. "She almos' always does."

Just then, Anne arrived at the wagon. "Thanks for waiting, Clarence, I had to go get my money."

"Thas' all right, Miz Gannon, I'll always wait for you."

"Clarence, I want two pounds of tomatoes, half a peck of snap beans, six ears of corn, a peck of peaches, and a watermelon. Do you have all of that?"

"Yes, ma'am." He got off the wagon and walked around to the rear of it, where a small shelf with a set of aging rusty kitchen scales was set up. While this was going on, Casey noted that Clarence wore a faded straw hat and a pair of overalls that looked as old as Clarence himself and a gentle demeanor. On his sockless feet was a pair of old rundown dress shoes with no laces. The toes were cut out in places to give his corns their freedom. He assembled her order, bagging some and providing woven baskets for the rest. "That'll be three dollars even. And who's this young man who says he might live here now?"

"This is my nephew, Casey Gannon. Mr. Gannon had a brother living in Montana, but Casey's parents are dead now, so he had come to live in Aiken with us. Here's three twenty-five. The extra quarter is for you."

"Thank you, ma'am. Master Casey, it's mighty fine to meet you. I hope you likes Aiken 'cause you got some mighty good folks to take care of you."

He climbed back up onto the wagon and prepared to leave. He said, "I'll see y'all agin on Wednesday." And he drove off.

Back in the house, Casey finally said, "That was a surprise, seeing a horse and a wagon on our street and a man bringing vegetables to us. Why did he call me Master Casey?"

Anne answered him, saying, "Colored people always call you boys Master this-or-that. Clarence will visit us this way all summer. It's just the way fresh vegetables are sold here. Didn't you eat vegetables and fruit in Montana?"

"Yes, ma'am, but my mama had to go to the store herself to buy stuff. Nobody brought it to us with a horse."

"Well, you'll just have to get used to it, I expect. It's the way Aiken works. A lot of nice people make a living by bringing things you need straight to your street, straight to your house," she explained.

Later that afternoon, Casey was in for another surprise. There was the steady hum of an engine running at low speed. He asked Anne what the noise was. She said, "Run outside and see for yourself."

Casey stepped onto the front porch in time to see one of Aiken's sprinkler trucks. Because so many of the streets were sandy expanses, any period without rain caused the dirt streets to become hot, dry, and dusty. It was necessary to sprinkle water on them to hold down the dust. Every unpaved street received the spray treatment at least twice a week in warm dry weather, and most of Aiken's streets weren't paved.

Anne asked Casey if he was aware they would be going to church tomorrow morning. He had not even thought about it since he was not accustomed to attending church services in Butte. He told her that he would go with them but professed ownership of no clothes worthy of going to church if it required dressing up to any degree. She assured him that his clothes would be fine, but privately she wondered if he was going to be embarrassed by the situation.

When Jake arrived home from work at seven o'clock, they ate a quiet dinner, after which he checked the mailbox. He reentered the house, waving an envelope with the name Iron Mountain Insurance Company printed on the outside. "Looks like your mama's insurance policy is finally gonna pony up some money. I bet it won't amount to much."

He quickly opened it, gasped, and broke into a very broad smile. There was a brief letter and a check, made out to Jacob Gannon, legal guardian of Casey Carter Gannon, in the amount of $8,500. "Holy cow," he exclaimed. It was worth repeating with more emphasis. "Holy crap!" His spirits were immediately lifted when he took it all in. The amount stunned and surprised him. He had expected no more than $2,500. A man could easily support a family for two or three years on $8,500. It was more money than he had ever seen at one time.

He went to the kitchen where Anne and Casey were finishing with the dishes. He showed it to his wife, and her face lit up. "Okay, y'all, the check came in the mail from Vera Gannon's insurance policy. This is a bunch of money and it needs to be put in the bank first thing Monday morning. This is all about your future, Casey. That's why your mama bought the policy, I'm sure. To make sure your needs were paid for until you can be a grown-up man on your own." Jake could not hide his glee and his relief.

"Does that mean I get to buy some stuff I need?" asked Casey. "I need some clothes for your church, and a bicycle, and a new lunch box, and a baseball cap, some things to play with, and some better shoes."

"Whoa there, boy, we can't let you have all of that at once," Jake said. "This money has to be managed carefully 'cause it's got to last you a long time, at least eight or ten years."

Anne said, "I have an idea. This is an awful lot of money. Why don't all three of us think all weekend about the best way to safeguard this money for Casey and at the same time think about the kinds of things to use it for as well as the kind of things not to use it for."

Jake had suddenly become relaxed about everything. His smile was wider than she had ever seen. He answered her, "That sounds like a good idea. Don't you agree, Casey?"

"Yes, sir," he said. Casey checked his feelings right then, and he realized for the first time that when he saw his uncle relax, it made him relax a bit himself.

"All right," Jake finished. "Monday, we put it in the bank, and Monday night, we talk about how to use it."

Anne worried privately about Jake and that large sum of money. She had seen a look in his eyes that she had never seen before, and it concerned her. Later, in the kitchen, she whispered to him, "Now, don't you get any ideas about that money. It clearly is not yours." He just smiled at her and nodded.

The next morning, they all woke up in time to have a big breakfast and get dressed for church. The most difficult things were two in number. First, to process that many people through the same bathroom in a short time, and second, to get Casey's good shoes and socks on the feet that had not been wearing shoes for most of the summer. His feet were wider than they had been last May by a noticeable amount.

At a few minutes before eleven o'clock, they walked up the steps of First Baptist Church at Richland and York. Casey was nervous because churchgoing was not a normal event in his life, and he also knew he would be meeting a lot of people for the first time. Even though he hated the idea of being in Aiken, he still reacted normally to certain social situations. Like most other ten-year-olds, he wanted others to like him. That had not changed.

Of course, Jake and Anne knew most of the people there; and before and after the service, they had a chance to introduce Casey to many others, both adults and children. Reverend Howard was the minister, and he delivered a timely message on the seven deadly sins of lust, gluttony, greed, sloth, wrath, envy, and pride. Casey admitted later that he had no idea there were that many sins. Anne nudged Jake with her elbow during the Lord's Prayer, prompted by the line "lead us not into temptation," and gave him a stern look while doing it.

Casey could only remember one name from all the new people he met that Sunday, and her name was Arlene something. Another vague recollection later was that he had met a daughter of the minister who was about his same age. Her name was Jane, maybe.

When they returned home, Anne followed her usual tradition in feeding her family on Sundays. That was to prepare ahead of time a very large dinner (lunch) of fried chicken, macaroni and cheese, mashed potatoes, gravy, and butterbeans, making sure that there would be generous leftovers for Sunday evening's supper (dinner). They would cut the watermelon too.

After lunch, Jake was more talkative and relaxed than usual. He joined Casey who was already on the back porch. "I have a hunch about your name, Casey. Why did your mama and daddy call you Casey? Did anybody ever tell you?"

"Yes, sir," said Casey. "Mama told me that when Daddy was little, he really liked the baseball story of *Casey at the Bat*. She said that he always liked the name after that."

"That's what I thought," Jake mused. "I remembered that from when we were little, Georgie always talked about that Casey story. You realize, don't you, Casey, that the batter, Casey, was not a good batter? You know the story is about him blowing his big chance. He struck out in a clutch situation."

"Yes, sir, I know that. That don't bother me none. If I play baseball, I'm gonna be a better hitter than him."

"Well, maybe so," opined Jake. "Both your daddy and me played baseball for Richmond Academy over in Augusta, but not at the same time. And we weren't too shabby neither. One day, I'll tell you about it. Hey, one night, when I feel like it, you and me can go see the Augusta Tigers play a home game. They're a pro team, farm club of the Detroit Tigers. You interested in doin' that?"

"Yes, sir, but I've never seen a real baseball team play." Casey was still very hesitant because he continued to see his uncle as potentially hair-trigger explosive.

Jake nodded his okay to that. Then he asked, "What do you think of Aiken so far? You been here all of two days."

Casey answered, "Oh, you know I want to live in Montana. But I guess I have to say it's okay for now, but I still don't want to be here. There's way too many trees here. In Butte, there's not many trees and you can always see a long ways away." He changed directions. "Why is it called Aiken?" Casey was irritated because he caught himself tiptoeing into every response to Uncle Jake, but he remained determined to show some dislike for his circumstances.

"Annie knows," said Jake. Turning his head toward the door into the kitchen, he said, "Annie, we need your help out here."

When she appeared, Jake said, "Tell Casey what Aiken means and who this Aiken guy was. I know you know that."

She started. "Yes, I do know that. Aiken is named after a man who never lived in Aiken at all. He was William Aiken, from Charleston. Remember that longest-railroad story I told you yesterday, Casey, the one from Hamburg to Charleston? Well, Mr. Aiken was the president of that railroad. It was called South Carolina Railroad and Canal Company."

She continued. "Aiken was given its town charter in December 1835 and got the name Aiken then. Unfortunately, William Aiken was not around anymore to enjoy the honor. He had been killed four years earlier by being thrown from a horse buggy. Sometimes you have to be dead to have something named after you."

"Ugh, that's too bad," muttered Casey.

"Yes, that's too bad for him," Anne said. "He never got a chance to see his namesake. The streets in Aiken had been laid out in 1834 by a Mr. Dexter and a Mr. Pascalis. The reason for this town even being here is that while that longest railroad was being built, this place had been set up as a construction camp, a staging area for the railroad builders to work from each day in laying the tracks. All of this property had been owned by three men—a W. W. Williams, a man named Rogers, and a William Moseley—until they deeded it to the railroad company and to the town."

"I told you she'd know," said Jake. "Any other questions?"

"Yes, sir. I've seen a lot of signs here on telephone poles about some man named Thurmond. Who is he, and is he important? His name is on just about every telephone pole."

Jake laughed. "I guess those signs are hard to miss. Let me ask you. Do you know who is president of the country right now?"

"I think it is President Truman," Casey answered.

"That's right, Harry Truman is the president. But right now there's an election going on all over the country, and two other people are running for president against Truman. Their names are Tom Dewey, from New Jersey, and Strom Thurmond, from South Carolina. In fact, if you stretch your imagination just a little bit, Thurmond is from Aiken, South Carolina. He's really from Edgefield—twenty miles up the road—but he hangs around in Aiken a lot."

"Wow, somebody from Aiken might be the next president?" asked Casey.

"No no," said Jake, "he won't win. He can't get enough votes to win. He's just trying to make a point, but he is sure screwing up a lot of people's ideas about running for anything in the South. He created a new political party called the Dixiecrats just to enter this election. Right now, he's the governor of South Carolina and has been since 1946. He'll still be governor after this election is all over, I suspect."

During the rest of the evening, Jake played his radio and listened to a hillbilly station playing Roy Acuff and Hank Williams songs. Casey went to bed that night feeling a bit better due to the arrival of the money, but he was thinking about Uncle Jake and that money and praying that everybody was honest when he finally drifted off to sleep. It seemed to him that Uncle Jake got a lot nicer the minute that money showed up.

The next day was Monday, and Jake deposited the insurance check in the Farmers and Merchants Bank across from the post office. Anne made some phone calls, asking a few friends some questions about what was involved to get Casey registered for the upcoming school year.

That evening, they sat around the kitchen table after dinner to talk about Casey's new wealth.

Jake started the conversation by saying, "Casey, I put your money in the bank today like I said I would. The check was made out to me, as your guardian, so it was natural for me to open it in my name. You're only ten years old and don't have a social security number, so they wanted the account to be in my name. You understand that, right?"

Anne jumped in to make sure Casey would relax about the arrangement. "I'll make sure the money is kept safe for you, okay?" She cut her eyes toward Jake and gave him a look.

"Yes, sir, yes, ma'am," Casey responded.

Jake leaned forward and placed a savings passbook in front of Casey. Yes, the number $8,500 was there all right.

Jake said, "I'm worried that we'll go through this money too fast. It's a good feeling to have it there, but let's be wise in using it."

Anne added, "Casey, how do you feel about this money mostly being in reserve for you? What I mean is let's not be picking at this bank account for every little thing that comes along. Jake mentioned that you could earn some money by doing little jobs. Does that interest you at all?"

"I've been thinking about it too just like you asked me to," Casey answered. "I don't want to spend it fast either, but I do need some stuff. I want to earn some of my own money so that I won't have to use this money here. I want to pay for my stuff myself if I can. But I've never done it before."

"What kind of things do you mean?" Anne asked.

"Well, I had my own bike in Butte, but I didn't bring it because it cost too much on the train, and well, anyway, I had about outgrown it. That's the other reason I left it there."

Jake said, "Yeah, you oughta have your own bike. I had mine before I was your age. What about this idea? I go to the bank and pull out $25 for you to have as your starting fund in Aiken. You can get a new bike for $12 to $13 and a basket for it for another $1.50. Your other school stuff can be paid for too. As soon as you earn enough money to pay for those things, we'll make sure you put the money back in the bank account."

Anne got excited. "Oh, Jake, that's a great idea. What do you think, Casey? If you need to buy something, we'll borrow the money out of your account with the idea that it'll be put right back in when you earn some. That way, your money could last a very long time."

"Okay," said Casey. "That sounds real good. I've been thinking about maybe a paper route."

"Oh, a good idea," replied Anne.

"Can I say something else?" asked Casey. "I need to say this." And his eyes got teary for a second. "In Butte, I had my own room at home. I've slept on this sofa here for four days. Do I have to keep sleeping in the living room? I don't have any place to put my stuff. Can we use some money some way to get us a bigger house or another room in this one?"

Jake and Anne looked at each other. At first, both of them thought for an instant that Casey was being ungrateful that they had taken him in. But in a flash, they realized that it was a worthy idea to consider.

Jake took a breath, brought his attitude under better control, and answered him. "Look, we don't own this house, Casey. We rent it for $44 a month. I guess we could think about renting a bigger house, but it would cost more." Jake looked surprised that these words came from his own mouth. "Anne, what do you think?"

She answered, "I heard about a house for rent over on Newberry Street about three blocks closer to downtown that's a lot bigger than this one and it's only $60 a month. Can we afford that much?"

"Not very well," Jake replied. He looked at Casey. "Casey, your money is in a bank account that pays 1 percent interest a year. The $8,500 will earn $85 each year, or about $7 a month. We could apply that to our rent. Also, your Mr. Grover is planning to sell your mama's car and send the money to us. That might give us another $50 or $100 to apply to a higher rent. We might be able to swing it if that's how you want to use some of the money."

"I would like to have my own room like I had in Montana if we can do it," Casey said. "I'll get my own job to help pay for it."

"All right, here's what we'll do. Tomorrow, I'll take $25 out of your savings account to pay for the things you say you need. And I'll set it up for the interest to be paid out to us every three months. Annie, you find out some more about that house for rent, okay?" Jake was rapidly adjusting his thinking and was moving toward being very much in charge of the plan.

Casey finished the conversation by saying, "And I'll start asking about paper routes in this town tomorrow."

Beginning the next morning, the small family acted as if a special mission needed to be accomplished. By ten o'clock in the morning, the house was empty. Jake had gone to work, and Anne and Casey were on a walking mission to pursue the tasks they had taken on for the day. While walking toward downtown, Anne steered them over to Newberry Street to at least give Casey a walk-by view of the house she had in mind. He got excited when he saw it because it looked much larger than the bungalow they had just left.

He said out loud, "Aunt Annie Lou, it almost looks like it's a two-story house."

She answered him while not slowing down, "Yes, I think it probably is. We're headed for the rental office of Eulalie Salley. She'll be able to tell us."

They spent almost an hour with Ms. Salley at her office on Park Avenue and learned that the rent of $60 a month was correct but that if they signed a two-year lease, the rate would be discounted to $54. The house had two small bedrooms upstairs as well as a full bath. The downstairs bedroom was the largest in the house and was set up to be the master bedroom. It also had a full bathroom. She arranged to see the house, with Jake and Casey, for the next evening.

Their next stop was to be Aiken Grammar School, but Casey persuaded his aunt to backtrack to Sears and Western

Auto. Casey begged to "just look" at their bicycles. They both had a large stock of bikes, already assembled, on display in the stores. It was determined that a good bicycle could be bought for $11.95 cash or $13 on layaway. That was good news as well.

At the school, the principal, Ms. Coleman, was in her office with an assistant on duty. Casey met her, thinking, *Boy, this is a woman in charge*, whose no-nonsense attitude reminded him of drill sergeants he had seen in war movies.

Anne had brought Casey's report cards from the last two years in the Montana school system. After reviewing them, Ms. Coleman agreed that he would be in the fifth grade and assigned him to the class of Mrs. Ellis. She reminded them that the first day of school would be the Tuesday right after Labor Day, or only eight days hence. The assistant took Anne and Casey to see the classroom on the second floor. Casey inhaled the familiar smell of freshly oiled floors, erasers, chalk, and textbooks.

As they were walking back home, Casey reminded his aunt that he wanted to stop by the *Aiken Standard and Review* offices to ask about a paper route. Their office was on Richland Avenue, adjacent to the Commercial Hotel. It faced a beautiful grove filled with magnolia trees with a few tea olives on the periphery. The scent literally filled the street with a pleasant aroma.

Casey learned something useful in his conversation with the person behind the desk there. The Aiken newspaper was printed only twice weekly on Wednesday and Friday and had a full staff of paperboys for delivery. But the lady referred Casey to the *Augusta Chronicle* and *Augusta Herald*, whose combined offices were located a couple of blocks away. She stated that one was a morning paper and one was delivered in the afternoon. She was certain that both of them used boys for delivery. Anne noted the address, and they left for home and a late lunch.

In the afternoon, Casey asked his aunt if he could go find the Augusta newspaper offices by himself. She thought about it for a second and answered him, saying, "Yes, that might be a good experience for you. If you can follow my simple instructions on a map I'll draw, you can do it by yourself."

When she handed him the map, he was out the door in a flash, with his shoes on. Casey found the small office downtown on Curve Street. He walked in and saw a man sitting at a desk on the telephone. The man motioned for him to sit down in a chair adjacent to the desk while he continued talking. Casey looked around rather timidly, seeing lists taped to walls and a stack of newspapers in the corner. After a minute, the man hung up and said, "Well, young fella, what can I do for you?"

Casey was nervous, but he managed to say, "I want a paper route so I can make some money."

The man smiled and asked, "Son, what's your name and how old are you?"

Casey responded, "Casey Gannon, and I'm ten and a half."

"Casey Gannon, huh? You related to Jake Gannon here in town? You live on Pendleton, near the cemetery?" He showed a hint of displeasure when he heard the name.

"Yes, sir, he's my uncle," Casey said.

"Did you just come to Aiken?" the man asked. "I heard something about Jake having a new nephew here. Is that you?"

"Yes, sir, I just came last week from Butte, Montana. I'll be living here from now. My folks died. I want my own paper route so I can earn my own money."

"Okay, son, it sounds like something you might expect out of Jake," the man said. "Let me talk at you for a minute or two and you listen. I need to explain how this works. My name is Mr. Johnson, and I'm the Aiken manager for the *Augusta Chronicle* and the *Augusta Herald*. The *Chronicle* is a morning paper and the *Herald* is in the afternoon. The *Chronicle* is seven days a week, and the *Herald* is six days. Only one paper is put out on Sunday, and it's delivered by the *Chronicle* paperboys. Ten years old is a little bit young for a paperboy—we like them to be twelve—but I can make exceptions if a boy looks to be pretty dependable. Since you're so new, you probably don't know the streets yet or your way around. You have a bicycle?"

"Not yet," Casey answered, "but I will get one in the next few days."

"All right, that's good. Here's what we'll do. I don't have any open routes to give you right now, but a *Herald* route is going to open up in about two months. It has over sixty customers on it. You go ahead, get your bike—one with a basket—and start riding all around Aiken near the downtown area. Get familiar with the streets and where things are. Stay in touch with me every week or two. Try not to let Jake lead you in any bad directions. If you do all that, you may be throwing papers in the afternoon after school in just a few weeks. You can earn $3 or $4 a week on this route."

"Wow, that's real money," exclaimed Casey.

"Yes, it is," Mr. Johnson answered. He reached out and shook Casey's small hand and added, "I'll see you in a couple of weeks." He half expected not to see this boy again, considering his home environment. He knew that Jake Gannon was pretty good at hardware, but left a lot to be desired in the dependability and sobriety departments.

Casey ran almost all the way home to deliver his news to Anne. Although he hated being in Aiken and he detested the circumstances that compelled him to be there, he promised himself that as soon as he got his feet squarely on the ground here, he was going to work like crazy and make more money than they ever dreamed about. He was gonna show them. He knew Jake didn't want him here, and Casey was beginning to hatch a plan to impress everybody in Aiken about their new resident from Montana, even his gnarly uncle Jake.

Jake walked through the front door at six thirty, as was his custom. During dinner, the conversation was all about going to a new school, possibly moving to a bigger house, and bikes and paper routes. He perked up considerably when he realized there was a possibility they might be paying $54 for rent instead of the $60 he had heard at first.

At the end of the meal, Jake fetched his wallet from a hip pocket and handed Anne five $5 bills. He said, "Annie is going to manage this money for you, Casey. You're only ten years old. It's for the bike, the basket, and anything you need new for school. As soon as we're sure you can tend carefully to money yourself, we'll let you do more. I'm counting on you to find some way to pay this money back to your savings account by Christmas. You're gonna do that, right?"

"Yes, sir, you just watch me."

Anne put the money away and reminded Jake that "Tomorrow evening, right after you get home from work, we'll go see the house on Newberry." Jake nodded his agreement. The next twenty-four hours were uneventful.

When he drove up the next day after work, he tapped the horn and Anne and Casey bounded out of the small house. In three minutes, Jake parked in front of the house they would be touring. Ms. Salley's car was already there.

The house was a large frame structure with a bold green tin roof that faced its sloping broadside to Newberry Street. They were very near a cut-through street, Henderson, which placed them within a block of Aiken High School. A feature that captured Jake's attention upon exiting the Hudson was a deep wide-as-the-house front porch. A newspaper or a bicycle could stay dry on that porch, he thought.

Ms. Salley showed them around the entire house, pointing out its good features. Privately, Jake had wondered for a long time if they would forever be confined in a small bungalow house. He never voiced it to Annie, but he was also tired of being too cramped too often. He visually took in the much larger master bedroom on the first floor, the bathroom that had its own doorway from the same bedroom, the larger kitchen with its own expansive eating area, and the large screened porch out the back.

He was more excited when he realized that the narrow driveway on the right side of the house led to a small outbuilding at the rear which could hold one parked car and all of his tools. He could fashion a workshop out of that space!

The upstairs of the house contained two smaller bedrooms and a full bathroom off the hall. Besides that, there was a large walk-in attic for storage. There were no upstairs windows to the front, but each bedroom had ample lighting with double windows at the sides of the house.

Casey was thrilled when he realized that if they leased the house he would be the only person living upstairs. He could certainly get excited about that.

After the tour, Jake asked Ms. Salley a few important questions. He discovered that he could get out of his own lease with a thirty-day notice and that he could move into the new house at any time but must sign a lease. A two-year lease would guarantee the $54 rate. No deposit was necessary since he was employed and was known around town to be a person who paid his debts, but he must, of course, pay a month in advance.

Jake asked Ms. Salley for a few minutes to huddle with his family. Jake could not help but think about the $8,500 sitting in the bank. If they ever had a time where funds ran short, he reasoned to himself, he could probably dip into that account to make up for it and then pay it back. They went to the front porch where Jake said to Annie and Casey, "I don't see a thing wrong with us living here, and it looks like it gives all of us a lot more space. What do y'all think?"

Annie had not assumed that Jake would agree this easily. She smiled exuberantly and said, "Oh, I love it. Let's take it. What about you, Casey?"

Casey jumped in with "Yes, ma'am, it answers all of the things I want. I want to live here. I might even start to like Aiken a little bit if we moved to here."

"Annie, how long will it take you to get us packed up to leave our house?" Jake asked.

She answered, "We could get out in two weeks, but let's not kill ourselves over this. It's late August right now, let's give ourselves until October first. That way we can get Casey in school first and not try to bite off too much at one time." Jake nodded in agreement.

He went back inside the house and gave the news to Ms. Salley. She asked Jake to meet her in her office at lunch tomorrow to sign all the papers. He agreed.

A few days later, it was Labor Day weekend. Casey had already bought his bicycle—a Schwinn from Sears,

Roebuck—and had begun to explore his part of Aiken, including the site of their new house. He had already learned how hard it was to ride on the streets. Almost none of them had a hard surface except for Laurens, Park, and Richland, and the only sidewalks were in the immediate area of downtown. A pair of automobile ruts on a street represented the worst examples, and unimproved flat expanses of hardpan represented the best. The main problem was the sand. Aiken's sand could be very loose and deep. A bike had to be driven hard to get through it in many places.

He rode to a nearby grocery store to ask if they would allow him to return empty cola bottles for money. One of the cashiers told him that they would pay him 2¢ for every bottle he brought them. "But don't come back unless you have at least a dozen at a time," she said. "It's not worth it to open the register for one or two at a time." Casey thought that this was very good news. He started being more alert as he rode around, and he picked up every stray bottle he spotted from then on.

For the weekend, Annie had announced that they were going to make homemade peach ice cream for the holiday. She told Casey that his job would be to help with the hand-cranked churn. He told her he had never done it before, and she promised to teach him all he needed to know.

The day before the weekend, Casey rode to the Western Auto store to buy a basket for his bike for $1.49. He figured that even if he did not get a paper route, he needed the basket to haul the drink bottles he was finding. The store helped him install it before he rode off.

So it was natural for Annie to ask him to go to the Colonial ice plant on Union Street to purchase twelve pounds of crushed ice. "Tell Mr. Summer to make it marble-sized pieces for churning ice cream," she said. She gave him the money, a small hand-drawn map, and a thick cloth laundry bag to transport the ice in.

On his way to the Union Street ice plant, he meandered around a bit to see as much of Aiken as he could. He went a block past Union and saw a colored man washing cars in front of his house. As he rode by, the man spoke, saying, "Hey there, young man."

Casey stopped. "I just moved to Aiken, and I'm just riding my new bike around to learn the streets."

The man talked while he worked and said, "Well, I'm just washing this car for a man so I can wax it for him too. You can watch for a minute."

Casey offered, "My name is Casey Gannon. Is the man going to pay you to do that?"

"Oh yeah, I definitely gets paid. My name's Farris Wynn. This is what I do. I washes and waxes cars. We call it Simonizin' cars," he said with a smile. He wore a military service-type cap, the kind General MacArthur wore when he waded in from the Pacific. And he seemed to smile constantly. Casey thought he was nice and friendly.

After a few minutes, Casey said, "Thanks. I better go. I have to get some ice at the ice plant."

"Come back any time," said Farris Wynn. "I'm here doing this almost every day."

Casey rode a block back to Union Street and bought the ice. When he got back home, they began immediately to churn the ice cream because the ice would easily melt if they tried to store it overnight. While they were working on it, he had a chance to tell Anne about meeting Mr. Wynn. She told him that it was a good example of the people you run into in Aiken. "They don't even have to know you much to treat you just like a friend," she said. "It's one of the main reasons I like Aiken so much."

In 1948, it was easier to store the resulting ice cream in their refrigerator than the ice itself. Ice had no shelf life because most refrigerators had very small freezer compartments.

Annie instructed Casey how to set up the churn, the ingredients, the ice, and the salt and churned for about thirty seconds before she turned the task over to him. He wore himself out for the next forty minutes but made a generous amount of peach ice cream, which they enjoyed over the next three days.

The weekend featured other highlights too. Jake said something about wanting to go to an Augusta Tiger baseball game before the season ended. He told Anne that he was going to Augusta to get a ticket.

She stopped him, saying in a low voice, "Don't you think we might want to go too?"

After a quiet, brief whispering discussion, he agreed to take them also. On Saturday, he took the day off. They loaded into the car and drove to Augusta, using the laborious two-lane road through the Horse Creek Valley. Casey was able to see for the first time the cotton mills just off the road in Warrenville, Langley, Bath, and Clearwater.

They crossed the Savannah River, going into Georgia using Augusta's Fifth Street Bridge. Jake turned right on Broad Street, the city's main business district.

"Wow," exclaimed Casey, "this is a really big town."

"Yeah, it is," said Jake. "This is where the Gannons come from. I was born and raised here."

They drove west on Broad until Fifteenth Street appeared, where they turned left, drove about a half mile up and over the Butt Bridge, which crossed Augusta Canal, an eighteenth-century offshoot of the Savannah River. Immediately after the bridge, they veered left and into the parking lot of Jennings Stadium, where Augusta's professional baseball team played.

When Jake parked, he told Casey and Anne to go with him so they could see the ball park. While he was talking at the ticket window, they walked into the stands to see the field. After a few minutes, Jake joined them, saying, "The season's almost over and there's only six more home games. I bought three tickets for us for a game here tomorrow night."

"Oh boy, a real baseball game," exclaimed Casey. "Thanks a lot, Uncle Jake."

"Y'all sit down for a minute," Jake requested. "I want to ask you a couple of questions." They sat. "Do you think you're gonna like baseball at all, Casey?"

"Oh yes, sir. I don't know how to play yet, but I always wanted to. Can I learn how in Aiken?"

Jake said, "Yeah, if I find the time, I'll teach you some. I was pretty good. So was your daddy. We both played the outfield, and we both could hit the ball better than most.

"Another question," Jake stated. "Have you ever heard of Ty Cobb or Babe Ruth?"

"Yes, sir," Casey answered. "Babe Ruth hits home runs for the Yankees. Isn't Ty Cobb the best baseball player ever?"

Jake laughed. "Yeah, you're right, but things change. While you were riding to Aiken on that train a few weeks ago, Babe Ruth died of cancer, so he's gone. And a lot of people do think Ty Cobb was the best. Did you know that he lived here in Augusta?"

"No, sir, I didn't know that Babe Ruth died, and I didn't know about Mr. Cobb being from here either," said Casey.

"On the way home, we'll drive by the house he grew up in. It's not far from here. It's up on the Hill on Williams Street. I'll show you. Let's go."

True to his word, Jake pointed out the white frame house as they drove by. Casey had an hour to think on the way back to Aiken. *Maybe this isn't going to be as bad as I thought*, Casey mused. *Maybe Uncle Jake might be okay after all. Maybe I can trust him with the money.*

The next day, they drove back to Augusta to watch the Augusta Tigers play against the Jacksonville Tars. Even though his uncle didn't spend any time explaining what was going on, Casey enjoyed it tremendously and vowed quietly to himself that he was going to learn this game.

Chapter 4

Tuesday, September 7, 1948, was Casey's first day of school in Aiken. The household awoke early to make sure he would not be late. The three had a quiet breakfast, and Jake offered to give Casey a ride "just this once," as far as the hardware store.

Anne spoke up, saying, "I was planning on walking him to school from here, but if you'll let both of us bum a ride in the car, I'll walk him to school from the store to make sure he doesn't get lost. Then I'll walk back home."

"Okay," Jake answered, "and one more thing. It's only three more weeks before we move to the new house. We have to start thinking about those details, right?"

Anne nodded, and Casey gave his usual "Yes, sir."

When Casey and Anne exited Jake's car and started their walk to school, she detected a nervousness in him and said, "Sweetie, everything's gonna be okay at school today. Just be yourself and they'll like you. I promise you Aiken kids will not reject you."

When they arrived at the nandina bushes outside the school, he swallowed hard and waved her away, saying, "Mothers and ladies don't walk ten-year-olds to school. Look around. You don't see anybody but us doing it."

"You're right," she said. She gave him a bit of a shoulder hug, handed him 25¢ for lunch, and added, "Good luck today."

He turned and walked into the school. She walked back to the edge of the street and crossed her fingers as she departed the area.

Seven hours later, Casey came in the front door of their house. Anne had been working on the packing-and-moving project all day to keep her mind off what Casey might be going through at school.

She said to him, "How about some cold ice tea, big boy?"

"Yes, ma'am, I'd like some."

After the drinks were poured, she nudged him toward the comfort of the back porch and said, "I want to hear all about your day at school."

"Okay," he said and started up. "There's about thirty people in my room. Mrs. Ellis is kind of strict. She doesn't let us talk to each other much. We start getting our books and some homework tomorrow."

Anne asked, "Can you remember any names of the people in your class? Tell me."

"I don't remember any last names, but I know a lot of first names. There's a Bo, and a Harold, and a Donald, and a Tommy, and a Brooks, plus two Jimmys. For girls, I think I heard two Beverlys, a Sissy, a Janet and a Jane, and a Rosanne. Oh, and an Arlene. I met her at church and she's in my class too."

"Were the other children nice to you?" asked Anne.

"Yes, ma'am, specially Arlene."

"What do you mean? What did she do that was special?"

Casey blushed a bit and said, "She wanted to eat lunch with me after she heard what I said in the morning class before recess." He paused, got quiet, and said, "Mrs. Ellis asked the class if we did anything special this summer. Then she went around the room to everybody one at a time. Because I was new, I was the last one. Everybody else had said something, so I had to think of something to say."

A small dread washed over Anne, but she tried not to show it. "So when your turn came, what did you say?"

"I told them that I went camping with the scouts and that while I was gone, my mama died. Then along with some other people, I buried her in Montana, and I rode a train for three straight days to come to Aiken."

"Oh, Casey, I don't know what to say. Was it sad to tell them that?" Anne asked.

"Yes, ma'am, it was. I think my voice hurt then and they could tell. It was real quiet in the room after that. I had to wipe my eyes once too. Some of the girls made a little sniffing noise then and the boys wouldn't look up at me."

He gathered himself and added, "I like Arlene. I don't know her last name yet. She was really nice and told me she would be my first new friend at school. She said she felt real sad about my mama."

Within a few days, Casey had endured a whole week of classes. Starting on the third day, he rode his bike to school and parked it in a rack provided for that purpose. Living in Aiken and going to school was all starting to smooth out.

He was still a curiosity because he was so new. All the others were familiar with each other from the past. On a very hot day during the second week, Casey decided to yield to his temptation to go barefooted. He arrived at the usual time but parked briefly out by the large clump of nandina bushes at the front of the school yard.

Crawling into the middle of the clump where he could not be seen, he removed his shoes and socks, stashing them off the ground, up into the middle of the largest bush. Then he crawled back out, dusted his pants off, and rode barefoot to the bike rack and parked it. He felt good. He did his best to get up to his classroom without being seen.

Like many educators, the principal, Mrs. Coleman, had eyes in the back of her head. Within a few minutes, she was on the telephone, talking to Anne Gannon. Thirty minutes after that, Anne entered the principal's office, breathing hard after the brisk walk from home.

Mrs. Coleman asked, "Are you having financial problems in your family, Mrs. Gannon? Your nephew arrived for school today without shoes and socks. Is there a problem we need to discuss?"

Anne immediately blushed to a deep red. "No, there's no problem. He left home this morning dressed correctly, including his shoes and socks."

"Okay," Mrs. Coleman responded. "Let's get his little rear end in here for an explanation." With that, she dispatched the hall monitor with a note to Mrs. Ellis's classroom. Within three minutes, Casey appeared, acting very subdued. He saw his aunt in the principal's office and knew he was caught.

"Y'all know I don't want to live in Aiken. I want to still be in Montana. I can go barefooted in Montana. I'm sorry. I just wanted to go barefooted here for one day. My stuff is outside stuck in the bushes," he explained.

Mrs. Coleman looked over her glasses at him and glared for a full thirty seconds. "Well, young man, without waiting any longer, I suggest you run out there right now and fetch them. Bring them back here while we watch you put them back on."

"Yes, ma'am." And he was out the door. Within two minutes, he was back and sitting on the floor, busily donning socks and shoes again.

Mrs. Coleman spoke again. "Mr. Gannon, there will be punishment for doing this. You have disrupted school and caused your aunt to come to my office. Tomorrow morning, I want you to hand me the assignment I am giving you. I want you to write one hundred times the following sentence: 'Casey

Gannon will always attend Aiken Grammar School wearing his shoes and socks.' Do you understand? Write that one hundred times, to be handed to me tomorrow morning."

"Yes, ma'am, I understand," replied Casey.

"Shoo! Back to class."

Anne left after a few pleasantries with Mrs. Coleman. She walked into the hardware store to inform Jake as to what had happened at school. He wasn't happy. "Tell Casey I'll deal with his little butt when I get home tonight."

Several hours later, Casey slowly walked in the door with his books. He started up quickly by saying, "Aunt Annie Lou, I'm really sorry about my shoes. I'll be careful not to do it again."

"I forgive you," she answered, "but you've got two other people to worry about—your uncle Jake and Mrs. Coleman. After you get a drink, I want you to sit down and grind out those one hundred sentences for her. That way, when Jake gets home, you're already done with that."

Casey worked on the sentences for the next hour. When Jake got home, he didn't say anything about the shoes right away. After dinner, he asked Casey to meet him on the back porch.

Jake started up. "You dumb little brat! I'm really disappointed and disgusted and mad as hell about what happened at school today. It shows a side of you I didn't know you had. What you did was dishonest and sneaky, no other way to put it. It tells me you're willing to do things behind our backs that we don't approve of. I don't like that one damn bit."

"Uncle Jake, I'm really sorry. I won't do it again."

"Listen to me for a minute, Casey. I've decided that I'm not going to pile on any more punishment to what the principal gave you. But I'm going to give you the best advice you'll ever hear from anybody. You're only ten years old and you've only been in Aiken a few weeks, but you need to hear it now. I've made plenty of dumb-assed mistakes in my life, and I'll be damned if I'm gonna let this pass without me reaming your rear end out about it. We are not rich people. We can't go out and just get anything in a store we might want. But we have our reputations whatever they are up to now. We are nothing more than a collection of what other people think of us, right or wrong. Other people in our lives judge us by our deeds, our behavior, the things they see us do every day. Sometimes, mine have not been perfect and I know that. I want you to be better than I was. You've embarrassed me and this family.

"If you get into the habit of doing sneaky things, the people around you start to not trust you. When you are around and about, they will keep their eye on you because of your behavior, which to them is unstable, can't be trusted. On the other hand, if your deeds are always above board, always on the up-and-up, always legitimate, never sneaky or misleading, after a while you get the reputation of a person with some honor, a person with some integrity, a person other people can relax around because they trust you. A wise man once said that integrity is the name of the thing that develops in a man by him always doing the right thing when nobody is looking. I want you to think about the kind of man you want to be when you grow up. You have to start deciding now if you want to be that sneaky, untrustworthy man or if you want to develop into that man that everybody trusts and wants to be around."

As he spoke, his voice faltered a bit as Jake realized that he was not only talking to Casey, but he was thinking of himself as well. He voice broke so he cleared his throat and added, "Is that absolutely clear?"

"Yes, sir." Casey had gotten very quiet, and a tear was running down one cheek. "Uncle Jake, I'm sorry you're so disappointed. I swear you won't ever have to feel that way about me again."

Jake pondered his own words for a long time afterward and wondered why that particular sermon came out of him just then. Since their nephew had come to live with them, Jake had begun to think about how much of his old ways would be told to Casey and whether he may have to explain his past life. God knows that not much of it could be carried with pride.

Casey laid low for a few days and spent his afternoons looking for drink bottles and checking with Mr. Johnson, at the newspaper office, and riding around the neighborhoods. On one of these trips, he saw Farris Wynn again, washing cars beside his house.

He recognized Casey from before and asked, "Hey, young man, you want to make a quarter?"

Casey parked his bike against the fence and answered, "What would I have to do for a quarter?"

Wynn pointed to a nearby car and told Casey, "I'm fixing to wash that car next. I will pay you 25¢ to vacuum it out, dump the ashtrays, and vacuum the trunk out."

Casey carried it all out in about twenty minutes and showed off the results. "Pretty good for a beginner. I like how you did that so fast," Wynn said. "Here's your quarter. Any time you want to work some more, just come on by here. I washes cars just about every day. Do you want to make some money regular, or do you just want to piddle around with workin'?"

Casey said, "I plan to work a lot. I like money and want to have some of my own. At first, I didn't want to stay in Aiken.

I wanted to run away. Now, I'm just going to stay around and do everything right. And I want to make me some money."

"Good for you," said Farris. "Maybe I can help. A little bit later in the fall, I know an old white lady on Columbia Drive who's got some pecan trees. She's gettin' too old to bend down to pick up the nuts when they start to fall. When the time comes, in a month or so, I'll take you over to her house so you can help her. She'll pay you a dollar or two to help. Might even give you some pecans too."

"Thanks a lot," Casey responded. And he rode off on his bike with a big smile.

Casey was calculating in his head and realized that between drink bottles and Farris Wynn, he had pocketed over a dollar in the past few days. His opportunities seemed to be growing.

Things were also going pretty well at school. At first, he was kidded a lot about trying to get away with being barefooted in school, but then the other children let up on it. Arlene continued to be his good friend and protected him from making any other bad mistakes. He liked her as his friend. They ate lunch together almost every day, and sometimes others joined them. He found out that her last name was Cushman and she lived on a farm south of Aiken.

School actually had two recesses, called first recess and second recess. Lunch was always served during first recess and it was forty-five minutes long. Second recess came an hour after the first one ended, lasted thirty minutes, and its purpose was to let the kids visit the restroom, run around, exercise, and burn off some steam. When they were finished with second recess, there was only an hour and a quarter left before the final bell dismissed them.

Later in the week toward the end of the month, Anne Gannon started to talk about going to the Cotton Festival.

Casey perked up and asked what the Cotton Festival was. He had never heard of it.

Anne said, "This year is the first time it's ever been held, but it will be in Aiken next Thursday, Friday, and Saturday. And they're planning to have the festival every September from now on. You should understand, Casey, that cotton is very important to Aiken County. All around, in every direction, you can find farms growing cotton. They'll even hire you to pick it, but I warn you, it's very hard work. Down in the valley, you have all of those cotton mills. The biggest ones are the Graniteville Company and Clearwater Finishing Plant. This county is a textile center based on cotton. Almost all of the farms around Aiken grow some cotton, and ninety percent of the workers in Horse Creek Valley work at one of the cotton mills."

She continued. "The festival is going to be a really good time, Casey. On Thursday, there will be all kinds of exhibits in all of those mills and in the Municipal Building at the fire department. That night there's gonna be a football game between the Aiken Green Hornets and the North Augusta Yellow Jackets. Can't you just see those two swarms of 'bees' flying around? We can go to that with Jake if you like. You've probably never been to a high school football game. On Friday afternoon, a parade with decorated floats and marching bands will be held on Park Avenue and Laurens Street. They'll march all the way from the passenger train station to Eustis Park. That night, they'll block off Laurens Street downtown to hold a street dance and crown a queen. Then on Saturday, a men's golf tournament will be at the Aiken Municipal Golf Course. We can do some of those things and have a good time with other Aiken people and the crowds that come."

"I want to go to the football game and the parade if that's okay. Does any of it cost money to go?" he asked.

"They'll charge 25¢ or 50¢ each for the ball game, but that's all. Everything else is free. Okay, we'll plan to go to the game," she responded.

Jake wanted to see the football game too so they drove to Eustis Park on Thursday night, parking just outside the gate. "Boy, they've got lights so they can play at night," Casey observed.

"Yep," said Jake. "Those were installed back in the spring of this year. I read in the paper that it cost almost $10,000 to light it. Before this year, they had to play everything in the afternoon or on Saturday morning."

During the game, Casey spotted his friend Arlene and pointed her out to Anne. They had a chance to speak briefly at halftime, and Anne saw that she approved of this very nice child. During the second half, she told Casey, "I see why you like her. She's very kind and respectful to everybody. She's pretty cute too."

Casey blushed. He started watching the football game more closely and noticed that Aiken was getting beaten by North Augusta. When the game ended, Aiken had lost by three touchdowns. For Aiken players, he kept hearing the names of Cupp and Hair and Cook and Ellis. He wondered if the Ellis boy was related to his teacher.

The next afternoon, Anne and Casey walked downtown to see the parade. They were standing on Laurens Street to get a good view when Arlene Cushman appeared again and spoke to them. After a few minutes of chitchat, she introduced her mother. Anne had a chance to see Casey again in her presence, and she determined that this little girl's friendship had already meant a lot to him.

Casey told Arlene that he was trying to get a paper route to make some money and that he had already been earning a few dollars by helping to clean up dirty cars and by collecting empty drink bottles.

Arlene said, "In a couple of weeks, the horses will arrive for the winter at the train station, and after that I'll be busy for a few months helping to move hay around in barns and mucking out stalls. If you want to make a few dollars with me, I can probably get you included on that."

"Wow," he said. "That'd be great."

On the way back home after the evening's festivities were over, Anne mentioned Casey's little jobs and reminded him that schoolwork would always have to come first and the part-time jobs would be second.

He nodded in the dark as they passed the standpipe and answered her, "Aunt Annie Lou, I've been thinking about this a lot. We are gonna move next week into a bigger house, all because of me. Y'all's costs will get bigger because of me. I'm gonna try to make sure that you and Uncle Jake don't worry. I've decided to make all good grades this year. I'll always do homework first. But I'll also work a lot of small jobs to make money. I think I'll get that paper route before Thanksgiving. I can help Mr. Wynn clean up cars any day I go over to his house. I can find Coke and Pepsi and Nehi and Grapette bottles all over the place. I can even do that on my paper route. A lady wants me to pick up pecans at her house. I'm gonna learn how to caddy at Highland Park. Arlene might be able to get me working with the horse stalls. I see a bunch of stuff I can do. After I fill the bank account back up, I'll have my own money and maybe you and Uncle Jake won't be worrying about me and the money."

She smiled to herself on hearing his words and acknowledged that she heard what he said but added, "Just remember that schoolwork."

The next Saturday came all too fast for all of them. Jake had arranged for Jackson Moving to send a truck and two movers to handle all of the big things in the move, but he had also leaned on three of his friends who had pickup trucks to help him. Anne had it all organized into some packed boxes; plus, she had a few tagged items indicating where in the new house to put the item. After the first part was loaded onto the trucks, she rode with one of them and spent the rest of the day at the new house on Newberry Street.

Jake and Casey supervised things at the old house until it was empty and then drove to their new address. Anne fed everybody lunch and then the helpers departed. The remainder of that Saturday was spent unpacking boxes, hanging things on walls, and making furniture adjustments in each room.

Casey's meager personal items and his trunk were easy to get upstairs into his room. Anne had spent a small amount of his money to buy a bed for upstairs, and Casey was immersed all afternoon in fully appreciating having his very own bed and his very own private room. He had been in Aiken for six weeks, and things had changed for the better pretty fast. When he said his prayers before bedtime, he had a lot to be thankful for.

The days of October 1948 rolled by pretty fast. Casey quickly established a work routine that included homework, hunting for drink bottles, and a ride by Farris Wynn's house to see if there was any work to do. In the middle of the month, Arlene told him at school that the horses would start arriving the next day. He met her at the freight station on Park Avenue after school, and they watched the annual unloading. Some were reloaded onto horse trailers, and others were saddled and ridden off toward South Boundary and the horse district. A few were walked by their handlers in the same direction.

Arlene saw a trainer she recognized and ran over to him. He gave her a hug as if he were greeting a lost friend. They talked for a minute and then Arlene looked toward Casey and waved him over. Presto, Casey made his first contact with a person from the Winter Colony. Within two days, both Arlene and Casey were spending an hour every afternoon sweeping out stalls, raking and grooming the stable area, and removing horse manure from the stalls. They weren't paid much to do this work, but they were paid for every day they worked and in cash.

South Boundary

One day, on the way over to meet Arlene at the stables, Casey took special note when he crossed over South Boundary about just how pretty a street it was. At times, he was mesmerized by the beauty of the tunnel formed by the hundreds of live oak trees planted alongside the traffic lanes. When he asked Aunt Annie Lou about it, she was full of information about the history of the street and its trees.

She started. "You've found the prettiest street in Aiken, in my opinion. It got that way because of one man and the ride he used to take to get to work. Mr. Henry Dibble was the president of the Bank of Aiken, which was in the downtown area. But he lived in Montmorenci and drove his horse and buggy to work every day right down South Boundary. The story is that he thought it was a drab ride and he wanted to make it prettier. He bought some live oak saplings from Beaufort—where this kind of tree thrives—and talked the City of Aiken into planting them all along South Boundary. That was in the year 1880. Well, you can see the result now. Just gorgeous. By the way, that was a dirt street until last summer. It was getting so much traffic on it, the horse community finally gave in and allowed it to be paved." Casey was always grateful that his aunt seemed to know the answer to everything.

A few days before the end of the month, Mr. Johnson called Casey's house and asked him to stop by the newspaper office downtown. When Casey arrived, he learned that the old *Augusta Herald* carrier was giving up the route in a week. Johnson asked Casey, "Son, do you still want this paper route? It's a lot of work. You have to do it every afternoon, six days a week. It'll take you about an hour a day."

Casey's answer was immediate and unflinching. "Yes, sir, I'm ready to do it if you let me have it."

"Okay," said Johnson. "I want you to ride with the old carrier every day for the next week to learn where the customers are and how to do everything." Casey made the agreement and set up the time to be there the next day. He was now in the newspaper business!

Suddenly, Casey's life was very full. He made a deal with his aunt, Annie Lou, to start doing his homework right after dinner every evening. He explained it very well to her when he said, "It's the only way I can make the day work out. I'm still gonna try to help Mr. Wynn with the cars, and cash in the drink bottles I find, and work the horse stables with Arlene, and deliver my papers, and pick up pecans whenever somebody asks me to. I can make it work out every day if you just let me adjust things around differently."

She temporarily approved his new schedule but stated that his report card was going to get extra scrutiny from now on.

Casey took a liking to the regularity of having a paying job every afternoon. During that first week, he learned that the majority of his customers were on Hayne Avenue, Richland Avenue, and the streets that connected them west of downtown, out to the hospital. It was ideal and was not very far from his house.

Finally, it was November and the national election was held on the second. At school, the teachers were explaining the election process to students. A mock election showed that Thurmond made a strong showing but that Dewey would win. After dinner that evening, Jake asked Casey if he wanted to walk down to the *Standard & Review* office on Richland Avenue to check the election results. Casey was nervous about being alone with his moody uncle for that long a time but agreed because he had an assignment to be ready to discuss the election tomorrow.

He was surprised at what he saw at the newspaper office. Two large temporary blackboards had been erected outside on the street and in the median, with two clerks running up and down ladders and constantly erasing and reposting numbers as new precincts were reported in. It was pretty exciting to watch this scene of democracy in action. A large crowd had gathered to watch. It was clear that all of these people knew each other and respected each other. Overheard were comments about how great the United States was and how South Carolina was a necessary part of it. Jake and Casey sat under a tree to watch it all. The mixed aromas of magnolia and tea olive served as a background in a beautiful fall setting.

Casey decided to tell his uncle about his plans to work a lot of small part-time jobs in order to make money. His primary goal, he said, was to repay the money he had borrowed from the bank account. Jake showed real interest as Casey was talking, but the only thing he said at the end of it was, "Well, we'll see, won't we?" Casey interpreted the comment as skepticism on Uncle Jake's part. On the spur of the moment, Casey decided to reveal more to his uncle than he intended.

"Uncle Jake," he began. "You got $25 for me from my savings account a while back." He reached into his pants pocket and pulled out a wadded ten-dollar bill that he was keeping in reserve to give to his uncle. "Here's a big part of it back. I am making money as fast as I can."

"Well, well, well," stated Jake. "You got yourself quite a start, I see. Good for you. This goes back into the bank tomorrow." Casey smiled quietly to himself.

It was clear that Strom Thurmond was not going to win the presidency, but he made a strong showing in the South. The next morning's newspaper showed that he won in four states and received thirty-nine electoral votes. The shocker was that the unpopular Harry Truman beat Tom Dewey for the presidency. All the experts had thought that Dewey would win. The nation would continue to say "President Truman" and not be using "President Dewey" anytime soon.

Chapter 5

In November 1948, Casey's life began to settle into an acceptable pattern. He and Arlene Cushman had developed a good relationship with the manager of one of the largest stables on Two Notch Road. If one didn't mind the physical labor involved in moving hay and oats around into the right stalls, and if one didn't mind the smell of horse manure, and if your gag reflex didn't live too close to the surface, a young person could accumulate a decent amount of money quickly. Casey pocketed 25¢ every afternoon he worked there, as did Arlene, and he was averaging three days a week.

He had taken a liking to his paper route because it gave him an enormous amount of independence for over an hour every day. As his supervisor, Mr. Johnson, had told him, there was a base of sixty customers who subscribed to the *Augusta Herald* for whom he was responsible. The customer paid 30¢ a week for the newspaper and 5¢ of that belonged to Casey once he collected it. So it was possible to earn three dollars a week or over $12 a month. The paper route was his core job and the basis for the financial plans he began to structure in his mind.

One Saturday while he was visiting with Farris Wynn, he explained that his family life had "settled down some" but that he still worried about Uncle Jake.

Wynn said to Casey, "I don't know him very well, but the word on him on this side of town is to steer clear. He can be trouble."

Casey explained that his aunt was very supportive and that he had made a few good friends at school. He told Wynn that he had decided that the best way to worry about his future was to work hard, save money, get some education, and be ready for whatever life was going to throw at him.

Farris Wynn said, "That's a lot for a ten-year-old to worry about. I be hepping you as much as I can, y'hear?"

"Yes, sir," Casey responded. "I want your help by letting me help you clean up cars. I'll always do you a good job. I promise."

Later, when he rode his bike back home, he found his aunt and asked her a question. "Aunt Annie Lou, do you ever do any putting up food? You know, what ladies do in the summer with vegetables to save them?"

"I think I know what you mean," answered Annie. "We call it canning or pressure cooking. Why are you asking me that?"

"Do you have any of those jars used to do that?" Casey asked.

"Yes, they're called Mason jars. Here, I'll show you one." And she pulled an empty one quart jar from a kitchen cabinet.

"Yes'm, that's them. Can I have three jars for myself?"

Annie responded, "What in the world do you need them for?"

Casey was ready with the answer. "I'm starting to need a way to manage the money I'm earning. I want one jar for the money that is going back into the bank to pay for the money I borrowed. I want another jar to save the money I need to put in the plate at church and to use for presents at Christmas. I want a third jar to save all of the rest."

"Oh, Casey, I think it's a wonderful idea! Here, you can have the jars and the lids that go with them." She gave Casey three quart jars. He took them straight up the stairs and into his room.

Later, when he got around to finishing his financial organization, he found a crayon and wrote "#1," "#2," and "#3" on the metal lids and on the sides of the proper jars. He placed $2.00 into no. 1 bank jar, $1.33 into the no. 2 church-and-presents jar, leaving only 85¢ for jar no. 3, his slush fund jar. He was happy.

As Thanksgiving Day approached, the lessons at school took on an air about the pilgrims and being thankful for what we have. On a day that the stables did not need to be worked, Arlene asked Casey to meet her in front of the school after he finished delivering his newspapers.

He asked her, "What's up this afternoon?"

She said, "It's a surprise. Just meet me here at five o'clock."

When he arrived a few minutes early, she had her bike and greeted him, asking, "Have you ever been to Hitchcock Woods?"

"I have never even heard of Hitchcock Woods. What is it and where is it?"

Arlene answered, "Oh, you're in for a treat. Follow me on your bike." She led them to South Boundary and turned to the east, toward Laurens Street. They continued riding straight until they got to a gate at the edge of a clearing. Arlene stopped and dismounted from the bike.

"This is the beginning of the Woods," she started. "I don't know why this big set of woods is in Aiken, but I can tell you that it is pretty special. When you get home, ask your aunt about it. She'll know. We have to walk from here."

For the next hour, they explored the west end of the total property. When they reached a large expanse of sand, she told him, "This is the Sand River. It has been here for hundreds of years, I was told. It runs the whole length of the Woods, about two miles. As you can see, it doesn't have any water in it. It's a dry riverbed." They walked deeper into the woods, using Sand River as their only pathway for at least twenty minutes. As Casey looked around, he became aware that this dry river did not see wet conditions very often. There was no sign of moisture anywhere.

Sand River

When the sand got deeper and harder to walk in, she suggested that they turn back but use another route to return to the entry gate. In a few minutes, she found a humped-up ridge that seemed to parallel Sand River. She announced, "We can use this to get almost all the way back to the entrance gate. It's called the 'Devil's Backbone.' It's a natural elevated hump that goes a very long way in the woods, just like Sand River does."

Eventually, they arrived back at the bikes and Casey was full of questions. Arlene's answer was, "I don't know the answers. But my daddy told me once about an old Indian legend about the woods and about Sand River.

"He said that an Indian tribe lived quite a number of miles west of Aiken a long time ago and the chief's daughter, a young princess of the tribe, got very sick and was close to dying. Her father had a dream that commanded him to build a cot to carry his sick child to the east, toward the rising sun. He did this, and the tribe traveled until they reached a particular pine forest. In this forest was a river of sand with no flowing water. They resettled there in what is now called Hitchcock Woods. In a short time, the new place and better climate restored the health of the princess. Beyond this small story you'll have to ask your aunt. She knows a lot more about Aiken, I think. Now we'd better get going. It's almost dark."

When he was with his aunt again, he told her about his new find of Hitchcock Woods as well as the Indian legend. He also asked her a lot of questions.

"Casey, please understand that I've only been there once and it was a couple of years ago. Jake and I walked through the woods on a Sunday afternoon. They occupy the whole southwest corner of this town. It's about 1,100 acres right now, donated to the city of Aiken in 1939 by the Hitchcock family. I was told that their family owns about 9,000 acres of land in that part of Aiken County. The Winter Colony people have all kinds of horse events there during the winter.

It was nice of them to give some of that land to Aiken so that everybody could enjoy it."

"I really liked being there," remarked Casey. "It's so different from Montana. Arlene and I plan to go back there on our bikes some more. We didn't see any signs telling us not to go in there."

"Oh, it's okay for you to be there. Just be careful when you're there," Annie warned. "You will see horses and horse trails in there, but I don't know if bears or deer or bobcats live in there too. There will certainly be snakes in there. Just always be careful and don't get lost either."

Soon, hunting season started and Jake Gannon started taking some time off from work to go hunting with a few of his friends. The second time he did it, he did not get home for his dinner until well after ten o'clock at night. He came in loud, stomping around, belligerent, and roaring drunk.

Annie tried her best to quiet him down. One reason was that her patience had grown thin the last time he had done this to her. The second reason was because Casey was still studying and had never seen or heard Jake like this. Jake was having none of her controlling him. He got louder, with more yelling at Annie, more boisterous noises of throwing things around, and finally Casey heard some drinking glasses breaking as they were thrown against the wall. Casey, scared and wide-eyed, tiptoed to the head of the stairs and was trying to see what was going on downstairs. Unfortunately, the top landing steps creaked and Jake heard it.

Jake screamed, "You just get your little tail back in your room! This ain't none of your business. Now git, you little sneaky bastard!"

Casey scrambled back into his room and made sure the door made a noise when he closed it. He wanted to make enough sound for his uncle Jake to know that he was gone. *It's too bad I can't lock my door*, he thought. The last thing Casey wanted was for Jake to come barging into his room while he was drunk. He had no idea what to do, and he was petrified about what might happen next.

Then he heard loud footsteps as they approached the bottom of the staircase. At the same time, it was possible to hear Annie's muffled voice and her lighter steps. Suddenly, a crashing noise jolted the house from downstairs and everything got still and was quiet.

The footsteps on the stairs got no closer, and all sounds from downstairs ceased except for the loud closing of a door, probably the bedroom or bathroom on the first floor. Had Uncle Jake hit his aunt? Casey couldn't tell, and there were no more distinguishable noises from the bowels of the house.

Casey stayed very quiet for the next hour and cried softly from his fears. Finally, as the time passed, he relaxed a bit, tiptoed into the bathroom, and brushed his teeth. He performed all of it as soundlessly as he could, finally edging into his bed. It took him a while, but he finally went to sleep.

Next morning, Casey got up to go to school on his usual schedule. Aunt Annie Lou called the hardware store and told them that Jake would not be at work until later, that he had awakened feeling ill. Of course, he was still zonked out in his bed. At the breakfast table, Casey looked for signs of injury to his aunt but saw none. She sat with him and talked quietly to him.

"That man scares me to death when he does that, and it's been a long while since he came in drunk like that. Casey, I swear to you, I thought he had broken that habit. He is still in bed, trying to sleep off the liquor. I won't apologize for him. He has to do that for himself. I guarantee you that he'll feel some deep sorrow about last night. He always does."

Casey finally found his voice. "I was really scared. He sounded like a wild grizzly bear. Didn't he hit you? I thought I heard something bad at the bottom of the stairs."

"Oh, when he looked like he was going upstairs, I ran over to try to stop him, but I tripped on the throw rug and fell down. It made a lot of noise and hurt like the devil too, but he never touched me. If he had hit me, I can promise you we would have left this house last night. No, Jake did not hit me. When I fell, it shocked him and took the steam out of him and he wandered off to bed."

Casey was relieved and said, "That's good. I was scared. I'm not big enough to fight him yet, but one day, I will be."

"Try not to think about it today. You get on off to school before he gets up," she said. "We'll try to talk to him tonight."

He went to school, and at first recess, he ate lunch with Arlene Cushman, as was his usual habit. He told her about his uncle Jake arriving home from hunting all day in a drunken rage. She listened intently and then sat quietly for a few minutes.

Finally, she said, "Casey, you are my best friend at school and I don't want to hurt you. But I need to talk to you honestly about your uncle, Jake Gannon, and what people here in Aiken think of him."

He said, "Okay, I'm listening."

"He is known as a rotten skunk, and people don't like him. Most don't trust him although a few do. I worry about you all the time, and my parents worry about you too. They like Anne Gannon, your aunt, and that includes almost everybody in Aiken. I can't think of any bad thing I have ever heard said about her. Everybody thinks that your aunt Annie will protect you from Jake and his temper and his rotten ways, but people are worried about you. Be careful around him."

"Okay, I'm worried about him too," Casey responded. "I can't tell if he's gonna be kind or mean when he gets home from work every day. I think about that way too much."

"Like I said," Arlene repeated, "just be very careful."

When Casey got home from school and had already delivered his newspapers, Anne met him at the porch. "Your uncle Jake is at work. He went in after lunch. You feel like talking about last night?" she asked.

"If you want to, I will," was the answer Casey gave. He quickly added, "I thought about it all day long in school. He really scared me."

They spent the next hour reviewing the events of last night, and Casey voiced his concerns about his safety and his aunt's. They talked about their options and plotted a strategy to confront Jake at dinner about his behavior.

By the time dinner was ready, not a word was uttered by any of the three. There was no eye contact, and the only words spoken during the meal were, "Pass the potatoes" and "May I have another roll, please." In their short time of living together as a threesome, there had never been a similar scene.

When it was obvious that the meal had been finished by all, Jake finally broke the silence, and it caused both Annie and Casey to flinch. "Annie, you and Casey please clear the dishes to the sink. When you finish, come back in here and sit down. I've got some things I want to say."

Annie looked at Casey and issued a slight shrug toward him as if to say, "Let's keep our agenda to ourselves until we hear what Jake has to say."

After the table was clear, they came back from the kitchen and sat down, furtively eyeing each other with trepidation. Jake started out, "I want y'all to listen to me for a few minutes before you say anything. I got a lot I need to say." He poured some more iced tea and began.

"I did a terrible thing to both of you last night and I wanted you to know first off that I know that. I swear, when I drink, I don't have the slightest idea what direction my behavior is gonna go, so the first thing I want to say is that I ain't never gonna drink again. I know, Annie, that I've told you that before, but this time I really mean it. God as my witness."

He cleared his throat, took another swig of tea, and continued. "Last night, I know I scared the senses out of both of you, but you also need to know this. I scared the same thing out of me too. So this afternoon, I went to the bank, Casey, and made some changes in the way they handle your account. I put Annie's name on the account with mine and made it so that she has the power to take my name off of it anytime she thinks it's necessary. Annie, if I ever drink again, I want you to change it so I can't get to Casey's money. This is how I plan to live up to my promise not to drink anymore."

Annie and Casey looked at each other with some amazement because Jake's punishment for himself was much worse and in a different direction from what they had planned to try to impose.

She finally spoke. "Jake, you really did terrify us both last night, and we couldn't see how we could ever get along with you if that was going to be your behavior. Nobody, me included, wants to live in such a home."

She looked at Casey and asked him, "Do you have anything you want to say to Uncle Jake?" She also gave him a look that implied that he should not hold back but should speak forthrightly.

Casey had been totally surprised to hear what Jake said. He realized that this might be his best ever opportunity to improve his relationship with his uncle and at the same time to air all of his grievances, so he waded in directly.

"I know I am only a ten-year-old boy, and yes, sir, you scared me bad last night. I knew that if you came up those stairs, you might even kill me and I didn't have any way to stop you. I cried some after it got quiet downstairs because I was worried about myself and Aunt Annie Lou. I hate it a lot when somebody makes me cry. I'm helpless and I know it. Nobody likes it to be that helpless. I promised myself last night that I would kill you when I grow some more and get big enough to do it. I don't like myself for thinking it, but that's the honest thing that was running through my head."

He looked up from where he had been staring at the table to see if they thought he was making any sense. Annie was wiping a tear with her napkin, and Jake was biting at his lower lip.

Casey was a little bit encouraged by what he saw and continued, "I want to say some more. Uncle Jake, if I ever get a chance in my life to know what a daddy is supposed to look like, this is it. So far, it don't look too good. Please, please, be telling the truth about doing better. I can't stand it being scared of you all the time. I hate it. I can't stand it when I worry about Aunt Annie Lou. I can't stand it when you treat me like I was nothing. You can have all of my mama's money if it will make you treat us better."

When Casey's outburst was finishing, he had begun to cry. He could not help himself. Annie placed her arm around his shoulder and pulled him closer to her. "All right, all right, it's gonna be all right," she purred.

Jake's face had become very long and incredibly sad. He finally said, half to himself, "That's what happens when you drink. You foul up everybody's world around you, including your own." He was not usually a very emotional man, but Casey's words had penetrated to his core. He found himself wiping at his own tears.

"Casey, you listen to me," he began. "That money and any money that follows you to this house is yours and only yours. I swear by Almighty God that I won't touch a penny of it without your knowledge and your permission. And another thing, I am going to try to be a daddy to you as long as you live here. I want you to be happy that you live with us and not afraid of being here. I will do better, I swear before God."

With that comment, Jake stood up and walked around the table to Annie and Casey. He placed his gnarly hands on their shoulders and squeezed them gently. "It's a new day in this house," he stated conclusively and left the room.

Annie looked at Casey, hugged him tighter, and managed a tight smile. "My little friend, I believe we got way more than we expected. Jake might have finally grown up just now, and I am so happy about that. We both heard his promises. Let's wait and see. I have a feeling all of our lives are about to get better."

"Yes, ma'am," Casey uttered in response. And he was thinking that she was probably right.

SMOOTHER SAILING

Chapter 6

Thanksgiving Day came, and Annie Lou Gannon busied herself with making it a feast that all of them would remember. She had already prepared the turkey for baking on Wednesday and had assembled all the things necessary to give Casey a meal he would not forget. He told his aunt that Thanksgiving at his mother's apartment in Butte had always been a small affair.

"She was not as good a cook as you and we never had very big meals during the holidays," he told her. "You make these meals special. I can tell."

The meal she put on the table was outstanding, he told her later in the kitchen. It had consisted of turkey, stuffing, cranberry sauce, mashed potatoes, butter beans, macaroni and cheese, homemade bread, iced tea, apple pie, and ice cream on top of that.

When Thanksgiving dinner was over, he still had to deliver his newspapers. On the way out the door, he made sure he touched base with Uncle Jake. Ever since the big confrontation and apology of several weeks back, Casey had tried to stay closer to him than before. It seemed to be working. Jake Gannon was indeed trying harder than ever before to be a father figure to Casey, and he occasionally reminded Casey that "you can count on me." Casey liked what he heard, but he kept a bit of skepticism in reserve.

After the *Augusta Herald* was delivered, Casey decided to ride by the Aiken Municipal Golf Club on Highland Park as a way of learning more about the downtown area of Aiken. He was surprised to see activity around the practice green, and a foursome was coming in on eighteen.

Parking his bike against a tree, he meandered toward the center of the activity beneath the clubhouse. A colored young man intercepted him and inquired, "Are you looking for somebody, young man?"

Casey answered, "No, sir, I was just looking around and wondering if this golf course uses caddies to take clubs around for the golfers."

The colored man smiled and said, "Yes, we use caddies here. Have you ever caddied before?"

That was the question Casey dreaded, and he looked down as he said, "No, I've never done it before. Does that matter?"

The man laughed and said, "Young fellow, my name is Bubba Moseley. I'm the assistant caddy master at this club, and if you ever want to caddy here, I have to know who you are and give you some basic training and my permission after that. How old are you and what's your name?" Bubba smiled as he said it.

"I'm Casey Gannon and I'm almost eleven years old. If you train me, I'll do a good job for you."

"What makes you think you can be a good caddy? You know, it don't pay but $1.25 a bag for eighteen holes. You ain't gonna get rich doin' this."

"Mr. Bubba Moseley, I'm a very reliable worker. Once you train me, I will make you proud."

Bubba laughed. "Casey, there's something about you I like. I'll be carrying a bag myself Saturday morning and another one on Sunday afternoon. Can you be here at either one of those times to walk with me so I can show you what to do? It's gonna take about four or five hours and you don't get paid for it."

Casey grinned broadly and said, "Yes, sir, I can be here Saturday morning. What time?"

Bubba patted him on the shoulder and said, "Be here at ten o'clock sharp, Saturday morning."

"I'll be here. Thanks a lot." Casey was grinning from one ear to the other all the way back to the house on Newberry Street.

One of the things Casey had worried about was being able to fit in some caddying time into his newspaper route schedule. Working as a caddy on Saturday or anytime on Sunday was going to work out fine, at least this once.

On Saturday morning, Casey was full of anticipation about learning about a new way to earn money, but he was also nervous. He arrived at the clubhouse ten minutes early and sought out Bubba Moseley. When Bubba saw him, he grinned and said, "Okay, Casey, you've made a good first impression. On time and even a little bit early. I like that."

Bubba explained the game of golf to Casey and gave an example of a typical day for a golfer. "When a golfer gets to the course, he wants to putt some on the practice green, he wants to hit a few shots on the practice range to warm up, and he wants to check to make sure he has enough balls, enough tees, and his glove and shoes. Then he starts on the first hole. After nine holes, he might want a bite to eat. Then he tees off on the tenth hole to start the back nine.

"After the round, he might have a drink with his playing partners before going back home. Your job as the caddy is to carry his clubs, to give him the club he asks for, to help him spot where his shot goes so the ball doesn't get lost, and to hold the flag when he putts if he asks you to. Today, I'll be doing all of that for Mr. Winans, and you'll be tagging along to see how I do it. I'll explain what I'm doing as we go along, but you need to stay out of the way and be as quiet as possible. I'll explain to Mr. Winans why you're here and he'll understand. He's playing with a young college golfer named PJ. I met him once too. They're both nice men."

"Bubba, I'm a little bit nervous 'cause I've never caddied before," Casey confessed. "I don't want to mess up in front of these people."

Bubba looked at Casey with some understanding and not a small amount of compassion. "You're new to Aiken, but you need to understand something about this place. People here want you to succeed. Most of the time, if you are trying your hardest, Aiken people will help you. Ain't in nobody's interest to see you fail. Nobody here wants Casey Gannon to mess up. You got that?"

"Yes, sir," Casey muttered and he was relieved to hear Bubba's words.

Within a few minutes, Mr. Winans and PJ appeared, and the day began and proceeded as Bubba had explained. Casey learned about golf etiquette, the rules of golf, more caddying functions, and how to watch the ball in flight so it would not be lost. During the early part of the round, Casey noticed that abutting the left side of the golf course was a railroad track and an extensive expanse of woodlands. At a quiet moment, he edged over to where Bubba was standing and asked about it.

Bubba said, "Oh, that's easy. The railroad track is the one that runs from Augusta through Aiken, all the way to Charleston. It goes through the railroad cut that you see running under those bridges. The woods are part of Hitchcock Woods. You know all about that, right?"

Casey nodded that he knew and said, "Thanks."

After two hours, they stopped for a bite. The young man named PJ pulled a small portable radio from his golf bag as they were eating. A football game between the North Carolina Tarheels and the Virginia Cavaliers was in progress. For the remainder of the afternoon, Casey not only learned more about golf, but he was also treated to college football at its best and a player named Charlie "Choo-Choo" Justice, who seemed to be the best football player in the country, according to the excitable announcer.

Casey noticed that the golf holes wound in and out of a number of sandy roads like Hillcrest, Dibble, Valley Green, Fairway, Bissel, and Forest Hills. He had never seen this part of Aiken and made a decision to visit on his bike in the near future. The sandy lanes would be tough to do on a bike though.

At one point during the golf round, a ball was temporarily lost to the right of the fifteenth hole in the front yard of a pretty two-story stone house. Mr. Winans had sliced his drive over Hillcrest Road, putting it out-of-bounds. Casey was polishing his new skills of following a ball in flight and was the first to discover it in a bed of camellias and azaleas. After the round, Casey was surprised to receive 25¢ from the grateful golfer. A nice and unexpected surprise! And the University of North Carolina had been good enough to stomp Virginia by three touchdowns.

After the golfers had departed, Bubba told Casey that he had done very well in his caddy training and that it would be possible for him to carry an occasional bag at the Highland Park course. Casey explained about his paper route and that he would always have it as his first priority but that he would love to caddy on Saturday mornings and all day on Sunday. Bubba wrote down the Gannon's home telephone number, and Casey finally departed with a happy experience behind him. He had to hustle all that afternoon to get his newspapers delivered on time.

The week after Thanksgiving turned cold and inched into December. Casey had learned how to shoot marbles at recess during the first three months of school, and suddenly, it became too cold to enjoy doing it anymore. One of the new friends he had made while learning about marbles was a left-handed shooter named Tommy.

The playground on the south side of the school was well equipped with swings, monkey bars, an eight-person merry-go-round, and a steel sliding board. He used all these along with Tommy and several others. Elsewhere on the front playground, several groups of boys busied themselves shooting marbles.

One day, Tommy unexpectedly asked, "You wanna come over to my house after school? My daddy owns a junkyard full of wrecked cars, and we could have a lot of fun playing there."

Casey told Tommy about his afternoon paper route and explained that he was sure that he could work a visit in sometime soon. It was finally a good sign, he thought, that somebody else besides Arlene was reaching out to him.

In the weeks leading up to Christmas, Casey worked hard at all of his pursuits. He visited Farris Wynn often and vacuumed, dusted, and dried. He picked up pecans on Columbia Drive. He toted bottles to Freeman's Superette once or twice a week. He cleaned out horse stalls and spread hay with Arlene. And of course, he delivered newspapers and studied as hard as he could when he could find the time.

Just before Christmas, he decided to count his earnings. For some reason, he had been content to slam as much money as he could into his three Mason jars, but he had never stopped to count it. One night, he sat on his bed upstairs and dumped out the contents of each jar, one at a time, and counted it carefully. He was surprised to find that his no. 1 jar—repay the bank account—had $33 in it. That was significant because he only owed $15 to pay the account back. He extracted the extra $18 from that jar and set it on top of his dresser. The $15 he owed the account he stuck in an envelope and labeled it "Uncle Jake, Bank Account."

For the no. 2 jar—church and presents—he counted out $12.52. He had used this fund sometimes to drop an occasional dollar bill into the collection at church but had not bought any presents for anyone. That would have to change in the days coming up.

When he dumped and counted jar no. 3—miscellaneous —he was surprised to see that it already contained $21.50

before he added the $18 from the top of the dresser. Suddenly, he realized that his financial plan was coming together faster than he imagined it would. It looked like a small fortune to a ten-year-old boy. He decided at that moment that no one but him ever needed to know the exact contents of these jars. He felt that having funds all by himself that nobody knew the depth of would somehow give him unknown advantages. His aunt and uncle did not have a need to know. He would use the funds as generously as he dared from time to time, but he would not expose his financial condition to them as long as he never needed to ask them for money. It was a decision that would serve him well into the future.

Whenever the subject of Christmas came up at the dinner table, Casey tried to feel them out as to what they might want for a present. And in their turn, they were asking him directly what kind of presents he would be looking forward to. It was a kind of family dance and hints and word games that parents everywhere play with their close friends and relatives. Casey wanted a good baseball glove, but he had not told anyone. As soon as warm weather returned to Aiken in mid-February, he wanted to find a way to start learning and playing that game.

Just before Christmas, Casey's relationship with Arlene took a distinct turn in a new direction. Since they met in September, they had become close confidantes. After all, they worked together in the horse stalls a couple of days a week. A classmate's birthday party in the third week of December changed the relationship.

There were a dozen boys and girls in attendance, and someone suggested playing a game of Spin the Bottle. This involved all participants sitting in a circle and one of them being appointed as the spinner. A Coca-Cola bottle was perfect because it seemed to spin eternally on its fat waist before it ever thought about stopping. Arlene was named as the first spinner, and when the bottle finally stopped spinning, it was pointing directly at Casey.

The crowd erupted, "You've got to kiss her, Casey," and they screamed it more than once. He had never played this game before and didn't understand. Casey's face turned a deep red, but he didn't move. Arlene quickly realized that he was extremely embarrassed, so she said, "I'll take care of it." With that she leaned over and planted a large kiss on Casey's cheek, but much closer to his mouth than she intended.

That set off the other children even more. Someone said, "Boy, she aimed for his mouth" and added, "Woo woo!"

Casey was briefly mortified but also realized that he had just gone through a rather pleasant experience caused by his being able to absorb her scent. Within a few more seconds, the bottle was passed to another spinner, and Casey and Arlene were relieved to no longer be the center of attention. When he had a chance, Casey cut his eyes covertly toward Arlene and was surprised to see that her eyes sparkled back at him. She reached over and patted the back of his hand.

The party lasted about two hours, and it was finally time to make their exits. Casey had ridden his bike, but Arlene was being picked up by her mother. She made sure she walked out with him and said, "I'm sorry if I embarrassed you, but since we're friends anyway, it's better for me to kiss you the first time instead of those other girls. It didn't hurt, did it?"

"No," he moaned, reddening. "Didn't hurt." And with that, he gave her a funny look, mounted his bike, and rode off.

On Christmas morning, which was a few days later, he was awakened by his aunt Annie Lou jostling him slightly. He finally opened his eyes, and she said, "I was beginning to think you'd sleep all day. Most children in Aiken have been awake for hours just to see what Santa Claus brought them."

"Oh, you know I don't believe in that stuff," he said. "But I'm happy it's Christmas. Let me get dressed and I'll come right down." As soon as she left the room, he sprang into action by dressing and rooting around in his closet for some packages he had recently bought at Blake's Drug Store and Mack's Five and Dime.

When he appeared a few minutes later in the living room, Uncle Jake put down the *Augusta Chronicle* he was reading and welcomed Casey to his first Christmas in Aiken. They had been getting along much better since the blowup and showdown of a few weeks earlier. Casey had a paper shopping bag in his arms. "Whatcha got there, Casey?" asked Jake.

"Just a few things I bought for Christmas," answered Casey.

"Sweetie, you didn't have to do anything for us," Annie Lou said with surprise in her voice.

"It's not much," Casey responded. "I just wanted to show you and Uncle Jake that I am thankful for being here." With those words, Casey handed one wrapped package to Jake and two to Annie Lou.

Jake opened his first and discovered a carton of Camel cigarettes that Casey bought at Blake's Drugs. "Just my brand. Thanks a lot. I really appreciate this."

Then it was Annie Lou's turn. She had two small wrapped items that Casey handed her. The first was a box of chocolate-covered cherries from Whitman. He had bought this item at Blake's too. The second present was a glass juicer from Mack's. "Oh, Casey, you're too good to us. You must have heard me say that I wish I could squeeze my own fresh orange juice from the oranges I buy. Thank you very much."

Jake rose from his chair while she was talking and went into the master bedroom. One could hear him opening the closet door. Soon, he returned holding a wrapped package in one hand and a wooden baseball bat in the other. Casey's eyes rejoiced as soon as he spotted the bat. Jake handed over the box, and Casey wasted no time tearing the ribbon off and then the Christmas paper. Inside, there was a box labeled Rawlings and the smell of new leather. Nestled in the pocket of the glove, Casey found two brand-new baseballs.

"Wow, wow!" was all that Casey could manage to say. He was surprised and overwhelmed.

After he had settled back down, Casey remembered the envelope at the bottom of the paper bag. He pulled it out and gave it to Jake, with the words "That's to pay back the other $15 to my bank account. Remember, I promised I would earn the money by Christmas. I did it. There it is."

Jake spoke up. "You did a great job, Casey, in putting this money back and I'm proud of you." He paused for a minute and then added, "The Aiken County Recreation Department doesn't have baseball yet for boys, but the city of Augusta does. As soon as warm weather hits, I'll take you over to Augusta and join you up in their program. You'll enjoy it, I know."

"Thanks, Uncle Jake," was the response by Casey. Today was another piece of proof in his mind that Jake had indeed changed.

During the holidays between Christmas and New Year's Day, Jake and Casey made the opportunity to play catch with the new glove and baseballs out in the middle of Newberry Street in front of the house. One day, Jake suggested that they take the new equipment, including the bat, to an empty Eustis Park. It was only half a mile away at the end of a rutted Barnwell Avenue.

Once at the park, Jake showed Casey the basics of the batting stance, throwing posture, and other ABCs about playing baseball. He also introduced Casey to a game he had played in Augusta called "Roll-to-the-Bat." This involved throwing a baseball for distance and accuracy to try to hit the bat lying on the ground. For the first time, Jake saw that Casey had a stronger than usual throwing arm for a ten-year-old boy.

His thought to himself was, *This dang boy has the same strong Gannon arm that George and me had.* And it made him smile to himself. This stuff of teaching baseball to Casey looks like it could be fun.

Just before the end of 1948, Casey was still enjoying his days off for Christmas vacation, when his friend Tommy from the marble games called the Gannon house to ask if Casey could come to lunch at his house. Aunt Annie Lou gave her permission after a couple of questions, and Casey was off on his bike. The house he sought was out York Street toward Columbia. Tommy had said, "When you get to the railroad track crossing the road, you're here."

Casey was amazed to find that Tommy lived right adjacent to a side track of the railroad and his house was surrounded on three sides by wrecked cars and trucks. His father owned a wrecking yard and tow trucks and the associated paraphernalia.

During a peanut butter and jelly lunch, Tommy explained that he had a surprise for Casey when they finished. They went outside and headed for the far end of the expanse of junked cars, which were neatly arranged in rows and stacked two or three cars high. There was a strange-looking vehicle sitting idle in one of the passages between cars. It was a vehicle frame with four working tires, a plywood floor bolted to the frame, and two bentwood kitchen chairs screwed down to the plywood. Only a steering wheel and gearshift protruded above the plywood. A naked engine dominated the front. There was also a brake pedal, a clutch, and an accelerator. No fenders, no hood, no trunk, no headlights, nothing else.

"Ain't it a beauty?" Tommy asked.

"I don't get it," Casey said. "What's it for?"

"Man, it's to drive around this junkyard. And it's mine. My daddy made it for me," Tommy boasted.

With that comment, Tommy jumped on the plywood floor and sat down in the wooden chair behind the steering wheel. He presses a button somewhere, and the engine came to life.

"Move back and watch me," said Tommy.

Tommy shifted into first gear and scratched off, leaving a rooster tail of dust and smoke in his wake. He disappeared around a pile of cars, and Casey could hear everywhere Tommy went around the property. Presently, he reappeared and skidded to a halt in front of Casey.

"Wow," said Casey. "You can drive. How old are you and where'd you learn to do that?"

Tommy answered, "I'm ten, same as you, almost eleven. Daddy taught me to drive it and shift the gears. Ain't nothing to it. You wanna try?"

Casey thought for a second and tried to imagine all the trouble with Jake and Annie Lou if they found out he'd been driving. He said, "I want to try it, but I don't want my folks to find out."

"Don't worry," said Tommy. "We'll be right here in the yard and nobody'll even see us. I won't tell."

For the next hour, Casey learned about the gears, the clutch, the gas pedal, and how to use each of them somewhat effectively. He drove the machine slowly around the yard, carefully staying in the back part of the large property so that no one but Tommy would see his efforts. Of course, his friend was riding in the passenger seat the entire time to give advice and assistance when it was necessary. When he got to a point of proficiency, he drove the buggy back to its original parking spot, thanked his host for the lunch and for the unusual time in the yard, and said, "I have a paper route, you know, and I have to leave now to go do that. Thanks for teaching me to drive."

Casey rode his bike to the end of Columbia Drive, which was nearby, turned onto that, and cut through over to Edgefield Road. Using this route was a big decision on his part since it was soft sand and rutted for the entire distance. It was hard riding. Along the way, he passed by the pecan trees that he had helped the lady with a couple of months earlier. She was in the yard, recognized him, and waved. Then he made a turn onto Laurens Street and headed back toward downtown. All the way to his papers, he kept amusing himself with this thought: "I'm ten years old and I can drive."

Later that day, while they were eating dinner, Casey mentioned how hard it was at times to ride his bike through the deep, loose sand. Annie Lou commented about that by saying, "Casey, my understanding is that where we are right now, Aiken, South Carolina, used to be oceanfront property. Think about that for a minute. Millions of years ago, the Atlantic Ocean was washing back and forth right here. It deposited all of that nice sand here, on top of the clay and rock that's underneath that. The horse people from the Winter Colony love Aiken because of the weather, but also because of that sand. I've heard that the sand is so soft and gentle to the horse's hooves that it's okay sometimes to not put on their horseshoes. It's one of the reasons Aiken is a horse town."

"I sure am glad for the horses," Casey observed, "and hope they enjoy running around where it's nice and soft. It's not so good for the bike riders. We have to work real hard here."

Chapter 7

The year 1949 began in Aiken with a few new freshly paved city streets—tar and gravel only—and the same old president in the White House, Democrat Harry S. Truman. One of the jokes of the day was that the *S* initial stood for a synonym for manure. But Harry himself had proven to everyone that it didn't stand for anything, that he had no middle name, and had simply selected an initial since everybody else seemed to have one.

Jake Gannon had backed up his insistence so far that he was deadly serious about turning over a new leaf. To Annie Lou and Casey, he had become refreshingly easy to be around. No more walking on eggshells in the house on Newberry Street.

Casey's schoolwork was hovering strongly in the B-plus category. He had a couple of As, many Bs, and no Cs or worse. Annie Lou had relaxed about him keeping himself so busy. He was still engaged first in his paper route, but also cleaning horse stalls with Arlene, vacuuming out cars for Farris, picking up empty soft drink bottles every time he saw one, and being always on the alert for new income opportunities.

His relationship with Arlene had remained just about the same even though she had stolen an almost-kiss from him in the Spin-the-Bottle game in December. He finally asked her directly about that. The way he put it was, "Now why in the heck did you do that anyway?"

She reddened and smiled back, saying, "Are we friends or not? Are we best friends or not?" She stopped raking and put her hands on her hips and added, "Casey Gannon, I happen to like you a lot. I'm not sorry about it either. It looks to me like you like me some too. It's just natural to show that to you sometimes. Did you mind so much?"

It was his turn to have a red face. This conversation was now headed in a direction that caused him to squirm. Finally, he was able to muster a response from somewhere inside. "Arlene, you are my best friend, but I'm not ready to get all mushy with you or anybody. Just stay my best friend, okay?"

She saw his obvious discomfort and said, "Okay."

On one winter afternoon, they both showed up at the horse barn only to be told that they were there on the wrong day. "You're supposed to be here tomorrow, not today," was what they heard. On the spur of the moment, they decided to spend the time together anyway. They discussed whether to meander into Hitchcock Woods or to go to a movie at the Patricia theater.

Casey was immediately persuaded toward the latter and said, "I've been wanting to see a movie there ever since I've been in Aiken, but haven't done it yet. Let's go to the movie. I'll pay."

Arlene was also game for a spur-of-the-moment activity. They rode their bikes to Laurens Street and parked them in the bike rack in front of the theater. The movie *The Boy with Green Hair* was playing, starring Dean Stockwell, and neither of them had ever heard of it. For children under twelve, the tickets cost 11¢ each. Casey fished a quarter from his pocket, paid, and went into the theater. He used the 3¢ change to buy candy.

Only a few people were inside since it was a weekday afternoon. Once, during the movie, Arlene allowed her hand to brush against Casey's, and it was done on purpose. She was

testing him to see if he would hold hands with her. Casey
didn't bite. He continued watching the screen and moved his
hand slightly away from hers.

By the time the movie was over, it was late afternoon and
the winter sun was getting low in the sky. He knew he had to
hustle now to finish his paper deliveries before dark. He said
goodbye to Arlene and rode off hard toward his duties.

After a few months of living at the new address on
Newberry Street, Annie Lou had settled into a routine she
liked. One thing hadn't changed though. Like most women
living in the South, she washed the dirty clothes on Monday
and ironed them on Tuesday. Right after the move from
Pendleton Street, she had gotten Jake to install a sturdy
clothesline in the backyard between two trees. True to her
rural roots, she still loved the smell of clean clothes that had
been dried outside by the sunshine.

She was still called on from time to time to
substitute-teach at Aiken Grammar School, and it made her
keep up with and to read any new book that came out about
Aiken or South Carolina.

She also had made a strong effort to renew the contact
with those tradesmen who knew her and brought goods to
her. Clarence and his mule, Bubba, for example, already had
found the Newberry Street house and had renewed his home
delivery of fresh vegetables when they were available. Claude
Brown, a grey-haired farmer who owned his own small dairy
in the Redds Branch section of Aiken County, had also
continued to deliver milk, eggs, and butter to her front porch
twice a week. He used an old blue four-door 1941 Ford sedan
to deliver to her. She liked Mr. Brown because he was always
punctual, honest, and totally stood behind his products.

A funny thing happened early in 1949 regarding Annie Lou's reputation for being an excellent cook. One of Casey's new acquaintances at school, a boy named Albert, had started to follow Casey home from school each day. Because Aiken is a very friendly place and any such behavior is treated kindly, no one questioned this new attention that Casey appeared to be attracting.

Casey's daily habit when he arrived home was to grab a quick bite in the kitchen before he weighed in on any other endeavor. Because Annie Lou made twelve corn sticks from scratch each day after lunch in two cast-iron corn-stick molds, Casey's snack was often a still-warm corn stick or two fresh from the oven. If Albert was present also, and he usually was, Annie Lou always offered the snack to him as well. And he never turned her down, but always exclaimed that she had to be the best cook in Aiken and "this is the best cornbread ever made."

Annie Lou finally wised up and realized that Albert was only visiting them for the corn sticks and for no other reason. She tested the theory one day by announcing that "this is my last day of cooking cornbread for a while and I'm taking the rest of the month off."

Sure enough, Albert did not appear the next day or for the remainder of the week. He finally quizzed Casey at recess as to when Annie Lou was going to resume her cooking of cornbread.

Casey's answer was, "I'll be sure to let you know, but it's not yet."

On a pretty Sunday afternoon in February, Annie Lou suggested that all of them should go to the polo game that was due to start at 3:00 p.m. Jake was first to answer by saying, "I don't know a thing about polo, and I'm not too sure I want to learn."

But Casey quickly added his comments to the discussion. "Arlene goes to them sometimes, and she told me that they're pretty much fun."

"Okay," Jake said. "I know when I'm beat. How much does it cost?"

Annie Lou answered, "The sign at Laurens and Richland says it's $2 a car. I guess that means no matter how many are in the car."

Casey decided to add to the conversation again. He offered, "I have an extra dollar, and I'll pay that toward our ticket. Can we go?"

"Yeah, I guess so," Jake answered.

They loaded into the Hudson, and Jake drove them to Whiskey Road and proceeded to Mead Avenue, where the Whitney Polo Field was located. Jake was a bit uneasy as he paid the fare because he had no idea what to do next. The attendant made it easier by saying, "You can drive on in and find any empty spot at the edge of the polo field and park at the wooden curbs facing toward the playing field."

When they parked, it was obvious that some people stayed in their cars to watch the game while others exited the car and stood around talking to each other. *Heck, I can do this*, Jake was thinking, *and it might even be fun.*

Within a few minutes, Annie Lou spotted a friend of hers from the Grammar School. She came over and met the Gannon family. Annie Lou explained that this was their very first polo game although they had lived in Aiken for a number of years.

The friend, Betty, said, "Oh, you'll enjoy being here. Let me tell you a little bit about polo. The game is divided into six seven-and-a-half-minute periods called chukkers. At halftime, which is between the third and fourth chukker, they will put us all to work. The horses run up and down the field and really churn up the sod and grass. We get to go on the field to fix all of the divots the horses have kicked up. That makes it safer for the riders. Each team has four players, and each player usually brings three or four horses to use during the game, saddling a new mount between the chukkers. The field is 300 yards long and 160 yards wide. The ball used is made out of wood and painted white. It's about the size of a baseball. Think of croquet for similarities. The player is trying to hit the ball between the goalposts at each end of the field. His team gets a point for each one. Highest score wins. That's about it. I hope y'all have a good time." She exchanged a few more words with Annie Lou and went back to where her car was parked.

Jake, Annie Lou, and Casey were impressed as the horses ran up and down the field, sometimes coming perilously close to parked cars. At halftime, they all ventured onto the field and repaired divots, as the public address announcer had requested.

The game restarted, and during the fourth chukker, a cold front started moving into the area. Within twenty minutes, the temperature had dropped fifteen degrees and the wind kicked up, making a slight misty rain almost unbearable. This was February and getting very uncomfortable.

None of them were dressed for the rapid shift of weather, and they first took refuge in the car but were already too cold to warm up rapidly. Annie Lou made a suggestion. "This looks like it's gonna settle in for the long term and I'm cold. Let's go home." Casey and Jake both nodded in agreement, and Jake started the car, joining a small motor procession away from the polo game.

When they got home, Jake quickly started the oil furnace that was under the floor of the downstairs hallway. For the next ten minutes, all three were huddled together, standing on top of the metal grating that separated the interior of the house from the floor furnace.

In minutes, all three were feeling much better and Jake offered, "It's too bad we all have to stand over the air flow, but it sure feels good, don't it?"

Casey appreciated the warm heat, but he had a different thought. "Uncle Jake, when it gets really hot this summer, how will we stay cool enough to stand it? Will this thing blow cold air too?"

Jake laughed and asked, "How can you even think of it being too hot when we're all standing here shivering?" Then he answered the question. "No, this thing won't blow cold air. I guess I'll have to put a window fan in the other bedroom upstairs or find a way to install an attic fan. That way, we can suck the hot air out of this house in five minutes." Casey liked it that his uncle Jake had an answer.

For quite a while, Casey had been itching to explore Aiken a lot more, both on foot and on his bike. On a warm March day after he had delivered his papers, he rode to the passenger depot at the corner of Union and Park and leaned his bike against a tree on the shady side. He walked across Park Avenue to the wooden bridge (called the high bridge) and went down the embankment to the railroad track.

He set out to the west, toward Chesterfield, Newberry, and the golf course where he had been caddying. He tried to note each of the six wooden bridges as he passed under them, pausing under Laurens Street long enough to hear the occasional *Brrrump! Brrrump!* as a car passed over his head. One thing that impressed him the most was how deep the railroad cut was all along the route. The track finally started coming out of the deep gouge as he neared the first hole of the golf course. He walked on, paralleling holes one and two. Once or twice he saw something in the Hitchcock Woods off to the left that motivated him to detour and investigate. But finally, he saw that light was dimming.

Rather than return the same way he came, he crossed the golf course on the third hole and, working his way back toward the downtown area, he finally recognized his surroundings on Highland Park Drive. He ran all the way back to the passenger depot, along Park Avenue. It was a distance of well over a mile to get back to his bike. As if he were checking off a list in his mind, he thought to himself, *Well, I've been there, and done that, and I'll probably do it again, maybe the next time with Arlene.*

A week later, Uncle Jake suggested that they drive to Augusta to talk to the baseball people who ran the youth leagues there. The prospect of finally getting started got Casey excited.

As Jake nosed the Hudson along U.S. 1 toward Augusta, they suddenly came upon a massive scene of construction about three miles out of downtown Aiken. Jake said, "I've been hearing that there was talk of a new Aiken-Augusta superhighway, and this looks like the beginning of it. Boy, that's pretty exciting to think that one day soon we'll have another way, a faster way to drive to Augusta."

As they drove on through the small towns, they bisected Stiefeltown, Warrenville, Gloverville, Langley, Burnettown, Bath, and Clearwater. Not directly in their path but nearby were also Graniteville and Vaucluse. Jake continued to talk about the prospect of not having to drive through the Horse Creek Valley and seeing all the cotton mills, the mill houses, and heeding the many speed zones. "I'll be a happy man when the superhighway opens up."

Casey decided to ask a question. "Don't a lot of lint heads live here in this valley?"

Jake's head snapped around. "Where did you get a question like that?" he asked.

"I heard it at school," Casey replied nervously. "One of my friends said that nobody but lint heads lived in the valley."

Jake shot back, "I don't want to hear you using that kind of language. It's insulting to these people." He paused and asked, "Do you even know what a lint head is supposed to be?"

"No, sir, I don't."

"Okay, listen to me for a minute," Jake responded. "Do you remember when we went to the Cotton Festival in Aiken a few months back, September, I think it was?"

"Yes, sir."

Jake continued. "Well, the Cotton Festival was a kind of celebration of the harvest of the cotton crop in Aiken County. When crops are harvested just about anywhere in the world, there's apt to be a wine festival, or a wheat festival, or a corn festival to celebrate it. Aiken produces a lot of cotton, and the mills in this valley are in the business of buying that cotton and turning it into thread and then cloth so that we can have bedsheets and towels and shirts and dungarees and anything else we might like that's made out of cotton cloth. The people who work in these cotton mills run the machines that change that cotton crop into large bolts of cotton fabric. They're called mill hands, not lint heads.

"I want you to have some respect for them. Any man or woman who has the gumption and the giddy-up to get out and get a job should never be picked on. Anybody who gets up every morning and goes to work to earn a living for himself and his family deserves your respect. If you just have to complain about somebody or to show disrespect for somebody, save it for the person who has the ability to get a job but decides to sit on his ass and stay home drinking beer and just lets the county welfare system feed him and his family. That's the bozo who needs his rear end kicked and who deserves your scorn, not the mill worker, got it?"

"Yes, sir," answered Casey. "I understand it." He was surprised at the level of his uncle's vehemence.

As soon as their car left Clearwater and was approaching North Augusta, again there were signs of massive road construction. Just before reaching Schultz Hill and the dirt airstrip on the right, there was a high bluff overlooking the Savannah River and the Augusta skyline. Road graders were plowing back and forth, creating the anticipated new right-of-way. Jake could not suppress a broad smile. Progress was finally heading this way, he thought.

When they arrived in downtown Augusta via the Fifth Street Bridge, Jake sought out a parking place on Broad Street, very near the entrance to Bowen Brothers Hardware. He had a friend working there who was "up to his eyeballs in youth baseball" in the city of Augusta.

After they talked for a few minutes, Jake walked back to where Casey was waiting and said, "He just told me flat out that we can't do what I was trying to do. He said that if you don't live in Augusta, you can't play in Augusta's youth baseball leagues. It's in their by-laws or something. We have to get you into baseball some other way. I'll find a way to do it."

On the way home, as they traveled near Clearwater, Jake was scanning the countryside as he drove. He spotted a herd of dairy cows, grazing on a rolling knoll. He tested Casey by asking, "Tell me what you see there."

Casey sensed that they were playing some kind of game, and he quickly responded without a pause, "I see seventeen brown-and-white milk cows and one brown bull."

Jake was not prepared for such a precise answer, so he shot back, "Just tell me how you know that?"

Casey answered again, "That's what I saw. I promise. Let's turn around and go back to count 'em."

Jake was game. He slowed and did a U-turn to backtrack. At the proper spot, he parked on the grassy shoulder, turned off the car, and they both got out. Jake was soon aiming his finger at the distant herd and ticking off his count. "I'll be damned. How did you know the answer so quick and so accurate?"

"I'm not sure how I do it," Casey said, "but I always try to see as much in one look as I can." Then pointing to the telephone line across the road, Casey expanded his explanation. "See those birds on the wire? While you were parking, I could see and count twenty-seven birds. I don't know what kind, but I'm pretty sure about the number."

Again, Jake pointed and counted. "Exactly twenty-seven. You amaze me. Just how good is your eyesight? You ever been tested?"

"No, sir," Casey answered. "But I've always been able to do this for just as long as I can remember."

The next morning, Jake told Casey and Annie Lou that it looked like there won't be any baseball team this year. But then he added, "Casey, I am going to spend my spare time this year being your baseball tutor. We'll talk baseball a lot and go to Eustis Park when nobody else is using it. We'll hit some and throw some, and I'll coach you how to do things in baseball. When you finally get to play on a team, you'll already know what to do. We won't waste this year at all. And if one or two of your friends want to be in our little training camp, they can come too."

Both Annie Lou and Casey thought it was a good plan. They were thinking that it seemed to be a continuation of Jake turning over a new chapter in his life.

Chapter 8

As soon as the days started to turn warm in late February, Jake and Casey could be seen playing catch out in the middle of Newberry Street. On Sunday afternoons, after church and lunch, they would walk in the deep ruts on Barnwell Avenue the half mile to get to Eustis Park. On occasion, there would be other boys and their fathers doing the same thing.

The adults pitched—at first underhand—to the young boys who were eager to find out if they had any kind of natural gift for hitting a baseball. Casey was able to connect right away, as he seemed to have unusual hand-and-eye coordination for a boy his age. Others had more difficulty, and their fathers would pull them aside to give more basic instruction. All who participated agreed that they saw improvement from week to week and that they should continue to do it.

During early March, Jake received a new letter from Willus Grover, Vera Gannon's old boss in Butte. The letter contained a check for $53 along with the explanation that he was finally able to sell Vera's old car for $50 and he even got $3 for Casey's old bicycle, which he had left behind.

The Grover letter went on to say that he had been interviewed several times by the insurance company about Vera's death, one time while under oath in an official hearing. He opined that they still were wrestling with the idea that her death was a suicide, but he had assured them that he knew her very well and for several years and that the death was an accident, pure and simple. After Jake deposited the check into Casey's bank account, he brought the deposit receipt home for all to see. Casey and Annie Lou smiled to see his account growing some more.

In the first week of April, Jake came home from work one day and asked Casey if he wanted to go to a golf tournament in Augusta. Casey was quizzical. "Does Augusta have a golf tournament, and who plays in it?"

Jake answered directly, "You've heard of Bobby Jones, haven't you?"

Casey said, "Maybe I have, but I'm not sure."

"Well," Jake started, "he's a very famous golfer from Atlanta who built a new golf course in Augusta about fifteen years ago, and he started an invitational tournament at it called the Masters. Somebody came in the hardware store today, gave me two tickets to go to it this Sunday, and if you want to go with me, we'll go. Usually, they have people like Ben Hogan, Sam Snead, Byron Nelson, and Jimmy Demaret playing in it."

"Yes, sir, I'd like to go with you," Casey answered.

After church on Sunday, the two of them piled into the Hudson and drove to Augusta to see the Masters. On the way there and back, Jake had another opportunity to see the progress on the Augusta superhighway. Casey loved seeing a golf tournament since he had never been to one. They watched Jimmy Demaret as he dropped the final putt at the eighteenth hole to win it and the $2,400 that went to the champion.

On the way home, Casey told Jake, "That was a lot of fun. I'd like to do that again sometime. How much did it cost us?"

"It didn't cost us anything because somebody gave me tickets they couldn't use. But the price printed on the ticket said '$3.00 for daily ticket.' Anybody can go if they just walk up to the gate and buy a ticket. I've been told that you can go for the whole week for $10 and tickets are always available."

A couple of weeks later, Annie Lou directed a question to Casey. "Do you plan to do anything in the Bicycle Rodeo?"

"The what?" Casey inquired.

"The Bicycle Rodeo," she repeated. "It's gonna happen for two days at Eustis Park toward the end of May. The Aiken Police Department is putting it on for boys and girls aged eight to sixteen. It's all about bicycle safety or something. But they'll have girl and boy races, by age, and riding an obstacle course. It sounds like fun, and some prizes will be given out. I'll bet somebody from your class will be doing it."

"Yes, ma'am, I think I'd like to do that," Casey finally answered.

The rodeo was conducted on the last weekend in May. Casey decided to enter only one event, the boy's race. He had ridden his bike a lot for the past few months, and quite a lot of it was on the sandy streets while delivering his newspapers. In fact, he often had to stand up with his behind off the seat in order to pedal the bike through the thickest sand.

When he arrived at Eustis Park, there were signs that directed him to sign up for the events he wanted to enter. The registration table was set up on the first row of the very large roofed green grandstand that dominated the right side of the grounds. A policeman who supervised his event explained the rules to a group of about twenty-five ten-year-old boys. The race for his age group would begin on the chalked first baseline of the baseball field, and racers were to ride toward the left field fence. In the outfield, a white rope was lying on the ground and riders had to cross the rope, execute a 180-degree turn, and ride back to the first baseline, which also served as the finish line.

Casey felt that he had a chance to win but decided to use his brain as well as his legs in the process. He grabbed a quick lead and calculated his turn so that he barely nipped across the rope in the outfield before heading back for the finish. He won by several yards. The officials huddled together and decided that they would not declare him the winner.

Casey complained quietly, "I did cross the rope out there, just like you asked."

The race official replied, "We expected you to ride across the rope, then turn around and ride back, just like all of the other riders did. You didn't do that in coming in first. You had an unfair advantage. We are gonna run the race again."

Casey was embarrassed and gnashed his teeth, promising himself to win by even more on the second race. But he said nothing.

The racers lined up again and started when the starter's pistol fired. Casey rode as hard as he could, standing on his pedals and pumping his legs at their maximum for the entire race. In the outfield, he carefully crossed the rope straight on, then made a sweeping turn while a nearby official watched, and tore back toward the finish line, still pedaling hard with no sitting and no coasting. He won again, this time with twice the margin of the first race. Casey felt a great relief with the result.

During the awards ceremony, the race official, an off-duty policeman, was effusive in his praise. "Son, I think you showed us for sure who the best racer was today. I'm sorry you had to do it twice. Congratulations, and you win a new bicycle basket as your prize."

Then he pulled Casey aside, lowered his voice, and added, "I figured you probably won the race that first time fair and square and by the rules, but I didn't want even one boy going home with the idea that you cheated to win. I didn't want you thinking that you took an unfair advantage of anybody either." The comment impressed Casey. Although he could have lost the second race or even fallen down, he saw the wisdom of the policeman in making them race twice. *Even the cops in Aiken are nice*, he thought.

Casey nested the new basket into his old one and, using a narrow sandy bike path that was part of Barnwell Avenue, rode the half mile to their house on Newberry, passing by Aiken Prep School on the way. Annie Lou was working in a flower bed in the front yard when he rode up. He told her the entire story, and she beamed at the details.

"I'm so proud of you for winning, but I'm even more proud that you kept your temper under control when they made you win it a second time. You already have a basket. What are you going to do with this new one?"

Casey had already figured out what he wanted to do. "I'm going to put it in the tool shed out back for a while. Then later this year, I'm planning to buy you a bicycle for a present and put this basket on it."

She was stunned by his generosity. "Casey, that's going to be expensive for you, but I love the thought. Thank you so much, sweetie."

As soon as the sun went down that evening, Annie Lou called attention to the small dots of light moving around in their yard. "Casey, have you paid any attention to the lightning bugs all over the yard? You haven't said a thing."

"I was about to ask you," Casey answered. "In Butte, we had something called fireflies."

"Lightning bugs are the same thing, sweetie. You interested in helping me catch a bunch of them in a mayonnaise jar?" she asked him.

"Yes, ma'am," he answered back.

They had fun for the next half hour chasing and capturing the bugs. While they were finishing up, she asked him, "You want to help me tomorrow catch a few June bugs to fly around?"

He was puzzled by the question, and his face showed it. She continued, "June bugs are out during the daytime right now. We'll catch a few tomorrow and tie some of my thread to them and fly them all around the yard."

The next day, they flew June bugs around after school. Casey could not remember a time when he had more fun.

School was out a week later, and Casey's report card showed two As and four Bs. Jake and Annie Lou were happy at his abilities to get good grades and be able to perform as many job-paying tasks as he had done. They had seen him grow from the slightly timid boy who had arrived scared and reticent in August to a more confident capable boy by the next June. He had also grown two inches in height.

During the first week of summer, Jake and Casey spent some time throwing and hitting the baseball at Eustis Park. It was starting to be evident to Jake that his protégé was getting to look more and more like a natural athlete. His throwing motion appeared to be more mature than boys three or four years older. And his stride when swinging the bat looked adult rather than boyish. Jake was happy with the progress.

Also, Annie Lou decided that Casey needed to get acclimated to being around water. She checked out the municipal pool farther downtown on Newberry but decided that it was too deep for a beginner. She abandoned that plan. On the next Sunday afternoon, she talked Jake into driving them to Scott's Lake, a popular swimming lake seven miles from town toward Columbia. On the way there, she started talking about the polio epidemics that seemed to take hold every summer, particularly in the South.

"Casey," she started, "polio is a terrible disease, and nobody knows what causes it. It seems to attack children before other people. It can kill a person in days. It cripples legs, ruins lungs, and destroys speech. It seems to have something to do with swimming places, warm weather, and germs that can pass easily from person to person. I don't want you to die or end up in an iron lung for the rest of your life. So if I say go wash your hands, you go and do it, or if I say out of the water or if I say stay away from those people, don't sass me, just do it. Polio doesn't play around, and I won't either. We already know too many people right here in Aiken who've been afflicted with this horrible disease. I don't want it to happen to you, you get it?"

Casey had never seen his aunt so serious. All he could manage to say was, "Yes, ma'am."

They got to the lake, paid the 10¢ admission fee, and had a wonderful time splashing around in mostly shallow water. Casey did not learn to swim well that day, but he got a good feel for everything that was involved, including how to hold his breath. Most important, he was no longer afraid of being in the water. All three agreed that they would have to repeat this day again before the summer was over.

The last week of June arrived along with a withering heat wave in Aiken. Casey could not believe how much the heat could build up in the top of their house compared to the relative comfort of the downstairs. He sweated his way through two very hot, still, stuffy nights and arrived downstairs each morning with wet hair. On the third afternoon, Jake brought home a thirty-six-inch electric fan and spent the next hour mounting it in one of the windows of the spare upstairs bedroom, the one that shared the upper house with Casey. After testing it and closing all the windows of the house down to a two-inch opening at the bottom, the fan was drawing the hot air out of the house as cooler air flowed from outside through the small openings provided by each window. Casey and the entire household were as comfortable on the third night as one could reasonably expect.

July 1, 1949, was Casey's eleventh birthday. As the date approached, Annie Lou announced that she would make one of her special "double chocolate" cakes to celebrate the event. Double chocolate simply meant regular chocolate cake accompanied by rich chocolate icing to hold the four tiers together. Casey told her that just his saying the words "double chocolate" made his mouth water. "Who would you like to invite over?" Annie Lou asked.

Casey thought for a minute then spurted out, "Arlene, Tommy, and Farris Wynn."

"Isn't Farris Wynn the colored man you help with the cars?" she asked.

"Yes, ma'am."

"Well, okay, that's who we'll ask," she answered him back. "I'll call Arlene's mother and Tommy's mother, but you'll have to invite Mr. Wynn because I don't know how to contact him, all right?"

"Yes, ma'am, I'll ask him tomorrow," Casey said.

The next day, Casey rode his bike to where he knew he would find Farris Wynn and he made the invitation.

Farris was puzzled. "You sure you want to do this?" he asked. "Y'know, it's not very usual for a white boy to ask a colored man to come to his house for a birthday party."

"It's okay. You're my friend. You've been nice to me. I want you to come." And he gave Farris the address and the time to come.

At 3:00 p.m. on July 1, Casey Gannon had his eleventh birthday celebration on the wraparound porch of their rental house. Annie Lou had guessed that Farris Wynn would be reluctant to come into their house and sit around a dining room table with three children and one adult to eat a birthday cake and some ice cream. She was right because he told Casey later that he was going to eat on the porch when he came. So she figured it all out ahead of time, was one step ahead of everybody, and set it up so that they all ate on the porch.

It was obvious that Farris liked Casey and had respect for him. He had on a starched shirt and his good shoes, but he did not leave the service cap which made him look a bit like General McArthur at home. He wore it but removed it when they sat down to eat. He never went anywhere without that cap.

The party lasted only an hour as it was mostly an opportunity for friends to see each other briefly to eat ice cream and cake in the middle of a summer afternoon. Casey received a small gift from each of them and thanked them over and over. Arlene was particularly happy to be there since she had not seen him for about a month. Farris ate quickly and left, claiming to have more cars to clean up.

Before Tommy left, he pulled Casey aside and asked, "Your paper route is mostly around Hayne Avenue and Dibble Road, right?" Casey nodded in agreement. Tommy whispered in a conspiring tone, "Meet me tomorrow at five o'clock at the corner of Forest Hill and Dibble Road. I've got a surprise for you. And we'll have some fun."

"Okay," Casey whispered back. "I'll be there."

The next afternoon, Casey finished his newspaper deliveries early and rode to the intersection Tommy had indicated. Tommy was standing at the corner, anticipating the arrival of his friend.

"Okay, here I am," said Casey. "What kind of surprise do you have?"

"Follow me," Tommy responded, and he set off down a dusty Forest Hill Drive in a slow trot. Casey followed on his bicycle as best he could, considering the deep ruts he had to negotiate with the bike. When they had gone about two hundred yards, Tommy turned left into another sandy lane and stopped.

"This is it. Welcome to Snake Road, my other playground and racetrack." With that, he pointed to some underbrush where his junkyard car—the one without the body—was parked.

Casey's face lit up. "How did you get that car over here? We must be two miles from your house. You didn't drive it here, did you?"

Tommy displayed a wide, proud grin. "Oh yeah, I drove it here myself, just before you got here."

"But how did you hide it from the police?" Casey asked. "It's not a legal car. They'll put you in jail if they catch you, won't they? And take away the car too?"

Tommy beamed. "I come over here a lot to drive it in the deep sand on Snake Road. I bet the Aiken Police Department don't have but about ten cops, and they're spread out all over the place, mostly where the streets are paved. When I leave my house, I just stick to all of the back roads, all of them dirt roads. In Aiken, that's pretty easy to do. I'm careful and I take my time getting over here. It's the best place in Aiken to drive this buggy because Snake Road has no trees on either side to run into, it's got good deep, loose, sandy ruts for almost half a mile, no houses anywhere in sight, big fun S-shaped turns back and forth, and nobody to bother us."

"But," Casey inquired, "what about the golf course? We're pretty close to the twelfth and thirteenth holes. Won't the golfers see us? Or at least hear us?" Casey was nervous about the idea of riding an illegal car out in the open. He immediately had the thought that he had just turned eleven yesterday and didn't want to be labeled as a criminal so young.

Tommy reassured him. "I've done this a bunch of times here and never been caught. We're safe because everything else is so far away. No houses. No cops. No traffic. For the noise, my daddy put a muffler on the tailpipe. We'll be okay."

Casey finally relaxed and got off his bike, stopping to lean it against a nearby sand hill. Tommy said, "Get on the buggy and I'll show you Snake Road." They sat next to each other on the bentwood chairs, and Tommy started the engine. It purred quietly as he backed it out of its hiding place.

He positioned the four wheels and naked chassis in the deep sandy ruts and dropped the stick shift into first gear, slamming his foot on the accelerator as he simultaneously allowed the clutch to rise under his left foot. Casey watched it all as closely as he could because he knew his turn to drive would come.

Snake Road was, in fact, flat and shaped like a snake that was in a hurry. It wove back and forth for a distance of about half a mile. It started as an obscure lane off Forest Hill Drive and exited back onto Forest Hill after seven or eight rather pronounced zigzags, all of them in deep sand and all of them potentially precarious for a young driver. At the far end, Tommy slammed on the brakes and slid the car into a 180-degree turn, positioning it for the return trip.

Casey only had time to say, "Wow, a great ride!" before Tommy accelerated again. At the end of the return trip, he looked at Casey, asking, "Wanna try it yourself? I'll ride with you."

"Oh yeah," was Casey's answer as they exchanged seats. For the next thirty minutes, they rode back and forth on their make-do racetrack. Casey was very nervous at first as he reacclimated himself and his feet and sense of timing to the task of engaging the clutch, shifting gears, and making the buggy ride smooth. By the end of their joyrides, he was almost as accomplished as Tommy at making it go hard and fast.

Casey was full of appreciation for the experience he had just gone through. "Thanks a bunch, Tommy. I really like doing that. But I have one question. Is this place really named Snake Road? And are there lots of snakes living here? I was looking, but I didn't see one."

Tommy laughed hard. "Naw, I've never seen a real snake here and I don't even know if this road has a name. I call it that because of the way it goes back and forth, shaped like a snake."

When they parted, they promised to do it again soon. Tommy drove off slowly and quietly in the general direction of the hospital and Eustis Park while Casey aimed his bicycle toward Hayne Avenue and the downtown area. He was smiling all the way as he replayed the experience in his head. He could not keep himself from laughing and having this thought: an eleven-year-old boy just taught another eleven-year-old boy how to drive and race a car. Wow!

During the next week, Casey decided to satisfy one of his curiosities about Aiken. Although he had attended Aiken Grammar School for an entire year, he had never explored much of the area south of the school. For example, although he knew that Chesterfield Street terminated at the school and a strange-sounding thoroughfare named Whiskey Road started at the school and extended farther to the south, he had never actually ridden his bike on Whiskey Road. He wanted to see what this unusually named road was all about.

One morning in mid-July, he took his bike and headed south toward the school and beyond. On the way, he was surprised to see an electric traffic light controlling the traffic at Aiken's primary intersection, Richland Avenue at Laurens Street. A stop sign had surprisingly been replaced by the installation of red and green lights facing all four directions. Drivers running the stop sign was about to become a thing of the past.

While he was riding toward the school and digesting the new downtown environment, he got to the Aiken County Courthouse at Chesterfield and Park and saw yet another set of new traffic signals there. *Holy cow*, he thought, *this place is being invaded by modernization.*

Finally arriving at the end of Chesterfield and the beginning of Whiskey, he noticed immediately that the street got a lot narrower and the houses a lot grander. The serpentine brick walls also were very different from the other parts of Aiken. He realized that he was now in the Winter Colony part of town and that most of the large houses he passed were vacant during the summer. The traffic was very light on the two-lane road. Occasionally, a dirt road would intersect with his paved, but potholed highway. He had heard of the Fermata Club and finally saw where it was.

Palmetto Golf Club

After he rode past the club, the road continued to be two lanes as it narrowed considerably, but the overgrowth of trees hovering over the sides of the road ceased. He was now riding out in the bright sun. He was surprised to see a golf course on the right as he continued. Nobody had ever told him that there was a second golf course in Aiken. He would ask his aunt about it. Suddenly, after the golf course, he was riding on a lonely, relatively deserted rural road with no houses or other signs of civilization. He was out in the country, and all of Aiken seemed to be behind him. When he came to that realization, he knew his exploration for the day was over. He turned his bike around and headed home, a bit disappointed that there wasn't more to see out Whiskey Road.

During dinner that evening back at home, he told Uncle Jake and Aunt Annie Lou about his exploration of Whiskey Road. He asked first about the golf course he saw. "I didn't even know Aiken had another golf course."

Annie Lou answered him, "That's the Palmetto Golf Club, and it's been there since the late 1800s. Thomas Hitchcock started it along with all the other things he started when he came here. It's a pretty well-known course. It was designed by the same Scotsman who built that course in Augusta. Ben Hogan plays there whenever he comes to this area to play in the Masters. Oh, and Bing Crosby and Fred Astaire play there whenever they come to Aiken. That's about once a year."

Casey said, "It looks like a good place from the road. I wonder if they use caddies there."

"You can always ride over there and ask," she said.

She looked at Jake and said, "By the way, while Casey was gone today, I heard all of these loud engines running and went outside to investigate. I followed the noise and walked on Newberry toward downtown and saw that it was being paved on both sides near the swimming pool and that log cabin where the Chamber of Commerce is. Did you know about that?"

"Yeah," Jake responded. "That started up today. I asked somebody who works for the City and he told me that other streets are being paved now too. He mentioned parts of Chesterfield and parts of Pendleton, near downtown. He said that it was part of Aiken's plan of trying to make the downtown area bigger. I guess that in due time, we'll see most of these back streets paved too."

Casey shifted topics. "I wondered what was out Whiskey Road. It looks like it just stops right after the golf course."

"Don't be fooled by that little two-lane road," Jake responded. "On out Whiskey Road, there's other roads crossing it like Silver Bluff and Pine Log and several others. There are some dairies out there and a bunch of farms. That road goes all the way to Ellenton and beyond." Casey made a mental note to ride out there again the next time he had the chance.

Late in the summer, Jake mentioned one evening at dinner that there was going to be a meeting that night at one of the other hardware store to discuss the coming of television and how it would probably change the world. "There's even talk around that hardware stores are the most natural places to buy television sets when they start to arrive, that there's no other natural place for people to expect to see one on display. I suppose that's about right," Jake added. "Now we listen to the radio to hear the Green Hornet or the Lone Ranger. We bought that radio, most likely, at a hardware store, or at Sears, Roebuck, which is just a glorified hardware store itself."

Chapter 9

Right after Labor Day, the public school system opened its doors for students again. Aiken High School and Aiken Grammar School were in session. Casey entered the sixth grade and was assigned to the room of Catherine McLeod, an experienced elementary teacher.

On that first day, several of the class members spoke of having seen television over the summer for the first time. One had seen it in a hotel room in Atlanta, and others saw it during a stay in Washington DC. Ms. McLeod offered the opinion that if television lived up to the promise it had at the moment, the entire country and the way we live would be forever changed. One of her friends told her that Charlotte, North Carolina, already had a working TV station that just opened during the summer.

She also spoke about the wider world and how it seemed to be changing rapidly. One of our allies in the Second World War, Russia, was becoming more and more belligerent as a country. She told the class that Russia had just recently detonated an atomic bomb in a test. Everyone had thought that the United States was the only country with this super bomb fully developed, but now Russia proved that somehow she had mastered it too. This was a scary thought only if Russia continued down its present road of cultivating an image of hostility toward the United States and its old allies.

Before first recess, there was a general all-grades assembly in the large auditorium on the second floor. Mrs. Coleman, the principal, wanted the opportunity to welcome the children back to school and to send out her annual warning about adhering to upstanding behavior and pursuing good study habits. Casey was sure that in the next life, she would come back as a drill sergeant.

She had some words to say about the state of the world (and South Carolina's place in it) and, as Ms. McLeod had done, mentioned the Russians blowing up an experimental atomic bomb.

Her final mention was about some local Aiken news. Over the summer, the City of Aiken had hired a new director for the recreation department. His name, she added, was Henry "Tot" Robinson, a son of Aiken who was born here, educated in the local school system, and recently returned from college. His plans included starting up midget football, basketball, and baseball leagues within the city. All the boys perked up when they heard this, and a low murmur moved through the crowd. The assembly was adjourned for lunch in the first-floor cafeteria.

Arlene's face lit up when she saw Casey. They had barely seen each other for three months, his birthday on July 1 being the only exception. At recess, she talked endlessly, trying to catch him up on all of her activities and trips over the summer. He had to admit to himself that he had also missed her. She was always obviously so supportive of him, and he appreciated it. He secretly wished that one day he might even be able to show her that side of him, but he wasn't ready now.

At home in the evening, Casey relayed the news of the day about school. Jake was particularly interested in the part about Tot Robinson. "I know him. I remember when he was in high school. He played all of the sports and was pretty good at all of them. But he's got to be real young, maybe twenty-three or twenty-four years old. No more than that. I'll call him up soon to see what Aiken's gonna do about baseball for boys your age."

This year, the adults at school seemed to be taking the world more seriously, or was it simply that Casey was maturing and listening more closely to what his teachers were saying about it?

Sometime in the second week, he heard all about something called the Iron Curtain and its cousin, the Cold War. At dinner that evening, he asked about them during the meal.

Annie responded, "Casey, the end of the war four years ago happened because the United States dropped two atomic bombs on cities in Japan that killed almost two hundred thousand people. Our scientists had discovered a way to split the atom in a way that unleashed an unheard-of amount of power and destruction all at once and all in one small space. We thought that the world would be very peaceful for a long time after that since nobody else had this type of bomb and we knew we would never use it again, except to defend the United States."

Jake cut in. "But Russia was jealous and wanted the bomb too. And somehow, a few weeks ago, they proved they had it by exploding one of them in a test. Right after the war, in 1945, Winston Churchill saw how the free countries in the west and the more restrictive countries in the east, like Russia, were lining themselves up as democracies on our side and Communist countries on the other side. Churchill called the imaginary border between them the Iron Curtain, and the name has stuck. Some people who are smarter than me call this condition a Cold War. It means we are on opposite sides but we are not shooting at each other. Both sides seem to be content just to be a menace to each other. The theory is, I guess, if we are both happy to just glare at each other and threaten one another, then maybe we won't ever bomb each other."

Casey had listened to their explanations and finally said, "Does our side trust the Russians? It sounds pretty scary if they decide to use that bomb on us."

It was Annie's turn to reassure him. "Look, we all hope and pray that won't happen. Russians are very different from Americans, but they don't want to die in a stupid way over small stuff any more than Americans do. We have to trust our leaders and their leaders not to do something dumb like bombing each other. You quit worrying. Let Jake and me do the worrying for you."

Casey appeared to be happy with their explanations and finally said, "Yes, ma'am." He admitted to himself that his aunt and uncle seemed to know as much about the unusual phrases and the general world as his teacher did.

The Gannon household continued to hum with the activity generated by the eleven-year old Casey. Not only was he continuing to deliver his newspapers—now expanded by eight new customers due to referrals by existing customers on his route—but he was still scooping up every soft drink bottle he saw, helping Farris with cars, caddying at Aiken Municipal on the weekend, and any other odd-job chore that came his way. His inquiry about carrying golf bags at Palmetto was met with some skepticism about his experience, so he had not succeeded there as yet. He was pounding the extra funds into his three Mason jars and was happy that he was never questioned by anyone about the size of his cash stashes.

Jake Gannon had met with Tot Robinson at Aiken Recreation Department to ask about the future of youth baseball in Aiken. Because it was out of season and Tot was busy with football, he did not show much interest in Casey or his abilities. But he told Jake to continue throwing with Casey and showing him the fundamentals of batting, baserunning, and the game's rules. He assured Jake that Casey could get involved in the spring when baseball started up.

One day at school in mid-October, one of his fellow classmates asked Ms. McLeod about the upcoming Clemson-Carolina football game and who she thought was going to win. She did not want to use classroom time to discuss it, and in dismissing the topic, she mentioned the state fair and a thing called Big Thursday. Casey was puzzled by this.

Again, he sought the answers to the day's questions at dinner at home. He said, "What is the big deal with a football game between Clemson and South Carolina? I don't understand."

Jake laughed hard. "My boy, you just wandered into one of the biggest sacred cows about living in South Carolina. First, you need to understand that college football, for whatever reason, is the tail that wags the dog almost all over the South in colleges. A lot of college students in the South think that having a good football team is far more important than having a good academic reputation. It makes no sense, but that's just the way it is and it's been that way a long time."

Jake continued as Casey and Annie Lou listened. "The state of South Carolina holds its state fair in the middle of October every year in Columbia at the fairgrounds. The centerpiece of the state fair, every year, is the football game between Clemson College and the University of South Carolina. This annual game is always played on Thursday of state fair week in Columbia. You probably know that most college football games are played on Saturday. This Thursday tradition started in 1896, I heard somebody say, so it's been going on a long time. Some newspaperman started calling the day 'Big Thursday,' and for the people involved, I guess it is a very big day."

Jake continued. "Some crazy ideas have come out of this arrangement. The Clemson people hate it, having to travel to Columbia for the game every year. For them, it's always an 'away' game, never a home game. Some of their fans have even suggested building a new football stadium midway between Columbia and Clemson and calling the place 'Big Thursday, South Carolina.' Can you imagine having a big stadium out in the middle of nowhere that's only used one day a year? Anyway, this is why it seems so important. It gives one set of fans bragging rights over the other set for an entire year. That's why it gets so much attention."

Casey sighed. "I was hoping it was something really, really important. But it's only about a game."

Later in the week, the University of South Carolina beat Clemson by 27-13, making half of the state happy and leaving the other half gnashing its teeth.

Chapter 10

The year 1950 literally started with a bang. Jake had been successful in shopping around Augusta and North Augusta for a mixture of powerful firecrackers. Casey had never been exposed to using fireworks, so his uncle had to go slowly in order to train him in using them safely.

They had cherry bombs, silver M-80 torpedoes with side-mounted red fuses, Roman candles, sparklers, and Chinese string firecrackers, both large and small. Casey also learned about fuses and their length of burn and which ones to trust and which not to trust. He had a blast and had to spend most of the day on January 2 cleaning up their part of Newberry Street.

During the cleanup, he was privileged to meet one of his neighbors, Carroll Watson, who was the football coach at Aiken High School. Mr. Watson asked Casey if they were finally out of fireworks and expressed great relief when Casey replied that they were.

During the holidays, it became obvious that Aiken was becoming more interested in television. A few stores stocked the Hallicrafters brand, and one story was circulating about a family on the north side of town that purchased a set for family viewing. Although the nearest TV station was in Charlotte, 120 air miles away, reception of a decent picture was still only a dream. To make this set work and be effective, the family had an electrical contractor erect a sixty-foot telephone pole in their backyard with a TV antenna atop it aimed toward Charlotte. Many of the neighbors laughed, but a few of them saw their first snowy television image on that very Hallicrafters television set.

There was a minor amount of excitement in mid-January when Aiken's second movie theater, the Rosemary, opened on Laurens next to the Patricia Theater. Arlene nudged Casey into taking her to one of the first shows at the Rosemary. It was a double feature of *My Friend Irma*, a movie in which Dean Martin and Jerry Lewis starred, and *Ma and Pa Kettle*. They both laughed long and hard at the antics of the very funny Jerry Lewis. As they were leaving the theater, Casey asked, "Isn't this theater named after a real person in Aiken?"

"Oh yes," Arlene responded. "Rosemary Ram. She goes to our school and she's in the class right behind us. She's in the fifth grade."

Casey nodded his understanding. He also said, "Aunt Annie Lou told me about her when I first came to Aiken. I think it's probably not very normal to name a movie show building after a young girl."

Arlene agreed and said, "Well, that's Aiken."

Spring arrived at last, and Casey was finally ready to try out for a baseball team. He had to work hard to fit his new activity into the already busy schedule of schoolwork, paper route, and his other money-making endeavors. The first practice was right after the school on the Grammar School playground that was directly behind the building, on the York Street side. Tot Robinson conducted the practice, and every boy—only fourteen had showed up—had a chance to throw the baseball multiple times with Tot and to take ten swings at slowly pitched balls.

Casey already knew just about every boy who came to the practice. From his own classroom, he recognized Tommy, Donny, Billy, Harold, Alvin, and Emory. A few others came from the other sixth-grade class or from St. Angela Academy, the Catholic school located elsewhere in town.

During the meeting before practice, Tot told them about midget baseball coming to Aiken County. "Our team will be called the Aiken Mites, and boys under thirteen years old will be eligible to play. Three other teams are being formed and will be in our league. Besides Aiken, there will be Warrenville, Graniteville, and Gloverville."

It was obvious which boys had been exposed to baseball and which had not. Casey, for example, threw the ball with more authority than any of the others and had the strongest arm. With the bat, he also excelled although he swung and missed at two of his ten pitches, causing him to register mental disappointment with himself. After all, he was thinking, *These are slow pitches and I'm supposed to hit all of them if I can.*

After the practice ended, Tot pulled Casey aside and asked him, "What's your name again, son?"

"I'm Casey Gannon."

"Oh okay, you're Jake Gannon's boy, right?"

Casey quickly corrected him. "He's my uncle, not my daddy. I'm living now in Aiken with my uncle and aunt. My folks are dead."

"I'm sorry about that. Son, you'll do okay in baseball if you work hard at it. You've got a real strong arm for an eleven-year-old. Where'd you get that?" Tot was clearly impressed by something he had seen.

Casey said, "Uncle Jake says it's in my family. He played baseball for Richmond Academy in Augusta, and I think my daddy did too. He told me they both played centerfield and liked to throw runners out at home."

Tot laughed. "We might need a center fielder on this team too. I'll see you at the next practice, right?"

"Yes, sir," Casey was quick to respond. "I'll be here."

He couldn't wait to repeat that conversation to his aunt and uncle at dinner tonight. Uncle Jake and Aunt Annie Lou were very interested in hearing about the first practice. Jake told him, "Remember, son, I'll help you as much as I can to be a good player."

He paused for a few seconds and then added, "I want you to know that I've gone into a quiet partnership with a friend who is a building contractor here in Aiken. We'll be doing remodeling jobs on houses and apartments and garages in town. Not much competition in doing that right now, and we see a good opportunity. My partner will do the work during the week, and I'll be helping as much as I can on weekends. I'm keeping my job at the hardware store because, well, we can always use the money and I can help us get discounts on wood, nails, and building materials if I just stay put where I am. I just wanted you to know it from me and not from somebody telling you on the street."

Another topic that evening was the new Korean War. Aunt Annie Lou asked, "Casey, have you heard about this new war going on in Korea?" She waited until he shook his head from side to side, indicating no, and then continued. "President Truman has decided to send a lot of our troops to help the South Koreans fight the North Koreans. General McArthur will be in charge. It looks like these wars never end. I heard it all on the radio this afternoon. Here we go again. Only five years since the last one ended."

During the rest of the summer, the small family attended half a dozen baseball games at Eustis Park and in Graniteville. Casey won the centerfield position and led the team in batting average. He actually threw out one base runner at third base. More important, his voice started to change to a lower range and he grew three inches during the summer alone. He was now almost twelve years old, five feet ten inches tall, and 125 pounds. He was growing rapidly.

One day at Farris Wynn's house, Casey learned about an almost brand-new full-sized woman's bicycle for sale for only five dollars. He was able to see it, ride it briefly, and make a decision about whether to buy it for his aunt Annie Lou. He rode his own bike to his house, extracted a five-dollar bill from his "gifts" Mason jar, retrieved the basket he won at the Bicycle Rodeo, and pedaled back to the available bicycle. He spent most of the remainder of the afternoon installing the basket on his new purchase and secretly pedaling it back to his house. He stashed it temporarily behind a row of hedges behind their garage.

On Sunday, after church and after lunch, Casey announced, "I have a big surprise. Follow me outside." After his uncle and aunt had joined him in the backyard, he brought the bike out and presented it to his aunt.

"This is for the best cook in the world," he announced.

"Oh, Casey, I can't believe you! Where'd you get this?" Annie Lou was delighted.

He explained that he had wanted to do it for a long time and the opportunity finally came. He also added, "Sometimes, I need somebody to ride with me and I guess you're it." She laughed and thanked him with words and a big hug.

Later in the summer, a quiet twelfth-birthday celebration for Casey was held in the backyard for just the three of them. Annie Lou's bicycling skills were rusty, but after riding around on the few paved streets in the area, she became confident as a rider. Everyone who knew her saw her personality change as she suddenly felt a freedom she had not felt in a long time. Casey invited her often to ride around with him and saw how it affected her. He was silently thankful that his generosity had been the key ingredient in her newfound freedom.

One of the secrets he kept from his aunt was that he got a special kick from riding his own bike in the gray cloud behind the DDT truck. Any time he was out with his bike, particularly in the late afternoon, he was apt to see or hear the mosquito patrol and the thick cloud of DDT spewing in its wake. He was happy to see that other kids his age experienced the same magnetic pull of this local rite.

After Labor Day, the changes arrived in the Gannon household almost weekly. First, Casey was now in the seventh grade and that meant Aiken High School, not the old Grammar School. He could now walk to school by going out the front door of his house and walking just one short block down the sandy Henderson Street to the large hulking high school on Laurens Street. The building contained grades seven to twelve since no junior high or middle school existed in Aiken.

Aiken High School until 1954

This represented a monumental but desirable change for all the seventh graders. Most of them had attended basketball games in the gym or theatrical productions in the auditorium, but they had never belonged here. They had been visitors only. Now for each of them, it was home. It was now *their* high school. They were no longer part of those pesky snot-nosed elementary school children; they were in high school. It said so in granite over the door on the front of the building.

James O. Willis was the principal, and he had been in the job for several years. The building was solid brick and had three connected wings. Classrooms and administration functions occupied the center wing, and that central wing was three stories high. A large auditorium with its spacious balcony was on the left flank, with its own front entrance, and the medium-sized gymnasium sat on the right. The complex did not have a cafeteria per se, but a large central hall on the third floor of the central wing served as the eating hall. A kitchen was situated in a large room off to the side, and cooks working there prepared the food; tables and chairs were set up end-to-end to capture the entire corridor as eating space. It was possible, therefore, for juvenile seventh graders to eat with, leer at, admire, and converse with all the other students of the school almost every day.

A "canteen" was on the ground floor facing the backyard of the school. It was supervised by algebra teacher and local legend Johnny Eubanks and staffed by students. There, the student body could buy Cokes and crackers (four crackers in a cellophane package for 5¢) for lunch if they desired. Behind the school was a dirt playground, bereft of playground equipment, and Pendleton Street. For most of the class day, school buses sat parked on Pendleton end-to-end, awaiting the need to transport the students back home.

The new setting represented a major adjustment for all the upcoming seventh graders. For one thing, they had to get used to having a homeroom teacher, plus learning the names of all of their other teachers who were specialists in specific subjects, like Civics or Geography. They had to learn how to change classes every hour and make it quickly from one classroom to another without getting lost. And they had to adjust to being on the bottom rung of the seniority ladder instead of the top rung as last year's sixth grade had been.

Football season was beginning as school started in early September. As it happened, the 1950 season's results turned out to be one of the best in Aiken High School sports in a long time. The town was excited to watch an autumn of eight wins against three losses. Philip Moody, a well-built fullback, finished a very good football career, as did Bobby Ashley, Len Yaun, and quarterback Bill Wenzel. Cousins Ed and Tom Moseley, as juniors, enjoyed banner seasons and excited the town with many very long touchdown runs and punt returns. They were very fast halfbacks and made it exciting to watch well over a dozen breakaway runs for touchdowns. Tom scored 114 points, mostly on long touchdown runs, to smash every scoring record in the area.

One of the interesting facts in the background of Tom Moseley was that he considered himself a poor student. As a result, he had already dropped out of school with no plans of returning. Carroll Watson, the Aiken High School coach of four sports, was seen on numerous occasions at the Moseley farm talking to Tom and trying to entice him back into the classroom and into sports settings. He was eventually successful. Watson was once quoted as saying that Tom was the fastest man he had ever seen and that his speed could easily be his ticket to a better life.

The seventh-grade boys, at least those who hung around with Casey, attended all the home games and experienced the whole gamut of high school life, from majorettes to cheerleaders to marching band to concession stands. They also proved to be typical boys and got into the habit of admiring the older upper-class girls up closely at lunch, particularly those they had already seen performing at football games.

One conversation, which was overheard by one of the teachers, went like this: "Can you believe how good-looking that Florence Galloway is? And Lord, that Julie Henderson? My gosh, aren't these girls gorgeous? Ain't it great being so close to them?" The answer among the group sounded like, "Man that ain't nothing. Have you taken a good look at that Matilee, and that Chartee and Beth and Gail?" Another opinion weighed in. "Boy, that Ann Brown girl is really cute, just my type! She's definitely in the middle of my strike zone!" Clearly, the new seventh-grade boys were smitten by the number and the attractiveness of the Aiken girls.

As this was going on, some of the upper-class boys took notice and decided to intervene and offer some friendly advice to them. They sent a spokesman, a very tall polite boy named Gene, who came over and sat down with them, looking intently at each one. Finally, he said, "Boys, you're just about embarrassing us. Put your tongues back in your head. Quit drooling. Yes, our girls are pretty, and very nice too. They appreciate being noticed and enjoying some attention, but you're being way too obvious. Those girls admire boys who *are* cool and act cool. It's hard to look cool when your slobber is running down your chin. Learn to respect what we have in Aiken but in a much nicer way than I see right now. Don't fawn. Don't let them see you get so excited. For gosh sakes, you're in high school now. Try to act like it. Try to grow up a little. Learn to control yourself, okay? I'll see you around, and I know you'll be better at this next time I see you at lunch." He smiled, stood up, and left.

All five of the boys reddened during the sermon and swallowed hard. One of them finally said, "I guess we overdid it. We probably needed that."

A few weeks later, after they had adjusted to controlling themselves in the larger environment of high school, they sometimes found themselves sitting at the same lunch table with Tom or Boozie Moseley or other Friday night heroes from the football team like Everett Baker. They found to their delight that these very popular older boys always had time to say hello or listen to a question or comment. It was almost impossible to find a student who carped at them or was harshly critical. They found that upper classmen were very nice people who always had a minute to spare for the younger members of the school. It seemed that a lot of upstanding people and good examples walked the halls of Aiken High School. It was nice to learn that and see it in action.

Late in the fall, the newspapers were starting to talk more and more about the Aiken-Augusta Superhighway. Jake Gannon was sure that it would be open between Thanksgiving and Christmas. He had already heard stories of drivers sneaking on it to try it out.

Finally, the *Aiken Standard and Review* stated that the road had been opened for traffic on Friday, November 24, 1950, and would be officially dedicated at a later date. Jake told Annie Lou and Casey, "Let's go to Augusta to do some early Christmas shopping. Hot dog! No more pokey slow trips through the valley."

When they used the road for the first time, it was even better than Jake ever dreamed. The new part began about three miles from downtown Aiken and ended three miles from Augusta, where the North Augusta airstrip was located on Schultz Hill. In between, the road was almost entirely limited access, was a four-lane divided highway with a grassy median, and had a fifty-five-mile-per-hour speed limit. The road cruised through some almost virgin territory of Aiken County, and kaolin deposits were visible on many stretches of the road. One crossroad was at Boogaboo and led to either Graniteville in one direction or Warrenville in the other. Another intersection later in the trip gave access to Clearwater and Belvedere, but no other interruptions or cross traffic existed. Jake was tickled to experience the new road. He knew it would change his life and the lives of those who resided and worked in the valley.

Less than a week later, on November 28, a group of Aiken and Augusta leaders and newsmen gathered for an important called meeting in the Federal courthouse in Aiken on Park Avenue. All the movers and shakers, reporters, and policy managers were in attendance, with Mayor Odell Weeks being the most recognizable person from Aiken's leadership.

The next morning, the subject of the meeting was revealed; the *Aiken Standard* told of massive changes that were about to affect life in the region. The headline of the local newspaper's November 29, 1950, issue read in large bold letters:

A. E. C. TO CONSTRUCT HUGE PLANT NEAR AIKEN

It was the last day of the old era. Nothing would ever be the same in Aiken after that. It was almost unbelievable that two such major events could happen so close together. The new Aiken-Augusta Highway was a major new factor all by itself, and now a huge atomic energy plant on top of that? Incredible!

Chapter 11

When the atomic energy plant was announced in late 1950, the city of Aiken was made up of original Aiken people who were born and raised there, plus a healthy smattering of Winter Colony residents. Cotton and peaches constituted the primary agricultural products, so farms and farmers dotted the countryside.

The original announcement stated that 250,000 acres would be purchased by the government on which to build the plant. The site of the plant would straddle the county lines of Aiken and Barnwell, and it would be operated by the E. I. DuPont de Nemours Company of Wilmington, Delaware, under a contract with the U.S. government. It was explained that the enormous tract would be necessary due to the need for "nuclear dispersion" of the various functions of the plant. Citizens soon came to learn that the concept of dispersion meant this: maintain a large separation of a few miles between key elements of the plant so that one Russian atomic bomb could not knock out the entire plant but just a small portion of it. What a message that was!

It essentially said that a site near Aiken would become a frontline participant in making hydrogen bombs for our national defense and, as such, would also, by default, become a major target for our enemies to destroy if it ever became necessary for them to do so.

The towns of Ellenton and Dunbarton learned right away that their entire existence must be relocated within eighteen months. This meant *everything*—schools, stores, churches, houses, cemeteries, *everything.*

For the next few days at Aiken High School, the "bomb plant" was the entire topic of discussion. Teachers and other administrators tried to translate the meaning of the new environment for the inquiring students. One of the meaningful numbers that emerged within the first few days was this: The initial number of construction workers to build the plant was eight thousand. They would all have to find places to live and schools to which to send their children. The City of Aiken had recently learned the results of the national census and discovered that at the start of 1950, Aiken had 7,000 residents. So the general region of Aiken, Barnwell, the Valley, and Augusta was about to be compelled to digest a number of citizens larger than Aiken itself within just a few months.

Mr. Willis spoke of the need for larger schools and more classrooms. Ms. McLeod wondered out loud where the desks would come from and where pupils would sit. Coaches spoke of getting more athletes and having better teams. Student-athletes spoke of teams being harder to make and maybe getting washed away by better players from somewhere else.

At home, Jake and Annie Lou discussed the new situation candidly with Casey. "We are about to see a long period of very choppy water and some turmoil. I hope our city leaders, like Mayor Weeks, keep their thinking caps on all the time. This place is gonna be overrun by strangers in no time flat. Today, in the Aiken paper, I saw ads from little Springfield, South Carolina, and Bamberg County, advertising for the ex-residents of Ellenton and Dunbarton to move there. The ads talked about their good farmland, good churches and schools, and friendly people. Those people have to move somewhere, I guess."

Casey asked a question. "Won't businesses get the chance to have a lot more customers? I keep thinking that some of these people will want to buy the *Augusta Herald*. I might get some new customers."

Annie Lou pitched in. "You're dead right, Casey. It's possible this might create more opportunities for the people already here, not less opportunity."

Jake perked up when he heard that. "Good thinking, girl. Aiken's gonna need a lot more stuff like houses and schools and places to eat and places to shop. We might be able to have some of that come our way. We're already here and we know the ropes here. I'll think some about that."

That afternoon, Casey went to Farris Wynn's house to help out with two cars. Casey asked him. "You heard about the bomb plant coming here. What will happen to Aiken, Farris?"

He smiled very broadly and said, "Farris Wynn's very happy about it. A lot more cars will be here and they'll get dirty too. Ole Farris gonna have more business than he can shake a stick at. All I gotta do is keep giving people good service. And you be hepping me." And he laughed.

The next day, Casey looked for Arlene at lunchtime on the third floor. He spotted an empty chair next to her and sat down. She sniffed a bit because he hadn't been paying much attention to her since the school year started. True, they worked at the same times in the stables but were frequently doing different chores in different barns.

Finally, she looked his way and said, "How you doing, stranger boy?"

"I'm fine," admitted Casey. "I need to ask a question. What do you think about this new stuff, you know, the bomb plant, and DuPont, and all these people they say are coming here?"

"I'm scared about it," she answered. "My parents say it will change our whole way of life. They're afraid that our quiet little Southern town will never recover and never be the same again. That scares me too."

He frowned when he heard her answer. "Listen to me a minute, Arlene. I finally got to where I think this is a pretty good place to be. I know I've only been here a little bit more than two years, but Aiken is really nice and has a lot of nice people, grown-ups, and kids. A lot of new people are gonna come. We need to make sure that we don't let them change us from our way to their way. We don't even know what 'their way' is. But we know what ours is. We need to hang on to that and let the new people see how good it is here and make them see it and like it along with us."

"I hear what you're saying, and I agree with you," she responded. "That's exactly what I'm afraid of—that we'll lose the nice, soft Aiken way and a hard old strange way will come here to take its place."

"I don't want that to happen either," Casey said. "We have to fight against that happening."

When Casey heard Arlene's concerns, he became concerned again himself. After his papers in the afternoon, he got home and asked his aunt about Arlene's worries. She said, "I see why she's worried about that, but listen a minute to me. Some of these people who'll come here are construction people who will be here a year or two, then they're gone—off to the next construction job somewhere else in the country. These people probably won't try to change Aiken very much."

She continued. "After they're gone, the people who will run the plant every day will come—the permanent people. I've heard there might be as many as fifteen thousand of them. They'll be engineers and scientists and nuclear experts who will be transferred here by DuPont. Now, these are gonna be some pretty smart people. They might have some of their own good ideas about Aiken that might even improve on what we already have here. I think we have to be careful not to let them run all over us, but also to listen to their view with an open mind. Let's not be ready to reject them right out of the starting gate. Let's listen and then decide. The mixture of our old ways and some of their new ways might be a benefit to all of us."

Casey nodded. "Okay, I'll stop worrying about it, and I'll tell Arlene what you said, that we should wait and see."

A local story that made it to the front page of the newspaper said that when Strom Thurmond left the governor's office in a few weeks, he was going to move to Aiken and work as a lawyer with Dorcey Lybrand and Charles Simons in their law office. That created some speculation about where the Thurmonds would buy a house. The Kalmia Hill area was everybody's popular choice as to where they would probably end up.

As Aiken prepared for another Christmas, many shoppers noted that Aiken seemed to be somewhat more crowded than usual. Weekends in December were prone to experience small traffic jams as more and more visitors were cruising the downtown area to look around. Early plant workers, maybe?

On Christmas Eve, Jake Gannon brought the day's mail delivery into the house as he arrived home from work. He noted that one envelope was from Vera Gannon's insurance company in Montana.

They must be finally getting back to us on their final decision about her death, he thought to himself. The Gannons had speculated from time to time about what the final outcome would be.

He opened the envelope and discovered a one-page letter and a check. The letter said,

> *Dear Mr. Jacob Gannon, guardian of Casey Carter Gannon:*
>
> *The Iron Mountain Insurance Company has made its final determination on the matter of the death of Vera Dudley Gannon. After examining all of the facts surrounding her tragic death, we have ruled that her death was accidental, and therefore, the double indemnity clause of her insurance contract with our company is being paid in full.*
>
> *Please find enclosed our cashier's check in the amount of $8,500.00.*
>
> *Merry Christmas to you and your family.*

When he examined the check, there it was: $8,500.00.

"Annie Lou, Casey, y'all come in here. Quick." Jake was very excited.

They arrived quickly from the kitchen. He said, "Listen to this," and he read the letter aloud.

Annie Lou broke into a wide grin. "I never dreamed that insurance company would do that. Boy, am I pleased!"

"Me too," echoed Casey. "I figured they'd just say no."

Jake said, "Casey, this takes all the financial pressure off of your future. Just like before, I think we should advise you to handle this money very conservatively. If you have any obvious needs, we should take care of those right away. But for the long haul, this is great news for you."

"Here's my idea," Casey said. "I really don't need anything right now. I have enough of my own money in my jars. Let's do the same thing we did the first time. Let's put the whole thing in the Farmers and Merchants account at the bank, and then all of us think about whether any special thing should be done with it."

"Good idea," Annie Lou answered. "We won't make any snap judgments or sudden decisions about this."

"Agreed," said Jake.

Christmas Day came and went. The weather stayed mild, and the daylight hours found Jake and Casey in the middle of Newberry Street throwing a baseball. During a break, they sat on the front steps of their house and talked. Jake asked, "Have you adjusted to the idea that your uncle has decided not to continue his wicked ways and is trying to set a good example for you and others?"

Casey reddened some, but recovered quickly. "I like the way you are now. I don't worry anymore about those first months after I came here."

"Good," Jake answered. "I'm enjoying having you with us and have started to realize that you won't always be here with us. You're twelve now and before we know it, we'll all wake up one day to find you in the army or in college or in a job somewhere else. I want to help you grow into a fine man and not see you change into a person with big problems."

The subject soothed Casey on the inside but made him jittery, and he wanted to change the subject. "Uncle Jake, can you throw a curve ball? Can you show me how to throw one? I figure that if I can learn to throw one, maybe knowing that will teach me how to hit one. Some of my teammates said it's almost impossible to hit a curve ball."

Jake laughed. "Yeah, I can throw a curve ball, and your friends are right, a curve ball can be hard to hit." He gripped the baseball with his thumb, index finger, and middle finger, turned the seams a certain way, and snapped his wrist downward as if throwing the ball. "A curve ball has to spin a certain way or it won't curve. The seams have to be held in a certain way too."

Casey perked up. "I can see the stitches turning when we play bat and catch. I already noticed that the spin goes a certain way on each throw. I can see the spin when a ball's coming toward me."

"Are you kidding me?" asked Jake.

Jake thought for a second and remembered the times when Casey could see cows on the horizon or birds on the telephone wire. He recalled thinking at the time that there must be something unusual about his nephew's very sharp vision. "You might find that you have a knack for hitting that other people don't have if you can do that."

The next day, the winter weather was still balmy; and they visited Eustis Park with gloves, balls, and a bat. They had the place to themselves. Jake announced in advance the pitch he was throwing, and Casey quickly graduated from catching them to swinging the bat at them. He connected with almost every pitch, at times very solidly, dead solid on the barrel of the bat.

After thirty minutes of batting, they went into the large green grandstand to rest and to talk. Casey admitted, "When you told me a certain pitch was coming, I adjusted my thought to what the stitches should look like as the ball came closer. I was able to know if the ball would stay straight or if it would curve, and I guessed right every time. I could really see the stitches on the ball good. Now I have to make my bat get to the spot where my brain tells me the ball will be. That's all."

Jake laughed. "That's all? That's all? You just nailed it what batting is all about. If you can teach yourself to do that, you will be the world's best batter. Every baseball player tries to do just that when he's batting."

Casey answered him, "I know it's easy to say but hard to do. I'll be trying to teach myself how to do it."

After church on Sunday, they ate their usual large lunch at home and retired to the swing and rocking chairs on the side porch. Jake asked, "What do y'all think we should invest Casey's money in? You know, you've got more than $17,000 in your account."

Annie Lou said, "I've been thinking hard, and I think we should save some of it for college. Other than that, I can't think of what he ought to spend it on."

Casey looked at the floor as he rocked and asked, "How much does a house cost?" He was embarrassed to put the question out in front of them.

"What does that have to do with anything?" Jake asked. "A twelve-year-old boy can't buy a house."

"I was afraid you were gonna laugh," Casey said. "No kidding, how much do houses cost in Aiken?"

Annie Lou jumped in to save Casey from more embarrassment and said, "Honey, tell us why you want to know that?"

"I'll answer the question, but first, how much would a house like this cost if it was for sale?" Casey inquired.

"Okay," Jake said. "I can give you a good guess. This house would cost about $9,500 to buy, but I know for a fact that it's not for sale and is not likely to be."

"All right, one more question, then I'll tell you why I'm asking. When somebody buys this house for $9,500, do they have to pay it all at once, or can you do layaway, like at Sears Roebuck?"

Everybody laughed at the reference to layaway for a house. "Generally," Jake answered, "you don't pay it all at one time, but you get a special house loan from the bank to pay it off in fifteen or twenty years. It's called a mortgage. With a mortgage, a buyer has to pay about ten or twenty percent down payment and borrow the rest for about twenty years of payments. That's how most people buy a house."

Casey started smiling when he heard Jake's answer and began to understand it. The idea he had hatched in his head might work, he was thinking. "We are renting this house from Ms. Salley, right? My idea is not about this house, but a different one. Why can't we use my bank money not to actually buy a house, but to get the bank to get somebody else to sell us a house we might want for ourselves?"

"Oh, sweetie," said Annie Lou. "We don't have the money to buy a house. We just can't do that."

"I know, Aunt Annie Lou," Casey said earnestly. "But with the money in my account, we do. We could do it."

Jake and Annie Lou both jumped in with negative reasons and answers. She said, "We're not taking any of your money, and that's that."

Jake said, "I made a promise to both of you that I would never take a cent of your money, and I haven't and I won't."

Casey was patient. "Listen to me for another minute. Everybody says Aiken is about to change from where we are now to something else, something bigger. If that's true, I want us to use the new thing to help us, not to hurt us. Workers are already coming here to find places to live. I saw some of them on Laurens Street. We can either stay in this house and keep paying the $54 a month, or we can find a good house to live in that we can buy, either now or later.

"The money in my bank account is mine, I agree with all of that. But I know y'all are both smarter than me. I really am happy that I have a place to live because of you. But I was hoping that if y'all think about it hard enough, y'all can find a way for me to keep the money, but for you to be able to use it to help us move to someplace else that we can own. A lot of new people are coming here. Can't you find a way for me to sign something that says the money's all mine, but y'all can use it for a little while?"

Jake and Annie Lou just looked at each other, unbelieving. They were both thinking the same thing: *This boy we have is no dummy. He has just hit on an idea that probably has some merit.*

Jake's attitude changed almost totally. "Do you mean to say that if we can find a way to use your money without actually spending it in order to buy us a house, you'd do it, that you'd be okay with that?"

"Yes, sir, that's it," Casey responded.

"Damn." Jake exhaled. "Annie, this boy is something else. What do you think?" he asked, directing the question to her.

She answered, "I think Casey is amazing me more and more, and his kind and generous side is showing more that I even knew he had. And it's about to make me cry." She sniffed, paused, and looked at the boy. "What made you think of this, Casey?"

He said, "To me, it just makes sense. Aiken is going to change a lot. We will always need a place to live. With my mama's money, it seems like we have enough to get into the best place we can afford. I think we have to do it before all of those new people get here."

"Okay," Jake said, "tell you what. When the bank opens tomorrow, I'll go over there and ask them for some advice. I'll tell them what we talked about today and ask them for their ideas about how to do it. My banker is pretty smart and maybe he can think of something."

"I think that's the perfect way to do this if it can be done," Annie Lou said. "Maybe they can think of a way to do it and protect Casey's account at the same time."

When Jake came home from work the next day, he told them that the bank was interested in helping them. "I agreed with the bank that the three of us will come to a meeting with them the day after New Year's Day."

Chapter 12

Jake and Casey had another big celebration with fireworks on New Year's Eve. The next morning, which was the first business day of 1951, Jake asked his boss at the hardware store if he could take the morning off and show up after lunch. Permission was given.

The meeting at the bank was set up for ten o'clock. Jake reviewed the situation for the group, making the centerpiece of the meeting the question of whether Casey's money could be used in any way to finance the purchase of a house in Aiken. The banker, a man named James McCabe, stated, "Jake, I'd say if you plan to buy a house in Aiken, you'd better hurry. The bomb plant has been in the news for only five weeks, but this town is already stirred up with people looking for livable real estate."

"I agree," Jake said. "I have my eye on a place already."

James McCabe addressed Casey directly. "Young man, you have a nice sum of money in your account. I checked it this morning, and the amount is slightly more than $17,300. Jake tells me that you are willing to use this money to help the family get into another house before the big rush on Aiken gets here. Is that right?"

"Yes, sir, I want the money to help us if there is a way, but I don't want to spend it too fast," Casey replied.

"Well, I need to ask a question or two, and I want you to be totally honest with me. Are you doing this totally of your own free will? Do you feel any pressure from your uncle and aunt to do this? Whose idea was this?" McCabe was uncomfortable asking the questions but felt he needed to understand this family before proceeding.

Casey bristled at the questions. "Yes, sir, this is my idea. Both of them disagreed and fought me on it at first. It's my plan, my idea. I want to help them like they helped me."

"Okay, okay, calm down," McCabe said smoothly. "I'm sorry I had to ask that, but I had to make sure of everybody's reasons and motives."

He continued. "I'm a pretty conservative banker, and I can help you design some plan to make this work. I advise you right now to commit no more than half of your funds to this house. Keep the rest of it in reserve for other things. Now that suggests that about $8,500 would be available to help secure a house. In Aiken, that can still buy a pretty nice house right now—three bedrooms, a couple of bathrooms, a carport, or maybe a garage. Is that about what you had in mind?" As he said it, he looked at Jake and Annie Lou.

Annie said as she nodded and looked at Jake, "Oh yeah, that would do nicely."

"Okay, let's use $9,000 as a planning figure. If you folks wanted to buy a $9,000 house and used Casey's account as collateral, that is, to ensure the bank that you would always be able to make the monthly payments, you could get our lowest-interest loan here at the bank, and you would only have to put five percent down on it, or about $450. We would want Casey to sign some papers for this, and we would want his name as one of the owners on the loan and the deed. Can you swing that down payment, Jake?"

"Yeah, it's tight," Jake answered, "but I believe I can handle that."

"Okay," McCabe said. "That's about it. Go find yourselves a house to live in, then come back. Any more questions?"

Jake said, "I know of a smaller house than you described, down in the Highland Park Drive area. I might want to buy it and add some rooms on to it as we move into it. Would that work for you and this deal, or is that too complicated?"

"Yes, with the safe kind of financing we will have on this transaction, we can do almost anything you want." McCabe was smiling broadly as they left. He knew that he was looking at the safest kind of loan the bank could make.

Outside, Jake told Annie Lou and Casey about the house on Highland Park Drive and asked if they wanted to ride by it before they went back home. Both of them agreed that they wanted to see it.

Jake drove for a mile or more from the bank toward the west, passing the golf clubhouse and some of the holes on the golf course. He slowed down as he approached an intersection with Dibble Road and pointed up a gravel driveway to the right.

"That's it right there. It's a ranch style, all on one level, with two bedrooms and a bathroom. I would want to change it to three bedrooms, add another bathroom, and put a garage on it and maybe a toolhouse out in the back. I know you can't tell much from here, but I'll get us in to see the house later this week. It won't last long in this new market that's gonna grow real fast."

Casey realized that he was somewhat familiar with the area. It was close to—within a few hundred yards of—the area where he and Tommy had wrung out the stripped-down buggy on Snake Road. He decided that this was not the time to talk about that or show them the twisting sand road. That was for another time.

Jake turned the car around at Dibble and came back by the house. "Look to the other side of the road, opposite the house. That's part of Hitchcock Woods. There won't ever be anything built across from us. And the railroad track between

Augusta and Aiken runs laterally down in that swale you see just before the woods. You can't see the track from here. We would have a lot of privacy."

Annie Lou asked, "What's the price of the house?"

Jake said, "As it sits there right now, they want $6,600 for it. I might be able to get it for just over $6,000. My building partner thinks he can add everything we need for another $2,800."

As they were riding home, Annie Lou said, "You know, Casey, you have enough money in the bank now that you can stop working. You don't have to deliver papers anymore or any of those other things you've been doing to make money. You can stay home and sit back and relax."

"I know," Casey answered. "I already thought of that, but I don't like that idea much. These little jobs forced me to meet a lot of people in Aiken I would have never met. I like working. I'll keep on doing it. It makes me feel good to do things people need to get done."

Jake drove them back home and dropped them off, exiting quickly to get to work. Casey was encouraged that things were trending in a good direction.

Later in the week, several things happened to move them closer to buying the house they had seen. First, they discovered that Eulalie Salley was the agent handling the house and she got them into the house for a tour very quickly. Annie Lou liked the house but realized that it would change her daily habits because it was farther from her downtown shopping places and habits. Her bike was going to be a handy necessity.

Second, Casey was unconvinced at first because it wasn't much larger than the Newberry Street residence. He rode his bike to the new location every day just to look at it again, and it started to grow on him.

Third, Ms. Salley assured them that they could be released from their rental lease with one month's notice. It was a fact that they had already fulfilled their two-year rental obligation. Because of the arrival of the bomb plant, she knew that the owner would be able to crank the rent upward as soon as the Gannon family vacated it.

By Friday, Jake, Annie Lou, and Casey were ready to make an offer on the new house and told Ms. Salley. She drew up the documents and included the offer of $6,000. The owner counteroffered at $6,400, and the Gannons countered with $6,300, which was accepted by the seller. Closing was set for forty-five days later in mid-February.

The next period generated flurries of activity, but the loan was quickly granted at the bank for up to $9,000, which included the money to immediately add on to the existing structure. Jackson Moving was hired to move the furnishings, and the relocation was on. Within another month, the Gannons were happily installed in the house, and carpenters were busy with the additions.

One of the first things Casey did after they moved into the new house was to explore how to find his way into Hitchcock Woods and, once there, how to quickly locate Sand River and the Devil's Backbone. He was tickled to discover that it was an easy task. Within the first week, he was thoroughly acclimated to his new woodsy environment and promised himself to visit there at least every week.

One late winter day, Casey finished delivering his newspapers early and decided to ride his bike on the Laurens Street sidewalk, just slowly cruising the stores. A tall man in a hat, a suit, and carrying a briefcase flagged him down in front of Julia's Dress Shop, asking if he had any extra copies of the *Herald* to sell. As he said "Yes, sir," he looked closer and realized he was talking to the ex-governor, Strom Thurmond. Casey gave him the newspaper and was handed a dime with the words, "Just keep the change, son."

A little bit in awe, Casey sat on his bike until Thurmond disappeared into a sidewalk door between Julia's and the Dinner Bell restaurant. Then he remembered that he read about the law office being upstairs in the Weeks Building, at the corner of Park and Laurens.

Casey was elated that he had met somebody famous in Aiken and rode to Uncle Jake's hardware to tell him about it. Jake was impressed. He said, "That's real good. I hope you were nice to him. I heard they're moving into a house on Shadow Lane in the Kalmia Hill area."

Casey nodded in agreement. "I heard that too."

Then Jake announced that since no customers were in the store, right then it was break time. "C'mon, Casey, you can do this with us."

They went to the business office where there was a Coke machine selling Cokes for 5¢ each. Five coworkers were standing by to participate with Jake.

"Okay, boys, this is my boy, Casey, he's gonna do this with us. He's never done this game before." Then talking directly to Casey, he said, "This is a game, a ritual, we go through every day, sometimes twice a day. Each man puts his own nickel in the Coke machine and buys his own Coke. Before we take the cap off and drink it, we look at the bottom of the bottle to see what city is printed there. The city that is the farthest away from Aiken has to buy the Cokes for everybody else. If you lose, it's gonna cost you 35¢ today because it's seven Cokes. You can afford that, right? That's the worst you can do. The best is that you get a free Coke."

Casey learned that the city where the bottle was made was embossed on the bottom of the bottle. On this day, there were two bottles from Aiken, two from Augusta, one from Atlanta, one from Charlotte, and one from San Antonio, Texas. He got lucky and had the one from Atlanta. Free Coke. This was a fun game that Casey learned happened hundreds of times a day all over the South.

Soon April was there, and the family, this time including Annie Lou, took a day off from everything to go to the Masters Tournament in Augusta. Annie Lou was finally able to see in person the famous golfers she'd heard about. Like most people who don't play golf, she was very appreciative of the trees, azaleas, redbuds, teaberry shrubs, and the beauty of the surroundings at the Augusta National Golf Course. They stayed until the awards presentation and watched as Ben Hogan accepted a $1,500 check for winning.

Right after that, the people of Aiken, being novices in the industry of building atomic weapons, read in the *Aiken Standard* that Julius and Ethel Rosenberg were convicted in a court in New York of stealing atomic bomb information from the United States in order to give it to the Soviet Union. Their theft was found to be the most critical factor in Russia being able to explode its own test bomb so soon after realizing that this technology existed in the United States. The Rosenbergs, who were American Communists sympathetic to Russia, had been paid as spies to steal these bomb specifications. They were sentenced to die in the future. A few Aikenites wondered if these events would ever affect its future as a bomb-making location.

Then later in the spring of 1951, Aiken High School experienced a rare degree of athletic success that brought pride to the area. The track team won the South Carolina State

Championship for Class A-sized schools. Again, the success was centered on the athleticism of Tom Moseley. Although he was still only a junior, he won first place in the 100-yard dash, the 220-yard dash, and the javelin throw, setting new state records in the process. The track meet was so one-sided that the other schools conceded the last event—the mile relay—to Aiken without actually running the race. Aiken's team score at that point was more than twice that of the second-place school.

Casey continued with all of his other activities—the paper route, bottle pickup, car vacuuming with Farris, and anything else he was asked to do. And baseball practice was starting, and that excited him all over again.

When time permitted, he and Jake threw baseballs and engaged in batting practice. Casey had thickened in his build and was getting stronger. Jake noticed that his batting ability had more power in the swing and that he drove the ball hard and straight every time he connected.

Tot Robinson asked Casey which outfield position he wanted, and he specified center field. The season would be similar to last year, with games at Eustis Park and at fields in Graniteville and Warrenville. The season was only twelve games in length. Casey, as the most effective batter on the team, was the cleanup hitter, batting in the fourth position. Although he was not an overpowering extra-base hitter, he collected an inordinate number of singles and doubles. When the season ended, he was batting a gaudy .695. His outs were few and far between and tended to be line drives hit directly at a fielder.

His right arm was getting stronger and stronger and more accurate. In the first three games, he gunned down two runners at home plate and another one at third base. After that, the opposing baserunning coaches held their runners at second or third base, not daring to tempt Casey's arm to throw them out. Word was getting around that he was one of the best players to come along for quite some time, and respect for his baseball talents grew in Aiken and in the Horse Creek Valley.

By the end of the summer, the Gannon's new house was finished. It had the three bedrooms, plus two and a half baths, an eat-in kitchen, and a carport large enough for at least two cars. Jake had also found a way financially to build a large tool shed and workshop behind the house, nestled against the woods. Casey was more than happy with his bedroom. It was the bedroom that had been added in the construction and contained its own bathroom within it. For one thing, he was able to better spread out his personal things in his room. But he still hung on to the footlocker chest that had accompanied him on the train from Montana. For some reason, it was still important to him to keep his report cards, birth certificate, pictures of his parents, and his other vital papers in one place—the same old place he always kept them. What was that lingering habit all about he wondered.

The house remodeling business had picked up substantially, and the small company owned by Jake and his partner hired several carpenters and handymen to keep up with a growing backlog of work. Aiken was booming, and the small firm was getting its share of the jobs. They decided to incorporate the company, and its new name became G&G Construction Inc. after the last names of the owners.

July 1 came and it was Casey's thirteenth birthday. He told Annie Lou that he wanted her to bake another double chocolate cake, one large enough to feed his entire baseball team. One of the team members was a member of the

Outing Club, way out on Vaucluse Road, about halfway to Graniteville. His father had offered to assemble the birthday party into a swimming celebration as a way to end a successful season. They all gathered there, and Casey was able to become a teenager in the company of most of his baseball friends. The only ones missing were Arlene and Farris Wynn. The families toasted the fact that another summer was passing without polio striking too close to their loved ones.

School started back up the day after Labor Day. Casey entered the eighth grade and, for once, was happy to see classes start. He and his old friends were in for a shock, however, because there were so many new students in class on the first day that teachers had to use folding chairs to contain everyone. Folding tables were also in use, and it was common to see six or eight students gathered around one table. He even saw one student using a windowsill as a desk in a math class.

There was immediate talk of building new schools and hauling in house trailers for classrooms. Many, if not all of the new people, were children of construction workers. Stories were heard of fathers who had just returned from Saudi Arabia after operating Caterpillar tractors there, developing oil fields for the Arabs. Casey had a new friend who always wore work boots to school. When asked about them, the answer was that they were "steel-toed" boots.

"Why would anybody wear boots with steel toes?" Casey asked. The answer was that children tended to wear what their parents wore, and for a construction family, that meant very durable boots that could survive small accidents and protect feet. It also meant woolen plaid shirts and Levi's jeans that could fit over the boots and wide leather belts. Aiken had never looked like this before.

The entire elementary school had to break into two shifts in order to accommodate the huge influx on students. Some of the children arrived for class at 7:00 a.m. and were allowed to go home just prior to noon. Then another shift of students and teachers arrived to use the just-vacated classrooms from noon to 5:00 p.m. A few teachers taught during both shifts.

Area churches were also in use to provide enough classrooms for students. The Baptists, Methodists, and Presbyterians made their Sunday school facilities available to the county school system during the worst of the crunch.

The Aiken High School football team had another banner year. When the dust settled in mid-November, they had won six and lost three. Coach Carroll Watson had been selected to be the new principal of Aiken Elementary School, which was already under construction. Coach Watson had coached football, basketball, baseball, and the track team very successfully for the past six years and would be giving it up to manage the city's newest school.

Casey and Jake had attended every home football game at Eustis Park. Again, they saw Tom Moseley and his cousin, Ed "Boozie" Moseley, now seniors, lead the team in scoring. Tom ran fourteen touchdowns in the nine games while Ed had another three touchdowns. Both boys were speedy halfbacks, and long breakaway touchdowns were the rule, not the exception. Aiken High School was sad to see them finished with football.

The quarterback was junior Hugh Forrest, and senior Clyde Summer possessed the unusual talent of being able to make dropkicks successfully for the extra point. Some of the other seniors on the team were Len Yaun, Marshall Cain, and Jerre Freeman, whose family owned the grocery store where Casey cashed in his beverage bottles.

Late in November, it was announced that Tom Moseley was an All-State selection and had been chosen to play in the Shrine Bowl. When Casey asked about the Shrine Bowl game, he learned from Uncle Jake that every year, in early December, the best football players from South Carolina were invited to play in a special game held in Charlotte against the best North Carolina players. Casey was among those adoring eighth graders who swarmed around the Moseleys in the cafeteria the day those announcements were made. As usual, the Aiken seniors were gracious, humble, and quietly appreciative of the attention.

The other football excitement in the fall was about the October Big Thursday game, won by Carolina 20-0 and a Carolina player named Steve Wadiak, who starred in the game. The University of South Carolina was not accustomed to being in the national spotlight for its football accomplishments. But the halfback, Wadiak, had broken all the conference rushing records of "Choo-Choo" Justice and was receiving national attention for the achievement.

Casey had gotten into the habit of looking at the major league baseball standings in the newspaper every day. Since early August, the New York Giants had been slowly gaining ground on the league-leading Brooklyn Dodgers, a great team with Jackie Robinson, Duke Snider, Roy Campanella, and Gil Hodges. They finally tied the Dodgers on the final day of the season, causing a one-game playoff the next day, October 3, 1951. It was a totally improbable finish, but in the last inning of the playoff game, Giant Bobby Thompson hit a three-run homer off Dodger pitcher, Ralph Branca, to win the game and put the Giants into the World Series.

Casey was so excited when it happened that he got on his bike to ride all the way to the high school just to tell someone, anyone, what he had just heard on the radio. He excitedly told it to a puzzled Mr. Willis, the only person he could find. Mr. Willis thanked him.

Housing for all the construction workers now building the bomb plant was stretching the cities of Aiken, Augusta, North Augusta, and Barnwell to their limits. A rumor circulated in Aiken that the federal government and possibly DuPont were exerting severe pressure on Mayor Odell Weeks to allow hundreds of house trailers to be placed in the parkways of the wide Aiken streets so that the construction workers and their families could live in town and not in trailer parks on the edges of town. Mayor Weeks reportedly said, "That'll happen over my dead body," and refused to seriously consider the idea. It was truly impossible to imagine a line of trailers in the middle of Barnwell Avenue or Chesterfield Street. Luckily, that idea never took root as the mayor successfully stymied it.

Sometime near the end of 1951 and the beginning of 1952, Robbins Trailer City became a reality on Pine Log Road. Also, the city fathers hustled and came up with a plan to restructure all the 150-foot-wide streets into travel lanes heading in one direction, other travel lanes aimed in the opposite direction, and separated by medians with shrubbery and trees. Paving the travel lanes and sometimes adding curbs, gutters, and sidewalks was final touch for some of the streets. The coming of the bomb plant was forcing Aiken to deal with a slew of its issues in a permanent, constructive, aesthetically pleasing way.

Chapter 13

Arlene Cushman pulled Casey aside one day in the hallway just before Ms. Ballard's English class and told him that she might not be in school for the next few days. Her mother had an accident the day before and had been hospitalized.

Arlene added, "She had a bad fall and broke her leg in two places; and I need to stay home with her to make sure she can get around and take care of herself again. She's coming home from the hospital this afternoon. Besides, the cooking and housework will fall on me for a while."

Casey nodded and said, "Let me help. I'll ride my bike to your house this afternoon to help you, but after my papers are delivered." She agreed that his help might be useful.

Arlene's farm and house were out on Silver Bluff Road so it meant using Whiskey Road to get there. He quickly discovered that riding a bike on Whiskey Road had become more dangerous since the last time he tried it. The workers coming home from their workday at the bomb plant clogged the roads more than ever before, particularly the main route between Aiken and the plant. It was especially busy in the early mornings and late afternoons. Aiken was finally starting to experience a "rush hour."

Casey was not sure exactly what support Arlene might need, so he told himself that he would do anything she asked including just listening to her conversation.

Mrs. Cushman had a full cast on her right leg and had arrived home in an ambulance bearing crutches and a special wheelchair. Once they got her settled in a corner in an oversized farmhouse kitchen, she was content to listen to her radio programs. Arlene tuned in *As the World Turns*, and once her mother had begun to listen, she waved them out of the room.

They went out the front door to the large screened area where two porch swings were hanging at one end. They faced each other about eight feet apart to facilitate face-to-face conversation. Arlene sat in one, and Casey took the other. They instinctively started to sway gently as they talked.

After a minute of chitchat about her mother's condition, Arlene changed the subject. She asked Casey, "We're both thirteen now, teenagers at last. I was beginning to think we'd never get there. Have you decided what you want to be when we're all grown up?"

Casey was surprised by the question. After he adjusted to her mood and squirmed once in the swing, he said, "If I'm good enough, I want to be a baseball player in the major leagues. Most people never get good enough to do that, but I'm gonna be trying my hardest."

"I suppose you'd make a lot of money if that happens, and that would be good for you." Then she frowned. "You would have to leave Aiken to do that, of course. Do you want to leave Aiken?"

Casey was torn about how to respond to the question, but decided to answer it to her and to himself as honestly as he could. She was not completely aware of his financial situation regarding the insurance money from his mama's death, and he did not want to address it head-on with too much detail even now. "When I first got here three years ago, I hated it. First, there was all that trouble with trusting my uncle Jake, but he promised us he would change into a new man, and he really has. I depend on him now and honestly believe he likes me. And I finally realized that I hated it only because my mama was dead and that was what caused me to be here. You probably guessed that I got some money from her life insurance. That has caused my uncle and aunt to quit worrying about paying for me and the stuff I need. When I met you at school, everything started to get better. Not all at once, but slow. Now after three years, I've still never been to a bunch of places, so I still don't know too much about the world. But some things about this town are pretty special and make me want to be here for a long time."

"Like what?" she said as his comment perked her up.

"Well, like the weather. It's never very cold here. We won't ever be shoveling snow, I don't think. And the winter people. They come here so they won't be shoveling snow either. And the old Aiken people like your family. Very friendly." He paused and decided to add, "I heard that people can be very jealous in other places. I have never seen anybody in Aiken who is jealous of me. It seems like everybody here wants to see me get to where I'm going—wherever that is. They want to boost me up some to help me get there. Nobody has rooted against me yet."

Arlene was beaming when she heard the compliments Casey was describing. She asked, "Sounds to me like you would like to stay here instead of going back to Montana when you get grown."

"Yeah, that's probably right," he answered her. "I haven't thought about those people in a while. The more I'm here, the more I like being here."

She decided it was time to shift gears. "You know what I want? I want to get as much education as I can, then I want to be the best mother any woman can hope to be. I want to do that right here in Aiken so that I will know the same people for my whole life. I love my parents, and they want me to be the best I can be. Daddy's always saying, 'Child, I don't care what you decide to do, just don't do it halfway. Be the best at it if you can.'"

Casey decided to say one more thing while they were baring themselves to each other. He said, "Arlene, this is not easy to say and I'm only gonna say it once. My being happy here has an awful lot to do with you and with us being friends. Thanks for being on my side since I've been here."

She blushed and realized that she had just gotten more of an admission from him than she ever dreamed was possible. "Thank you so much for saying that and for helping me today. You're very special to me. I think you know that." They got up and went back into the house. After helping Arlene check on her mother, Casey said goodbye and left.

The next day, she caught him in the hall at school and said, "Thanks for helping out yesterday with my mom, and I liked our little talk on the porch. But I forgot something I wanted to ask you. The church is having its annual winter hayride tomorrow night and I'd like for you to go with me."

"What's a hayride like? I've never been on one." Casey was genuinely puzzled.

She was ready with the answer. "A big truck filled with hay in the back will leave the church at seven o'clock tomorrow night, filled with couples and a chaperone. The truck belongs to Bo Coward's father's business, you know, Coward Seed and Feed. Well, it drives out to Aiken State Park, about fifteen miles, around Windsor. Out there, we have a wiener roast and hamburgers and marshmallows and then ride back to the church. You'll be home by eleven o'clock. Please go with me. We'll have fun."

He thought for two seconds and said, "Okay, I'll go." And they had a terrific time talking together some more and playing ping-pong at the cookout shelter. And they enjoyed themselves even if it meant having to watch some other couples necking in the dark. They just ignored the necking teens and talked all evening.

Jake's home construction sideline business had really taken off along with the new year. One night over supper, he told his family that he was getting ready to leave the hardware business and work full-time to run G&G Construction Company. He said, "We are already making good money with several projects we have going on, and more people every day are asking me to take on their new house project or their add-on project. I need to start working in my company full-time to give everybody the good service they're looking for."

Annie Lou answered him, "Honey, you have to decide what's best for the family. We'll support whatever you decide."

"I'll give my notice at the end of this week," Jake said. "Somebody has bought the empty lot next door to us and they are begging me to build their house for them. I think they believe they'll get a better house if the man next door, who happens to be a home builder, does their construction. As a matter of fact, it would be real convenient for me to supervise it from right here." Jake told Casey that he would not allow the change in his work status to interfere with whatever came up in their lives pertaining to baseball.

Somewhere about this same time, Casey was told about a great American hero from World War II named Chuck Yeager. The intriguing fact that emerged from Yeager's story was that as a fighter pilot, he had become "an ace in one day," meaning that he had been personally responsible for destroying five German Messerschmitt fighter planes in a single day! Casey was able to find a reference to this in the school library. He sat there and read about the achievements and became enthralled to read that Yeager had indeed achieved this rare feat and that his own opinion was that his outstanding eyesight had provided a key tool to enable him to do it.

Yeager related in the story that his twenty-ten vision in both eyes enabled him see airplanes in the sky well before they could see him. He spoke of being able to see "disturbances in the air as far as two hundred miles away," and within minutes, these disturbances would turn out to be a squadron of airplanes. In other words, he couldn't exactly see the enemy airplanes, but he could see that something was stirring up the air at that same spot. He trained himself to recognize that disturbed air meant there had to be airplanes there.

This discovery excited Casey. He finally had read something that helped to explain his own ability to recognize things that most other people did not see. He could observe the seams turning on a baseball, right after it left the pitcher's hand. He could quickly determine if the spin was side to side or diagonal or top to bottom. And finally he knew that other players did not see this much detail when waiting for their pitch.

He told his uncle as soon as he realized what had facilitated Chuck Yeager to be a great American hero. Jake immediately saw that his nephew was on to something important. He told Casey, "You take good care of that eyesight. I'll work on teaching you where to swing the bat based on the kind of spin you see coming. If I can get your muscles and your brain trained to position your bat's swing as early as you see the stitches, you can be the most incredible batter you ever dreamed about."

Just as baseball practice was cranking up for the spring, news spread very quickly around Aiken on March 9 about a real tragedy that occurred just outside of town. The South Carolina Gamecock All-American Steve Wadiak was killed in an auto crash between downtown and Scott's Lake. The car he was riding in with five others took a curve too fast, ran off the road, and rolled over several times, ejecting the famous player. He died on the way to the hospital. He had finished his playing days at Carolina and had been drafted by the NFL's Pittsburgh Steelers. Several hundred Aikenites visited the scene of the accident over the next few days, and the sharp curve in Route 215 was quickly renamed "Wadiak Curve."

The baseball season came and went, and Casey was once again able to put up some impressive numbers for a thirteen-year-old boy in the Pony League. For one thing, the pitcher's mound was moved back to fifty-four feet, and this gave batters more time to react to whatever pitch was being thrown. It was a hitting feast for most of the season for Casey. He was still growing rapidly as his voice began to change and gaining more weight and overall strength.

Toward the end of the season, Jake spoke to Casey about how well he was swinging the bat and gave him this important advice. "Everybody sees you as the best hitter on the team and doesn't really question how that came to be. You and I know that one of the biggest factors is your eyesight. Nobody else needs to know that little fact but us—you and me and Annie Lou. I'm worried that if opposing pitchers learn that you're able to see their pitch so well because of better eyesight, they'll start trying to bean you to injure you and destroy it. Let's keep this little eyesight secret all to ourselves. Even your coaches don't need to know how you're able to do it."

Casey agreed with Jake. "What should I say if people ask me about how I hit so well? What do I tell them?"

Jake thought for a minute, then said, "Tell them this: 'I work really hard on my swing and my hand-eye coordination, and I see the ball pretty well.'"

"Okay, that sounds good," responded Casey.

Jake's business had really taken off, and his activities now involved several building projects at one time. He had followed through and resigned from the hardware store and was keeping busy twelve to fourteen hours a day.

On a Sunday afternoon in midsummer, he suggested to Annie Lou and Casey that they should go for a ride on the south end of Aiken. He knew of multiple housing projects going on in that part of town.

They rode slowly out Whiskey Road and took in all that was going on in that area. A few new houses were being constructed on Boardman and Brandy Roads, as well as other side roads in this neighborhood. Part of Whiskey Road had already been extended to four lanes wide, and the remainder had road construction sawhorses and paving work underway. Aiken Estates, which was nestled in the edge of Hitchcock Woods, was heavily into the building of several single-family homes; and a few families had already moved in and were trying to install shrubbery and to replace their packed-down hardpan, but sandy front yards. Farther out on the left, Virginia Acres had somehow leapt out of the ground with scores of ranch-style houses mounted on slabs. Again, owners were toiling to establish a yard out of the sandy soil.

The construction and population explosion was creating gashes in the rural countryside and was evident wherever a person chose to look. Annie Lou finally caught her breath and said, "Well, everybody tried to warn us that Aiken was about to change, and they were so right. I don't think I've ever seen so many houses being built at one time."

Jake agreed. "I think we'll be able to ride the front edge of this growth current for quite a while. And I'm so glad we got ourselves settled into a bigger house before all of this stuff hit the fan. Casey, you were pretty smart to start nudging us out of that house on Newberry Street when you did."

Casey smiled and took it all in. They rode farther to the south and finally turned around at College Acres, a new development that all had heard of but were puzzled to learn of its whereabouts. It seemed to be the end of the development of outer Aiken. But of course, that didn't count New Ellenton, a town that was also sprouting up to absorb the citizens of Ellenton, all of whom had been forced to move out.

Many new businesses had appeared on the landscape associated with Whiskey Road and the expanding south side of Aiken. A strip mall called Mitchell Shopping Center had suddenly popped up near Aiken Estates. Also, a Dairy Queen franchise was erected at the corner of Pine Log Road and Whiskey, just beyond Virginia Acres. On out Whiskey Road appeared a new drive-in movie theater and a bowling alley properly named Aiken Bowl.

"Do you know how to bowl, Uncle Jake?" Casey asked.

"No, never done that," was the answer. "Maybe we'll do that sometime soon."

They never did get around to bowling, but the family did spend an entire Sunday afternoon driving to the Clark Hill Dam and reservoir to see construction in its final stages. The project had started in 1948 by the Corps of Engineers. The Savannah River valley, and the city of Augusta in particular, had always been prone to flooding during heavy rains and when annual rainfall exceeded expectations. The huge project, which backed up an artificial lake for ninety miles, was finishing up in mid-1952 and would permit better control of the river's flow. A good side benefit? It generated electricity too.

Toward the end of the summer, the Gannons met their new next-door neighbors Wade and Zachary Kessler. There was no Mrs. Kessler, as she had passed away some years earlier. Wade Kessler was a pensive, aloof engineer who was moving into Aiken directly from Oak Ridge, Tennessee, where he had been associated with the nuclear plant operated there by the Atomic Energy Commission. Prior to that job, he had been associated with subcontractors performing nuclear work at Hanford, Washington.

Oak Ridge was identified in 1942 as the premier site of the Manhattan Project, a U.S. government undertaking to develop the atomic bomb. It was still an active location and was being run by the Atomic Energy Commission.

Hanford, Washington, was named in 1943 as a second participant in bringing the Manhattan Project to a fruitful end in 1945. It was common for the most senior participants in the national nuclear industry to have hands-on experience at either Oak Ridge or Hanford or sometimes both. It was about to become common for everyday people to say "Oak Ridge, Hanford, and Aiken" all in the same sentence.

The son, Zachary Edward Kessler, was the same age as Casey when they met—fourteen years old. Where Casey's birthday was July 1, 1938, Zach had been born in a Knoxville, Tennessee, hospital three days later, on the Fourth of July. It was a coincidence that would make them fast friends. They also discovered that they would both be entering the ninth grade when September got there.

The Kesslers had moved in at the tail end of Jake's work crew, performing the final touches on their house. It came out very quickly that Zach was an avid basketball player and an average baseball player. Since the Gannon backyard had a separate toolhouse including a workbench, Wade Kessler had asked Jake to build an identical one for his yard and place it close to the property line, adjacent to the Gannon toolhouse.

This left only three feet between the two toolhouses. While this final detail was being carried out, Zach asked his father for a basketball goal to be placed in their backyard also. This goal was installed well away from both residences but near the toolhouses. Before too long, Zack and Casey could be seen in their spare time playing "horse," shooting baskets, and playing one-on-one games while listening to a portable radio playing the popular tunes of the day. Zach was a better player than Casey, but the daily games made Casey into a more competitive basketball opponent.

For the rest of the summer, the two boys became almost inseparable. Zach has his own bicycle and occasionally rode along as Casey delivered his afternoon newspapers. Zach kidded him about "still doing this little boy chore" although Casey was a strapping six footer who weighed 175 pounds. For the first time, Casey started to consider whether he should give up the paper route.

One day, while they were taking a break from playing basketball, Zach surprised Casey by asking, "When do all of the colored people here stir things up? In Tennessee, I heard that we'd see and hear nothing but trouble from the colored people down here."

Casey responded quickly with "Who in the hell told you that?"

"Oh, just about everybody in east Tennessee told us we'd be fighting with the Negro people all the time—that all of them carried switchblade knives and like to fight white people every chance they get." Zach said it as if he believed the fights would start any minute now.

Casey guffawed out loud and said, "Boy, somebody told you a big bunch of lies. That stuff does not happen in Aiken, nothing like it." Casey continued by telling the stories of how

Clarence and his old nag Bubba rode from street to street selling vegetables off the back of an old wagon.

And he eagerly told Zach of his relationship with Farris Wynn and how much help Farris had been in making him feel welcome in Aiken. "Heck, I owe Farris an awful lot. He's one of my best friends here, and he's a grown man, and a black one at that. Good Lord, Bubba Moseley is another one. Nicest man you'll ever meet. Soon, I'll take you over to Farris Wynn's house so you can meet him. You need to meet Bubba too. He can get you some caddying jobs at the golf course. Somebody has told you all the wrong stuff."

Zach's face reddened in embarrassment at Casey having to correct his statements so completely. "You're right," he said. "I'm sorry. I want to meet them if you like them that much."

They also spent some time and explored Hitchcock Woods from one end to the other, running up and down the "backbone" ridge and walking the full extent of the Sand River. Zach had a .22 rifle and took it deep into the woods to show Casey how to fire it. After brief instructions from Zach, Casey was able to hit his targets dead center with greater regularity than his teacher. His immediate thought, which he kept to himself, was that "it's my eyesight again, letting me excel."

Casey talked Zach into trying out for the high school baseball team next spring. "I play baseball a lot," Casey said, "and it would be fun if you could make the team too."

Zach's answer was, "You can see I'm pretty serious about basketball, but I like baseball too. I've already heard that you're one of the best hitters around. That about right?"

"Yeah, I guess so," Casey responded. "But the pitching gets faster every year. I hope I can keep up with it as I get older."

During the next week, Casey made it a point to ride with Zach over to Farris's house so that he could see for himself what a nice man he was. Then on the next Saturday, they went to the golf course where Zach's introduction to Bubba Moseley was done. Casey used the opportunity to ask Bubba if he could carry any bags anytime soon, and Bubba answered, "Be here at noon tomorrow for a Sunday afternoon round with me and Mr. Winans." Casey grinned at his success and nodded. After they got back to their homes on Highland Park, the two boys talked about black and white relations in Aiken.

Zach admitted, "Those people in Tennessee were lying to me. The colored people here are really nice. I haven't met a single one I don't like and I don't feel threatened by anybody I met."

Later that same day, Zach and his father, Wade, were discussing Aiken and what revelations he had discovered that day by just visiting a couple of black men. Wade asked Zach, "I've been thinking about hiring a maid or a cook to help out here. Do you think either one of these men might know somebody we could hire?"

"I would bet that Farris Wynn would know somebody. Do you want me to get Casey to ask him?"

Wade answered, "Yeah, let's see if he can help us."

Within the next week, things happened fast. Casey asked Farris, and Farris came up with a name—Katie Wilson. Katie called Wade Kessler, got an interview one evening, and was hired to start the next day. Her job was three days a week—cleaning, cooking, washing and ironing the household clothes. Mission accomplished.

Sometime during 1952, the *Augusta Chronicle* decided that "the Augusta area" and "the Savannah River Basin" was no longer descriptive enough to name their coverage area properly. They sponsored a contest and asked everyone in the area to suggest better names. After hundreds of suggestions and months of consideration, the editors decided on Central Savannah River Area, which was quickly reduced to CSRA.

In the course of their conversations, Zach probed Casey about whether he liked popular music or not. Casey answered in a way that sounded lukewarm or noncommittal. Zach went on. "This past year, I really got into music on the radio a lot. There's a bunch of new stuff being played on some of the Tennessee stations that I really like. There's a station, WLAC, in Nashville that's playing a totally new sound that all of us in Oak Ridge liked. Try to find it on the dial late at night. It's at 1510. You can get it here in Aiken but only after eleven o'clock at night. They're playing what they call 'rhythm and blues.' It's mostly colored singers singing some really sad and moving kind of music. Ever heard of Clyde McPhatter or Roy Hamilton or Chuck Berry or B. B. King or Joe Turner? That's some of the names you hear. I swear I think people are getting tired of Johnny Ray and Perry Como and Patti Page and Bing Crosby, particularly people our age. Something is happening. Listen to WLAC and see for yourself."

Casey told Zach that he would try to find the station on Uncle Jake's radio.

Annie Lou asked Casey if he would ride his bike downtown to pick up something for her at Liles Drug Store. His answer was, "I don't know where Liles Drug is, and besides I thought you always got our stuff at Blake's, in the corner of the Commercial Hotel."

"Normally, I do," she said. "But Liles is pretty new and I want to give them a try. They're supposed to be a little cheaper than Dr. Blake. It is right across the street from Blake's, at the opposite corner, where Hahn's Grocery used to be. Just go to the drug counter and ask for Mrs. Gannon's package. I'll call them to say that you're coming."

As Casey arrived downtown and found the store, he also noticed that a poolroom had opened up right behind the drugstore. A sign said, "City Billiards." He parked his bike by the poolroom entrance and went in, climbing half a flight of stairs up to where the business operated. He walked in, saw half a dozen new pool tables, and spotted a middle-aged man behind a short-order restaurant counter. The man smiled and said, "Can I help you, young man?"

"I'm Casey Gannon," he answered. "I just saw this place for the first time and wanted to check it out."

"Good for you. I'm A. R. Edwards, and this is my place. We just opened a little bit ago." There was more small talk where Edwards said he had moved to Aiken from West Virginia because other family members were working at the bomb plant. Casey contributed that he was a paperboy, a baseball player, and a rising freshman in a few weeks at Aiken High School.

"Casey, you're welcome here anytime to just hang out, or shoot pool, or eat hotdogs. I make a darn good hot dog, and nobody ever turned them down. They're made with my special chili with mustard and onions. Just remember my name is AR, not Mr. Edwards." Casey said that he would come back another time.

Everything went smoothly at Liles Drug next door. A gray-haired man was behind the counter, and it was he who retrieved the small bag that they had ready for his aunt. "Are you Dr. Liles?" Casey asked.

The man smiled and said, "I'm Mr. Liles and I'm the owner of the store. I'm not a pharmacist myself, but I have a couple of them who work for me. I recently moved my family here from Dalton, Georgia, to open and operate this drugstore. I've got a boy about your age named Pierce who'll be starting at the high school when it reopens. Maybe you'll meet him."

Casey responded, "Thanks, I'll be on the lookout for him. Aiken's a good place to be."

When he got back home, he could hear music playing outside from quite a distance away. He rode up the driveway that his house shared with the Kesslers and saw that Zach was out back shooting baskets and listening to his portable radio. The Kitty Wells song "It Wasn't God Who Made Honky Tonk Angels" was blasting into the yard. Zach had already said more than once that he liked music. Maybe the hillbilly stuff too.

Chapter 14

The first day of school in September 1952 was a shock to everyone involved. Scores of new students had arrived in town over the summer, and scores more were attending their first day in the seventh grade, having been promoted out of Aiken Grammar School, and these transferring students seemed to wander around their new school on Laurens Street in a daze that first day.

Casey offered his assistance to his new friend, Zachary Kessler, in not only getting to school but also to meet new friends there. Both boys were freshly minted fourteen-year-olds and entering the ninth grade. Arlene Cushman appeared in front of them right after they entered the building and warmly greeted Casey because she had not seen him all summer, having spent the three months entirely in the Great Smoky Mountains.

After Arlene met Casey's new friend, she left the brief conversation and Zach was quick to say, "Hey, buddy, you didn't tell me you had a girlfriend. She's very sharp looking."

Casey flinched and his head snapped around upon hearing the word *girlfriend*, and he immediately stopped Zach from going any further. "Arlene's not my girlfriend. But she is probably my best friend in Aiken. We go back a long way, all the way to my first days here. But it's a mistake for you to call her my girlfriend."

Zach thought for a minute before continuing, but finally plowed ahead as gently as he dared. "Have you ever paid close attention to how she looks at you when she's talking to you?"

"No, why should I?" Casey responded.

"Let me break it to you gently and put it this way," Zach began. "If you were an ice cream cone, she would be taking a big slurp out of you when she talks to you. Maybe that girl's not your girlfriend, but she thinks you're definitely the boy in her life."

"Oh, come on, Zach, let's go meet some other people and get to our homeroom."

Ms. Inabinet was their homeroom teacher, and they discovered that Arlene was also in this room and was seated near them. The pupils learned that this would be a very difficult year for the entire Aiken County school system, but it would be particularly trying for Aiken's city schools. For example, there would be seven classes being conducted at the same time in the school auditorium, one class in each of the four downstairs corners, one class in the middle, and two in the balcony—one on the left and one on the right. And this would go on for six periods a day every day.

The gymnasium was not much better off. Chairs and folding utility tables were set up in each of the four corners for simultaneous classes. Other students would be leaving the school grounds every hour to attend classes in nearby church auditoriums. New schools were under construction, but they were not far enough along to provide relief for the 1952-53 school year.

There was an assembly at 10:00 a.m. in the auditorium, and its purpose was to welcome the students for the new school year and to pass on some general orientation information for those who were new to Aiken. Mr. Wrenn, one of the teachers, was at the podium; and as part of his presentation, he asked where people were coming from. Most of the new students were the offspring of Dupont employees, and answers of "Wilmington, Delaware" and "Charleston, West Virginia" and "Richmond, Virginia," as well as "Camden, South Carolina" were heard from those in attendance.

He also asked specifically if anyone was from Hanford, Washington, or from Oak Ridge, Tennessee. Three students raised their hands for Hanford; and four, including Zach Kessler, identified their origins as Oak Ridge, Tennessee. The high school population had changed in ways that were unimaginable just two short years before. That first day was pretty chaotic, and everyone was relieved when it was over and done.

At the Gannon dinner table that evening, Casey was relating stories of his first day at school when Jake brought up a new subject. "Casey, you've been fourteen for two months now and you haven't said a word yet about getting your driver's license. I thought all South Carolina boys were just dying to drive as soon as they turned fourteen."

Annie Lou perked up and said, "Jake, you've never asked me that question, not once. One day, I want to drive too."

"Honey, we'll get to you eventually, but right now I want to hear what Casey wants to do about driving, if anything."

Casey sat up straighter in his chair, swallowed his current mouthful, and said, "Yep, Uncle Jake, I want to get my license soon, but I also want to do something else at the same time."

"What's that?" Jake and Annie Lou asked together.

"I've been thinking about having my own car too," he spat out rapidly without looking up.

Annie Lou gasped at the idea. "You don't even know how to drive and now you want your own car too?"

"Yes, ma'am, I do. I can drive a little bit, and I have enough money saved for a cheap used car." Then he told them about his driving experiences at Tommy's house and on Snake Road.

"Damn," was all the response Jake could muster about learning of Casey's previous driving experience.

Casey continued. "Farris told me about an old 1947 Ford coupé that he knows about and that he'll help me get running right. It only costs $125 and I've got that much saved up."

"Oh boy, here we go," Annie Lou said. "We've got ourselves a teenager."

Jake finally caught his breath and said, "Okay, we can talk about that. I have to admit that you've never been an ounce of trouble, if we ignore that barefoot business right after you got here a few years back. I trust you with a lot of things, maybe even with everything. You think maybe we can get to trust you with driving and cars too? I'll bet you don't know anything about that Ford model Farris is talking about. It's not a family car. It's really more like a one-person car, or at most a two-person car. No real backseat. But on a lot of them there's a rumble seat for extra passengers and it's outside the car, back where the trunk is on most other cars. Ain't no place for a person to ride when the weather's bad."

"That sounds kind of interesting," Casey opined. "I haven't seen it yet. Farris is waiting for me to say if I'm interested in looking at it or not."

"Well, tell him you're interested in seeing it, and I want to go with you when you do. By the way, where'd you get $125?" Jake had been surprised by Casey's claim to have that much money.

"Oh, I've got more than that," Casey volunteered. "I've been busy with all of my little jobs for several years making money and stashing it away in my Mason jars. I promised you a long time ago I would pay for my own expenses, and I have. I always make a lot more than I spend."

"That's a good way to be," Annie Lou offered.

"Uncle Jake," Casey asked, "will you take me for a test drive in the Hudson soon so that you can check me out to see if I'm a safe driver? There's a driving test I have to worry about too."

"You got a deal," Jake said. "We'll do it after church on Sunday."

The next day at school, Zach Kessler had a good look at the older girls during lunch on the third floor. He was trying not to stare, but Julie Henderson and Gail Sloan had him riveted in his chair, with him gawking at them more than he should. Finally, Casey decided to act by saying, "Yes, my boy, there are some very good-looking girls in Aiken, but your drool is about to ruin my lunch. Cool it. Don't let them see you with your tongue hanging out like that."

"Sorry," moaned Zach. "But these girls are making me forget about Tennessee women. Man oh man!"

To change the subject and get Zach's mind off the girls, Casey asked, "How's that new colored lady working out? You know, Katie Wilson?"

"She's doing great. My dad likes her a lot and that's really important. Dad doesn't always like the people around him and it's a problem when that happens."

Casey saw an opening and waded in. "I haven't been around your dad very much, and you almost never talk about him. What's he like?"

"My dad's kind of a loner, and he's always been sort of like that. He's an engineer and very smart, and he doesn't always like small talk or people he thinks aren't as smart as him. His job is not with Dupont but with one of the subcontractors. He travels a lot for the nuclear business, and I really don't know what he does at the bomb plant. He never talks about work. Sometimes, he goes to meetings back in Oak Ridge and

Hanford, and once in a while overseas to London or Brussels. Part of the reason for hiring Katie was so that somebody can be there to take care of me while he goes off to those meetings. When my mom died in Tennessee a few years back, he changed to being even more distant and more of a loner than before."

Casey changed the subject. "I finally got around to listening to that Nashville station, WLAC. Boy, you're right about that 'rhythm and blues' label. The announcer seems to use that phrase a lot. I really liked the music even more than I thought I would. You didn't tell me about Fats Domino or the Drifters and songs like 'Lawdy Miss Clawdy.' Do you really suppose we'll ever hear this music on a local Augusta station? Since all of the singers are Negroes, the announcer said that if a white singer ever came along who sounded like them, look out. It might be the next big thing. He might be right."

"I told you it was different," Zach said.

"Oh," Casey added. "I found another station on that end of the dial called WCKY. It's from Cincinnati and it's at 1530, right next to WLAC. It seems to be the home base of hillbilly music. I heard as much of Hank Williams and his 'Jambalaya,' Roy Acuff, and Webb Pierce as I could stand. Again, it's one of those stations that you can't get in the daytime, and it even fades in and out late at night. I guess you know about that one."

"You almost can't listen to WLAC without knowing about WCKY too," Zach said.

On Saturday, Farris took Jake and Casey to see the 1947 Ford he thought Casey might like. The first thing they saw was the rumble seat. Yes, it had one, and it was in good shape. No leaks and no tears in the seat cover. Jake checked it all over, drove the car briefly with Casey riding along. Casey saw that it had a radio, turning it on and determining that it worked okay. They went back and talked to the current owner and made the decision that Farris could fix everything that needed fixing for about $30. Casey agreed that he could afford that too.

Jake couldn't let the opportunity go by without kidding about the radio. "Of all the things that could be wrong with the car, you had to check the radio first."

Casey had an answer. "It's the only thing I could test and decide whether it worked or not." Jake just laughed.

The next day after church, Jake and Casey took Jake's Hudson out on the Augusta superhighway, and Casey showed Jake that he knew how to work the gears and all the other controls. Jake was surprised that he was as relaxed in the driver's seat as could be expected. He drove all the way to Schultz Hill in North Augusta and back. At the end, he told Casey to drive all the way to their house.

Once they were parked at home, Jake said, "This week, get yourself a South Carolina driver's manual, and study it so that you can pass the written test. There's also a driving test with a state patrolman. You can use the Hudson when the time comes for the test. Usually, they're tough and people don't pass on the first try. During the next week you can practice parallel parking here at home with my car. Get yourself ready, old boy. Once you've done all of that and actually have your license, I'll let you buy that Ford."

"Thanks, Uncle Jake. I'll get all of that done. I won't let you down or embarrass you."

The next few days were like a blur for the Gannon family. Casey was still doing his balancing act with school, bottle pickup, delivering afternoon newspapers, and now he was studying the driver's handbook and practicing his parking.

Finally, he felt like he was ready to take the written and the driving tests. Jake drove them to the testing office on Richland Avenue, and Casey passed both tests on his first attempt. It was not without a minor scare, however.

When the state patrolman, who was riding shotgun during the driving test, shouted, "Stop! Quick! Right now!" during the middle of it, Casey slammed on the brakes and virtually stood on the brake pedal since he hadn't been expecting it. The patrolman was slammed forward into the windshield and dropped his clipboard to the floor.

Once he was able to gather himself, he stared at Casey and yelled, "What in hell did you do that for?"

Casey nervously said meekly, "I thought you meant for me to stop as quick as I could. You just saw it. That was it—me stopping as quick as I could. I thought you were grading me on how quick my reflexes were."

"By God, you snot nose, I ought to flunk your ass for throwing me into the windshield like that! You pass, dammit, drive us back to the office and get your permit."

When Jake and Casey departed the licensing office, they were in possession of the new permit—a three-inch-long piece of bright, shiny brass stamped on both sides with Casey's home address and his vital statistics such as date of birth, height, weight, race, and the date of expiration for the license. A handy hole was drilled in one end so that the license could be easily mounted on a key ring.

Jake congratulated Casey and said, "You get to drive us home. We'll start getting your car tomorrow. Get your money ready." Casey could not stop smiling for the rest of the day.

The next afternoon, Jake drove them to Farris's house to buy the car and pay for it. The final repairs had been made overnight by Farris. The owner accepted the cash, which

Casey had carefully counted out, and gave Jake the title for the car. He studied it to make sure it was correctly made in the name of Casey Carter Gannon. It was.

Casey had also brought extra money with him to gas up his new purchase on his way back home. He often visited the Gulf station on Richland Avenue, directly across the street from the Commercial Hotel and behind Wise Hardware. It was usually to buy a quick snack or pick up stray soft drink bottles. He winced a bit when he had to pay 22¢ a gallon because he had seen it somewhere recently for only 20¢.

After gassing up, he drove straight to the highway department offices on Richland to purchase his first South Carolina license plates. He had even remembered to bring pliers and a screwdriver with him to attach them while still in the parking lot. Today, he would deliver the *Augusta Herald* using his new car!

At the dinner table that evening, Jake wanted to make some special points about the responsibilities of car ownership. He said, "You know, Casey, one of the primary mileposts in life for a man happens when he gets his first car. That just happened to you today, and you're just barely fourteen years old. You probably realize that I was in a position to stop this from happening, but I had to admit to myself that of all the fourteen-year-old boys I know, I prefer to see you driving your own car over all of them. You have completely earned the right to what you have today."

Casey was not expecting the compliments, and his face blushed. "Thanks, Uncle Jake."

Annie Lou pitched in with "You really deserve this, dear boy."

Jake continued. "We had a rough start there for a while back in 1948 when you first got here, and I admit, most of that was my fault. I wasn't ready to share my house or my earnings or my assets with you. Truth is, I was way too greedy. I saw you as a monkey wrench thrown into the gears, a handful of nails tossed onto the road. You have managed to have just the opposite effect in our lives. You have lived an almost perfect life since you've been here, and I want you to know that I have so much admiration for you that I want to say it out loud. You have been a great example for me, and it was an example I apparently needed."

Casey was beginning to feel his emotions edge up to the surface, and he tried to clamp down on them. He failed. In another second, he felt tears running down his face involuntarily. He grabbed his napkin to try to hold back the flood. Again, he failed.

Finally, he gave up any attempt to continue eating. He sat back and used the time and the napkin to regain some control. Annie Lou sat by quietly, not knowing what might come next.

Eventually, Casey was able to say, very softly, "I'm old enough now to know that when I got here over four years ago, I was an orphan. No parents. No other place to go. Probably no future either. I know now that y'all could've said, 'No, we won't take him, send him someplace else,' but you didn't. You took me. It was a long time, but I finally got the picture. I like it a lot that I live here with you. I won't ever be able to tell you what it means. Y'all are my parents. That's what I tell people. Because of y'all, I have a life. I have a place to be. I have a future. I have something now after having nothing then."

Now Annie Lou was melting as well. "You have meant so much to us, Casey, we can't thank you enough," she said as she wiped at her eyes. "I don't think there's anything you could ever do that would make us change our minds."

Jake finally was able to talk again. "What I was trying to say before I lost control of things is that you have special responsibilities when you drive a car. It's a three-thousand-pound weapon if you don't take care of it and use it just right. Always obey the law, don't go running off too fast, learn where the risks are, and drive in a way to protect everybody around you. That license you got is the state of South Carolina giving you their permission to drive on their roads. They take the position—and rightly so in my opinion—that they can take away that permission if you don't follow their rules. If that happens, you'll end up selling your car and riding that bicycle again."

"I understand, Uncle Jake, thanks for everything you said."

Shortly after dinner was over, he walked next door to see Zach. When he answered the doorbell, Casey said, "Hey, you want to see my new car? C'mon outside."

Zach liked the car, even the rumble seat. Casey said, "Tomorrow morning, I'll drive it to school for the first time. I'd like you to ride with me."

"Oh boy," Zach answered. "You've got a deal."

On the way to school the next day, Casey offered to show Zach a tour of Aiken in their new ride as soon as school was out at three o'clock. Zach immediately accepted.

After school, and before newspapers had to be delivered, Casey took the car and Zach to the parts of Aiken that were favorites and those he may not have seen yet. It started with his driving straight to Eustis Park, where baseball would be played in the spring. And it involved, as it always does near downtown Aiken, in crisscrossing the myriad of scenic double streets. Zach fiddled with the car radio as they drove and was able to receive at least three Augusta stations—WGAC, WBBQ, and a colored station, WAUG. They drove to Bethany Cemetery, which had an unusual pull on Casey even though he did not know a single person buried there. He just liked the way it seemed to preside over things from one end of Laurens Street.

He liked South Boundary and wanted to make sure Zach had seen it for himself. The arcade of live oak trees was a signature site within the city limits. While they were in the neighborhood, he wanted to guarantee that the unpaved streets made an impression on his friend. They rode the washboards of Magnolia Street, Two Notch Road, Powderhouse Road, Audubon Drive, Mead Avenue, and Grace Street. Before Zach could complain out loud about the rough ride or kicking up so much dust and dirt, Casey told him that the residents in this part of town wanted it this way. "They want their horses to be handled gently, and providing dirt roads is one way to do that."

Track Kitchen

While still on the south side, they drove toward the bomb plant far enough to see where the Fox Drive-In movie theater was located and checked out the homes under construction on Brandy Road, Boardman Road, and Barnard Avenue. Jake Gannon's construction company was involved in several of the projects.

Hopelands Gardens

Casey drove his car over each one of the six wooden bridges that spanned the railroad cut, and he showed off the passenger depot as well as the freight station a few blocks away. After an hour of cruising around, he realized he had to stop the touring and deliver his newspapers.

"We'll do some more of this in a few days. I want you to see where we swim. That means Scott's Lake, Johnson's Lake, and a place we call the 'blue lagoon.' It's at a kaolin digging site out the back way from south-side Aiken toward Warrenville, actually off Howlandville Road near Pine Log."

When Zach was dropped off at home, he thanked Casey for the tour and said that he looked forward to the next one.

The country moved slowly into the autumn, and some weeks later, retired general Dwight D. Eisenhower was elected to be the new president of the United States, bringing his vice president, Californian Richard Nixon, into office with him. Ike had proven to be a very popular politician after his successes as an army general during a time of war. He was widely credited for crafting the plans for the Normandy invasion on D-Day 1944, and the execution of his plan led directly to winning the European part of World War II. Adlai Stevenson was the Democratic nominee who had been defeated in the 1952 presidential election.

Locally, Mayor Odell Weeks had decided earlier in the year to retire from office. He was replaced in the election by Charles Jones, a local businessman.

When Casey got around to visiting Arlene Cushman in his car, she was captivated when she saw it for the first time. "Oh, Casey, it's such a cute car. You must take me for a real ride in it." He had driven it to her house at the farm to show her. They made a date to attend a movie together after seeking and getting permission from Mrs. Cushman, who had just been released from her final leg cast. She gave her permission reluctantly, saying, "Just remember, you're only fourteen and you don't have a lot of driving experience."

The next Saturday evening, they drove to Augusta for a movie at the Modjeska Theater. On the way, Arlene noted that Culler's Half Acre was doing a booming business for a Saturday night.

"Must be selling a lot of furniture to all these new bomb planters, she said." Casey was complaining lightly about the slow traffic and congestion between the Aiken County Hospital and the beginning of the four-lane road three miles west of Aiken. The widening of this old two-lane section of Route 1 was scheduled to begin in 1953, but not much had been done yet in preparation for that. The continuing bottleneck frustrated the entire area.

They stopped to eat hamburgers and drink milk shakes at the Dixie Lee Drive-In restaurant, which was about halfway between the two cities. It was the only restaurant on the superhighway between Aiken and Augusta and was already very popular with teenagers. Casey privately wondered how someone had planned so well and so far in advance as to have this wonderful monopoly aimed at hungry teenagers at about the halfway point between Aiken and Augusta.

Both of them enjoyed being together and having the freedom and privacy to simply bask in their time together. Casey even held her hand as they walked from the car to the theater. Arlene smiled to herself.

They had one more date together in 1952, and that was at the end of the first week of December. Casey had read a Henderson Hotel ad in the *Aiken Standard and Review*, which stated that in their upscale dining room, one could eat lunch for 85¢ each and dinner for $1.25 each. He asked Arlene to go to dinner with him there and to attend the Christmas parade afterward. She was thrilled to be asked and agreed. It was among their first experiences of eating in a restaurant instead of eating at home. They enjoyed meat loaf, a salad, and chocolate cake, feeling very grown-up.

The crowds attending the parade were huge. The newspaper said later that over thirty-five thousand people were watching the parade on Park, Laurens, and Richland. The big draw was Santa Claus, of course, and several marching bands and decorated floats. Newcomers to the area were beginning to be more obvious.

Chapter 15

The new year of 1953 began with all three Gannons at home enjoying the time off from work and everyday activities. The radio was tuned to an Augusta station that was playing a mixture of Bing Crosby and Perry Como Christmas standards and a smattering of hillbilly tunes.

The announcer broke in during a song to state, in a fully emotional voice, that singer Hank Williams had died in the backseat of a car traveling through West Virginia. When she heard this sad news, Annie Lou started weeping quietly and saying over and over, "But he was so young, he was so young." She listened to hillbilly music during some part of every day. Her habit was to keep the radio on at low volume all day long.

Over the next few hours, it was completely verified that Hank Williams, master of "Cold, Cold Heart" and "Your Cheatin' Heart," had succumbed to too much alcohol and drugs in his body. He was only twenty-nine years old.

Within a few days, Aiken was returning to normal from the holidays. The talk was of television, which was arriving in cities all over the United States, and would be affecting the Aiken-Augusta area before the year was over. Sears, Roebuck and most of the hardware stores were beginning to stock floor model sets. Names of Dumont and Hallicrafters, Emerson, Admiral, and RCA were on the minds and the lips of potential buyers.

Early in the year, Aiken discovered that it was not immune to tragedy. On Tuesday morning, January 27, 1953, someone working at Jones Electric & Gas on Laurens Street smelled gas vapors and asked Jimmy Jones, the owner's son, to run downstairs to the basement to check out the odors. He descended the stairs, and upon reaching the bottom, he flicked a fan switch to allow him to exhaust the fumes. That act of turning on the switch created a tiny electrical arc that ignited the gas vapors. Jones Electric, and at least two other businesses in each direction, blew up and started a roaring fire. Jimmy Jones was blown totally out the rear of the building and was burned seriously, but he survived to tell the authorities how the explosion happened.

The destroyed businesses were Platt's Rexall Drug, Diana Shops, Jones Electric, McCreary's, and Liles Drug. Others, including Holley Hardware, were damaged badly. Almost every storefront window across Laurens Street was broken from the shock wave of the explosion.

Casey and Zach were both in Mr. Dobson's civics class in the balcony of the high school auditorium. An audible

WHUMP sounded throughout the building, and students looked at each other, saying, "What was that?"

Within three minutes, Mr. Willis was making an erroneous announcement on the PA system. He said that some chemicals at Liles Drug Company had somehow blown up and caused severe damage downtown, only a block from the school. Pierce Liles, son of the owner, was also in the class. He immediately jumped up and ran out of the class, heading for the explosion. He learned of Mr. Willis's error as soon as he saw where the damage was located and saw that his father was assisting the injured and those trapped.

For the next several hours, the Aiken Fire Department, plus some other departments from Augusta, North Augusta, Williston, and the Horse Creek Valley, fought the fire and were able to bring it under control. Even the new fire department under Dupont's supervision, located on the bomb plant site, sent a portion of their department.

Unfortunately, ten Aiken residents were killed that day, and most of them were well-known. They were David Rutland, May Weeks, Emilie McCarter, James S. Watson, Charles Long, Mrs. W. M. Dunkin, Jack Neibling, Jack Holley, Ruth Madrey, and James "Bubba" Moseley. Almost all of them were employed by Jones Electric or in some way associated with them, except for May Weeks. She was a long-term employee of McCreary's next door.

May Weeks was sorting some merchandise near the front of McCreary's when the blast occurred, and she was pinned beneath a large timber and other fallen wreckage. Attempts were made by several rescuers, led by William Liles, owner of the drugstore, to free her as the fire edged closer, but brick walls began to crumble around them and they finally had to retreat. She told them that they should save themselves while they still had the chance. "Just give me a shot to ease my pain and make the end come easier for me." They did not have time to do even that as a crumbling wall collapsed on her and entombed her as the fire swept over the area. She had been more than heroic. Her body was the first one to be recovered the next day because the searchers knew exactly where to look.

The news of who had died downtown on Tuesday hit the Gannon household very hard when they read the names in the Aiken newspaper on Wednesday. Jake knew almost all of them, but Annie Lou lost a good friend in May Weeks and one who had served her needs at McCreary's for years. The details about her being pinned and then being covered alive by a falling brick wall was almost more than she could bear.

But Casey was not easy to console about Bubba Moseley either. They had been friends for four years, and Bubba was one of the first people to believe in him when he was new to Aiken. As the weekend caddy master at Aiken Municipal Golf Club, they had caddied together half a dozen times and ribbed each other about anything and everything.

Casey asked Jake if he could go to Bubba's funeral. Jake's answer was, "Sure, I'll take you."

In the funeral parade on the way to the cemetery, Casey saw for the first time that incidental cars not involved in the funeral were pulling over to the shoulder of the road, allowing the funeral to pass. Cars in both directions did the same.

Casey finally asked, "Why are those cars pulling over to the side? I don't get it. Is it just to get out of the way?"

Jake said, "No, it's the way we bury people in the South. It's about reverence for the dead. It's each driver's way of showing respect for those going into eternity. Learn it well. When you become a driver, you'll do it too. It's a way to tip your hat to your friend, Bubba."

Casey felt the tears form quickly in his eyes when he heard Uncle Jake's words. It was weeks before he came out of the low spot about the death of his colored friend.

The city of Aiken sadly went about the business of burying its dead and beginning the massive cleanup in the middle of downtown.

As spring approached, Casey and Zach found themselves alternating between shooting baskets in the backyard and playing catch with gloves and a baseball to get ready for trying out for the baseball team. On occasion, they would take Zach's .22 rifle into Hitchcock Woods and engage in target practice. Both were amazed at Casey's growing accuracy in hitting very small targets.

Zach said, "I even told my dad I thought you could shoot the left eye out of a bullfrog. He just smiled and changed the subject on me. He told me he had to take one of those trips to Belgium, Brussels, I think it is. He said he asked Katie to come every day to work for the next week while he's gone. So I'll be there by myself for a week."

"Okay," said Casey. "I'll help you stay out of trouble."

A couple of days later, it was Saturday, and Katie and Zach were still in the house. A strange blue car drove up, and Casey could read the word *Kaiser* on the front fender.

Damn, he thought, *I never heard of a Kaiser*. A kindly colored man parked in the Kessler yard, and Casey spoke to the man when he got out from the driver's seat. "Can I help you, sir?" he asked as nicely as he could. Casey judged him to be about fifty or sixty years old.

The man smiled sweetly and said, "I's looking for the Kessler house. I's here to visit my good friend, Ms. Katie Wilson." And he giggled softly.

Casey was quite sure he had never seen a man like this. He had a perpetual smile on his very approachable-looking face, which was clean shaven. He wore a Ben Hogan-type of soft white cap, with a short bill buried in the softness. He removed the cap as he spoke and held it across his heart. He had solid white hair, worn in the short tight curls found on almost all colored men. A neat, freshly pressed blue sport shirt was closed at the neck where there was a bright green bow tie. Khaki pants, neatly pressed, completed the picture, and he was wearing black-and-white saddle oxford shoes.

"My name is Ross Howard, and I's looking for Ms. Katie Wilson. Did I come to the right place?" And he giggled softly again in an almost tittering sound, not at all unpleasant.

Casey answered him finally, "You're almost at the right place. That's the Kessler house right there." He pointed at the house next door. "Mr. Howard, I never saw a Kaiser car before. Where'd you get that?"

Ross Howard smiled again. "And what is your name, young man?"

"I'm Casey Gannon. My good friend is Zach Kessler, and he lives there next door."

"Well, Master Casey, it's mighty nice to meet you," he said as he bowed slightly over his arm and cap. "This is a 1947 Kaiser made by the Kaiser-Frazier Car Company of California. And you call me Ross please, not Mr. Howard. I drove over here from Augusta. Will you excuse me while I knock at the house next door?" And he laughed again.

As he walked toward the Kessler house, both Katie Wilson and Zach came out the back door toward Ross's car. Katie was smiling as she saw who was there, and she shook his hand as she gave him a slight hug.

"Ross Howard, what in the world you doin' here, and on my workday at that?" Katie was sounding mad, but it was easy to see she was pleased.

"I tole you I'd be comin' to see you on my day off, and here I is," Ross answered. He looked toward the two boys and added, "Ms. Katie don't always agree with me, but I's courtin' her as hard as she'll let me." He was smiling and laughing lightly as usual.

As the neighbors and their guest walked toward their house, Casey heard Ross say, "And yo name is Master Zachary, I understand. Are you named for that Zachary fella from the Bible?"

Casey went into the back door of his house and was going through the kitchen when his aunt Annie Lou asked, "Who's that visitor you were talking to? He looks real interesting."

He laughed, thought about it for a second, and said, "I swear I think I've been talking to Uncle Remus. He says his name is Ross Howard, but he's the exact image of what I think of when somebody says 'Uncle Remus.'"

"Well, okay," Annie Lou answered.

About an hour later, Casey heard his neighbors in the backyard again and decided to join them. When he had the chance, he asked, "Ross, tell us what you do in Augusta, and tell Zach and me why you call us 'master' and you only want us to call you by your first name?"

"Of course." Ross started his answers with his laugh, which had the ability to put everybody at ease. Then he said, "Down heah in the South, where we live, calling you boys 'master' is what I was always taught to do. Oh, you'll get to be 'mister' soon enough when you gets older. I have always lived in Augusta, and I works in a auto supply store, one that sells tires, and spark plugs, and windshield wipers, and car batteries, and seat covers to put in old cars. I sometimes works on seat covers or fixes flat tires for customers. That's what I does." The entire time he was talking, he had a wide smile on his face as if he enjoyed telling you all about it.

"Now I got to go, got to get back to Augusta. Ms. Katie, I'll see you on Wednesday evening to take you to yo' church over heah. I enjoyed meetin' you, boys. I'll see y'all again next time." And he got in his Kaiser, started it, and drove off.

As they watched him leave, Casey said to Katie Wilson, "Katie, that's a really nice man. I like him."

She answered, "I think I do too," and went back into the Kessler house.

Soon, baseball practice started, and Casey was one of the first freshmen students to sign up for tryout for the team. He talked Zack into trying out too. In a few days of practicing with the team, they both realized that Casey was a shoo-in to make the team and Zach was a "maybe." Although the pitching was faster, Casey was still able to make contact on just about every pitch in the strike zone, and the coach quickly maneuvered him to think about playing right field and batting toward the bottom of the lineup.

Casey quickly made the acquaintance of Hugh Forrest, a senior who was the regular center fielder. Hugh told Casey that he already knew a lot about him. "I know you'd rather play center field than right field. But center field is mine for this year, just like it's been last year and the year before that. But I promise you two things for this year. I'll teach you everything I know about playing the position, so you'll be ready for next year, and I promise you that I won't let anybody on the team mess with you. Know what I mean? Nobody's gonna pick on you if I have anything to say about it."

"Thanks." Casey was surprised, but he added, "Nobody in Aiken has ever tried to mess with me. I don't think the people who live here are like that."

During the season, the whole world noticed that on March 5, Joseph Stalin, the Russian leader, died of a stroke. Communist leadership was changing over to Nikita Khrushchev after years of Stalin's despotic rule.

A very important news item also hit the newspaper on March 26. A doctor from Pittsburgh announced quietly that after years of trying, he had created a successful vaccine against polio. Had Dr. Jonas Salk come up with the cure that would block summertime fears at last? Finally, a terrible scourge of childhood was about to disappear from the American scene!

The baseball season was a successful one for Casey. He became the regular right fielder and played every game, throwing out runners on base twice during their attempts to stretch doubles into triples. He began the season as the eighth batter in the lineup but was promoted upward as his hitting became more dependable and more of a factor during games. He finished the season batting in the fifth position and had been able to drive in some key runs in testy game situations. He struck out only twice during the season and had batted for a .370 average, one of the best on the team.

Hugh Forrest had been true to his word. He became a good friend and supportive teammate, always helpful and never critical. Casey was thankful that he had been able to watch an excellent center fielder from a close viewpoint. Zach had not made the team but was hopeful for the next year.

During April, permanent new families were quietly moving into Aiken, and they were becoming part of the huge Dupont operation for the long haul. More than one family was moving from the Dana, Indiana area.

Dupont operated a small but critical facility in that town that had fewer than one thousand people as its total population. The Dana operation, in 1945, had developed some of the earliest processes for making heavy water, essential for the production of hydrogen bombs. The technical phrase was that they had mastered what they called the "Girdler sulfide chemical exchange," which was an essential step for making heavy water. Some of the Duponters who were transferred to Aiken in 1953 were sent, two years prior to that, to work at the Dana facility to be exposed to the necessary technical thinking and experience they would need at the Aiken plant.

One of these families was the Cavanaughs, whose members included sixteen-year-old Fred Cavanaugh and a younger sister, Judy. Fred brought with him a 1939 Ford purchased at his former home in nearby Illinois for $75, plus a desire to play baseball, and a strong motivation to be a success in life. Two other families who came to Aiken through the Dana plant were the Christines and the Caneys.

In the major leagues, New York Yankee Mickey Mantle, playing in his third season, had hit one of the longest home runs ever hit. On April 17, he hit a ball out of Yankee Stadium that landed in the third deck in left-center field. It was measured at 565 feet the next day.

The middle of 1953 was marked by several key events in the Aiken area. First, the bomb plant became operational during the summer. Construction was winding down, and the production of nuclear materials was ramping up. Second, Julius and Ethel Rosenberg were electrocuted by the government on June 19, bringing anguish to Communists everywhere. But they had, after all, been found guilty of stealing atomic bomb secrets from the United States. That deed, more than any other single event, forced the United States into its decision to expand its nuclear arms capability into a place such as Aiken. Third, the Korean War was finally declared ended on July 27, after months of negotiations in Panmunjom. Finally, Chevrolet announced the production of its Corvette, making it the first true American sports car. It was also the first American car whose body was made of molded fiberglass rather than steel or aluminum.

Casey's baseball career on the Aiken High School team had to be addressed in an oblique way during the summer of 1953. Some of his *Augusta Herald* residential customers had complained about late delivery on those days when he had to play an afternoon game. Aunt Annie Lou had offered to help, but she could only do so much from a bicycle. Casey finally undertook the project of teaching his aunt to drive his blue Ford coupé.

He drove her to his old venue on Snake Road, which was only a few hundred yards from their house. It was still a sandy unpaved stretch of S-shaped turns just off Forest Hill Drive, near the golf course. He told her that it was here that he did his first driving outside of the junkyard owned by Tommy's father. She frowned as she realized that in spite of her best efforts, Casey had been able to take chances and engage in risky behavior that she would not know about or be able to prevent.

Annie Lou had some trouble with the clutch and accelerator timing at first, but then quickly caught the hang of the whole thing. Within two weeks, she was very confident and could drive on a city street, and within a month, she was tested for her license and passed with ease. Jake was skeptical at first but quickly saw the benefit of having three drivers living in their house.

When school started back up after Labor Day, everyone noticed that the halls, classrooms, and cafeteria seemed to be less crowded. Could it be that with the winding down of construction at the bomb plant, Aiken's infrastructure would also begin to breathe a bit easier?

Zach still rode to school with Casey, and he still seemed to be no less entranced by the girls just ahead of him in age and class. "Have you taken a really good look at that Sally Busbee girl?" he asked one day as they parked the car on Barnwell Avenue. "She's just about the cutest thing I've ever seen, but she doesn't even know I exist."

"Yeah, I agree," Casey muttered quietly so that nobody would hear. "She's a real good-looking girl. Good cheerleader too. I asked you not to drool in my car about somebody who doesn't know you exist."

"One more question, okay?" Zach asked and kept on rolling. "Do you know the girl named Sissy Slayton? I think she's one grade ahead of us. She's been really nice to me. Is she that friendly to everybody, or is it just me?"

Casey laughed. "She's pretty much nice to everybody, even wise guys like you. I don't think she's picked you out for special treatment."

Zach decided to change the subject. "Did you know that our high school has a boy in it named Catfish? I met him the other day when I was walking near the golf course. He's a golfer and plays on our school team."

"Yeah," answered Casey. "I met him once last year. His name's really Harold Kneece, and he's a really good golfer here. He plays basketball too."

On the weekend of the fifth annual Cotton Festival, Casey took Arlene to the parade downtown. That night, a tragedy occurred that rocked the city of Aiken and the high school to its core. One of its seniors, honor student Boyce Bell, was accidentally gunned down and killed by an Aiken police officer, who was working part time as a security guard.

The story was this. A drive-up restaurant called the Dairy Bar was the usual place of employment for the boy, but he had not worked that evening because he had also attended a Cotton Festival event. Casey and Arlene occasionally stopped at this same Dairy Bar to buy milk shakes while on their dates. It was in the 1000 block of Richland Avenue, a few hundred yards below Aiken County Hospital, on the way to Augusta. On his way home, Boyce was driving by and saw that someone had left an inner light on when they closed up. He stopped briefly to enter through the back door (the only door) to extinguish the light.

Unknown to him, a known thief had been spotted casing the area before closing. The owner called the police to ask for help, and they sent an off-duty officer to sit inside the small building in case the thief decided to follow through with a burglary. Boyce Bell was shot and killed by the officer as he entered and refused an order to stop. A hearing the next week cleared the officer of any wrongdoing. The popular student was buried within a few days with the entire senior class of Aiken High School in attendance. It was a tragic misunderstanding.

During the next month, the United States conducted its first H-bomb test during the Cold War. This test placed an exclamation mark on the fact that the Aiken area was now a frontline player in the nuclear age.

Things were changing very fast in 1953 in the United States generally and in the central South Carolina area specifically. On November 7, WIS-TV went on the air as an active new television station broadcasting from Columbia. Just two weeks later, on November 23, WJBF-TV went on the air from downtown Augusta. Aikenites now had good reasons to be shopping for those large floor model TV sets and "rabbit ears" antennas at Sears and the hardware stores. Sets with the screen size of seventeen inches was the norm, but a few fifteen-inch sets were also available. The talk at work and at school was of late-night television starring Jerry Lester, Dagmar, and Broadway Open House, sponsored by Anchor Hocking Glass. It came on five nights a week after the local news. And within the first month, every male in the area had seen wrestling (Is it fake or real?) and professional boxing. The ladies could watch *The Guiding Light* and other soap operas in the afternoon. It was all live TV. There was nothing else but that and amateurish local news and morning test patterns. Every TV station signed off with some version of the "Star-Spangled Banner."

Only a month later, at the end of the year, Hugh Hefner published the first issue of *Playboy* magazine. Almost unnoticed in the new media blitz of 1953 was that during the middle of the year, Aiken received its first radio station. In June, WAKN, an AM station, began broadcasting from its modest studio on Laurens Street during the daylight hours. Will the world ever be the same again? The answer was a loud and emphatic NO, but there was no way to know that yet.

Zach had made the basketball team but had to ride the bench for most of the season. Several newcomers from Dupont families won most of the starting positions on the team, and they included Bill Farmer, Sam Christine, and Pete Wallace. The transfers knew how to play the game well.

Chapter 16

The city of Aiken prepared itself to go through a massive upheaval in the school system in 1954. School construction had begun in 1952 on several fronts, and it was all nearing completion as the new year started.

The new high school opened finally on Rutland Drive on April 21, 1954. The administration had made a promise to Boyce Bell's class that they would be the first class to graduate there, and the promise was barely kept. In time, other school openings and students being shifted around occurred. The most significant shift was that the old high school building on Laurens Street, near downtown, would become Aiken Junior High School.

Less than a month after the high school opened came another bombshell announcement, this one being national in scope. The United States Supreme Court, on May 17, 1954, handed down its long-awaited decision in the *Brown v. Board of Education* case. The ruling outlawed the separate-but-equal racial school systems that were prevalent throughout Southern states, making them totally illegal. From this point forward, the schools would be forced to have integrated public schools. This represented a change in the way schools were run in the South and created a brand-new environment.

None of these new events had any effect on Casey Gannon's baseball season. The new diamond adjacent to the new school was not ready for play, so all the home baseball games were still played at Eustis Park. One new member of the team was a pitcher with a good fastball and a deceptive curve. He was Fred Cavanaugh, who was one of the team's three regular pitchers during the year. He had good control and struck out his share of batters.

Casey became the regular center fielder with the departure of Hugh Forrest, and the new baseball field was carefully being built on Rutland Drive. Besides growing taller and thicker with pure muscle, Casey continued his ability to hit the baseball almost at will. He was now six feet three inches tall, still growing, and would not reach his sixteenth birthday until later in the summer. He batted third in the lineup and was beginning to attract attention from local colleges.

The catcher, Ed Cortez, batted in the cleanup position because he was such a dependable power hitter and loved to come to bat with runners on base. Casey's batting average hovered near .420 for the year, and he was beginning to hit for extra bases with some regularity. Again, he struck out only twice during the season. Both occurred on heavily overcast days when it was more difficult to see the ball. By chance, he faced a knuckleball pitcher in one game and went hitless for the first time in several years. He attributed his difficulties in that game to the lack of spin on the ball to guide him as to where the ball would likely go. Knuckleball pitches can dance around erratically on the way to the catcher, and even the pitcher is not sure where it will end up.

His friend, Zach Kessler, became the regular right fielder and batted in the sixth spot, contributing positively to the team. Jake and Annie Lou always attended the home games, but Casey noticed that Zach's father, Wade, came to only one of their games and stood along the third baseline fence by himself for the entire game. He was a loner for sure.

An unusual highlight toward the end of the baseball season was that the *Augusta Chronicle* sent a sportswriter and photographer to Aiken to do a feature article on Casey. He was beginning to be recognized as a significant up-and-coming talent not seen often. They wrote an impressively complimentary feature story, accompanied by a spread of accompanying photographs. Jake and Annie Lou were pleased by the recognition, and even Casey was impressed by some of the things the article said about him and his potential. He was now a known player all over the CSRA.

Casey had finally decided that he had to give up the *Augusta Herald* paper route because it deeply conflicted with his desire to spend as much time as possible concentrating on baseball. To replace the dependable income he had received for almost six years, he went to Sears and purchased their top-of-the-line twenty-inch self-propelled power lawnmower. On weekends, he began to knock on doors at every house in his neighborhood where he saw a lawn and asked if he could cut their lawn on a regular basis for $1 for the front and $1 for the back. He was successful well over half the time and quickly built a sizeable clientele.

Jake's home construction business had grown so much that he was now in the position of hiring out most of the jobs and no longer did much of it by himself. This often led to windfall income for Casey during the summer. It was not unusual for Jake to ask Casey to work full days as a construction "gofer" for his work crews. Neither of them wanted to put him on the payroll as a regular employee, so Jake simply paid him out of his own pocket, usually the equivalent of the minimum wage, which was 75¢ per hour or $6 per day. Between this job and the grass cutting, Casey was making as much as $50 per week during the summer.

When he could, he would call Arlene to ask her to go with him to Scott's Lake. Their friendship could not be classified as romantic, but most of their friends noticed that they never dated other people. In the heart of the summer, going to Scott's would be a splashing and musically hopping good time, filled with teenagers that everyone knew. He allowed his friend Zach to ride along in the rumble seat, which was windy, but he didn't seem to mind.

During the summer of 1954, Joe Turner sang "Shake, Rattle, and Roll" from the jukebox for five cents (and seemed to do it endlessly) while the kids shagged deep into the afternoon. Roy Hamilton was also hot that summer, and his "You'll Never Walk Alone" and his "Ebb Tide" dominated the slow music on the dance floor. When they finally left late in the day, Zach sang "Earth Angel" and Rosemary Clooney's "Hey There" to Casey and Arlene all the way home.

Ross Howard also visited their neighborhood as often as possible that summer. Wade Kessler was on one of his trips, and Ross appeared every day or two like clockwork. He had a good mind and memory and greeted Casey with "Howdy, Master Casey, howdy Master Zachary."

"Are you here again, Ross?" asked Casey, as he winked kiddingly. Casey had learned quickly that anytime he saw Ross's blue Kaiser or heard the trademark giggle, he was in for a fun time. He liked being around Ross.

Ross giggled lightly. "Yessir, I's here. If Ms. Katie let me, I be here every day," Ross answered. "But she don't want me here every minute. I think she worry about Mr. Kessler gettin' mad if he find out."

Annie Lou came out the back door just then for the exact purpose of meeting the unusual Ross Howard. When he met her and shook her hand, he smiled, giggled, bowed, and told her, "Miz Gannon, you be the prettiest thing I seen all day." And he laughed his contagious, quiet laugh. Annie Lou thanked him for the compliment and added, "I've heard so much about you from Casey, I just had to meet you." With that, she went back in the house.

Ross had been eyeing Casey's Ford coupé. Finally, he asked the question, "Whose cute lil '47 Ford is this? Master Casey, this yo car?"

"Yep, Ross, that's mine," Casey responded.

"It shore be a cute one," said Ross. "Maybe even be cuter if you come to Augusta and get some fender skirts for it. I'll put them on for you. Won't cost but $10 to $12. And we got a blue just about that color."

"That's a good idea, Ross, maybe I'll do that."

Ross had one more idea. "You might want some of our dual exhausts put under yo car too. Makes a mighty nice sound with them two mufflers and two tailpipes."

"Ross, I can't afford all of that," was the answer.

When July 1 came, Annie Lou and Jake decided that Casey and Zach needed to have a combined birthday for the two friends and for the USA as well. Jake cooked hot dogs and hamburgers outside, and Annie Lou gave out birthday presents. Zach got a new basketball especially made for the outdoors, and Casey got his own Winchester 62 .22-caliber rifle and a multibladed pocketknife. Both boys turned sixteen years old during the week. Wade Kessler missed the party due to working late.

The next day, they spent several hours setting up a safer target shooting area inside Hitchcock Woods. Both were aware that shooting their guns in the woods was probably not in strict adherence to the laws but decided that if they ever got caught, they would be able to demonstrate that no one would or could get hurt there. They arranged the target area so that they would always be shooting directly into a steep embankment.

Uncle Jake had finally gotten around to buying a car to replace the old Hudson he had been using for a long time. He bought a new 1953 Ford sedan from Holley Motors, the Ford dealer, downtown on Laurens, just as the newer model 1954s were coming into the showrooms. Annie Lou was the proud recipient of the Hudson while Casey kept his '47 Ford running well.

Big political news in Aiken was that former governor Strom Thurmond was getting itchy to run for office again and was planning to switch from Dixiecrat (or conservative Democrat) to the Republican Party. His sights were set on the United States Senate, and he felt that he was now out of alignment with the philosophies of the other Democrats. In 1952, he had endorsed Dwight Eisenhower for president instead of his own party's Adlai Stevenson. This led the Democrats to block Thurmond's nomination to the U.S. Senate as his punishment. So he opted to undertake a write-in campaign against his more entrenched opponent. The strategy and his efforts met with a huge success. For the first time in United States history, a national senatorial candidate was elected by this method, as Thurmond stomped opponent Edgar A. Brown 63 to 37 percent in the November 1954 elections, and he remained a Republican for the rest of his life. Dorcey Lybrand and Aiken would be losing a lawyer, but Washington DC would be receiving another Aiken resident, this time as a senator, for large portions of the year.

In August, Casey followed up about the fender skirts. On a free day, he drove to Augusta one morning and found the auto supply store where Ross Howard worked. He said hello to Ross and ordered the fender skirts placed on his car and went into the customer service area to wait.

There was already one person sitting there watching channel 6, and she was an attractive young woman—in fact, one of the best-looking women Casey had ever seen. As he sat down and picked up a *National Geographic* to read, she asked, "Excuse me, but aren't you Casey Gannon?"

"Yes, ma'am, I am," answered Casey, surprised.

She smiled broadly and said, "I thought so, and don't you call me ma'am. I'm not much older than you are."

He was puzzled. "How did you know my name?" Casey asked.

"The *Chronicle* ran that big article on you back in May, and I just remembered what you looked like. I was so impressed with how good a player you are and only fifteen years old," she exuded.

"Well, I'm sixteen now, just had a birthday in July," he corrected her.

"Isn't that something?" she cooed. "I'm only twenty-four myself."

She wanted to continue the conversation although Casey had lowered his head and was busily flipping the pages in his magazine. "Frankly, Casey, I was so impressed with you because of the way you looked and the way you answered the interviewer's questions. Now seeing you in person, you're even more handsome and sexier than I thought."

Casey reddened deeply, being clearly embarrassed by the conversation. "I don't even know you," he said, eyeing her with puzzlement.

"We can fix that right now," she responded. "My name is Denise Slaughter, and I'm twenty-four years old. I've been married but got divorced last year and moved back in with my dad, who is a doctor at university hospital. My mom died three years ago, and I need to look after him. We live on the Hill, just off Walton Way, in a great big old Southern house. I'm in here having my wheels rebalanced, and you're getting fender skirts installed. What else do you need to know? Oh, and one other thing, I'm incredibly attracted to you and I think it's gotten worse since we've been talking."

Casey's embarrassment deepened even more. He looked at her and said, "Look, I don't even know how to answer you."

"Then don't," she said. "Just tell me that when we're finished here in this store, you'll follow me home in your car so that I can feed us lunch at my house. We need time to get to know each other better. Just say yes, and I'll take care of the rest."

He looked at her very intensely and long and wondering what she was all about and realized how inexperienced he was and that there was no easy way out of this. He finally said, "Yes, okay, but I can't stay long. I've got to get back to Aiken."

Thirty minutes later, he approved his new fender skirts, which were surprisingly a good color match, and followed her in his car to Thirteenth Street, then to Walton Way and up the Hill to her house. She prepared a simple lunch of peanut butter and jelly sandwiches, plus a large glass of iced tea from the refrigerator.

She asked him, "Are you truly only sixteen years old? The article in the *Chronicle* said you were almost six feet four inches tall and weighed 180 pounds. I must say that sounds man-sized to me, and you sure look like a man. Are you willing to try to see if you are?"

Casey was still a bit puzzled. "I don't know quite what you mean."

She stood him up, placed her arms around him, and pulled his head down to hers and kissed him deeply. He went along with her reluctantly but felt himself getting worked up as a result of her efforts. She pressed herself firmly against his body. He finally said, "I'm sorry but I don't have any experience with what you're trying to do. Zero."

She had all the answers, and this time it was, "You don't need any experience. I have enough for both of us. Pretend we're dancing. Just follow my lead and you'll do just fine, big boy." She grabbed his hand and led him upstairs.

Later in the afternoon, they were sitting in her living room downstairs and he was preparing to leave. "I don't know what I'm supposed to say at a time like this, but I guess I'm supposed to say thanks," he muttered.

She laughed in a knowing deep-throated way and answered him, "Yeah, I think 'thanks' works for right now, and I should also tell you that you did just fine for your first time. I can teach you how to do this, you know. I can tell after that one time that you will be even better at it when you get more experience, and I want to be the one doing the teaching and getting the benefits of you mastering it. You are very strong in all the right places, and you have the instinct to do the right things at the right times. So I have to thank you as well."

"Well, I gotta go," he said.

"Will I be able to see you some more after this?" she asked with a slight pleading in her voice.

"Maybe. I gotta think about it. You're confusing me. I don't know," he said. Then he added, "Write down your name and phone number for me, just in case."

She wrote the information down on the back of one of her father's appointment cards and handed it to him. She added with as much of a throaty voice as she could muster, "If you really had a good time this afternoon, just remember there's more of that for you in the future. Be thinking of what we'll do next time." She kissed him hard, patted him on his backside, and pushed him out the door.

He drove back to Aiken slowly, contemplating everything that had happened this day. *Boy, life changes faster than you can imagine*, he was thinking. *This is probably not a good idea, but I might have to come back over here again.*

When he arrived back home, Zach was shooting baskets, and Casey joined him for a quick game of H-O-R-S-E before going in the house. Compliments were forthcoming about the new look of the Ford, but Casey just nodded absentmindedly and kept on shooting. His mind was a million miles away.

The entire incident in Augusta had jolted him from his core outward. He noticed that he became self-conscious around his aunt because he was thinking about what women looked like without their clothes on. It was all new, totally new.

He tried to immerse himself in his grass cutting and his chores for Uncle Jake on the construction sites. No matter how he tried to distract his mind, it kept returning to Denise Slaughter and the way she had used herself with him inside her house. It was all so new and so mind-numbing.

Within a week, he had waited until no one else was around his house and called her. She answered and gushed into the phone that she knew he would be calling her. "We are too good of a fit to ignore each other," she said. "I'm anxious for more of you, and you've just got to be about the same way for me. I mean, God, you're sixteen years old. You have screaming hormones at sixteen." And she laughed and told him to come on over right now, that she was alone. He agreed to come.

When he got to her house, she met him at the front door dressed in nothing but a wide smile. He blushed and slipped in. She kissed him passionately for almost a minute and tested his readiness to be intimate with her. Satisfied that he had reacted quickly enough for her, she led him up the stairs to her room.

She was overly excited, and this had the effect of getting him overly excited. And the entire encounter had such an effect that he was done less than half a minute after he started.

He was disappointed, and she saw it. "Don't worry about that," she said. "I'm not letting you out of here until you feel happy about it, and I feel happy about it. You just rest up some and we'll give it another shot."

That seemed to make him feel better so he gave in to her suggestion. He told her he wanted to ask her some questions about what they were doing. She nodded and he continued. "Why did you pick me over other men or boys? I can see how good you look and what a perfect body you have. Why me? I'm just a sixteen-year-old boy with no experience at this."

She smiled and rubbed her hand briefly on him, and it gave him a start. "That's one reason right there. It takes just a little work on my part to get a great reaction from you. I realize that you react from my touch not because of me, but because of how nature works in a sixteen-year-old. The second reason is that you are a damned attractive boy and one day you're going to be one hell of a partner for somebody. If I train you right, that somebody might be me. I love this stuff, or couldn't you tell? My ex-husband couldn't keep up with me because I seem to have a large appetite. That's why he's my ex. My guess when I first saw you that day in the auto shop was that you might enjoy this as much as I do. Do you? Tell the truth now."

Casey blushed and answered her, "Yeah, it's okay so far. I always wondered what it would feel like, and so far it's pretty good. But I see one problem with it."

"What's that?" she asked, feigning being insulted.

"I have thought about this way too much since that first time we did it. I can see how being with you like this can distract me from everything else. That worries me."

"Oh, don't be ridiculous," she said and laughed. "You will also find out that it's a great relaxer. One day, you'll come in here all tight as a drum and you'll leave two hours later all wobbly from being so relaxed."

Denise left the room for a few minutes and busied herself nearby. When she returned, she tested him again, and he immediately reacted. "Oh boy, you're just about ready. Let's try it again. Just follow my lead and do things when I tell you."

A while later, after doing everything he was asked and in ways that seemed to please them both, he was finished, exhausted, and flopped over on his back. Within a few minutes, she was finally able to say, "Fantastic. I haven't felt that good in a long time. You're definitely catching on. You were amazing."

After a brief nap, Denise slipped out of the room and into a robe. She went downstairs and came back with some milk and Oreos. They sat up in bed and had a snack, joking and poking each other with some level of familiarity and enjoyment.

Finally, Casey said, "I've got to go back to Aiken. People at home will start worrying about where I am."

"Honey, are you sure you don't want to test yourself one more time? It might make everybody in this room happy if you found out you could go three rounds in an hour." She playfully flicked her hand at him as she spoke the words.

Casey smiled and said, "I think that this little boy has had enough for one day."

She was quick to challenge his comment. "Don't call yourself little. You're anything but that. You're a man."

As he dressed, Denise did her best to distract him and get him excited again. "How about one more for the road?" she asked and seriously tried her best to divert him from the business of leaving. He squirmed away from her direct touch, sat down, and put his shoes on.

"Oh, you joy killer," she moaned. "I was just getting warmed up." He led her down the stairs and to the front door.

Once again, she made him kiss her deeply before he left. She reminded him, "There's nothing quite like an afternoon of good close-up intimacy. You be thinking about that on your way home and for the next week. When you are aching for me again, call me for some relief. I will be here with open arms."

This time, he drove back to Aiken with four thoughts heavy on his mind:

> *This is an awful lot of fun with somebody like Denise.*
> *Her appetite for it overwhelms me.*
> *How will I ever be able to play good baseball again?*
> *I've got to stop this.*

Casey dived headlong into his friendships with Zach and Arlene and tried to make as much money as he could for the rest of the summer. He asked Uncle Jake to get him as many workdays as he could until school started back. Even Jake could see a slight change in Casey and thought that his mind seemed to be grinding away on some problem he had.

He lasted for over two weeks and would have lasted longer, but one day late in August while checking the mailbox out on the street, he saw Denise driving by in her car. *Darn it,* he thought. *I didn't think she knew where I lived in Aiken.*

She stopped her car beside him and said, "I really miss you, stranger. Why don't you get in my car and go home with me? I'll bring you back in a couple of hours."

He was upset that she had found his house. "How did you find me? I never told you where I lived."

"No, you haven't," she snapped. "I saw it on your driver's license when you put your keys down on the table at my house."

"Oh," he answered back. "I can't go with you right now. We're about to eat supper."

She hardened her expression and said, "I'm not leaving until you promise me you'll come see me tomorrow. I mean it. I'll sit right out here all night if I have to."

Casey looked around nervously, afraid that someone in the house would see them. "Okay, okay, I'll be there for lunch tomorrow at noon," he said, under obvious pressure.

She smiled at his words and relaxed noticeably. "See you tomorrow, lover boy."

When he went in the house, his aunt asked, "Who were you talking to out on the street? I've never seen that car before."

He winced and looked away from her so that she could not see his face. He answered, "Oh, just somebody from my old paper route, stopping to say hello." Boy, he hated lying to her. It was his first time.

The next morning, he did his best to stay in bed and try to avoid everybody. When he finally appeared, he told his aunt another lie, saying that he needed to drive to Augusta to get a part for his car. He drove off by eleven thirty and arrived at Denise's house at noon sharp.

When he was let into the house after ringing the doorbell, he was not particularly in the mood for what she had in mind. "We need to talk," he stated coldly.

"Okay, what's wrong with you, sweet man?" She was cooing to him, sensing that he was in no mood for what she had in mind.

He was adamant in wanting to have his say. "This whole thing we have going is about to wreck my life. I lied twice to my aunt in the last twenty-four hours about you. I can feel my whole life about to spin into a ditch, all because of you and what this sneaky activity is doing to my brain. As much fun as it has been—and it has been terrific at times—I want to end it today. My life is getting too messed up because of what it's doing to me. You agree with me, right?"

"No, I don't agree with you," she said firmly. "I need what you do for me. Can't you tell I have a sort of fixation on you and certain things we do together? Why can't you see what I need?" She was almost to the point of hysteria.

"Look," he said in a lower tone, trying to calm her. "I will make you as happy as I can today, but this is my last visit here. I know that sounds crazy. Most boys I know would love to have a friend like you, somebody to do this with, but I can't handle it beyond today. I have to get my life back to normal."

"Oh, all right," she said with resignation and surrender. "But let's get to it. I've been rubbing against the furniture for days, waiting for you to call." She started to remove things and nodded to him to do the same.

When they were ready, she used her hands to get him primed and noticed that he was less responsive than he had been in their other sessions. She had to work more aggressively, and he was not doing anything active other than giving her the freedom to do what she thought was necessary. Finally, everything was ready. She pushed him onto his back and pounced on him. He watched incredulously, almost totally detached, as she continued to please herself but using him to achieve it. He finally got slightly aroused himself but bit his lip hard to try to stay under control. He finally lost it though.

She had succeeded in bringing herself to a peak and beyond and needed several minutes to collect herself when it was over in order to have enough energy to separate from him. After a while, she found the strength to ask, "Are you seriously telling me that you want to give this up? That we have done this for the last time?"

Casey was resolute in his determination. "I can see that you have serious needs. I'm not telling you to ignore that. I'm simply saying that you can't look to me anymore to satisfy yourself. Yeah, I have had fun and enjoyed it at times. But I'm smart enough to see the future very clearly. If I let you, you will have me doing this stuff every day. If I do this with you as much as you want, I won't have any time to go to school, or play baseball, or be with my family. We are stopping right now while I can still think clearly. Find somebody else please. Not me, not anymore."

The tears welled up in her eyes, and she dabbed at them with the edge of the sheet. "Oh, all right, I'll let you go. You've been better than you had any right to be. But I'll certainly miss you and our wild times."

She got up and started dressing, throwing his clothes to him as she proceeded. The room was quiet, and both were finally fully clothed.

She smiled, walked him to the front door, and said, "Mr. Gannon, it has been my pleasure to know you. If you ever change your mind, you'll know where to find me."

He decided to play along to be able to exit without further upheaval on her part. "Ms. Slaughter, the pleasure has been mine and mine alone. Your company has been most enjoyable." And he kissed her on the cheek and departed as quickly as he could.

As he drove back to Aiken on the superhighway, he was thankful again and again that she had not been difficult at the end. His dominant thought was, *I've got my life back. I can make it into what I want. And I will never let myself get boxed in like that again. Never ever.*

He spent the next several days luxuriating in being totally free again. He cut as much grass as he could, visited Farris every day and worked some with the cars there, and carried bricks for a bricklayer on one of Uncle Jake's construction jobs.

But every time he looked at his aunt Annie Lou across the supper table, he was remorseful about something and felt strong pangs of guilt. He did not understand it at first, but finally a big truth hit him and it was this: he needed to get the entire Denise Slaughter episode behind him and off his mind and out of his soul. He felt that she still contaminated him. He needed to tell his aunt all about it and get her advice about what it all meant. The minute that thought hit him, he decided it would be most unpleasant to do, and one part of his consciousness fought with another part about whether to tell her at all. Finally, the "confessional" part of his brain won.

When they were alone in the house the next day, he started the conversation. "Aunt Annie Lou, do you have time to talk to me about a problem I'm having? I need to talk to you about it."

"Of course. What's the matter?" she asked.

He decided to tell her everything about how it started, where it was done, and how it had affected him and was continuing to affect him somewhat. He was not going to go into any detail about what they did in private. He started with "I've been having intimate relations with a woman in Augusta" and proceeded with his story.

Annie Lou was riveted from the first moment on and tried not to be too shocked at anything she heard. It was difficult. She decided that she would not ask questions either.

Casey wound up his story with this: "And I'm telling you now because I feel so guilty about what I did. It involved me lying to you a couple of times, and I'm sorry."

"Oh my, that's some story, and I must admit I'm shocked. I had no idea about this," she exclaimed.

"I found out that I'm not ready for that stuff yet. I kept telling her that I was only sixteen. I feel better already just getting it off my chest to you. Am I terrible for doing it?"

"No, sweetie, you're not terrible for doing it. She came after you very hard, and I dare say that no sixteen-year-old boy could have handled it as well as you did. All on your own, you decided that it was wrong and you got to stop it. I'm so proud of you for that. That was a very grown-up decision to have to make, and you made it. But it is quite unexpected."

Casey was relieved by her answers and her reaction. He felt a tremendous weight lifted from his body. "Aunt Annie Lou, you are the best. Please don't tell this story to Uncle Jake or anybody else. I'm not ready to tell anybody but you about it. I don't know why, but I needed you to know about it."

"You have no worries, sweetheart. Your secret is safe with me. Why do you think you wanted me to know?"

Casey swallowed hard and looked at his shoes while he answered. "I felt like I was cheating my family by doing it, and my family is you. I don't ever want my actions to hurt you and Uncle Jake. Y'all are protecting me and I wanted to protect you." And as their eyes met, they both seemed to realize that their nurturing love and friendship had just reached a new plateau.

Chapter 17

The Aiken area had swallowed the huge lump called "the bomb plant" and was still in the process of digesting it and all of its repercussions, growing in various new directions as a result of it. It had never been easy, but with everybody working more or less for the same lofty goals, the job of newcomer assimilation was more or less getting done somehow.

The new high school on Rutland Drive was proud to call itself a "school campus" because it was comprised of several separate buildings that were connected by outdoor covered walkways and sidewalks. Even the gymnasium was connected in this way but was otherwise detached from the classroom wings.

Major shifts and adjustments had to be made for all of the high school's athletic programs because Eustis Park was no longer the center of attention. A new football facility, Hagood Stadium, named after school superintendent L. K. Hagood, had been built on the west side of the school and was located between the school and Teague Drive, named after Elizabeth Teague, school librarian. Seasoned players were so accustomed to being tackled on the hardpan of the old field that they couldn't believe that the proper grass surface could feel so nice to fall on. One of them was heard saying, "I just love to be tackled at practice. It's like falling on a nice, soft cushion."

The first game played on the new field did not go very well for the Aiken Green Hornets. It was against Augusta's

Richmond Academy. Over five thousand enthusiastic fans attended the contest, but Aiken was unfortunately defeated 20-0 by the larger, stronger Musketeers. The cheerleaders, led by Chartee Muckenfuss, did their best to offset the opponents, but to no avail. The student body turned out at a high level for games at the new facility. Aunt Annie Lou spoke of sitting near Sissy Slayton, Ed George, Ellen Busch, Manning and Betty Owen, and Rosanne McNair at the first game.

After the game, Casey met with Arlene and asked her if she wanted to go to the nearby "Hornet's Nest" drive-in restaurant for a hamburger. She agreed and was happy anytime Casey sought her out to be his companion.

They had not been together much during the summer, which just ended due to conflicting activities. Casey had been very careful to not even hint about his experiences with Denise in Augusta. He discovered something about himself in the process of getting back together with Arlene. He did not take her for granted any longer, and he was genuinely happy to be with her every time they ended up together. He found that he was more comfortable with her than with anyone else outside his family. *I wonder if that means anything*, he often asked himself.

They attended all the other games together and watched as George Wilson and Benny Knight led the teams to some memorable performances while Beverly Driver was named football queen at halftime of the homecoming game. The new football stadium was a much more comfortable place to watch the local team than Eustis Park had been. Parking for visitors was also far more plentiful and better organized.

Casey's autumn was filled with odd jobs and the continuation of stashing money into his three Mason jars. He was happy to be living within his own means and never having to rely on the bank account that held his mother's insurance proceeds. On occasion,

Jake would make a declaration aloud across the dinner table that Casey was one of the best money managers he had ever known. That comment made Casey feel some pride.

Any time there was a need for funds at school (lab fee, class pictures, school picnic, junior prom, etc.) he took the money from a Mason jar and never asked Jake or Annie Lou for it. He also provided gasoline, insurance, and maintenance for his car without asking for help.

Luigi's, a new restaurant owned by an Italian family, had opened on Broad Street in Augusta; and it served pizza, spaghetti, and lasagna. He got into a habit of taking Arlene there for any special event. They both found that Italian food suited them well. They also patronized the Varsity Drive-In on the east side of Augusta, as well as Greene's in the same general neighborhood. These drive-ins were where Augusta's teenagers hung out and cruised endlessly.

There were new restaurants in Aiken as well, and they patronized them also. Places like Jean's on York Street, operated by the Jeancake family, and A&W Root Beer on Richland Avenue, run by David Neilson, who had recently graduated from Aiken High, followed by his finishing at the University of South Carolina.

Sometime during the fall, Casey discovered parlay cards, the method for betting on college football games, but he had no idea how to bet. He discovered that A. R. Edwards, at the poolroom right behind Liles Drug, was the place to get a parlay card. He went in and asked AR how to use the cards. AR told him that to bet cost one dollar and that he had to select three teams to bet on or to bet on the other team while taking the "points" offered as the betting differential. Casey understood. As he left, he asked, "AR, I've always wondered. What does the AR stand for? What's your real name?"

AR chuckled and answered, "My real name is Amidee Rose Edwards. Now you know why I'm just AR. Now don't you go spreading that all over this town." Casey chuckled too and left.

Sometimes, a movie was scheduled that they wanted to see and they had added the Fox Drive-In Theater on Whiskey Road to the Patricia and the Rosemary theaters downtown. Early in the year, they saw *East of Eden*, which starred a new performer, James Dean. All of Aiken's teenagers were impressed by him as he seemed to be a new definition of what it was to be "cool."

Later in the year, before his second movie *Rebel Without a Cause* was shown in theaters, James Dean was tragically killed in a high-speed crash in his Porsche. The young people of America learned all at once what it was like to be suddenly whipsawed between exhilaration and tragedy.

As their relationship matured more and more, Casey sometimes thought about Arlene in a sexual way. After all, they were young and attractive, possessed normal hormones, and he already had experience due to Denise's persistence in teaching him. No sooner had the thought formed in his head than he discovered that something blocked it every time.

He respected Arlene more than any female he knew other than his aunt, and he decided that he did not want to know her in that way, at least not yet. If it was meant to be, he was sure that it would happen naturally whenever the proper time came. So he never pushed her beyond what they were both comfortable with, and that didn't even include kissing yet! He did occasionally hold her hand when they were totally alone or riding in his car, and it always had the effect of lifting her spirits.

Jake Gannon's home construction business had prospered along with others like it in postatomic Aiken. He was continuing to build fill-in houses in Aiken Estates, College

Acres, Kalmia Hill, Dunbarton Oaks, Boardman Road, Brandy Road, and even Crosland Park, which had been one of Aiken's earliest subdivisions.

Annie Lou's life changed when she started driving, and she got involved in many efforts involving history and the preservation of it in town. Plus, she still was a substitute teacher in fifth-grade history.

When baseball season came around again, Casey and Zach were ready for it. Not only had they been playing catch all winter in their backyards, they had also set up a net and batting cage so that they could practice their swings and keep a sharp batting eye during the off season.

In class, both of them had to work hard in Ms. Barlow's class and that of Dr. Guy, the chemistry teacher. And Mrs. Bobo's English instruction once each day was the summit of their challenging high school day. It seemed that the arrival of the bomb plant was accompanied by the toughest teachers in South Carolina. There was a lot of talk around the high school that the engineers and physicists of Dupont had lobbied the county hard for tougher schoolwork for their children, and some of it appeared to be true.

The telephone began to ring often with college baseball coaches on the other end of the line. Casey was not sure what to say to them, so he usually handed the instrument to his aunt or uncle with the words, "Another baseball coach."

The coaches who called wanted to express their interest in having Casey play for their college baseball programs after his high school graduation. And they always asked how they could get the team schedule so that they could attend his games in person.

An interesting discovery he noticed about Aiken during his junior school year was that some of his male classmates actually drove school buses, transporting children to the public schools. He found it hard to believe that the school administrators trusted sixteen-year-old boys to drive the students to and from school. And they were paid $35 a month to do it! A couple of his teammates were often late to practice because they were driving their school bus routes in the afternoon.

When his junior year was over, Casey had been scouted by the University of South Carolina, Clemson, the Citadel, the University of Georgia, Georgia Tech, and the University of North Carolina. He had a superb year at bat and in the field. One scout told him, "You have the strongest arm I have ever seen on a high school outfielder." Another coach told him, "Your batting eye is very mature and the best I've ever seen on a teenager. I like the way you're so picky about which pitches you swing at." Casey batted an even .575 for the year, going 38 for 66 in the fifteen games. And he was walked intentionally twelve times. He batted fourth in the lineup and banged out seven home runs, driving in a total of twenty-seven runs. Opposing pitchers hated to see him come to the plate.

Zach and Casey became closer friends during the season. Zach became a dependable right fielder and contributed noticeably at the plate. They were almost inseparable during March, April, and May. Whenever they weren't playing baseball, they were hiking through Hitchcock Woods or shooting at targets there. Life was full, and much of it was outdoors.

There was a period in April when the weather was rainy for a long period and baseball practice almost disappeared. Then a member of the Winter Colony came to the rescue. A mansion on the south side, just off Whiskey Road and Coker

Springs Road, with the name of the Pillars, had an indoor tennis court with a red clay surface. It was not being used by the owners—in fact, it had not been in use for tennis for several years—and they made it available to Aiken's baseball team for the period of the rainy days. The team loved it because it was out of the wet elements totally. It even had a large fireplace at the side of the playing area. The tennis net and posts to hold it in place had already been moved and stored, so for all practical purposes, they were using a gymnasium-sized facility with an outdoor clay ground surface. It was an unusual experience to say the least.

Players were told to leave their spikes at home and to wear their sneakers. The team showed up in Keds, Sears sneakers, and Converse All-Stars basketball shoes.

To be sure, the team was not able to have batting practice at the Pillars because of the confined space, but they were able to throw, practice their baserunning, sliding into bases properly, and running wind sprints up and down the court to stay in shape. Also, pitchers were able to do complete workouts consistent with the pitching position. This was important because a couple of key games were coming up against the strong-hitting Graniteville Rocks team.

Admittedly, Graniteville was a much smaller town than Aiken and, in a normal world, should have fielded weaker baseball teams compared to the Hornets. But they had a strong tradition for baseball and currently had at least three high-caliber players (Verley Swygert, Danny Marchant, Jimmy Hays) who always made Aiken play to its maximum ability in order to win.

The summer of 1955 was a hot one, and Aiken's teenagers spent their quality time at Richardson's Lake and Scott's Lake. Casey was pretty popular since his 1947 Ford was often filled with two riders in the front with him and another two in the rumble seat.

He also continued to cut grass, caddy at the golf course, and work when Uncle Jake needed him on a construction job. Arlene stayed in town during the summer, so it was possible for them to see each other as often as they wished during the hot months.

The Fox Drive-In Theater was open several nights a week, showing relatively current movies that were making their second pass through the area. The Dixie Lee Drive-In restaurant, in the Langley area on the superhighway, had become very popular with Aiken teenagers, and it was common for Casey and Arlene to drive to it just to sit in the car and drink milk shakes.

Birthdays were coming up in the first week of July for both Zach and Casey when they would both turn seventeen. Annie Lou convinced Jake that they should throw a big birthday party for the boys. She wangled access to the Outing Club on Vaucluse Road for the occasion, which was a cookout of hot dogs, hamburgers, and marshmallows. Over thirty of the boys' friends were in town and able to attend. The guests included Rosanne, the Beverlys, Harold Price, Brookie Wyman, Clyde Davis, Carole Evans, Bo, Ellen, Foley, Sissy Cothran, Herndon, and of course, Arlene Cushman. The party was such a roaring success that Annie Lou wondered why they had not done it at least every three or four months.

During the next week, Annie Lou had a need to visit a hardware store for a couple of items. Jake was no longer in the hardware business and was not at home, so she decided to handle the errand herself. She had heard that Franzblau's Hardware, across Richland Avenue from the poolroom, was interesting and specialized in having just about every item imaginable. She drove the Hudson there and parked in front of the store.

For the next five minutes, she had one of the most unusual times she had ever had in Aiken. Here's how she told it that evening over dinner.

"I was amazed when I went in and saw the biggest mess I had ever seen in a retail store. Hardware boxes and bags were stacked everywhere, even in the aisles. There was a little Jewish man in there wearing a carpenter's tool apron. He welcomed me to his store by gruffly saying, 'I'm Finkelstein, and who are you?' He spoke with a very strong East European accent. When I told him my name, he asked me how he could help me. I told him I needed two washers for some bolts I needed to use in the kitchen and that I wanted some sandpaper.

"That's when the trouble started. He asked me for the bolts. I told him they were at home. He barked at me, 'Mrs. Gannon, you are a terrible customer that you could not even bring the bolts for us to see. How will I guess what size to sell you? I won't, that's what. I cannot sell you imaginary washers for imaginary bolts. Now what sandpaper do you want? Will it be fine or ultrafine or medium or coarse or double ought or what?' I know it was the wrong answer, but I told him that I didn't know, that I wanted him to recommend something to me. He got really agitated then and said, 'You want me to make all the decisions to run this store and you want me to make all the customer decisions too. You ask so much of an old Jewish man. It's more than I can handle. Oh, to be so responsible as to make all the decisions this world needs to make. It is all on my shoulders, just as my dear departed Jewish mother always told me.'

"That's when I realized I was in the wrong place for this day, and I said, 'Mr. Finkelstein, I humbly apologize for being such a terrible customer today, and the next time, I will be better prepared to shop. Thank you for your valuable time.' And I got out of there as quickly as I could."

All Jake could say through his laughter was, "Well, that's Finkelstein. In true form. But I have to tell you. He knows where everything is in that store. He's legendary around Aiken."

Halloween came and went, and Spooky Weeks celebrated his sixteenth birthday. The funny thing was that Odell Weeks's oldest son was born as a "junior," but because his birth was on Halloween, the Weeks's neighbors saw fit to think of the event as somewhat spooky and gave him that nickname, which replaced his real name Harry Odell in perpetuity.

A funny thing happened on this Halloween of 1955 on the newly widened Kalmia Hill. Some high school seniors had swiped a small truckload of softball-sized pumpkins and had driven them to the top of the hill, parking in the woods just off the pavement. At opportune times for almost an hour, they ran to the middle of the four-lane highway and bowled their farm-raised missiles down the hill into oncoming traffic. Luckily, no accidents occurred, but several drivers later reported having to dodge the rolling pumpkins by zigzagging in the road.

Football season came and went, and the local team had a so-so season of wins and losses. Quarterback Herndon McElmurray and backfield runners Billy Molony, Johnny Wingfield and Ronnie Upton made their mark on opponents. Several other players from the newcomer community, such as Cliff Herrick, Foley Thornton and Pierce, were on the starting team. And old Aikenites—head cheerleader Sissy Cothran and head majorette Beverly Driver—performed almost flawlessly on the sidelines. A junior beauty from a Dupont family, Jane Christine, was named football queen at halftime of the Boys

Catholic game. Students from bomb plant families were having a significant impact on events in Aiken.

During the fall, it was time for the seniors to order their class rings. Almost everyone in the class decided to place an order for one. They would not receive them until just before graduation the next spring.

AHS Class Ring

Casey and Zach had been talking for some time to getting dates and going to a rhythm and blues show in Augusta. These shows came to town from time to time and were always staged at Bell Auditorium on Telfair Street.

Finally, a show was announced that would feature Chuck Berry and Roy Hamilton, and they decided to go. Casey asked Arlene, and Zach asked a classmate named Carole. At the Bell, as it was referred to by almost everyone, concerts of this nature were always Negro events primarily, and white patrons could participate as viewers only. The main floor was set up as a colored dinner dance, featuring tables for six to eight people, with a dance floor near the stage. White people could attend, but only as spectators who would be accommodated in the balcony.

Casey asked Aunt Annie Lou if he could borrow the old Hudson for the evening so that no one would be forced to ride to Augusta in cold weather in his rumble seat. She loaned the car to them for the event.

While the four were eating dinner at Luigi's prior to the show, Arlene told the group the information about how concerts were done there. She also told them that the Bell also had a smaller five-hundred-person theater, with fixed seats and a balcony that was behind the main ballroom where larger events were held. Both venues were served by the same stage and dressing rooms. She knew this because an uncle was a gospel-singing fan who often attended events called "Sings," which were held four or five times per year in the smaller auditorium, always on Sunday afternoons, lasting for several hours.

When they got to the main auditorium and found their seats in the first row of the center balcony, they were looking at a sea of colored people on the main floor, some dancing to the orchestra, some eating, some talking between tables, and some just sitting and waiting.

Eventually, the curtain opened and the show started. Chuck Berry played his guitar, comically duckwalked a few times across the stage while playing, and sang "Maybelline," his most famous song at the time.

Then it was time for the headliner, Roy Hamilton, to perform. He had several Top 40 songs at the moment, including "You'll Never Walk Alone" and "Ebb Tide." The sellout crowd ate it up, and the Aiken group decided that the show was worth every penny of the $5 each admission fee. All four wanted to do it again whenever the next concert came to Augusta.

All the way home, Zach was crooning,

Maybelline, why can't you be true?
Oh, Maybelline, why can't you be true?
You've started back doing the things you used to do.

He seemed oblivious while the others were laughing at him and trying to talk over him.

The Christmas season of 1955 finally arrived, and the students who took the break just before the holiday returned to school two weeks later into a vastly changed teenage world. Over the holidays, Elvis Presley, who had been a relatively minor popular rhythm and blues singer up to that time, suddenly was on everyone's lips. His first major hit burst upon the radio and into music stores. "Heartbreak Hotel," introduced during the holidays, was being heard at least three times an hour on the radio, and 45 RPM copies of it became the hottest record in the history of popular music. The rock-and-roll era had started and progressed with full intensity after that first no. 1 Elvis song.

Chapter 18

For the beginning of the New Year, Jake had visited his fireworks supplier to get his usual mixture of cherry bombs, M-80s, sparklers, and Roman candles. Zach helped Casey decimate the entire supply on New Year's Eve and the next day. Of course, Aunt Annie Lou was on them all day after that to clean up the mess around the two houses and in the street out front.

The boys talked in their spare time about how they were in the middle of their senior year and how high school baseball would end in a few months. Just the act of talking about it caused them to extract their gloves from winter storage to start limbering up dormant arms.

Casey finally said out loud the thoughts he had about being already well-known in the Aiken-Augusta area for his baseball skills. "I know that the pitchers will be gunning for me this year. They don't like it that I hit their best pitches as well as I do. My goal this year is to be the best hitter in the state and to get a baseball scholarship offer from every top college in South Carolina and Georgia. I want to be the best outfielder too. Zach, you are a good right fielder and better-than-average hitter. You can improve even more this year and get some scholarship offers too."

Zach was quick to answer. "If I can do that, I'll go to whatever college you pick. Maybe we can be a package deal, a 'two-fer.'" They both laughed at the possibilities.

As soon as the weather turned warmer in early February, both boys, with Uncle Jake as their mentor, were already working out hard, taking batting practice wherever they could find a field and generally preparing for their final high school games. College coaches were already calling and positioning themselves with Casey's aunt and uncle. Area newspapers touted Casey's abilities and predicted a great future for him in baseball.

Games were scheduled with Richmond Academy, Boys Catholic, North Augusta, Graniteville, and teams as far away as Carlisle Military Academy, Brookland-Cayce, and Greenwood. The team had graduated its best pitcher from last year, Cavanaugh, and was going to be relying on sophomores and juniors to staff the mound. This meant that good hitting was going to have to win most of the games, placing strong pressure on Casey, Zach, Don Smith, and Billy Molony.

The Gannon household tried to maintain an orderly routine and an organized way of dealing with the baseball scouts who wanted to influence Casey's future selection of a college. Finally, Jake had to lay down the law to them by saying, "We're only going to talk to scouts and coaches on game days and only after the games." That rule quickly brought about more order in the recruiting process. The family refused to take calls for Casey and simply hung up the phone.

The season finally got underway, and the team got its chance to perform. There were sixteen games, and the Aiken team won ten and lost six, which was not too bad considering that it was short of high-quality pitchers. Casey batted fourth in the lineup and led the team in every batting category. He batted .737, going 56 for 76.

As he often told Uncle Jake after they returned home from the games and the aftermath, "The baseball has never looked bigger to me. Sometimes, it looks as big as a cantaloupe. I have begun to focus on whether I want to hit the ball square on the nose or slightly under the center of the ball in order to get it into the air or slightly over the center of the ball to hit a very hard ground ball through a gap in the infield. It's amazing to me that I can control that now."

Amazingly, Casey only struck out once during his senior season and that particular time at bat needed footnotes to explain it. The game was in the valley, and the day started out warm and sunny, making short sleeves and basking in the sun the order of the day. Aiken jumped out to a big lead on the strength of Casey's home run and double, driving in six runs. The score was 12-0 in the sixth inning, when a severe cold front suddenly moved in from the west. Temperatures dropped twenty-five degrees, in a matter of minutes, the wind started to kick up, and an icy light drizzle began blowing sideways. All the spectators left. The umpire, shivering in his mask and short sleeves, urged the pitcher to hurry up and throw. Casey was the first batter in the sixth.

The first pitch was in the dirt, and the ump said, "Strike one." Casey winced but ignored the call as best he could. The pitcher wound up quickly, delivered again, this time two feet outside the strike zone. "Strike two," said the umpire. Casey stepped out of the box, looked back at the ump, and muttered aloud, "That was way outside, had to be a ball." The ump, still shivering, lifted his mask, spat on the ground, and said, "Aiken is up twelve zero. Sixth inning. Everybody's gone home. Freezing our asses off. Ain't gonna be no more balls."

Casey stepped back into the box, the pitcher threw again, this time two feet over Casey's head. He swung and missed. The next two batters suffered the same fate, and the umpire called the game due to the weather.

Zach became the most improved player on the team. He started the season batting sixth, but before three games had passed, he was the lead-off batter. It seemed that every time Casey drove in a run, Zach was the one who scored. That's how effective he was at getting on base. Their individual performances paid off because Casey was selected as first team All-State, and Zach was named to the All-CSRA team.

Late in the season, the University of Georgia invited both Casey and Zach to visit their campus in Athens. They encouraged parents to accompany them. Wade Kessler begged off, asking Jake to stand in for him. The four of them—Jake, Annie Lou, Casey, and Zach—went for the visit late in April. On Sunday of the visit weekend, the coaches asked for a meeting at the main field house.

After ten minutes of small talk and introductory comments, the Georgia athletic director placed some documents on the table. His comments were, "Casey, we love the way you play the game of baseball, and we want you to play for us for the next four years. We may be able to win the Southeastern Conference with you on our team, and the NCAA championship is also within our reach with you here. These papers in front of you represent a full four-year scholarship, including tuition, room and board, and all student fees. We really want you here."

He continued. "Zach, we also like the way you play and we can see that the chemistry between you and Casey makes both of you more effective. The papers in front of you represent a scholarship for tuition for four years, but we want you or your family to be responsible for your own room, board, and student fees. Well, what is your reaction to our offers?"

Casey looked at his aunt and uncle and could see that they were pleased with the offers, and he answered, "Coach, UGA has been high on my list for a long time. I would like to come here to play, but let us have a few days back at home to talk about it."

Zach jumped in as soon as Casey stopped talking. "If Casey comes here, I'm coming too. Thanks for the scholarship."

The athletic director was pleased with their reactions. He said, "Take your time in deciding. It's a big decision, but just remember, we really want both of you. Take the scholarship contracts home with you and after you have permanently decided, sign them and send them back to me. You will both love it here in Athens."

After a few finishing comments, the Gannons departed along with Zach and headed back to the parking lot to their car. When they were out of the office and out in the hall where no one was looking, Casey stopped and hugged his uncle Jake.

"Thank you so much, Uncle Jake. This could have never happened without you coaching me." Jake had to bite his lip to keep from going all emotional. Annie Lou was all smiles. All the way back to Aiken, the two boys showed their mutual excitement about both of them being able to continue playing together for another four years. Zach added, "Hey, we can even be roommates. Casey, you wanna be my roommate?"

"Oh yeah, of course I do," he quickly answered. He shifted his attention to the adults in the front seat. "Uncle Jake, Georgia is what I wanted all along. Can you make all of those other scouts and coaches leave us alone? You can tell 'em we've already decided and we're going to Georgia."

Jake smiled and Annie Lou did also. "I think it's a good choice, Casey," Jake said. "You won't be but a couple of hours from Aiken if you need to come home. Georgia has a strong baseball program, and you boys will fit right in. It's decided then." While he was talking, Annie Lou was nodding eagerly in agreement.

During the next week, the boys and the adults in their lives signed the scholarship agreements and mailed them back to Athens. It was a done deal.

The rest of the school year was anticlimactic. More baseball games followed, Beverly Jones was named "Miss Hornet" when the yearbooks came out, and the class of 1956 prepared for graduation. It came on May 31, and 147 seniors were proud to receive their diplomas in the new arched-ceiling high school gymnasium.

Everyone, it seemed, had different plans for the next several days. A large group, including Zach and Arlene, were going to a slew of different parties at Myrtle, Pawley's Island, Edisto, and Folly beaches. On the day of graduation, the death of Annie Lou's favorite aunt, out in Sandersville, Georgia, put a damper on things and meant that she and Jake must drive to central Georgia the next day to attend to family matters.

Suddenly, Casey found himself at home alone shortly after breakfast on June 1. Annie Lou told him as they drove off, "We'll be home late. We don't know what kinds of things we'll be faced with in Sandersville." Wade Kessler had just returned from one of his frequent European trips and was presumably asleep next door, shaking off the lag time of crossing multiple time zones.

Casey decided to spend the day tending to things he had been putting off for a long time. He wanted to organize his Mason jars again and inventory his funds; he wanted to reorganize the important papers that he had in his mother's attaché case, adding in his new diploma and scholarship papers; he wanted to take his car to the Gulf station

downtown on Richland for retuning the sparkplugs and to gas
it up; and he wanted to go into Hitchcock Woods for some
target practice and to evaluate how hard it was going to be for
him to disassemble the target shooting area he and Zach had
erected there. A full day was in the works for sure.

By late afternoon, he had everything accomplished and
walked back through the woods and across Highland Park
Drive and up the familiar driveway to his house. He saw the
basketball lying idle under the goal and decided to shoot
a few baskets before going inside. He laid his .22 rifle on
its side between the two toolhouses and proceeded to shoot
short jump shots, gradually increasing the length of the shot
as he progressed. Finally, he took a really long shot, which
he missed badly, with the ball clanging clumsily off the rim
and bouncing erratically into the small space between the
toolhouses, ricocheting rapidly from one toolhouse wall to
the other, in rapid succession, making a loud clatter in the
process.

As Casey sidled into the tight space to retrieve the ball, his
eye fell on three small booklets lying on the ground which had
fallen out of a small crack between two siding elements of the
Kesslers' toolhouse. Up high, under the eave, he spotted where
they had fallen from. He sat on the ground, was puzzled,
and picked the booklets up, noticing that the first one was a
maroon color and some strange foreign letters making out a
word he couldn't read.

ПАСПОРТ

was embossed in prominent letters on the front cover. The
second booklet had the unknown word

REISEPASS

in the same place on a royal blue cover, and the heading
DEUTSCHE DEMOKRATISCHE REPUBLIK near the top.

The third booklet had the single word

PASSPORT

at the center of its blue cover, and the words United States of
America, beneath that.

Casey stared hard at them as he digested the information
and then started to slowly flip through each of the booklets.
He quickly realized that all of them were passports, made out
to the same person, but issued by three separate governments.
He saw the picture of Wade Kessler, Zach's father, in each one,
but he was named Vladamir Propov in one, Wilhelm Koch
in one, and Wade Kessler. He gasped, leaned back against his
toolhouse, and took another deep breath. He felt dizzy and
nauseated and dreaded the thought that his life was about to
change and he had no control over it.

His surmise was that he was holding a Russian passport because he recognized the word *Leningrad* in a stamped entry. *Holy cow*, he thought. *It looks like Mr. Kessler was in Leningrad just five days ago.* Casey couldn't believe his eyes. Was it possible that his best friend's father was a Russian? Or a Russian spy? Didn't he claim that he was going to be in Belgium?

He heard a slight noise and looked up to see Wade Kessler approaching him from his house with an object hanging down in his right hand that looked an awful lot like a weapon. Instinctively, he grabbed his .22 and held it in a ready position.

Kessler rounded the corner of the small structure and saw Casey with the three passports fanned open in front of him. He held his right arm behind his right leg to shield his hand's contents from view. At last, he spoke. "I believe you have something there that belongs to me. Let me have them please." He clearly saw the rifle in plain view in Casey's hand, more or less pointing in his general direction.

Casey's first inclination, only because an authoritative adult had just made a request of him, was to hand the small booklets over. But he quickly realized that it would be a huge mistake. He said, "Mr. Kessler, please explain to me what I have in my hand. It appears that you have some explaining to do, that you are not what you seem. It appears that you go to Russia when you say you're going to Brussels. Please explain that to me in a way I can understand and I will give them to you."

Wade Kessler squirmed uncomfortably. "So you have read the entries too. You are not old enough to understand the world yet. You don't need to know what that is about. Let me have them now."

"Mr. Kessler, are you a Russian? Are you a Russian spy working at the bomb plant and living here in Aiken? Please tell me why you need three passports from three different countries in three different names." Casey was getting bolder, but also realized that he was in a very bad situation. "Please explain this all to me, sir. I will accept just about any explanation that makes sense." He was virtually pleading in a plaintive voice. He felt his heart racing.

Kessler quickly raised the pistol up and fired off a shot at Casey's head that missed and sailed over his left shoulder. Casey fired the rifle quickly, first into the hand holding the pistol, and then through Wade Kessler's right ear, puncturing through the cartilage and hitting the backboard just above and behind him. Casey scrambled up and seized the pistol, which had fallen to the ground.

Kessler screamed, "You shot me, you crappy little asshole! You just tried to kill me. Now you're in real trouble! I'll get you, boy!"

"Look, Mr. Kessler, I was not going to shoot this thing until you shot at me with that pistol. I'm afraid you got what you deserved. If I was going to kill you, the shot in your ear would have been in the middle of your head. Be thankful I know how to shoot." Casey continued to aim his rifle at the man.

"Are you going to just let me bleed to death, you pig?"

Casey grabbed a small cloth from the butt of his rifle and threw it to Kessler.

"That's all you get for now," Casey said.

Kessler applied the rag scrap to his ear and then to his hand to stem the small amount of bleeding. He said, "Listen, boy, you don't even realize how badly you've screwed up by seeing those passports. Your life is over. You are as good as dead, boy."

Casey shivered. "How is that?" he asked. "Seems like I'm the one holding the gun, and seems like I'm the one who's gonna turn you in to the police and tell them that we probably have a Russian spy living right here in Aiken."

"I just said that you are as good as dead. What you don't know is that just before I came outside, I called my local contact and he is coming over here to visit with me within the hour to debrief me. Yes, you stupid boy, there's more than one of us. There's a slew of us. You just walked into a buzz saw. You'll be dead before this day is done."

Hearing those words threw Casey into a near panic. He had not even thought of there being more than one of them in Aiken. Wade Kessler saw the effect of his words on Casey and pressed forward with more of the same. "I know your folks are out of town but will be back tonight. We'll have to kill them as well. And yes, boy, we know how to make it look like a murder-suicide. It's over for you and for them. That's how far we'll go to avoid being exposed."

Casey had heard enough. He realized he had to think and do it fast. There wasn't much time. "Get up, Mr. Kessler, and get inside your toolhouse." He prodded with the rifle, and Kessler saw a small opportunity to grab the rifle away from Casey so he lunged for it. Casey was faster and pulled the weapon out of reach, rotated it rapidly in the same motion, and hit Wade Kessler flush in his left cheek with the rifle butt, opening up another bloody wound.

It stunned Kessler. "Damn you, you son of a bitch, you'll pay for that, boy!" he screamed.

"Sir, please don't call me boy anymore. I'm way bigger than you, and you get into the toolhouse." As soon as Kessler was safely inside, Casey activated the locking hasp that ensured the door could not be opened from inside. Then he said, "I will get you a first-aid kit and bring it to you. If you move, I'll shoot through the door."

As he ran toward the back door of his house, his mind was racing about what he should do and when to do it. He had massive confusion running through his normally well-ordered mind. He ran into the kitchen and grabbed the first-aid kit from under the sink and then instinctively ran to his bedroom and looked around, not being too sure what he was looking for.

He rushed back to the Kesslers' toolhouse door and said, "Mr. Kessler, get back away from the door. I am prepared to shoot you in the head as soon as I open the door, so don't try anything. I will throw the first-aid kit inside when I open the door. Do not try anything. If you do, I'll be forced to kill you this time."

Kessler grunted his "Okay, I'm back."

The kit was thrown in, and the door quickly reclosed and relocked. Before Casey could go too far away, he clearly heard Kessler start talking again, this time in a more measured voice. "You are panicked, boy. I can see it in your face and I heard it in your voice. Listen carefully to me before you decide your next move. I am important to my contacts in the Soviet Union and elsewhere. They will not allow my exposure to stop them, and they will not stop until you are dead and your aunt and uncle are neutralized. Even if you give the three passports back to me, you are going to be killed for what you already know. No matter where you try to hide, my people are the best at tracking you down and eliminating you. There is a network of them in Aiken and all over this country. And there is no rational way to prevent the liquidation of Jake and your aunt once you have told them about this little incident. You have made a very expensive mistake and it will cost you your life. And don't think for a minute that you can ever turn me in to the police. I am a well-known nuclear engineer. I have worked for my country for years. No one will ever believe you over me."

Casey had heard enough, and his mind was beginning to come to some conclusions. He could only see one way to resolve the situation. He said to Kessler, "I have one question for you. Does Zach know you are working for the Russians?"

The answer came back through the door. "No, he has never known."

Casey had decided. "I am keeping your passports because they are my proof of what a traitor you are and what you've done. I love these people here in this house and this town and this country much more than you will ever understand. But I will never allow you to continue what you have been doing. It is impossible for me to think of living next door to you. I would not be able to hide my disgust of you for more than ten seconds. I am making a decision to leave Aiken tonight, but it will be with your secrets in my possession. Your passports are going with me. If you ever lay a hand on my folks, I will walk into the nearest FBI office I can find. If you ever go back to Russia to tell those people any more about our bomb plant's secrets, I will turn you in. It's obvious I don't trust you about my safety. I see that you need me dead, so I will leave here and let you wonder when your secrets will be revealed and when your life will be exposed as traitorous to our country, when it's your turn to burn in the electric chair just like the Rosenbergs. You can just twist in the wind until that happens. I don't give a crap about how you explain all of this to your son or your Russian friends. That's your problem. Goodbye, Mr. Kessler."

Wade Kessler tried to play one last card. He yelled out, "That little girl friend of yours, Arlene, who runs around with you and my son, will never be safe. I know where she lives. My people are all over this country."

Casey shrank back and ran quickly into the house. He remembered why he went in before. The first thing he reached for was his pocketknife, stuffing it into a pants pocket. Then he grabbed his Mason jars and dumped the contents of all three into just one of them. He joggled the three Kessler passports into one stack and inserted them into an empty Mason jar, making sure to tighten the lid snugly, and thrust it into his duffle bag, along with some undershorts, socks, and alligator golf shirts. The Mason jar full of money was wrapped in a towel and stuffed in too. The third Mason jar, empty now, he opted to leave in the middle of his bed. He badly wanted to write a note to put in this jar but had no time to do it. He grabbed his mother's attaché case, closed it up, and walked it into the kitchen, stacking it and the duffle bag next to the back door. Everything else in his room he had to leave there. Baseball glove, bats, everything.

He took his bags and cases outside and placed them on the seat of his car. Remembering the rifle and the pistol, now on the stoop leaning against the house by the back door, Casey retrieved them and placed in the rumble seat of the car. He had one final thought—get a small shovel, a spade, from Uncle Jake's toolshed. He retrieved that and placed it in the rumble seat also. He could not think beyond these actions.

He went to the Kessler's toolhouse door and said, "Sir, I am leaving now. Maybe your cohort will arrive soon to unlock this door. My folks will be home eventually tonight, and if you make enough noise, they will probably let you out as well. I seriously warn you. Do not harm them. Do not even think about it. Remember how well I can shoot. I won't be too far away. I will know it if you try to do anything. I can track you down also, and I won't reveal myself. You will be dead before you hit the ground. I will make sure of that."

He ran to his car, greatly relieved that he had managed to leave before Mr. Kessler's colleague arrived to interfere. He looked carefully up and down Highland Park for other signs of life, seeing none. He turned the Ford into the street and drove no more than three hundred yards where he knew of a place where he could hide the car for a few minutes in the edge of the woods, totally out of sight.

Out of the car, he quickly found the Mason jar containing the passports, the rifle, the pistol, and the shovel. Casey ran as hard as he could deeper into Hitchcock Woods to where he knew the Sand River to be, carrying the four items with him. In the sand, he knew of a large tree that had fallen halfway across the "river," which was about forty feet across at that point.

He found it and stood for a minute to suck in some air after his hard run. Sweat was running down his neck. He placed the items in the sand and began to dig as close to the horizontal tree trunk as he could manage. At the two-feet-depth mark, he stopped and carefully placed the pistol, his Winchester rifle, and the Mason jar in the bottom of the hole and filled the sand back in, tamping it firmly as he finished. He stepped into the woods and found a freshly fallen pine branch, which he used as a broom to brush over the area, obliterating his footprints and all other proof that he had been there. One last careful look around was made to try to remember the spot because he knew that he wanted to come back here sooner or later.

While he was digging, his mind was already racing toward the next step. *When I get back in the car and drive off, which way do I go?* He saw the compass in his head and wondered, North, south, east, or west?

He eliminated north because Washington, New York, and Philadelphia were in that direction and there was no interest for them. *Don't go east,* he mused, *because you run out of land pretty quickly at the Atlantic Ocean.*

That left the south and the west. He placed the shovel in the rumble seat, closed it, jumped in his car, and headed toward Whiskey Road, Silver Bluff, Beech Island, and on toward U.S. 25 via south Augusta. It occurred to him that he was subconsciously avoiding going anywhere near the bomb plant for fear of crossing paths with any of Wade Kessler's cohorts. While driving, he would have to think of the specifics of where he would head. His life had already changed too much too fast, and he was reeling mentally and emotionally from those changes.

Tears flowed freely from his eyes for the first few minutes on the road. He was acutely aware that the police will be looking for him because he had actually shot a man, not once but twice, and rifle-butted him as well. He felt that he may be able to explain his actions to them, but Wade Kessler had made it clear that someone from his Communist comrades would not only be searching for him, but their orders would be to kill him on sight. For every mile of distance between him and the city of Aiken, he was potentially creating more safety, but he was leaving behind all the things that were dear to him: His aunt and uncle, his best friends Arlene and Zach, his baseball scholarship at Georgia, his entire way of life, and what had been a promising future. Gone in a flash. Tears were called for, and he wanted to get that part over with.

He drove hard and fast through the darkness. Hours later, he stopped to gas up at an all-night service station as he passed through Statesboro, Georgia. Three hours after that, he pulled the old Ford into a parking space in North Florida and grabbed the only remaining possessions from his life in Aiken—the duffle bag containing his money and his mother's attaché case with his vital documents. When he stuck his thumb out at the first passing semi, it was 4:00 a.m. and the driver stopped. He jumped in the cab. "I'm heading west," Casey said.

"So am I," said the driver. "Get in."

THE WILDERNESS

Chapter 19

Wade Kessler sat on a toolbox in his toolhouse, dabbing at his ear and cheek and contemplated his situation. He was not too badly injured, but he did need medical help. He had been very foolish to continue using the flawed siding of the toolhouse to hide his passports, but he did not want to run the risk of Zach or the maid finding them accidentally inside their house. What's done was done, now was time to make the best of a potentially disastrous situation.

He believed everything Casey had told him—that he was going to keep the passports as insurance that Wade would not harm his aunt and uncle and that he would not continue giving atomic information to the Russians. He was thinking about that last part and formulating a plan to deal with it. His contacts in Moscow and Leningrad had always been demanding but had complained on recent trips that the information from him appeared to be gradually diminishing in value and was not as significant as it once was. Were they trying to tell him something? He needed to come up with a new way of dealing with the Russians. He felt that maybe he could create some breathing space to arrive at a new strategy with them.

Casey had bought into the idea that Wade had a cell of confederates in Aiken, but that was a necessary stretching of the truth. Wade had always worked this business best when fewer people were involved. He liked working alone if he could because his career of stealing and selling a country's atomic secrets was much safer that way. He had adhered to this philosophy from the very beginning in Hanford, Washington, and throughout his time in Oakridge too.

When he heard Casey's car drive off, he started to actively break out of his confinement. He needed to get to the hospital for treatment. A short-handled sledgehammer sat on the floor in the corner. Wade picked it up and battered the hinged side of the door, breaking through to the outside in four or five blows against each hinge. He was able to shove the remainder of the door to one side and step outside into the gathering darkness.

He drove to Aiken County Hospital and walked into the emergency room, telling the nurse on duty that he needed to be treated for gunshot wounds and from being assaulted by the butt of a rifle. He tried to make it sound like "no big deal" because he realized that the police would be getting involved very quickly once the cause of his injuries was revealed to them as the medical staff was obligated to do. Treatment began at once, but members of the Aiken Police Department showed up within five minutes, waiting outside the treatment room until he was finished.

Eventually, he went back to the waiting room and greeted the police team. "I know you have to talk to me about this, but I really want to go back to my house to do your interview. Can you follow me over there and do your inquiry there? It's not far. On Highland Park Drive."

"Yes, sir, we can do that. Give us your name and address and we can follow you to your home." He did, and they all left together, driving to his Highland Park home.

When the cars pulled into the driveway, Jake and Annie Lou were just getting out of their car as the police car parked just behind them. "Good evening, Wade, what's up with the police?"

"Jake, I'm about to be interviewed by these policemen about something that happened here earlier today. I think both of you should come over here to sit in and listen to what I have to say because it involves your boy, Casey." Wade was firm and more serious than they had ever seen him, and they were curious about the bandages on his ear, his cheek, and his hand.

They looked at each other with some dread and Jake said, "We're coming. Let us put our stuff down in the kitchen." Annie Lou noticed the broken door on the toolhouse and feared what was coming. *I wonder where Casey is,* she thought to herself.

Everyone was seated in Wade Kessler's living room—Kessler himself, two Aiken policemen with notepads and pencils, Jake, and Annie Lou. The police lieutenant began. "Mr. Kessler, can you tell us how you got your injuries and when and where they happened?"

"Yes," Kessler answered, "I can do that. This afternoon, I was taking a nap in my easy chair when I heard this ruckus outside and some gunshots. I grabbed my .38 caliber pistol, made sure it was loaded, and went outside. I immediately saw Casey Gannon, who lives next door and is related to these people, who seemed to be totally drunk, shooting his rifle wildly into the air and just carrying on in a generally belligerent out-of-control fashion. I was very uneasy because it was not normal to see him like that. He has always been calm and mostly well behaved. He is my son's best friend. My son is at the beach right now and not here.

"Anyway, I asked Casey to calm down and give me his gun before somebody got hurt. He refused, got even more belligerent, and pointed his rifle at me in a threatening manner. When he did that, I got very upset and raised up my gun and fired off a shot over his head, thinking that the noise might make him come to his senses. Instead, his reaction was to shoot my hand, sending my pistol flying to the ground. Then he aimed the rifle directly at my head and fired again. I sensed what was coming and jerked my head to one side, making the bullet hit my ear instead of my forehead, where he aimed. I was damned lucky, I tell you. I rushed him then because it felt like he was determined to kill me. He swung the butt around and caught me flush on the cheek and down I went. It dazed me. When I sort of came to myself, he was dragging me into my toolhouse, where he locked me in. I heard his car leaving later. I used a maul inside the toolhouse to break the door down. He was gone, and my pistol was gone too. Then I drove myself to the hospital. That's about it."

While he was talking, Jake and Annie Lou looked at each other with shocked expressions, and Annie Lou started to cry quietly. When Wade stopped with the account of the day's events, she said, "Oh, Wade, we are so sorry for what happened. He's never done anything like this before. Are you okay?"

Jake quickly added, "We've never seen that side of him before. We can't understand it. We're sorry. He'll have to give us some satisfactory answers the minute we see him."

The police lieutenant spoke. "Give us a few minutes to write this up, Mr. Kessler. We will want you to sign your statement, and we assume you will want to press charges."

For the entire time Kessler was giving them his oral statement, he had avoided looking at the Gannons. He had been afraid they would see through him and see his story as a lie. Now that he had the first telling behind him, he looked

at them for the first time. He said, "Yes, I'll press charges. We
can't just allow a boy to run around Aiken shooting nuclear
engineers, now, can we? But I hope you can charge him with
the most minor of the offenses and not ruin his entire life
with the most grievous of them."

"Wade, thanks a lot for that," Jake said.

"Mr. and Mrs. Gannon," the second policeman said, "why
don't y'all go back to your house and wait for us to finish
here? We need to get some more information from you about
Casey. Do you have any idea where he is right now?"

"No," Annie Lou answered. "We had to spend all day
arranging a family funeral out in Georgia and haven't been
here all day. He was here when we left this morning."

"Okay, we'll be over in a few minutes," the policeman said.

Jake and Annie Lou walked slowly back to their house,
detouring slightly to peer inside the Kessler toolhouse. She
finally said, "Jake, what in the world do you think happened
to our boy?"

"I don't know," he responded. "I don't think I've ever
been this shocked over anything in my life. It's just so out of
character for him. I won't really believe it until he tells me
himself."

They both went into Casey's bedroom with the idea that
maybe there would be some kind of clue to his whereabouts.
Annie Lou spotted the empty Mason jar first and quickly
looked for the others. Not there. She looked at his closet and
determined that almost everything looked normal, except that
the valise where he kept his important papers was gone and
his duffle bag was missing.

"Jake," she said in a worried tone, "this looks very bad to
me. All of his baseball stuff is here, but his money is gone and
all of his historical papers from Montana and his daddy's war

medal and the things that can identify him are gone. But his toothbrush is still in the bathroom. Oh, and his rifle is gone, and of course, his car. It looks like he left in a big hurry."

"That's really bad news," Jake said. "I'm gonna be surprised if we see him again tonight. Looks like he's decided to hide out somewhere for a while."

They heard a knock on the back door and saw the two policemen standing there. Jake opened the screen and invited them into the kitchen, where the four of them sat down around the kitchen dinette.

The lieutenant asked, "Where do you think Casey is?"

Jake answered, "We really don't know. If we did, we'd tell you. He's never done anything like this before. You realize who he is, don't you? The baseball player who's supposed to go to the University of Georgia in less than three months?"

"Yes, sir, we are aware of who he is. Probably the best baseball player ever to come out of Aiken."

Annie Lou said, "We're really puzzled and, of course, really disappointed. We can't explain it, didn't see anything like this coming."

The lieutenant said, "We need to ask some questions. What's Casey's full name, date of birth, and birth place?"

Annie Lou responded, "Casey Carter Gannon, July 1, 1938, in Butte, Montana."

"Next question, what's his social security number?"

Jake answered, "I'm pretty sure he doesn't have one yet. He works for me some, and when it came up, I just paid him out of petty cash. I asked him to get registered with social security, but I don't think he ever did."

"I'm pretty sure he didn't," Annie Lou added.

"Okay," the policeman said. "Do you know his height, his weight, any birthmarks or other identifying marks, and can you give us a current picture of him? We also need his car license plate number if you know it."

"Yes," Jake said. "He's six feet four inches tall, 190 pounds, no birthmark, no other marks, and we have his senior year picture from Aiken High School. You'll have to get his car stuff from DMV. I don't have it. It's registered in his name, not mine. What's all of that for?"

"Mr. Gannon, since he's not here to talk to and since he did shoot your neighbor, Mr. Kessler, we need to talk to him about all of this. I think that when we file our report, Chief Hanna will want to put out an APB for him and charge him with at least assault and battery and firing a weapon within the city limits. I hope we can talk him out of attempted murder, but that's what this case looks like. We have to start looking for him to bring him in for questioning. You understand that, don't you?" The policeman wanted to make sure that the Gannons properly judged the seriousness of Casey's predicament.

"Yes, I think we understand it," Jake said. "Annie Lou, get them a picture of Casey."

She brought the picture and handed it over, saying, "We have looked through Casey's room and it looks to us like he won't be back tonight. He has taken some things with him that we don't fully understand. One of those things appears to be his Winchester rifle. It's gone too."

That fact got both of the policemen's attention. "Did he use it a lot?" one asked.

Jake answered, "Yes, he did. He is a very good shot, one of the best I've ever seen."

"The chief is gonna want to know that," the lieutenant responded. "Anything else?"

Annie Lou said, "When you find him, he won't give you any trouble. I promise you that. He'll be cooperative."

Both of the Gannons slept miserably during the night. The next morning, after a very subdued breakfast, they went outside to look around, hoping to find any kind of clue to answer the hundreds of questions that had formed in their minds. Annie Lou looked all over the backyard for any evidence of where the incident happened. She wanted to see the drag marks for herself, this place where Casey slammed his rifle butt into Wade's face, and then dragged him into his own toolhouse. She looked and looked but saw nothing that backed up that part of the story.

When she looked in through the broken toolhouse door, she saw some blood on the floor and spotted the remnants of a first-aid kit plus a bloody rifle-cleaning rag, the kind that's used to ream out the bore of a gun.

When she went back into their house, Jake was still drinking coffee and watching the *Today Show* on television.

"Jake, do me a favor please. Check out our toolhouse to see if everything looks okay to you."

"Okay," he said. "Looking for anything in particular?"

"No, just see if everything looks normal."

He was back in a few minutes. "Hey, you know how all of my tools are organized, hanging in certain places on the wall? Your garden spade wasn't there. Did you leave it around the side of the house in that rose bed?"

"No," she said. "I haven't used that thing in several weeks."

"Well," Jake said. "It's not in its place on the wall. Missing in action, I guess."

When she heard his answer, another nagging thought nagged at her again. She looked under the kitchen sink where she always kept their first-aid kit. It was not there. *That's odd,* she thought. *It's always there.*

The next day, they had to return to the funeral in Sandersville, so they could not follow up on any of the questions they had.

On the morning of the day after that, the police lieutenant knocked on their door with news. "Mr. Gannon, Casey's car has been found. It was in the parking lot of the train station in Jacksonville, Florida. Casey was not with the car. We have no news of him. The car has yielded nothing in the way of clues. It was empty except for a garden shovel in the rumble seat. We don't know the significance of that. He could have bought a rail ticket to somewhere, maybe Miami. Or he could still be in Jacksonville. Do you know what the shovel was for?"

"No," Jake said. "But I think it all means we're not going to see Casey anytime soon. I expected that you would find the rifle in the car. Since you didn't, it's either still with him or he dropped it off somewhere, maybe even buried it with that shovel. Will we be allowed to have his car back? When he returns—and I know he will—he's gonna want that car again."

The policeman answered, "You can have the car, but you will have to go down there and get it yourself or just pay somebody to drive it back to Aiken. You'll have to pay some towing and storage charges down there, but yes, you can have it back unless we find out he committed some crimes on the way down there."

"Thanks. Keep us posted if you hear anything."

"Same here."

That afternoon, Annie Lou called Arlene Cushman's house and told her the bad news. It made one more person in Aiken extremely unhappy.

Chapter 20

A week after leaving his car in a Florida parking lot, Casey was staying in a cheap roadside motel near the middle of downtown Tucson, Arizona. He had been fortunate to get a continuing series of long-haul truckers to carry him from Jacksonville, along U.S. Route 90, through the Gulf Coast, and all the way to Tucson. Most of them even paid for his meals, saying that he was good company and made the miles go by faster. He had been able to visit a Salvation Army Thrift Store in order to supplement the meager clothing he had in his duffle bag. They even had a cheap suitcase for him to put them into. A nearby drugstore solved the problem of toothpaste and a toothbrush.

He had settled on using the name "C. C. Cannon" anytime he was asked for his name. He figured that if someone inadvertently saw any of his personal papers, he would be able to explain the name Gannon as just a typographical error. By the time he had given that name to more than one truck driver, he was beginning to like it.

One night, he opened the attaché case and spread out the contents on his motel bed. He also prepared his pocketknife for use and positioned a lamp to provide good light for the remake of his identity. He had decided to change his name to Casey Carter Cannon and to use "CC" as his everyday name.

He had to labor over every paper, every document in his possession, using the sharp point of his knife, to expertly pick off or in some cases scrape off the serif of the *G* in *Gannon* to change it to the word *Cannon*. He started by practicing on the report cards from elementary school back in Montana, figuring that if he botched the first few, no one was likely to look back that far anyway.

He worked his way through all report cards, ID cards in his wallet, his new diploma from Aiken High School, and finally to his Montana birth certificate. In time, all of them were changed to his new identity. The last name *Gannon* was magically changed to *Cannon*.

Another chore he tackled once he was settled into the motel room was to count his money. He had left in such a hurry and comingled the funds from three different jars that he could not remember the exact amount he had when he departed from Aiken. He was more than a little impressed that the total came to $1,865, mostly in $10s and $20s, but with a few $50s thrown in. He jettisoned his Mason jar and found a secret snapped pocket in his new suitcase to hide his funds, always keeping about $10 in his wallet for immediate use.

Several times per day, the enormity of his radically altered life swept through his mind. He missed his aunt and uncle and his room at home, as well as his Aiken friends. He had a miserable time adjusting to losing all that if he allowed his thoughts to run too far in that direction for too long. He was fortunate that he could force his mind into other directions.

It was time to think about finding some temporary work so that he would not burn through his small treasure too fast. But first, he would finally need a social security card before he applied for work anywhere. The motel owner, who also served as desk clerk, told him where the federal building was.

He walked to it, as it was only a mile away, and found the office that issued the cards. He was a little nervous because he had no idea how many lies he might have to tell to explain why he had no card and where he lived. He had remembered to bring his birth certificate, guessing that you must prove you were born in the USA to secure a card. He told the clerk, "You can see what my full name is, but everybody just calls me CC. I want the card to say C. C. Cannon, not my whole name."

He was uncomfortable when he had to talk them out of mailing the card because he had to explain that he had no permanent address, only the motel. The lady behind the desk said, "Well, we just can't give you the card right now because they get produced at night by a night-shift machine operator. It won't even be available until tomorrow."

"Can I come back in here tomorrow and get it from you?" Casey asked plaintively.

"Yes," she said. "Come back at the same time tomorrow."

The next day, he walked back, got the card from her, and checked it to make sure it was just as he ordered it. It was. He was worried that the Russians might find some way to search new social security numbers, and he didn't want Casey Carter *Anybody* to stick out like a big "come find me" sign. So C. C. Cannon it was.

When the social security clerk gave him the card, she also told him, "I noticed that your eighteenth birthday is on July 1. That's only a couple of weeks away. Don't forget, as a male you have to register with selective service within five days after that birthday. That way, the government and the military knows about you so that you can be drafted if they need you. You can come back here to do it or go to a post office and do it."

"Oh yeah," Casey answered. "I knew all about that but had forgotten it. "Thanks for the reminder."

He was worried about staying in one place for too long and had already made the decision to leave Tucson. The next day, he checked out of the motel and hitchhiked to Phoenix. His ride told him all about Glendale, a town nine miles northwest of Phoenix. Casey decided that larger towns like Phoenix probably should be avoided for their smaller bedroom communities on their outskirts. He did not want to be too conspicuous and to be seen by too many strangers in the large cities every day.

In Glendale, Arizona, he found a cheap motel on the bus line and very near restaurants and another thrift store. The U.S. Post Office was in the next block. He asked the thrift store if they ever hired temporary help, and the manager said, "I'm looking for a warehouse person right now. You look good and strong. I can pay you the minimum wage, a dollar an hour. The rate just changed earlier this year from seventy-five cents. You can start tomorrow. I can promise you twenty-five hours a week. What about it?"

Casey said, "Yeah, I'd like to do that. My name is C. C. Cannon. I need the work." So just like that, he had found a job and filled out their application for their personnel file.

He appreciated being able to have an income and to start adding back to his slowly diminishing funds. Having no idea how long he would be working there, he told the manager that he would stay "until we can't stand each other anymore." That line brought a laugh.

Casey's birthday was on Sunday this year, so on Monday, July 2, he went to the post office to register for the selective service board. He took his social security card and his modified birth certificate with him. The process was easy. He asked the clerk when he might expect to be drafted or classified. She said, "It only takes a week or so, and you can come back in here to pick up your draft card."

On the way out, he passed an army recruiter's desk, which was idle of any activity. The master sergeant on duty was smoking a cigarette and leaning back in his chair. Casey sat down across from him and started the conversation. "Sir, can you tell me why I would want to join the army?"

The sergeant laughed. "Son, it will make a man out of you so fast your head will spin." And he laughed at his own line. "Seriously, if you are a high school graduate and can prove it, you can enlist in the army for three years and I can promise you either Europe or Korea, if you're inclined to like the travel, or the warm Southern United States if you don't want to go outside the USA. You have to pass some interviews and a physical and be ready to give us three years."

Casey had been thinking about the army being a good place for him to hide out in his new identity but did not know quite how to do it. "I just graduated from high school, and I need to think about a job and what to do with my future, and I was thinking the army might be good for me."

"Yeah, that's true," the sergeant said. "What about your folks? They care one way or the other?"

""My mom and dad are dead. I've been an orphan for eight years," Casey said truthfully.

"Boy, that's tough. Sorry about that. Then you get to make all of your own decisions, right?"

"That's right," answered Casey. "If I tell you I want to sign up for three years, what's the next step?"

"Well," the man said. "You show me that high school diploma, we sign some papers, you take a physical, we check you out to see if you're wanted for murder or anything else, you get approved, and then you wait for your orders."

"How long does all of that take?" Casey asked.

"Here we are in early July. You could be at basic training in Colorado by the middle of August."

"I just signed up for the draft an hour ago in there," he said, pointing to the post office. "I don't have the draft thing yet."

"Don't worry," the sergeant replied. "I'll rush that draft card along. I have connections in there."

For the next hour, Casey filled out the required paperwork, making sure that every entry reflected his new name and his local address at his motel. When it was all finished, they shook hands and he left.

Oh my, he thought as he walked out of the building. *Life sure comes at you fast in my situation when you're trying to hide and change everything in that life.*

Within six weeks, he had passed the army's physical exam, cleared out of his motel and his job at the thrift store, and was on the way to basic training. He had to tell the manager at the store that "military service has intervened."

And he still had times when he missed all that he had left behind in Aiken. *Keep moving forward*, he told himself several times a day. *Just keep moving forward.*

At Fort Carson, on the outskirts of Colorado Springs, Colorado, Casey found himself temporarily in the 9th Infantry Division to learn how to be a soldier.

Back in South Carolina, in the immediate aftermath of the shooting of Wade Kessler, Annie Lou and Jake were reeling from the rapid changes in their lives. The incident had been mentioned briefly in the local newspapers, but they had been reluctant to make a big splash about it because Casey had become a visible role model with how well he had handled the publicity of being an All-State and All-CSRA baseball player. The word about the shooting incident was spread more by word of mouth than by the news media.

One morning, Annie Lou and Jake had a serious conversation about Casey's incident and where he was. Annie Lou said, "He's been gone a week now, and I just wish he'd call to tell us what happened, where he is, whether he's all right, and when he's coming back. I really love that boy and this thing worries me to death."

Jake said, "You don't love him any more than I do. I want him back here too. He grew on me slowly at first, but he turned into such a fine young man, I wouldn't be any prouder if I was his own daddy. I know him well enough to say that if he shot Wade Kessler twice—and I don't doubt for a minute that he did—then he probably did it for a good reason. It just don't make any sense for him to do something like that just out of the blue."

"Jake, I agree with you," Annie Lou responded. "I want to do something to try to help find Casey and help find out what might have happened. Would you mind if I got some of his best friends together to talk about what could have happened? Maybe there was something going on in his life that we didn't know about." She was silently thinking about the Denise Slaughter incidents when the idea crossed her mind.

"Yes, you go ahead," Jake answered her. "I want him back. He's my boy too. Do what you think will work. I'll support anything you can think to do."

That afternoon, she telephoned several people and asked them to meet her for lunch the next day in the lunch booth area at Liles Drug. The next day, Arlene was there, as was Zach, plus a member of the faculty at Aiken High School, as well as a member of the church who knew Casey better than most.

Annie Lou started by saying, "Thank you all for coming on such short notice. We have not heard a word from Casey since he left on the night of June first. I am hoping that by talking about this among his best friends, we may be able to shed some light on anything out of the ordinary that was going on in his life that Jake and I could have missed. Do any of you have any ideas about what might have happened to make him snap?"

Zach was first to say anything. "I know it was my dad who got shot, and I don't know of anything about either one that could have caused it. I asked Dad and he doesn't talk much, but he just says, 'Casey just got drunk and started shooting.' I don't know a Casey who would do that, but I don't know a dad who would make it all up. It's totally out of character for both of them, but especially Casey. He'll come back. I know him. He'll be back. He's got to come back. We're gonna play baseball at Georgia, and he's gonna be my roommate."

Arlene offered her thoughts. "Casey is one of my very best friends and I would trust him with my life. I can't imagine that he could get so drunk or so mad to do such a thing. I have never seen him take a drink, and if I haven't, then I don't believe anybody has. There's something here that we don't understand yet. We don't know the whole story yet. I will bet you that when we find out what really happened, we'll all be understanding of it and not be into condemning Casey. This town does not want to judge somebody like Casey—somebody who has never misbehaved—without having concrete proof of his guilt. If he never comes back, I'll go to my grave believing in him."

The teacher responded, "Arlene, that's a pretty strong statement, but I also agree with you. A leopard can't change his spots without showing some sort of inclination to do it. That boy was good down to his core, and I will give him the benefit of the doubt until I see some hard proof to the contrary. In the meantime, I don't even have a guess as to what happened. I don't know of anything strange he had going on in his world."

Annie Lou spoke up. "It looks like y'all knew the exact same person I did. That boy has not led a hidden life in any way. John," she directed her question to the man from their church, "can you shed any light on this discussion? You taught his Sunday school class."

John said, "I think all of you have pretty well nailed it. If Casey is totally guilty of this incident as the police are charging him, then it's all about a person none of us know. Something happened that we don't fully understand. If Casey were to walk back into town right this minute, Aiken would pause and give him the time and the place to explain himself and then Aiken would render its judgment. Not one minute sooner. We knew him too well and too positively to make any kind of condemnation until we know more than we do now. If I was a betting man, I'd bet he didn't do anything wrong, not intentionally, anyway."

Annie Lou dabbed at her eyes and said, "Y'all have said the nicest things about Casey. I didn't know what I would hear today, but what I heard is this: Y'all believe in Casey and his character and integrity as much as I do. Thank you for that and for coming today. Arlene sweetie, you and I need to stay closer in touch with each other."

Back at home that afternoon, she related the entire meeting and comments to Jake. He beamed as he heard the words. "I'm so proud of that boy. I wish I had told him how much he meant to me before he left."

"Oh, I think he knew," Annie Lou answered. "In that boy's mind, you had become his coach and his daddy."

When Zach saw his father again that evening, he related the meeting to him. Wade said, "Zach, it's like I told you, I never saw anything in Casey that would've made him go berserk like he did. In my mind, it was just an aberration, a one-time thing." Then he poured on a logical lie. "If he walked back in here right now, he would apologize, we would be friends again, and life would go on as normal."

Wade had given a lot of thought to their confrontation in the backyard, and he was coming to two hard conclusions: Casey was too afraid to be in too close proximity to Wade and Aiken, and Wade himself was afraid to act against those Casey loved like Jake or Annie Lou or Arlene. A true standoff existed.

Zach had the final word. "Well, I wish he'd get his butt back here. He's my best friend and we've got to be thinking about college and Athens and the future."

Later in the summer, Jake Gannon called the athletic director at the University of Georgia to tell him that Casey was missing from the family and may not be available to attend in September. Zach called them separately and somewhat later and notified them that he had changed his mind about coming and that he would be attending Clemson instead.

Chapter 21

Casey stayed at Fort Collins for basic infantry training, followed by advanced combat training. Several months had gone by, and his adjustment from civilian life to military life was almost complete. He discovered that the friends he made in the army were not very different from building a family from scratch. You find those who are the most compatible with your interests and make the strongest friendships you want. It was not a replacement for what he had felt for Jake, Annie Lou, Arlene, and Zach, but it would do for the moment. He adjusted well, but he knew he could never tell any of them what had happened in Aiken that sent him scrambling away from his life there. That story was locked up in his soul and would have to stay locked up. Simply too much risk to everything otherwise. And yes, he recognized the rural nature that Aiken had, but he still missed his life there tremendously. It surprised him, but he missed Aiken even more than baseball. Keep moving forward.

He had never been trained formally on firearms and how to shoot until his training in Colorado. He discovered what he already knew, but to a finer degree. Casey was the best shot in his training company of 120 soldiers and improved his marksmanship to a level he was proud of. Even he was surprised at how accurate he was at the five-hundred-meter distance. He would make a great sniper if he ever needed to do it.

Another facet of his days at Fort Collins was intramural softball, played on Saturday afternoons. In his first twelve at bats in two games, he hit the ball out of the park each time. He saw that his batting prowess was attracting too much attention, as word of mouth caused spectators to show up for the third game just to watch him perform with the bat. When that happened, he lied to his squad leader, saying, "I've hurt my shoulder and need to sit out the game." After that, he did not play any more softball. The last thing he needed was to have his identity uncovered because he was too good a hitter.

Just before Christmas 1956, he had finished his Colorado training and got orders for West Germany. In no time at all, he disembarked from a TWA Constellation after flying for too many hours all night across a cold, dark ocean from Fort McGuire, New Jersey, to Rhein-Main Air Force Base in Frankfurt, West Germany. He had departed from a frigid northeastern area and landed in an even colder foreign land, where the language was an immediate barrier to his rapid assimilation.

An army NCO met his flight in order to company him to his assigned company in Heidelberg, about thirty miles away. Casey had attained the rank of private first class (PFC) as he graduated from advanced training in Colorado. This meant he was moving along on a "fast track" from a superior's perspective. He was tall, trim, and fit, and he quickly learned from his squad leaders that the military singled out that particular profile to keep an eye on prospects for future leadership positions.

Since his own father had died at the hands of the German army only twelve years earlier in Belgium, he was prepared to feel strong animosity toward all Germans. Therefore, it surprised him that just about every German he met in those first weeks he liked. Casey found that they were industrious people, always clean and neat, and kind and friendly toward

Americans. To be sure, his first contacts were employees on his military base, people who drew their paychecks from American sources, but it was still remarkable that he liked them in spite of his previous biases.

He had become friends with one particular German man who worked at the PX and who seemed to be the salesclerk in several of Casey's transactions there. They became friends, and on Christmas Day, he was invited to the man's home for the main holiday meal. He gladly went, enjoying the unusual day in a new land for the first time.

On his first venture into this German's home, he had his eyes opened when he learned that there was still widespread suffering and a very simple life from the lingering effects of the war. His host was an uncomplicated man, married, and had a child. They also owned two cows that lived partially on the outside and partially inside the house.

Christmas dinner was served on the family dining table that was located on a concrete platform in the back of the house, under the roof, inside the walls of the house, but in an unheated area. It was more like an elevated loading platform than anything else but had barn doors to the outside that could be closed from bad weather. At the foot of the dining room platform, the cows fed at their own trough and on the hay laid out for them. It was interesting to eat this special meal of sauerbraten and dumplings with this family while being exposed to the odors and aromas that this unusual setting provided. It was a unique experience for an American and not one he could have ever foreseen.

He was thankful for the experience and the setting and realized that scenes like this would not be around much longer. He had also noted that here and there, there were rubble piles from Allied bombing that had yet to be cleaned up, as well as bullet holes in many of the buildings in the villages around Heidelberg. These scenes were possible even though the war had ended more than twelve years earlier. The world was changing fast, but war damage was still present in Europe.

Back in Aiken, Jake and Annie Lou were having the saddest holiday they had ever had. Casey had been gone for seven months, and they had not heard a word from him or from those who were searching for him. He had simply dropped from the face of the earth.

Annie Lou asked Jake if he thought they would ever see him again. Jake's eyes teared up as he answered, "Honey, I swear we will. I know that boy, and I know how he felt about us and about this town. He'll come back as soon as he can. For some reason, he doesn't think he can come back right now. Whatever that reason is, as soon as it clears up, he'll come back."

"I pray you are right," she said. "I'm at loose ends, don't know what to do with myself. I've been thinking about asking the J. B. White store for a job after the New Year starts. What do you think?"

"It'll give you something to do," he said. "I think it would be a good place for you. They're nice people there at that store."

When the holidays were over, she followed up by applying for a salesclerk position at White's, next door to the *Aiken Standard and Review*, on Richland Avenue. She had several friends who worked there, and it included the manager.

He was surprised to see her applying for the job. She explained it this way. "I need to do a job that I will really like, and I am sure that this is it. This is a wonderful store and I've always loved coming in here to shop. Now, I want to be part of the service that I have enjoyed for years. And yes, I am trying to invest my time in something really worthwhile instead of sitting around moping and waiting for Casey to come back to us. We don't know when that will be. I want to make more of my life while he is gone from us." The manager admired her outlook despite the adversity in her life and hired her at once, recognizing he would be getting a quality employee for his store.

Arlene Cushman missed Casey much more than she ever anticipated. When September arrived, she found herself in Columbia, registering for classes at the University of South Carolina. In the South of 1956, most girls sorted through a few obvious basic choices; they could get married if someone special were in their lives; they could go to secretarial school, learn to type, take dictation, and make coffee for the boss; or they could go to nursing school, apply to be a teller at a bank, or work in the retail industry. Arlene decided to go to college and learn how to become a schoolteacher.

She had never fully examined her feelings about Casey Gannon and how deep they went, even though she had had plenty of time to do so. Casey had never said anything to her that led her to believe that they would be a permanent couple one day. They had both approached the relationship as a "he's my best friend or she's my best friend" topic, and both of them took the other for granted, figuring that there would eventually be time to sort out their true feelings for each other. Of course, that assumption turned to empty fluff the instant Casey disappeared. There was no time to say goodbye or I love you, or I don't love you or any other meaningful expression. She felt empty without him and slowly began to realize that she had drifted into an assumption that Casey was the man in her life and for her life. She decided that she would therefore cautiously prepare to wait until he returned. Then they would make the hard decisions between themselves. In the meantime, becoming a schoolteacher was the goal.

Jake Gannon was having a difficult time adjusting to not having Casey in his life. His emotional pendulum had swung in a far greater arc due to his involvement with his talented nephew. At first, when Casey arrived from Montana in 1948, Jake had been vehemently against having him in the same house. But then, Casey had proven to be so industrious, so appealing, so athletic, and so determined to make the relationship with his uncle succeed that Jake now loved him as if he were his own son. Casey's financial backing had made it possible for them to move into bigger and better houses, which led to Jake having his own construction company, a company that was booming and providing a handsome income for their family. All of it was accomplished without ever spending a cent of Casey's insurance money, which still sat in the bank, earning interest.

Jake knew enough about baseball to realize that his nephew was one of the few talents to come along every few years, who sets records at each stage of his development. Casey's superb eyesight and his ability to swing the bat productively was probably going to open the doors into major league baseball in the future. But where was Casey? Wherever he was, would he be able to keep his abilities sharp and competitive, or would they fall into disuse? Jake missed the thought of the future and the desire to watch him play for the University of Georgia. All of that was on hold until Casey returned. More than anything else, Jake missed the intangible X-factor that Casey had, the one that led Jake himself to become a better person and to stay that way permanently.

He credited Casey with his improvement because no one else in his life had ever made that much difference that quickly. Casey had been his anchor for several years and probably didn't even realize it.

Zach made the adjustments in his life as well as they could be made under the circumstances. He enrolled at Clemson, and the athletic department pressed him to think about being a "walk-on" for the baseball team in the spring. He answered that he would think about it but did not encourage them.

When he traveled back to Aiken for the Christmas break, he was painfully aware that his best friend, Casey, was not there and was not likely to show up anytime soon. He asked his father if there had been any changes or developments in the Casey assault and battery case and was told no. "Where do you suppose Casey went? Any ideas?"

Wade Kessler squirmed upon hearing the question, but finally managed an answer: "I have no idea where he went." Then he rethought the circumstances of that fateful day and added, "I can't imagine that he went very far away. Didn't Aiken and his friends here and his folks mean a lot to him?" Zach agreed that they did.

Casey was an ocean and a continent away, but nobody suspected it. He was as safe as he could reasonably expect to be.

Chapter 22

After his first few months in Germany, Casey had settled into a few semipermanent decisions about the army and about his future. He saw it as a safe parking place for himself, given that he was wanted by the U.S. authorities under his Casey Gannon name, and given that a Russian assassination squad had to be looking for him as well.

He decided to stay in the army for a while—he had obligated himself to three years anyway—and sought out ways to better himself for that day in the future when he might be able to live out in the open again as himself. The distance of several thousand miles between Aiken and West Germany offered him a measure of security that he would not have felt anywhere in the United States. He spent a considerable amount of time analyzing his situation and discovered several facts about his current life in this regard.

First, there were correspondence courses available for Americans in Europe for all types of college-level courses. The University of Maryland seemed to be the most advanced institution in offering these courses. Not only were courses offered through the mail, but several cities in West Germany had brick-and-mortar facilities for on-site courses in the evening. Heidelberg was one place where they offered classroom courses.

Second, his superiors, at every level, seemed to like him and encouraged him to be the best soldier he could be and to consciously seek and qualify for promotions as they came along. As a PFC, his opportunities for financial reward were few, but sergeants, platoon sergeants, and master sergeants made levels of take-home pay several times greater than his. In his army life, that was one of the things he missed—having his own relatively unlimited amounts of money to spend. He chose to try to get promoted as soon as possible.

Third, he longed for some type of social life that approximated what he had in Aiken. He suffered from the losses in that regard. It meant having his own car and a girlfriend or two to take to the movies or out to dinner. He often thought of his old blue Ford and whether it was still sitting alone, rusting at the Jacksonville train station, and he thought often of "his people" there.

He pursued all of these interests with renewed vigor and enthusiasm. In short order, he received a promotion to specialist fourth class, which paid him more money while expecting more from him in the area of leadership and responsibility. After a few months, he had saved enough money to buy a used 1954 Volkswagen from an NCO who was strapped for cash in another company in the regiment. After passing the test for a European driver's license, he received the permit that freed him up to travel around the Heidelberg area and widen his vistas considerably. Of course, he frequented the abundant gasthauses with his friends and met enough fräuleins to satisfy his curiosity about German girls.

He learned that not only was Germany divided into four geographic sections as part of the settlement of World War II, but that the four annual seasons were also divided for purposes of training and war games for the use of outdoor training areas. Unfortunately, the assigned American season was the wintertime, and it was a permanent fixture of his life. As long as he was in West Germany, he would be spending most of each winter training outside in the cold, in places called Grafenwöhr, Hohenfels, Baumholder, and Wildflecken. He learned also that Heidelberg was located so far above the equator that it would be situated in far northern Canada if it were on the American continent. A very cold place in the winter!

As things developed, his unit trained in Baumholder every January; and during their three-week stay in the area, he met a colonel who saw the potential that Casey offered to his battalion and also to the army. Colonel Nason convinced him that if he were to transfer to Baumholder, he would find a friendly place to build his military future. Casey was impressed by what he heard. He liked the colonel and his wife, plus the nearby twin cities of Idar and Oberstein, which were only a few kilometers from his quarters. He decided that he wanted to transfer to the Baumholder post.

When the unit returned to Heidelberg, he carefully checked about transferring and whether he could continue the college-level classes he had signed up for. His commander agreed to allow him to apply for the transfer, which he did promptly. Also, his courses would be available by mail.

He applied to be a member of the 16th Infantry Regiment in Baumholder, which was a part of the 8th Infantry Division. They needed to fill some empty slots in several rifle platoons, and he was eagerly accepted.

In April 1957, he drove his small car packed with his personal belongings into the Baumholder post. Within a few days, he was completely relocated and oriented into his platoon. His first discovery was that the weather there was totally crazy. He experienced one spring day where the day started with a driving snowstorm, but by noon it had cleared and the sun came out, heating the area up to a mild sixty-five degrees. Then in the afternoon, a front moved through and it returned the post to blizzard conditions before the sun went down. When he asked his platoon sergeant about it, the answer that came back was, "Welcome to Baumholder, son."

No sooner had he settled down in his new quarters than his platoon sergeant told him that the unit would be traveling the next weekend to a small town in the small country of Luxembourg named Ettelbruck for the purpose of helping them celebrate the anniversary of their liberation from Nazi hands some thirteen years before.

"Why do we help them celebrate this day and not help other cities in the area?" Casey asked.

The NCO answered, "You know who Major McCluskey is, right? Our head of Regimental Operations? Well, during the big war, Major McCluskey was then Sergeant Joseph McCluskey, and he was the first American into Ettelbruck in 1944 to liberate their citizens from years of occupation by the German army. Major McCluskey is a hero in that town, so because of that we help them celebrate with something they call the Day of Remembrance."

Casey immediately understood and was enthusiastic about being a part of it all. He checked out his road maps and determined that the town was almost due west and only seventy-five miles from Baumholder. He asked the sergeant if he could drive his car there instead of riding in the deuce and a half, and he received the platoon's permission.

He gassed up his VW—only 13¢ a gallon at the quartermaster station—and drove into Ettelbruck three hours later. Germany had its famous autobahns, but not in the rural southwest corner of the country, so his drive was almost entirely on two-lane roads. It was a festive weekend, and Casey enjoyed the friendly people of Luxembourg. He even saw a poster-sized picture of Sergeant McCluskey, as he marched into town in 1944.

On Sunday afternoon, as he was driving back out of town to return to Baumholder, he decided to stop at the American military cemetery on the outskirts of Luxembourg City. He had been told during the weekend celebration that General George S. Patton was buried there, and he decided that he wanted to see the gravesite. Casey's own father had served under Patton, and he realized that most of the graves in this particular cemetery were for soldiers who had died in the Battle of the Bulge. After parking the car and going through the gate into the cemetery grounds, the very first grave he saw was that of the famous general. Other Americans had the same interest in seeing it, and a small group was gathered around it taking pictures.

Casey decided to find the caretaker's office to inquire if there was some sort of registry for those who were buried there. He discovered that the office was closed on Sundays and he would not be able to see a list of the dead there. So he had some extra time and decided to stroll through as much of the grounds as possible, looking for his father's name on gravestones.

Over five thousand American soldiers were buried at this one location, and he had been told that over a dozen American cemeteries were scattered around Western Europe. As he was quietly walking between the rows and rows of tombstones—some made of the familiar Christian cross and others the Jewish Star of David—his eye suddenly locked on to something entirely too familiar.

As the enormity of the moment washed over him, he dropped to his knees, emitting a quiet sob, and put his hand to his mouth instinctively. On a tombstone, he was able to read through his blurry vision the name and accompanying information:

George Gray Gannon
Sergeant First Class   99th Infantry Division
Montana   December 22, 1944
Silver Star

It was him—unquestionably the gravesite of his father. He had never dreamed that one day he would actually see it, but there it was in all its sunlit glory. Oh God, did he want a camera right then, but he had none. Casey said a quiet prayer for his father and for all the soldiers buried there. He concentrated very hard to make sure the entire scene was burned into his brain. If he could ever get back to Aiken, he wanted to make sure he could relate every detail to Uncle Jake and Aunt Annie Lou.

Once he thought of them, homesickness for Aiken and Arlene and their house and his car and Zach washed over his mind and body and made the scene even more intense and memorable. He decided right then that some way, somehow, he would eventually make it back to his adoptive hometown.

On his way out of this sacred place, he stopped by the visitor's welcome center and read the displays and maps affixed to the walls. He learned that the Battle of the Bulge was fought in December 1944 and January 1945, in Luxembourg, and nearby Belgium. The center of the battle action was Bastogne, Belgium, fewer than forty miles from this cemetery. Knowing that fact somehow added to the peace of mind he could feel forming inside his body. A sense of finality about his father and his death was meticulously being constructed in his thoughts.

He left the cemetery much more slowly than he had entered it. And the scene played over and over in his mind all the way back to his post in Baumholder. He was positive that he had just experienced a day he would never forget. It made him feel a breadth of love and pride for his family and for the bravery his father displayed in his last acts. After all, he had been awarded the Silver Star for his heroic actions in combat. Unfortunately, he would never be able to tell his buddies in the barracks what he had seen because his name was Cannon and not Gannon, and he did not want to discuss the reasons for the difference.

Back in Aiken, Annie Lou had become adjusted to her new role as salesclerk for the J. B. White department store on Richland Avenue. Many of her friends visited her in the store in the first year, making sure to secure their purchases through her, just in case it contributed to her income and her in-store reputation in some way.

Jake's business was thriving as well. His small construction company had earned a quiet niche in the Aiken housing market, one based on always finishing projects on time or even finishing early, and never being over budgeted costs. He often had to turn business away because of his stubborn refusal to overcommit to completion dates.

Arlene had buried herself into her studies and rarely allowed herself to think of the incredible sadness of her plight. She felt as if she were caught in the purgatory of having strong feelings for another person, not being able to admit to it to anyone, and not even being sure if that significant "other person" even knew or cared how she felt. She quietly gnashed her teeth more than once over never having asked Casey if he had any romantic intentions aimed in her direction. Her personality, which was easygoing and approachable, had worked against her better judgment regarding him. She vowed that in her next life, if there was one, she would definitely be more assertive and aggressive.

Chapter 23

In September 1959, it was time for Casey to either get out of the army or reenlist for another long hitch. He felt a bit safer about the threats in Aiken but was not ready to think about going back there, at least not yet.

Too much danger. During his time in West Germany, he had figured out a way to constantly exert a minor amount of pressure on Wade Kessler back at home.

Every few weeks, someone in his military life was exiting from the army and going back into civilian life. This always meant a trip back into the United States. Using his company's typewriter on a weekend, Casey had prepared a series of letters to be mailed to the Kessler home in Aiken. Each envelope was addressed simply by typewriter and had no return address. Inside was a single sheet of paper that said, "Still watching over you and your passports."

Casey would give one of the prepared, sealed, and stamped letters to the departing soldier and say, "I have a friend in the USA, and we are always playing small tricks on each other. Please drop this letter in the mail after you get back home. I have to keep him guessing as to where I am. It's a game we play." No departing soldier ever turned him down.

In his investigation about reenlisting, he discovered that the army would pay him a sizeable bonus to reup and would entertain any ideas he had about transferring to another post in Germany. In the three years he had been in Europe, he had tired of some of the small German towns and was ready to try out the big city life. He discovered that there were army units in West Berlin that would welcome him eagerly with open arms. He thought hard before reenlisting for five years, but he did it and transferred to one of the Berlin groups. He was twenty-one years old, had a good reputation as a solid soldier, was unattached, and was making good money as an E-5 staff sergeant. Within a few weeks, he had the unusual experience of driving the lonely East German/Russian autobahn across the bleak landscape of East Germany, traversing through the cumbersome border checkpoints along the way. In time, he had settled down in his new situation at Andrews Barracks in the exciting divided city of Berlin. And he was able to resume his college-level courses almost immediately. He was currently involved in basic marketing and business management.

He made friends easily in his new situation and was appointed as a squad leader in a rifle platoon, part of the occupation and the defense of Berlin against Russian uprisings or invasions. Nightlife was far more desirable here than in his old situations in Heidelberg and Baumholder. Quickly, he discovered two favorite hangouts, the Resi Bar and the Rex Casino.

Resi Bar was a one-of-a-kind nightspot, featuring the ultimate in communication systems between tables. Each one was equipped with a telephone, a pad and pencil, a vacuum-tube message system, and personal couriers. If a customer at one table eyed a customer at another table who seemed attractive and eager, it was easy to call the person by phone or send a message in another way since the table number was displayed prominently over each table. Hustling a girl at another table was made almost as easy as snapping a finger.

The Rex Casino was more traditional. It had been a gambling casino in the earlier days of Hitler's Third Reich, but now it was simply a popular bar and dance floor catering mostly to American soldiers, with no gambling. A disk jockey was on duty to play records. Casey preferred it because it was closer to his barracks and was generally a quieter place to socialize.

He met a German girl at Rex Casino named Greta Ohlow and spent quite a lot of time with her. After their third encounter, which was a formal date, he had a visit the next day at his work location from army CID agents, whose job it was to investigate matters of security. They asked him if he had long-term intentions with Fraulein Ohlow, and he immediately took offense, saying, "What business is that of yours? That's my own private business."

They calmly delivered their answer, and it was disturbing to him. "Sergeant Cannon, she is suspected of being a Russian agent, or at least she is known to feed the information she gathers at the Rex Casino to the Russians. We simply wanted to warn you to be careful in what you say to her and what information you give her."

Oh my God, Casey thought. *I'm taking a bad chance and didn't even know it.* He changed his attitude quickly and calmed down. "Thank you very much for the warning," he said. "I won't be spending any more time with her. You can count on it." Little did they know just how much he appreciated their timely contact with him. The last thing he needed was to be noticed by anyone who talked frequently to Russian agents. The incident spooked him so badly that he stayed away from the Rex for weeks.

Months later, he met another Berlin girl who took a special interest in him. After two dates, he contacted the same agents and asked them if she was okay. The answer came back that she was clean. Her name was Annalisa Schule. She was attractive and let him know early that she planned to marry an American soldier so that she could move to the States to live.

Her marriage plans put him off to some distance, but she was persistent. She told him, "You are very attractive and I will sleep with you anytime you want, but you must marry me first." He laughed every time she said it, but apparently she was serious about it. Eventually, several weeks after they met, he was at her house in East Berlin and her older brother showed up. She introduced him as a priest although he was not dressed as one. She said, "CC, I have asked my brother here to marry us, and that's why he is here today."

The brother, Herman, laughed and said, "I started to be a priest and studied for more than a year, but I have dropped out of the seminary. It was too demanding and too serious and I decided to do other things with my life."

Annalisa persisted. "Herman, you will please marry us now."

Casey looked at Herman, who winked at him, while saying, "Okay, stand here in front of me." They did as they were told, and Herman said a few words, ending with "I now declare CC and Annalisa to be man and wife. You may now kiss Annalisa and treat her as your wife." And he laughed as he said it.

Annalisa took Casey by the hand and disappeared with him into a nearby bedroom, where they spent the remainder of the afternoon.

When the day was over, Casey didn't know what to make of it all. Before they parted and he traveled back to his barracks, she said to him, "Casey, I am now your dutiful wife and will love, obey, and be your wife when you need me to be one. Thank you for everything. See you the next time."

Arlene Cushman was flourishing as a student in Columbia and found that she was popular among her classmates, friends, and sorority sisters. An attractive boy from Spartanburg took a fancy to her and asked her out for every fraternity party and every sports event held at the stadium or at the gymnasium. And they went and had enjoyed herself when she was with him, but something inside her made her withhold a part of her. This relationship went on for the better part of three years until he finally pushed her to elevate her closeness to him to a point that might lead to intimacy or to a marriage proposal.

She sensed his intentions but had always cut him off when he got too close to declaring himself. Finally, she sat him down on a Saturday afternoon after a football game to clarify matters.

"Tom," she began. "I have always had gobs of fun with you and you will always be one of the best friends I've ever had. We've been all over this campus and seen everything together and experienced all that it has to offer. But I can tell that you want to take our good relationship to another level, another plateau. I think I need to tell you that I'm not ready to go beyond where we are right now. You are so much more mature about what you want to do in the future, and I am so childish and uncertain about the same things. You pretty much know what you want out of the future, and I don't. I don't see myself getting there anytime soon, and I'm sorry about that. Can we at least always be good friends?"

Tom was downcast with her answer but smiled and said, "Of course." Later the same day, after their date was over and she was back in her dorm room alone, she wondered to herself and actually said it out loud, "While I was saying those words to Tom, why was the image of Casey stuck in the front of my mind?"

Casey was progressing nicely in his army career and was promoted to SFC E-6 and was an important squad leader in his unit. His superiors were pressing him to make a declaration of his intent to stay in the army for twenty years. This meant another extension of his enlistment contract. If he did as they asked, he might be able to hide out safely in Berlin for another number of years. He was almost finished with his business courses and had done well with his education by correspondence. Of course, in Berlin, many of his courses were taken at night and in person with real instructors in real classrooms.

The international political situation had also imposed itself on the city of Berlin. The Russians and East Germans had recently built the Berlin Wall, effectively cordoning off the East Berliners from fleeing into the West or even visiting the West. One major effect on Casey was to separate him from his "wife," Annalisa. To him, it looked to be a solution to a growing problem. She still wanted to move to the United States with an American soldier, but it had become clearer to Casey that just about any old American soldier could fill that need. He learned that he was not all that special to her, that he had simply filled her need at the time. She was trapped in East Berlin by the new Wall, having no realistic means of escape. And he felt pretty sure that they were not really married. She had kidded about it when they talked on the telephone and seemed to accept it as well.

There were other immediate effects of the Berlin crisis. Thousands of American soldiers were sent to West Germany as a show of force to the Russians, and a few thousand of these were assigned to West Berlin. Also, President John Kennedy visited the divided city in the summer of 1963, and security issues got very serious for a time to ensure the president's safety. Casey's battalion was fortunate to not be directly involved in his historic visit. Television cameras were everywhere, and Casey began to realize that he was exposed to their view several times per day for over a week. He did not want his location to be discovered by viewers back home in the States so he hid out at every opportunity.

This brief crisis in his life ended without his exposure, but later in the year, the president was assassinated in Dallas by Harvey Oswald, and all troops in Europe were placed on permanent alert status for a while. A lot of American troops were coming and going from the United States as the country's military leadership seemed to be uncertain as to how best to organize itself to provide both Europe and our home country with security.

One day in 1964, he heard another sergeant, a friend from another company in a nearby kaserne, speak jokingly of a new lieutenant in their organization whose name was Lieutenant Spooky. Casey's antenna went up, making him respond, and he said, "That's pretty funny. This new Lieutenant Spooky, is that his real name?"

The answer came back. "No, they just call him that. He said that's been his nickname for his whole life. The name tag on his uniform says Weeks. So I'm guessing he is really Lieutenant Weeks."

Casey's blood ran cold for a few seconds. He tried not to overreact, but finally said, "Interesting. Where's he from? What's he like?"

The other NCO said, "He's pretty nice. A Southern boy, product of ROTC. Maybe North or South Carolina or even Georgia. Southern accent. Can't tell much yet."

Casey was focused as he had not been for a while. Before the day was over, he sneaked away from his duties and walked to where he knew he would be able to observe the other company in a mandatory afternoon formation, about five hundred yards away. He took binoculars with him and stood in the shadows in a copse of trees at the edge of the parade grounds. He scanned the leadership positions of platoon leaders with the binoculars until he stopped suddenly.

"Bingo," he mumbled to himself. "There he is. Spooky Weeks, Harry Odell Weeks Jr. of Aiken, South Carolina, oldest son of former Mayor Weeks." *Boy,* his thoughts continued. *What bad luck. I can't let him see me in Berlin. If I'm discovered, all of Aiken may know by tomorrow that Casey Gannon has been found.* He shivered at the thought. And he sneaked back to his company area almost in a panic and with his mind racing.

Fortunately, the last day of his current enlistment was scheduled for three weeks in the future. Casey knew that he would have to lie low and hide out as much as possible until then. He immediately visited the first sergeant of his company and told him of his plans to leave the service and go back into civilian life. The sergeant said, "Cannon, the boss is gonna be upset. You are really good at this stuff. Are you sure? Are you positive you want me to start outprocessing you? You've got a good future in this man's army."

Casey answered him, "Yes, sir, I think I'm done. Best eight years of my life though. It's time to move on to the next big thing."

Two weeks later, having successfully dodged being seen by Lt. Spooky Weeks, Casey had turned in all of his equipment, sold his car, and quietly said his goodbyes to his friends and his troops. Then he flew out of Berlin Tempelhof to Frankfurt, then on to Fort Hamilton, New York, for his final departure from the army. He was back in the United States for the first time in more than seven years. While the paperwork processing was being finalized, he sat in his hotel room on the base, watching out a large window, the Verrazano-Narrows suspension bridge being completed just overhead.

He had thought long and hard about what to do next, and he was certain of his decision as he boarded a jet flying from the recently renamed JFK Airport on Long Island to Phoenix, Arizona, where he hoped to melt into the landscape, continuing to lead a life safe for himself and his aunt and uncle. He departed the army with a final check for over $4,000, mostly from unused leave he had cashed in. A new life awaited.

REVELATION AND RESURRECTION

Chapter 24

Casey celebrated his fifty-second birthday in July 1990, and his employees gave him a small birthday party in their "break room" in the back of the main store. He had owned High Sierra Trading Company for a dozen years, having bought it from his old boss, who had retired.

His civilian life had mostly followed a straight line toward success. After returning to the States in 1964, Casey returned to the Phoenix area to continue his life there in some form to be determined after he got there. He brought with him the equivalent of three years' credit in college courses aimed at business management, accounting, and marketing. He was hired during his first interview and started out as a salesclerk in a store specializing in Western wear for men and women in the southwest. It was an upscale one-store operation called High Sierra Sportswear.

After a few weeks there, the store owner realized that he had found a gem of an employee in C. C. Cannon. He began to groom him for larger duties, and within a year, a new store was opened in nearby Scottsdale, and Casey managed it successfully to the point that it outgrew the main store in Phoenix. Each time the company tried a new ploy, a new product line, or a new marketing approach, it seemed to work. Over a number of years, rewards came in the form of salary increases, more responsibility, and a minority ownership position in the company. As retirement for the owner neared, Casey was given the opportunity to buy the entire corporation over a ten-year period, which he seized upon, moving the headquarters from Phoenix to Scottsdale.

By 1990, the operation had grown into a small chain of eight stores, all in Arizona and New Mexico. Casey had found his own understudy, one Randolph "Randy" Rivers, who was so invaluable that Casey had already sold him a 20 percent stake in the business. Life was good and the business was continuing to thrive.

The day after his birthday party, his secretary walked into his office in midmorning and said, "Casey, someone is here to see you. Says he's an old friend. I can't swear to that because I don't recognize him."

"Okay," Casey said while not even looking up. "Show him in."

Zach Kessler walked into his office and said, "Hey, good buddy, I'm so glad it's you." Casey almost fainted from the shock when he heard the voice and saw who it was. He had been hiding for so long that the suddenness of Zach's appearance stunned him into silence and fear.

Zach held both hands and arms up and said quickly, "Please don't run away. I can see the shock on your face, but please relax. You're totally safe. We have a lot to talk about." Then he paused for a few seconds and added, "I was 99 percent sure that when I rounded that corner at the door I was gonna see my old buddy and friend, Casey Gannon. I am so relieved to see you and see that you're looking so good and prosperous."

Casey caught his breath and allowed the tension to subside a little. He finally was able to say, "Zach, I think I want to say that I'm happy to see you, but it all depends on what you meant when you said, 'you're totally safe.'"

Zach sensed that he needed to go slower, but he quickly said, "I need to give you some time to adjust to seeing me. Let me say clearly and quickly that my daddy's dead and that nobody from Russia or the KGB or an assassination squad is looking for you. Does it make you relax some to hear me say those words?"

Finally, Casey grinned very broadly and deeply when he heard those last words, and tears quickly formed in the corners of his eyes. "I can't tell you what a relief it is to hear somebody say that, and especially to hear it from you, of all people."

Zach stepped over to Casey's desk to shake his hand, and both now were standing face-to-face. Zach threw his arms around his friend and hugged him warmly, saying, "I now know everything that happened that day in 1956 and I'm so sorry for what my father did to you and to our country." Casey was hugging back as Zach's words spilled out.

Casey invited Zach to sit down. He looked at his friend, now thirty-four years older since he had last seen him, and said, "I'm still in shock. Can you tell me how in the hell you came to be sitting here in my office? I have to say I had no idea when I woke up this morning that my life was about to change again this drastically. How did you find me? How long did it take you to find me? How long have you been looking for me?"

Zach started his answer. "You probably remember that I was never very close with my father as I was growing up. That never changed at all after you left. I was never able to build that close relationship that most children can do with their fathers. We just went our separate ways. Several weeks ago, I got a phone call at work from University Hospital in Augusta. They said that Wade Kessler had a bad heart attack and didn't have much time to live and that he was asking for me. They said he needed to talk to me before he died. I live in northern Virginia and work in Washington DC, so I jumped on an airplane that afternoon and flew to Augusta.

"When I got to his room in the hospital, he was hooked up to all kinds of machines in the CCU and could barely talk beyond a whisper. He was already pretty far gone, but he was conscious. He made the nurses leave the room so that we could talk privately. Then he told me everything that happened that first of June 1956. He told me that he had been working for the Soviets for a long time, selling them nuclear information, and that you had accidentally found his three passports there in Aiken. Casey, I wanted to punch the son of a bitch right then, but I kept listening. He told me that he tried to kill you when you wouldn't give the passports back, but his shot missed. He told me that you happened to have your rifle with you and had shot him twice to neutralize him, and rifle-butted him when he tried to charge at you.

"He told me that he made threats to you about your own life, about Jake and Annie Lou's life, and even Arlene Cushman's life. He convinced you, he said, that Soviet agents would be chasing after you until they caught you and killed you and that they might just kill your aunt and uncle anyway even if they didn't find you.

"I asked him why he spied against our own country, and his answer was that he had been influenced toward Communism and against capitalism when he was in college. I asked why he didn't make things right with you, and he said at first he was afraid of the repercussions of getting caught as a spy and that toward the end, he wanted to make it up to you but had no idea where you were or how to find you. He told me that the fall of the Berlin Wall last year finally convinced him that Communism was a failed system and that it was never going to succeed as he originally thought it would.

"He also surprised me with a really interesting piece of information. He said that my mother, whom I had always been told died in childbirth while trying to have a sister for me, actually died of a suicide. She had discovered that my dad was spying back in Oak Ridge, and she couldn't bear the thought of having married a spy. So she ended her own life to escape from the situation. That was all new information for me.

"He remembered that just before you left him alone in the toolhouse you asked him if I knew that he was a spy, and he told you that I didn't know anything about it. That was true. I didn't know anything. Maybe I should have, but I didn't. One last thing he told me was that he had tried to become a more religious man in his later years—he called it the Aiken influence—and that had led him to having a guilty conscience about spying and particularly what he had done to you and your family. He said, and these are his exact words, Casey, 'I want you to find Casey Gannon for me and apologize to him. I should have never let this thing go on this long. I ruined that boy's life.' And then he told me that he had rewritten his last will to leave some money in it for you. He left you $50,000 I found out later when his will was read."

The story paused there, and both men sat back and absorbed the words just said. Casey sighed and said, "Zach, I can feel the tension leaving my body right now. It's a healing thing to hear what has happened and realize that the long, hidden part of my life just ended. The employees I have in this company, all seventy-five of them, have no idea about my Aiken life or my life as a young baseball player. I've had to hide all of that. They only know that I came out of the army and ended up in this business. My background has been unspoken."

His mind came back to practical matters. He asked, "Does anybody in Aiken know about this and about what you just told me?"

"No," Zach answered. "I haven't told anybody but my wife and my boss in Washington about why I needed to take this trip. I wanted to make certain that I had found the correct man first."

Casey asked, "Zach, I think I need to go to Aiken right away. Are you prepared to go with me?"

Zach answered, "Yes, I figured we would need to do that pretty quick. We need to clear your name there and let certain people know what happened. By the way, have you had any news about your aunt and uncle?"

"Of course I haven't. How would I know anything about them?"

"Oh right," Zach said. "You haven't exactly been in close contact, have you? When I was in Aiken recently to settle my dad's affairs, I found out that they don't live next door to the Kessler house anymore. They sold their house and moved somewhere into downtown. I was also told that Jake has some kind of health problem."

That comment got Casey's attention. "I'm sorry to hear that. I want to go to Aiken as soon as possible to see my family. And I need to dig up those three passports. They will verify everything you said and all that happened that day."

Zach was surprised. "You mean you still have the passports? Where are they?"

"They never left Aiken. We need to visit Sand River one more time together, this time with a good shovel and maybe a metal detector."

He called in his no. 2, Randy Rivers, and told him that he would be flying east to South Carolina the next day and would be gone for at least a week.

Randy answered him, "Not a problem. You know I'll take care of everything."

Casey called in his secretary and asked her to make the flight arrangements from Phoenix to Augusta, Georgia, for the next day. She assured him that she would do it.

She also took orders for lunch to be brought in for Zach and Casey.

When lunch arrived, she set it up on his small conference table and left the room, closing his office door. "You look like you all want to talk some more, so I'll leave you alone and hold all your calls."

They chatted their way through lunch while munching on sandwiches and sipping on Cokes. They were slowly but surely getting back to the close relationship they had known years ago. Casey spoke up. "I thought I was well hidden and had just about convinced myself that I couldn't be found. How in the world did you find me?"

Zach laughed and said, "You did a good job of hiding, so it wasn't that easy. And once I gave it some serious thought, I realized that I am one of the few people with the resources to find you as quickly as I did."

"How did you?" Casey insisted again.

"You don't know this, but I majored in statistical analysis at Clemson. Never did make it to Athens. When I graduated, I took a number of actuarial jobs at insurance companies, but somehow, after a few years, I ended up working for the Social Security Administration in DC. My wife and I live in Alexandria, just south of Washington.

"My father died, and that happened the day after he told me everything, but he had begged me to go find you somehow. I discussed the need to find you with my staff and my boss in Washington without giving them the exact reasons. I just told them it was important to me personally. They suggested that I could use the huge data banks of the millions of people paying into Social Security to see where you were located. So I took their advice, and at nights and on weekends, I started searching, first for Casey Carter Gannon. Well, that guy does not exist anywhere in our files. So I looked for various combinations, using initials, or no initials, etc. Nothing. Then I remembered that I knew your date of birth to be July 1, 1938, so I printed out a list of every person in the USA who was born on that date and who paid into Social Security, or who had paid in but was already dead. There were hundreds of these to look through, but still no Casey Gannon anywhere. After working with these files for a week or two, I kept seeing the name 'C. C. Cannon' on the list, but it meant nothing to me. Finally, in desperation, I looked at that specific file in greater detail and discovered that the full name of that person was Casey Carter Cannon. I'm thinking to myself that this is too much of a coincidence because my old friend was Casey Carter Gannon. Very close. I was able to reconstruct that Cannon didn't even get a card until right after the important June 1, 1956 date, the date you made your escape out of Aiken.

"Then I saw a steady pattern of social security contributions first in Arizona, then in Colorado, and ultimately from army sources in Germany. After Germany, everything shifted back here to Arizona."

"I finally surmised that it had to be you, but I couldn't prove it. I have an old buddy from college who lives in Phoenix, so I called him and asked a favor. Go over to this High Sierra Company in Scottsdale, I asked him, and find out if the owner is a big guy, around fifty years old, about six foot four, and weighs about two hundred pounds. He came to your store and identified you as Cannon, the owner, and verified your size and approximate age. He called and told me what he found. I concluded it almost had to be you. Soon after that, here I am in your office. I was afraid to call first because I didn't want to scare you into disappearing again. How'd I do in tracking you?"

"Good God, Zach," exclaimed Casey. "You ought to be a detective, not a statistician. You didn't miss a thing."

They spent the remainder of the afternoon comparing notes and catching up with each other. After Aiken High School, neither one of them had ever played baseball again. Then Zach asked a big question, "Casey, are you married or have you been?"

Casey laughed and said, "Yes, er . . . uh, no."

Zach laughed too. "Just what the hell does that mean?"

"I had a Mulligan marriage," Casey said and laughed again.

Zach was puzzled. "Wait a minute. A Mulligan is the first shot on the first tee of a friendly golf round. It's a stroke that doesn't count against your score."

"That's what I said. I had a Mulligan 'marriage' in Germany over thirty years ago that did not count. No real marriage, just a Mulligan."

They both enjoyed a big laugh over that. Zach got serious again. "Tell me why you didn't just go back to Aiken and take your chances with going up against my dad. Couldn't you have taken those passports to the cops anywhere or the FBI or any number of law enforcement agencies? Or when you were in the army? Or when you got out of the army? Didn't you have a large number of opportunities to turn him in?"

Casey's entire exile turned on this very point, and he had given it a lot of thought ever since that June day when he disappeared. He was ready with his answer. "Yeah, I guess you could say that I had opportunities. But your dad was very, very convincing when he told me about the larger Russian operation in Aiken and the worldwide assassination squads who would kill my uncle Jake and my aunt Annie Lou without batting an eye. I was overwhelmingly sold on the idea that my turning in your dad was the same thing as allowing my aunt and uncle to be killed, if not immediately, then at any convenient time later. As simple as that. I was totally protective of them because of the way they took me in back in 1948, when I became an orphan. My only leverage was keeping Wade Kessler's passports and holding them over his head forever. In my mind, that would keep all three of us alive indefinitely."

Zach said, "Well, it worked. My dad said he had heard from you several times over the years, particularly at first. Is that true? He said he got some letters from you. How did you manage that and not have him track you down?"

Casey explained the letter ruse he had used by asking departing GIs to mail letters for him once they were back in the States. Zach thought it was a clever thing to do to remind Wade Kessler that the pressure was still on him to stay in line and not revert to his old ways. It had to be disconcerting to get a letter like that from Texas, then Delaware, then Tennessee, and Alabama.

Chapter 25

Late the next afternoon, their Delta flight landed in Augusta, and Zach rented a car at the Hertz counter. In a few minutes, they were driving toward Aiken on the once-familiar Aiken-Augusta highway. Casey noted very quickly that the limited-access highway had become almost the opposite—it was now unlimited access with businesses and driveways and crossroads running in many directions.

As they drove into Aiken, Casey recognized where he was most of the time, but he was also struck that changes were everywhere. Zach drove straight to his old house on Highland Park Drive because he owned it now that his father had passed away. Nostalgia swept over both of them as they parked at the top of the driveway. The basketball goal was still there but had seen better days. The net was rotted out and gone.

Once they were inside, Casey finally realized that he was finally home in Aiken. "What do you want to do first, Casey? This is your party, your homecoming, not mine. What's first?"

"I really want to see my aunt and uncle first. I owe that to them, to make them first on the list. Where do they live now? Do you know?" Casey asked.

Zach already had the phone book in his hand and was looking for Jacob Gannon. "Here it is. Sand River Court. I'll call them for you."

Casey interrupted. "Tell them you're in town for a quick visit and want to come by for a few minutes to bring a surprise."

"Good idea," Zach said and dialed the number. Annie Lou Gannon answered, was thrilled to hear from him, and agreed to see Zach for a few minutes.

They drove to downtown Aiken, only a mile or two away. Casey was drinking in the sights as they moved along. Sand River Court was the only street in a small neighborhood called Sand River Condominiums, just off Laurens Street. It was near the post office and just behind the federal courthouse. He noticed that something was missing. "Where's the Presbyterian church? It's gone."

Zach answered, "Don't know. Remember, I haven't lived here for a long time either."

He parked the rental car in front of the Gannon home, and both men went to the front door. Casey stood to one side, smelling the tea olive nearby, while Zach rang the doorbell. They could hear footsteps inside just before Annie Lou opened the door.

She smiled broadly at the sight of Zach and said, "Just having you in Aiken is a big surpr—"

And that was the first second she saw someone else standing off to one side. She looked. "Oh my God, oh my God, I can't believe it. Casey, is it you? I'm dreaming, I know it. Thank you, Jesus, my prayers are answered." And she buried her head into his chest as he wrapped his arms around her.

She sobbed into Casey's chest for a full five minutes, with Zach standing by like an extra thumb on a butcher. He finally asked, "Hey, y'all, can we go inside to do this? My foot's gone to sleep."

Annie Lou stopped crying and started to laugh. "Oh God, it feels good to laugh. I haven't laughed for such a long time. And you," she said as she punched Zach's arm. "You just about gave an old woman a heart attack. You and your surprises!"

They went inside and sat down in the living room. Annie Lou could not stop grinning. Still holding Casey's hand, she offered Cokes for everybody and then sought them in the kitchen. "So where do we start, boys?" she asked. "How do we pick up all the pieces? I don't even know where to start. I'm so overwhelmed. And I'm so happy to see both of you."

"Aunt Annie Lou—" Casey started up, when she interrupted him.

"Casey, I'm now seventy-four years old and you ought to be fifty-two. I wish I could get you to call me Annie from now on. You too, Zach. I'm just Annie."

"Okay," Casey said. "That feels strange, but you've got a deal. Annie, I want Zach to spend the next few minutes telling you why I left all those years ago and how I am now free to come back. It's better if you hear it from him first. I'll jump in to fill in the parts where he gets off track or messes up the details."

Zach started up with "Take a deep breath. This is gonna shock you, Annie, but it turns out that my daddy was a Russian spy and Casey was the one who found out his secret on that sad day after graduation in 1956 . . ." And went on from there.

A full thirty minutes later, he was winding down his explanation after multiple questions by Annie and numerous insertions by Casey. "So you're telling me that my life was in great danger all those years and Casey's possession of the three passports is all that stood between me and being murdered by the Russians?"

Zach answered by saying, "That's about it. I really don't know how much real power my daddy had in being able to cause the assassinations of Americans that he threatened because he never elaborated on that part to me, but there is no question that he was a spy for the Soviet Union and that he traveled there at least once or twice a year to sell them secrets. He admitted that much to me as he was dying."

She looked at Casey for the hundredth time that afternoon and said, "Casey, Jake and I knew, *we just knew*, that you had good reasons for shooting Wade Kessler and that you had good reasons for staying gone and not contacting us, and you are telling me that we were right all along. You were protecting us the whole time. We should've known that it was about some kind of threat to all of us, but we never dreamed the truth about Wade. How could we have ever guessed that?"

"The truth is that you couldn't," Casey answered. "When I learned it that day, I had an impossible time even believing it. I can't wait to tell Uncle Jake. Where is he?"

Annie looked at him sadly and said, "Oh, Casey, he's in Mattie Hall Nursing Home. He had a stroke about four months ago. He's not in good shape, but he will want to see you and hear about all of this. I'm so worried about him, but your being back here will cheer him up for sure. He's partially paralyzed and has lost a lot of his ability to speak, but his mind is still there. We'll go see him tomorrow morning and tell him everything."

Annie insisted that Casey stay with her in one of the upstairs bedrooms in her condominium. He accepted immediately, asking Zach to please understand. They drove back to Zach's house to get his suitcase and made arrangements to meet the next day for visits to the police station and to do some digging in Sand River. Zach dropped Casey off at Annie's front door and left.

It was almost dark when she said, "I don't feel like cooking tonight. Why don't we go out for supper so we can talk some more?"

"Sure," he said. "What do you have in mind?"

She explained, "Downtown Aiken changed a lot in the years since you've been gone, and we have several good restaurants within walking distance from right here. I was thinking we could eat at Up Your Alley."

"That's a restaurant?" Casey asked. "Pretty catchy name."

"Oh yes," she said. "And the food's good too."

"Okay, Annie," he answered, "but I'm buying."

They departed from the condo and walked to Laurens Street and then toward the downtown shopping area. As they passed across Park Avenue, he pointed left and said, "You sure don't have to walk far to the post office."

"That's not the post office anymore. That has moved. This is now a photography studio. Can't mail stuff there anymore."

As they passed by Julia's Dress Shop, Casey said, "Hey, you know what's different? Parking meters. This place used to have a meter in front of every parking place. That's a big improvement that they're gone."

When they turned right at Lionel Smith Ltd. into the Alley, Casey smiled when he saw the changes. He couldn't resist saying, "This was once the dirtiest, filthiest part of Aiken. Look at this! It's beautiful now!"

The Alley

Before they entered Up Your Alley restaurant, he paused and looked around. Pointing, he said, "The Aiken Police Department used to be right there. Gone, but gone where?"

"Not too far away, on Laurens. This building here is still city hall, or at least the rear of it, but the police and fire departments merged about twenty years ago and moved to a new building on top of the hill on Laurens. It's called Aiken Public Safety now, and the cops and firemen are cross-trained to do each other's jobs. The police chief is Carroll Busbee."

Over a dinner of steaks and baked potatoes, they caught up on a lot of small talk. He told her all about his life on the run and how afraid he was in the beginning. He had gambled with regard to Wade Kessler and the passports and he was never sure if he had escaped free and clear, or if a team of Russian assassins were only a step behind him. He spent a good part of the evening reminding her that he had always wanted to return to Aiken, and he missed them terribly. Now it was a reality.

She said, "I know that tomorrow you have to visit with the police to clear your name, but we need to go see Jake first. He's going to be so glad to see you."

"I'll be happy to see him too. First thing tomorrow morning. Now, different subject. I'm almost afraid to ask," Casey timidly said. "But have you kept up with Arlene Cushman? Is she still around here?"

"No, I haven't seen her for several years. Last time I heard anything, she was teaching English at South Aiken High School. Oh yeah, we have two high schools now. South Aiken is out where Robbins Trailer City used to be."

As they were walking the short distance back to her condominium, Annie asked, "How long are you planning to stay in Aiken? I realize you have other responsibilities in running your clothing business."

"I'll stay a few days for sure, maybe even a week," he answered. "I want to make sure I do all the unfinished things I can think of. I don't want to leave anything or anybody out."

"I understand," she said. "And I want to catch you up on the changes in Aiken since you left. There has been a bunch of them."

After breakfast the next morning, she drove them to Mattie Hall to see Jake. Annie made Casey wait in the hall while she went inside Jake's room.

"Jake, it's Annie," she said quietly. "I'm right here to see you. I brought you a little surprise this morning."

Jake was immobilized, lying on his back. He opened his eyes from a light sleep. "Hey, lady," he said slowly with a pronounced slur. "What surprise?"

She continued. "You know, Jake, how we always prayed for a miracle that would bring Casey back to us, and how we never understood why the prayers didn't work? Well, they did work." She beckoned to Casey. "Come on in here and let Jake see you."

Casey walked in and went straight over to the bedside, leaned over, and kissed Jake on his forehead. "I have really missed the two of you," he said quietly.

The joy on Jake's face was unmistakable. The corners of his mouth turned up slightly, and tears ran from the corners of his eyes. "Casey, Casey, where you been?" he uttered very slowly.

Annie spoke up. "Jake, Casey wants to tell you himself why he left Aiken so suddenly and why he came back. Do you want to hear the story?"

"Story? Oh yeah, oh yeah," he slurred. "Tell story."

Casey pulled a chair up close to the bedside, grabbed Jake's hand, and started talking. "That day after I graduated, I was home by myself and was shooting baskets outside when the ball banged against the Kesslers' toolhouse and dislodged three little booklets from a crack in the siding . . ."

Casey then led Jake and Annie through shooting Wade Kessler, his threats against the Gannon family, driving madly through the night to Jacksonville, the days of hitchhiking to Arizona, joining the army, spending almost eight years in Germany, seeing his father's grave in Luxembourg, almost getting married in Berlin, and resuming his life in the

Southwest that resulted in owning his own business there. He spoke for over half an hour before stopping.

Jake was attentive until the very end. He finally said, "Baseball, no more baseball?"

Casey shook his head from side to side. "Never got to play baseball again," he said quietly.

Jake wailed as if in pain. "So sad, so sad," he muttered, with tears once again running down his face.

"Jake, I was happy to be able to protect you and Annie. If that meant no more baseball, so be it. It was worth the sacrifice to keep you safe from those Russians. I would do it all again to keep all of us safe. You and Annie had loved me with no conditions while I was with you back then. The least that I could do was to protect you and show you that I loved you right back."

Jake calmed down after that and allowed silence to prevail for a few minutes. Then he slurred a few words directly in Annie's direction. "Car. Farmers Merchants."

She picked up on his meaning. "Casey, Jake wants you to know that he got your car back from Jacksonville and we stored it for a while, but it was deteriorating rapidly and not being driven, so Jake sold it for two hundred dollars and put the money in your bank account. Also, your mama's insurance money that we put in the bank when you first came here? Well, it's still all there, plus the interest it earned. We did pay taxes on the interest for you, but there's a tidy sum in there just waiting for you to claim it."

Jake had listened as closely as he could and had one more thing to say. "Police. Go see. Fix all of it."

Casey understood. "I will go clear things up with them today. You are right, I have to clear my name with them for the laws they think I broke in 1956. It's very high on my list."

Casey leaned down to the bedridden Jake and hugged him as best he could, and Jake tried to hug back. Then the visit and reunion was over for now with Jake.

When they arrived back at Sand River Condominiums, Zach was waiting in his car for them. Inside the condo, Casey took the time to call his company in Scottsdale to check on everything there. They had it all under good control, he was told.

Annie had already decided that she needed to accompany the men to the police station because some of the policemen knew her personally and she could vouch for the pair, who would possibly be strangers to almost everyone they met.

When Zach parked the car out in front of the Public Safety Building, on Laurens, Casey had an immediate question. "Annie, where is that old standpipe I used to play on? Wasn't it right here, in that median?" he asked while pointing. "And the Marvin house was right over there where that building is. Am I remembering it right?"

She answered him, "Yes, you are remembering it correctly. The standpipe came down in the early 1970s. I heard somebody say it was rusting out. And the Public Safety Building was put here at about that same time. I heard that the Marvin house was infested with termites, but nobody ever proved that to me. It was such a beautiful Victorian house. That building sitting there is now our main post office."

The three went inside and asked to speak to the ranking policeman on duty. Within a few minutes, a uniformed lieutenant came out and recognized Annie Gannon.

She told him that the three of them were there together and needed to make some statements that would clear some old crimes off the books. "Could we have a meeting with you in a conference room with a stenographer to take notes? All three of us will be making extensive statements, sworn statements if you want." She introduced Casey and Zach and indicated that the "criminal" was Casey, but that it was an old complicated case.

He led them to a conference room and called for a team to join him in order to record sworn testimony and statements. When everyone was assembled, Annie started the process by saying, "Casey Gannon is my nephew, and he was accused in 1956 of assault and battery, using a firearm in the city, and some other things. He has returned to Aiken and wants to clear his name. He and his friend, Zach Kessler, will be doing most of the talking, and it is a very interesting story. The crimes were committed against Wade Kessler, an engineer out at the plant. Zach is his son and, Zach, I think it makes more sense for you to talk first, then, Casey, you can add yours."

She sat back as Zach started his narrative. Within ten minutes, he stopped and Casey told his version of June 1, 1956, and what he had done afterward.

When they were finished, the police lieutenant said, "Quite a tale. Casey, in your statement, you indicated that you believe you can lead us to the passports buried under the sand in Sand River in the Hitchcock Woods. Are you ready to look for them today? It would make the entire story more believable if we had those passports."

"Yes, sir, I believe I can. As you know, it's been thirty-four years. But if you also have a metal detector, it might make everything go easier and faster."

"Okay, prepare to go over there with us in a police car, thirty minutes from now. That will give me time to round up the equipment, plus a photographer to make a complete record of what we'll be doing."

Annie was dropped off at her condo, but a two-car caravan followed Casey's instructions about driving on Highland Park

Avenue and stopping and parking at a certain point, the same place he temporarily parked his Ford the night he buried the rifle and Mason jar. Two policemen, one stenographer, one photographer, and Zach and Casey made up the entire party entering Hitchcock Woods.

Casey led the way because only he knew where he was going. He was nervous because it all looked so different now. Trees were large, some were missing, new shrubs had appeared, and new mature trees had grown up. He finally reached Sand River and turned toward where the fallen tree had lay part of the way across the sandy expanse. The tree was totally gone, totally rotted away, and no longer in evidence. The sand also looked different. Was there less of it? he asked himself.

The small party sensed his uncertainty. He decided to look all around in a more general sense and tried to place himself in a spot that would be on top of where he had actually dug his hole.

He said to the metal detector operator, "Turn your detector on and scan ten feet in every direction from where I'm standing."

While this was going on, Casey walked over to the side of the riverbed and looked along the bank for where the base of the tree might have been when it fell. He thought he saw a depression where the root ball could have popped out of the ground and eventually rotted. This made Casey recalibrate his bearings. He spoke to the operator. "Move about twenty feet more to your right, and scan like mad. As they say in the artillery, 'fire for effect.'"

The operator did as he was told, and within seconds, he said, "Something's right under here."

Zach had brought a short-handled spade and started to dig. "How deep did you dig that night, Casey?"

"About two feet," Casey responded.

Within one foot, the spade struck a hard object with a thunk. One of the officers moved in and took the shovel. "This might be evidence so let me take it from here," he said.

He dug a few more spades of sand and dropped to his knees, using his hands instead. In another few minutes, he had extracted a very rusty Winchester rifle and a corroded pistol. More sand and more elbow grease were in order.

Casey said, "There should be one more thing in there. You're looking for a full-sized Mason jar. Don't cut your hands if it's broken."

Another two minutes of hand digging was rewarded with the appearance of a very dirty Mason jar. Casey donated a clean white handkerchief to the officer, and the sides were wiped clean enough to see three small curled booklets inside, still dry!

The lieutenant took the jar and immediately tested his ability to open it on the spot, even though the metal cap was badly corroded and discolored. It yielded on his second attempt, and the top was removed. He snaked two fingers inside it and plucked the passports out.

"Casey," he asked, "take a look at these. Are these the same booklets you found at Wade Kessler's house, and the same booklets that you placed in a Mason jar on June first, 1956?"

Casey took the booklets and leafed through each one, examining the photographs and the stamps of each one. "These are the same passports. I stuffed them in this jar years ago in 1956."

"Congratulations," the lieutenant said. "I believe that every judge in the country would say 'case dismissed.' We'll take this evidence to the chief and the head prosecutor, and I believe they'll be dropping all charges as soon as they hear the entire story."

That is precisely what was accomplished, and by the end of the day no less. Zach dropped Casey off at Annie's condominium and drove away, happy in the knowledge that some stories, tedious and haphazard and swinging from one extreme to the other, do end happily. His friend, Casey, was fully exonerated and had his name cleared that same day.

Casey gave Annie the news, and she was not surprised. "After I heard the whole thing myself, I knew how it was all going to come out. There's no way a logical person could decide otherwise."

It was close to dinnertime, and Casey said, "Annie, I'm getting pretty hungry, and as much as I'd like to wolf down some of your great cooking, I feel like a little bit of a celebration. Just you and me. The food last night was excellent at the Alley. You got any more good places like that?"

She was ready for the question. "There's a new place I've been itching to try but didn't have a good reason. It has Italian food, and it's over near the courthouse and the old Grammar School on Chesterfield, right next to the railroad cut. It's called Olive Oyl, you know, spelled O-Y-L, like Popeye's girlfriend. Let's go there."

Casey answered, "You've got a deal. I'm buying again."

While they were eating lasagna and linguini and sipping on Chianti, Casey asked if he could use her car the next day to do a few personal things. "I'm planning to be gone all day." She agreed.

Chapter 26

The next morning after breakfast, he drove to Farmers and Merchants Bank and introduced himself to a vice president who was on duty. Within an hour, he was able to establish his identity as Casey Gannon, the account holder, even though he carried identification that showed the Cannon name. Phone calls to the police department from the bank straightened this kink out to the satisfaction of the banking officials.

Casey told them that he was leaving all of his money there for the time being. He was also able to ascertain the amount of interest that Jake and Annie had to pay taxes on for all the years he was gone. He wanted to repay them. His account had grown in size tremendously between 1949 and 1990.

Casey had a strong desire to ride around the area all by himself to see how it had changed during his thirty-four-year absence. He drove by the first house the Gannons lived in on Pendleton, then the second house on Newberry, which had been near Aiken High School. Then he drove his paper route and over to Farris Wynn's house. He drove Whiskey Road and the dirt streets in the horse district. He saw what was left of Eustis Park and checked out USC Aiken, which did not really exist during his years in Aiken. On the spur of the moment, he decided to ride to Augusta to check out a few of his old haunts there. In short, he spent several hours driving to every place he had ever visited within the confines of Aiken and Augusta. The changes and the growth amazed him.

He stopped at a gas station and refilled the tank and finally drove back to Sand River Condominiums and parked the car, full of questions about the changes he had seen. He said to Annie, "I just drove all over the place to see what had changed. I even went to Augusta. I'm overwhelmed at how everything looks and feel different now. What happened? What can you tell me about what I saw?"

"I knew this was coming," she said, "from the time you reappeared. I've been trying to organize my thoughts so that I can answer your questions. In fact, many years ago, when I realized you weren't going to come back very quickly, I started clipping things from the paper and throwing them into a file. I need to go get that and then we can talk."

Casey settled down on the sofa and got comfortable while Annie was shuffling her papers and notes. She said, "You mentioned that you went to Augusta. That's a good place to start. I can tell you what's happened to Augusta, and then we can be done with them and move on to Aiken. Except for the Masters Tournament, my opinion is that Augusta is slipping backward some. They're losing a lot of population to Martinez and Evans and even North Augusta and Aiken. People seem to not be flocking to Augusta but to its surrounding area. It has something to do with their politics—the leaders are about half white folks and half black folks—and they never can seem to agree on anything.

"Now the Masters is just the opposite. When you left in 1956, it was a good tournament and an important one, but it was not at the top. Today, in 1990, the Masters may be the most popular golf tournament in this country, maybe even the world. Golfing people can't seem to get enough of it. People come from Europe and Japan just to see it. Tickets are always sold out—heck, you can't even get on the ticket list. They closed the list years ago and said, please don't apply for tickets anymore."

Casey cut in. "I've noticed that CBS television treats the Masters like royalty, and they seem to love to air the action live every year."

"You're absolutely right," Annie agreed. "Let me mention shopping and stores in Augusta. Augusta Mall opened up about three years ago, and it looks like the downtown stores dried up and blew away at just about the same time. Another mall, Regency, opened up and made it even worse. Downtown, Cullum's is gone, J. B. White is gone, Belk's is gone too. And the movie theaters—remember the Miller, the Modjeska, and the Imperial? I believe they're all closed downtown now. Those places you used to take dates to eat? The Varsity and Greene's? All closed up. Gone."

"Boy, I saw that Broad Street looked pretty slow today, but I didn't realize that all of those landmarks were closed or just plain gone." Casey was glum about it.

"Okay," Annie said. "I'll end the Augusta thing by saying this. Remember when everybody in Aiken would drive to Augusta for movies and restaurants and entertainment? Well, it's just about the reverse today. It's common now for Augusta people to drive to Aiken to do things and see things, and even to eat out. Let's move back this way from Augusta and check out Schultz Hill and the valley. On top of the hill overlooking Augusta, I guess you might have noticed that the little airstrip was not there anymore. Bulldozed and ready for other stuff. No more airplanes will be landing there. In the valley, most of the mills have closed or will be closing in the near future. Foreign textile imports are just eating them alive because of cheaper labor overseas.

"On the Aiken-Augusta Road, you might have noticed a complex called Aiken Tech, for Aiken Technical College. That was built in about 1975 and started with two-year programs in nursing, computers, and X-ray technicians. By now, I think they have over a thousand students taking classes there, and it has grown beyond the two-year courses of study."

Casey wanted to interrupt with a thought. "Annie, can you remember when that road was a pretty high-speed limited access highway? I can't believe how they've overexposed that thing with gas stations, drugstores, barbecue joints, and muffler shops. It's pretty crowded and hard to go fifty-five all the way to Augusta."

"Yep, you're right, and it's getting worse," she answered back. "As you get nearer to Aiken, you had to notice Aiken's Beltway, or at least that's what I call it. A road that goes all the way around Aiken. It has different names like University Parkway, Rutland Drive, East Pine Log Road, and Hitchcock Parkway, but they're all connected. Sometimes, it has two lanes and sometimes four, but it makes a complete circle around Aiken of right at seventeen miles. That was put in place in the late 1960s and early 1970s. It comes in very handy at times.

"Casey, you said you drove by USC Aiken today. You passed by it when you drove on the University Parkway part of the Beltway. When you ran away from Aiken, it wasn't even a gleam in the educator's eyes yet. By 1961, it had started up with about 140 students in a few classes at Banksia, one of the Winter Colony houses on Newberry Street. Just eleven years later, they moved into the campus they have now, three miles from downtown, on University Parkway. The student body is several thousand students, and by the way, they have a very good baseball team.

"Right across that same parkway is Aiken Regional Medical Center, which is another way of saying 'the hospital.' Aiken County hospital finally got too crowded and antiquated and had to expand and modernize. They relocated in 1976. You might remember that the hospital was on Richland Avenue, where Vaucluse Road starts. That building now houses most of county government's offices. That's where people pay county taxes and get licenses.

"And speaking of that area, you wouldn't recognize Eustis Park, right behind the old hospital building," she proposed.

"Why?" he asked. "I rode through there today. I couldn't figure out what happened to it."

"It is not an athletic field any longer. No grandstand, no bleachers, no football or baseball fields. Just trees and bushes growing where the infield once was and a few one-story buildings."

"That's so hard to believe," Casey responded. "Back in the day, just about every sporting event and outdoor activity took place in Eustis Park. Where do people go now?"

"Several places," Annie said. "Of course, Aiken High and South Aiken High have their own fields and facilities. Little League and Pee Wee football and county recreational leagues play at a new place called Citizen's Park. It's on East Pine Log Road near Banks Mill Road. Tons of fields and diamonds there.

"I spoke about two high schools. South Aiken opened for business in 1980. I think I told you it was built on the old Robbins Trailer City site on Pine Log Road. Aiken High just got too crowded, and some of the kids had to travel so far to go to school. The county did a lot of things right then with new schools and renaming schools, and closing a few."

She paused for a few seconds and shifted directions. "Have you ever heard of William 'Refrigerator' Perry?"

"Just about everybody knows about him," Casey answered. "He's that huge football player who scored a touchdown for the Chicago Bears in one of the last Super Bowls, and he does Coke commercials on TV, right? Why do you ask?"

Annie laughed. "You don't know, do you? He went to Aiken High just like you did, then on to Clemson, and was a first-round draft pick of Chicago."

"Wow," Casey hooted. "I never heard he was from Aiken."

"That's not all," she continued. "He has a brother, Michael Dean Perry, who graduated three years after his brother, but he went to South Aiken, then on to Clemson. Both of them are still in the pros right now, William in Chicago and Michael Dean in Cleveland."

"Okay, that's pretty impressive. Y'all have been busy making good athletes while I was gone."

"It's true," Annie said. "Henderson Johnson even took a Pony League baseball team all the way from Citizens Park to the Pony League World Series in Cincinnati in 1969. They didn't win, but they came pretty close.

"This is all good stuff, Annie. I'm glad you were paying attention and taking notes for me while I was gone so long. Let me ask you something. When I was riding through the valley, I saw a mention of Midland Valley and Midland Valley High School. I never heard of either one. What's that all about?"

Annie laughed and answered, "You know those valley people, always changing things. I told you there were some changes in the school system. Translate Midland Valley to Horse Creek Valley, and translate Midland Valley High School to the old LBC (Langley-Bath-Clearwater) High School."

Casey answered her. "I'll bet that two old baseball players I played against, Ray Sease and Charles Cromer, weren't too happy with that. They were pretty sure they played for LBC back in my day."

Annie asked a question. "Have you been able to keep up with anything related to the bomb plant?"

"No, I haven't," he said. "Has anything interesting happened out there?"

"Several things have evolved over time," she said. "For example, when you were here in the '50s, everybody called it the bomb plant, and Dupont built it and ran it. When it was finished and was a working facility, everybody called it the Savannah River Plant. Last year, the management of it changed from Dupont to Westinghouse, and we are all now calling it the Savannah River Site, or sometimes SRS. The number of employees changes, too, based on their changing mission within the Atomic Energy Commission. Whoops, there I go again. Now it's the Nuclear Regulatory Commission, not the AEC. Employees fluctuate between thirteen thousand and twenty-two thousand. I heard that right now, it's about twenty thousand. It is still the largest employer in this area by far. At one time, the security was provided by Pinkerton, but I think that duty has changed to Wackenhut."

Casey thought out loud for a moment and said, "Annie, do you remember when we worried—you and Arlene and me—about whether the new intrusion and infusion of people from everywhere would change us and change the character of Aiken? Or whether our nice sedate way of life would instead rub off on them and change them? Remember that? Did that ever settle out one way or the other? How did that all come out?"

"Oh you," she exclaimed. "You always ask tough questions." She thought for a few seconds and said, "I think you're gonna like the answer that I believe.

"At first, the construction people were here and everything was pretty rough for quite a while. They didn't try to change anything. They just wanted a steady paycheck and then off to the next big construction project somewhere else in the world. Then the scientists and the engineers and the physicists came, and they knew they were here to stay for the duration if they liked it enough here.

"Well, it turns out they liked it here quite a lot. Nobody has done any actual studies of how things changed, but at least one writer wrote about the changes. Do you know who Pat Conroy is?"

Casey was prompt to answer. "Isn't he from South Carolina somewhere, and didn't he write *The Great Santini*, and a movie was made about it that had Robert Duvall in it? And didn't he write *The Prince of Tides?*"

"Yes, okay, so you do know who he is. He graduated from the Citadel and played basketball for them. Before that, he grew up in Beaufort and was coached in high school by a man named Jerry Swing. Jerry Swing moved to the valley and was coaching at LBC when Conroy came here for a visit. That was in 1973, about seventeen years ago, when Conroy had never published anything you ever heard of and he probably didn't know a thing about Aiken.

"After staying in the area for only two weeks, he wrote a piece about Aiken and about the coming of the bomb plant called 'Horses Don't Eat Moon Pies.' A funny title, but he accurately nailed it as to how it was that old Aiken and new Aiken got along with each other. I have a copy somewhere, and I'll let you read it.

"Conroy talked about the original Aiken people and the Winter Colony people and how they related to each other. But he also saw clearly the other facets of Aiken—the Duponters, the scientists, the black people, the horse people, and the academic people at USC Aiken. The only ones he left out were the retirees, but they hadn't really gotten here in big numbers as early as 1973.

"I guess everybody has his own opinion about the changes. My personal feeling is that Aiken has been able to keep its best values intact, and the new people who came to work at the plant have been able to impose some of their most treasured values on us as well. The effect has been to improve Aiken, but like I said, that's just my own opinion. After you've been here for a while longer, I'd like to hear what you think."

"Okay," he answered. "I'll start paying close attention and I'll tell you later what I think."

"I just thought of something I need to tell you," Annie said. "You remember that it never snowed in Aiken while you were here and you were happy about that? Well, in February of 1973, that all changed. We got sixteen inches of snow all at once, and it shut this town down for several days. Never saw anything like it."

"I'm impressed," Casey exclaimed. "That's hard to believe."

Annie switched directions again. "Do you have any idea who the mayor is now?"

"No," Casey responded. "When I left, somebody named Charles Jones was mayor, and he had replaced Odell Weeks. Now I have to tell you, I got mighty confused today when I was expecting to see the neighborhood called Virginia Acres out on Whiskey Road and saw something called the Odell Weeks Activities Center instead. What is that, and how did it come about?"

Annie smiled and said, "I just happen to remember that, and it was a big deal when it happened. In 1956, not long after you left, Odell Weeks ran for mayor again and was elected, beating out Charles Jones. And Mr. Weeks has been our mayor ever since. He's still the mayor today. Impressive, huh?

"He got very active about Aiken's recreational shortcomings in the 1970s and was instrumental in the city buying out the homeowners in Virginia Acres to turn the space into parks, tennis courts, a gymnasium, and so on. When the grand opening came in the spring of 1975, the name was going to be Virginia Acres Activity Center, but city council had secretly voted to name the entire park after Mayor Weeks without his knowledge. He was so humbled and pleased that he didn't fight the council too hard about it. So today, with him still our mayor, it has his name on it. It's called Odell Weeks Activities Center.

"By the way, Casey, when you ride around Aiken and look into all the nooks and crannies, you'll find quite a few new neighborhoods. The first ones that come to mind are Woodside, Houndslake, and Cedar Creek. Retirees have discovered Aiken and they are settling everywhere, but these three developments seem to get the lion's share of them. I had a woman stop me on Laurens Street a few months ago, and she asked me if I was from Aiken. I told her that I was. Then she said something that has stuck with me. She said, 'My husband and I were riding through Aiken on the way to Greenville to look at a house we thought we would buy and retire to. We saw this town and this area and decided then and there to stop our search. We couldn't imagine that we were going to like Greenville more than this. We bought here and settled here. And we love it here.' Other people around here have heard similar stories."

Casey pondered her words and finally said, "I have to admit that there's something in the air here, in the mood of the people that says, this is a happy place, this is where friendly people live, this is where keeping up with the Joneses is not on the front burner."

Annie asked, "What do you think about Aiken's downtown area? Have you formed any opinions yet?"

"Not really," he said. "I noticed that an awful lot has changed downtown. I didn't see any shoe stores or any hardware stores, but I can't decide if that's good or bad. Sears is gone, Owen-Thomas has disappeared, Julia's Dress Shop is still there, but for how long, and there're no dime stores. I loved dime stores if you recall. I'm seeing gift shops and things like that."

She answered, "Downtown Aiken has gone through some of what other small towns have experienced. You know, when the malls are built in the suburbs, downtown just dries up. That happened to Aiken a little bit a few years ago. Somebody said back then that you could fire a cannon down the middle of Laurens Street and not hit a soul. That was true for a little while but not anymore. Downtown Aiken is showing a lot of spark and life lately."

Casey spoke up. "I noticed when I was riding around that the poolroom had moved and is now where the Colonial Store grocery once was. All these past years, sometimes I have gotten obsessed about having a couple of poolroom hot dogs. A. R. Edwards made them better than anybody else in the world. While I'm here, I'm going to walk over there to see AR and get him to fix me up with two of his best."

Annie frowned and said, "Old boy, I think your age is showing and you forgot how much time has passed. A. R. Edwards died a long time ago in about 1975, when he was already seventy-five years old. I saved his obituary for you."

Then Casey frowned too. "Oh, I'm sorry he's gone. He was always so nice and helpful to me, and others as well. I forgot that people I might want to see might already be dead. Who else died while I was gone and wasn't looking?"

"I kept a little list of those who died," she said, "just in case you showed up one day and wanted to know." She shuffled through some papers in her file, finally announcing, "Here it is. First, high school officials: Mr. Willis, the principal, died in 1978. He was only sixty-five. Johnny Eubanks died the next year, in 1979. He was eighty-five years old, never married, and they still call his old house on Park Avenue the Eubanks House. And Mrs. Bobo, your old English teacher, died in 1977 at age sixty-nine."

"I'm sorry about all of those. This is good information, and I need to know it," Casey said. "Any students die that I would know?"

"Unfortunately, yes," she answered. "Two boys you knew both died in car wrecks when they were only twenty-four years old. Danny Bradley, a year ahead of you in school, had an accident that killed him around Wagener, in 1962. He had gone to Clemson and was living in Aiken, running his father's plumbing and heating business. The other boy was Charles Ricks, from the class just younger than yours. Charles worked with his father at their freezer-locker business out near Montmorenci. He also went to Clemson and was driving his new Porsche on the Augusta Highway when he slammed into the back of a tractor trailer. That was in 1964. Like I said, they were both twenty-four years old. Very tragic and very sad for Aiken."

"I'm sorry to hear about those deaths. Yes, I knew both of them pretty well," Casey offered.

"I've got one more," Annie said. "This one's really bad, and I saved it for last. It's a boy from your own class. Brookie Wyman was intentionally shot and killed around

Thanksgiving 1971 by his own nineteen-year-old stepson. Brookie was only thirty-three years old. His stepson also killed his own mother and a half brother at the same time. Happened in the Columbia area, where they lived. Brookie and his wife were both teaching in a technical school. The boy who did the killing was found innocent by reason of insanity. It was a very sad case for Aiken. Brookie's father had been the mayor of Aiken some years before Odell Weeks. Their family was well known here."

"God, that's awful," Casey muttered. Then he added, "Oh yes, I knew Brookie quite well. If I remember correctly, he was an Eagle Scout. We had several classes together. What a waste! I'm really sorry for all of them."

"As you might guess," Annie began, "quite a few more Aiken people died in your absence than just these few. In fact, both of Arlene's parents are gone as well as many I haven't mentioned. Which brings me to a point of interest. Do you have any intentions of trying to find out anything about Arlene while you are here? You've barely said a word about her."

"Annie, the short answer is yes, I want to find out more about her and how she's doing. The long answer is that I am petrified as to what I might find out. I'm scared to death she got married. I'm scared of how I'm going to feel when I see her. I tucked memories of Arlene way back in my brain so far that I wouldn't have to look at them very often. She was my very best friend, as you know."

"Well, well, well! Aren't you a surprise? I never thought I'd live to see the day that you would admit that much about Arlene."

"Annie, my memories of Arlene are very good ones, but they are old as hell. When I finally see her, she will either appear as a total stranger, which won't be a good sign, or we'll just pick right up where we left off, which I would prefer. But I need to go find out."

"Yes, you do," Annie said firmly. "While you were running around in my car yesterday, I poked around for you by making a couple of phone calls. She lives on Colleton Avenue, only about four blocks from right here. I drew you a little map. You can walk over there any time you want to," she added as she handed him the map.

Casey took it, smiled at Annie nervously, and said, "Thanks."

Chapter 27

The next morning, he called his partner of High Sierra to make sure that the business did not need him for any emergencies. Randy Rivers assured him that things were running very smoothly in his absence and that sales were even running higher than they expected. Casey was calmed by the call and assured himself that the stores were in capable hands.

After one of Annie's hearty Southern breakfasts, they got in Annie's car and drove to Mattie Hall to look in on Jake. The visit was brief, but both Casey and Jake took some pleasure in seeing each other again so quickly. They stayed only a few minutes before leaving.

When they returned to the condominium, Casey told Annie that he was going to walk over to Arlene's house. "You mean you're not going to call her first?" Annie asked impatiently.

"No. No warning," he said. "I'm afraid she'll say no or put me off until tomorrow. My mind is set on doing it today."

At eleven o'clock, he walked out the door, up Hoods Lane to Newberry, on to Colleton, where he passed in front of the Willcox Hotel, which looked better than the last time he had seen it. Then a short dash across Chesterfield and over by the old Grammar School. In only another five minutes, he stood anxiously in front of her house. It was surrounded by mature tea olives and crape myrtles, which nearly obscured the house from the sidewalk. But he could tell that the house was white, with dark shutters, and had a wraparound porch that was positioned well above the sidewalk and the street. At least eight steps confronted him.

Once he was on the porch, he could see that it was a private front and side porch combination with comfortable cushioned chairs, a wrought-iron coffee table, and two swings at the corner, hanging from the ceiling. He knocked lightly on the door. He waited, listening hard. No response. His spirits dropped some as he knocked again, this time appreciably louder than the first attempt. He finally heard footsteps approaching and the words "Just hold your horses, I'm coming."

Again, he stood off to the side so that he could not be seen by the approaching occupant of the house. The door opened, and Arlene appeared, still safely behind the latched screen. She spoke. "Yes, can I help you?"

At that moment, Casey took a step that positioned him directly in front of the doorway. He answered, "I was hoping I would find one of my dearest old friends here."

Arlene heard the voice and was stunned into a long silence. In time, she edged closer to the screen and peered at him. "Casey Gannon, is that you? It sounds like the voice of Casey Gannon!"

She was clearly taken aback and was at a loss for any other words. It was an uncomfortable moment, but she fumbled to release the latch as he was saying, "Yes, I believe Casey Gannon has returned to Aiken." She opened the screen door outward, stepped onto the porch, and timidly threw her arms around him as he was doing the same to her.

She finally said, "I'm sorry, but I'm in just a little bit of shock. I was beginning to think I would never see you again." Then she started to laugh and smile and tried to say, "Just who in the heck do you think you are, dropping out of our lives and then suddenly dropping back in thirty years later? Don't you ever call first? Don't you know how to write a letter or make a phone call?" When she got that basic thought out of her mouth, she started to sob quietly, and he hugged her until it subsided.

Arlene backed away from him at arm's length and said, "I guess I had just about given up on you. Are you here for a while, at least long enough to tell me where you've been?"

He smiled at her and said, "I'm here for as long as it takes to mend all of the fences, make all of the appropriate explanations and apologies, and try to make it right with everybody again. In your case, I will stay here all afternoon and into next week if I have to until you have heard and understand everything about what happened. Do you have time to listen to me? Or did I just pop in here on a bad day for you?"

"Casey, I'm a schoolteacher at South Aiken and I'm off for the summer. My time is wide open right now. And I would always have time for you, or have you forgotten that? As we sometimes say here, I'm not lettin' you go nowhere 'til you 'splain things to me."

"That's great," Casey said. "Can I take you to lunch somewhere close by so that we can talk?"

"You could, but I have a better idea," she said. "I can fix lunch for us right here and we can eat it on the porch and talk all afternoon if you want to."

"Sold," he answered. "Let's do it."

She invited him into her house and showed him around on their way to the kitchen. He sat on a barstool while she made sandwiches at the counter with her back to him. He realized that he should ask a question or two in order to frame the conversations in the correct way. "Arlene, where is your husband? Is he at work today?"

She smiled to herself at the question and answered him honestly and directly, without turning her head in his direction. "I am an old-maid schoolteacher. I have never gotten married."

He was glad she was not looking at him because he was positive that the relief showed on his face as he digested the response. "Pity for the boys of Aiken on that one, not realizing what a prize was here among them all the time," he said carefully.

It had been many years since Casey had seen Arlene, and he was emphatically struck with what an attractive woman she was. No, she was not beautiful in the Miss America sense, but she had a glow about her, a mature aspect to her personality that radiated quiet confidence and charm and allure. He admitted to himself that he was more than casually attracted, well in excess of what he remembered when they had been teenagers. He was enjoying being in her house and in her presence. He instinctively liked her as a grown, mature woman. If he had seen her for the first time walking down the street, he would have said to himself, "Now there's a woman I'd like to meet."

She had summoned the courage to ask him a similar question. "Did your wife come with you on this visit to Aiken?"

He purposely delayed long enough to make her nervous and ultimately said, releasing the words slowly enough to intensify her worry, "My wife . . . has yet . . . to make her appearance in my life. I . . . don't have one at the moment."

It was Arlene's turn to feel the relief sweep over her in the wake of the answer she heard. "Oh, and have you had one in the past? A wife, I mean."

"No, not really," he responded. "But in our conversations this afternoon, remind me to tell you about what I call my Mulligan marriage."

She finally looked around at him and said, "A Mulligan marriage? Okay, I'll ask later."

He helped her push the food cart from the kitchen to the side porch, where they enjoyed the lunch she had prepared. After they had eaten, he asked if they could sit in the porch swings that faced each other while they talked. She agreed and added, "Do you realize that these are the same swings we used to have on our porch at the farm? They were always my favorites, and when I sold the farm, I brought them with me to this house."

On a hunch, he asked, "Why were they your favorites?"

She blushed and said, "Because of that conversation you and I had while sitting in them so long ago."

He definitely liked the answer, saying, "I was hoping you had a good reason like that."

"Okay, my old friend, I think it's time you told me where have you been. You've certainly taken your sweet old time getting back to Aiken. I'm filled with curiosity."

He smiled at her that she seemed to be trying to feign a snit, and he began with "You are about to hear an incredible story, one that's almost preposterous, almost too hard to believe. But every bit of it is true and provable. Zach Kessler, my aunt Annie, and the Aiken Police Department can vouch for just about all of it if you were to ask them.

"Listen closely. Wade Kessler, Zach's dad who died a couple of months ago, was our next-door neighbor if you remember. He was a nuclear consultant out at the bomb plant, but he was also an atomic bomb spy for the Soviet Union, and I discovered it all by myself the day after we graduated from high school while y'all were all at the beach and I was home alone . . ." And he went on from there for the next hour.

Arlene listened to the story in amazement as Casey recounted shooting him in self-defense, burying the weapons and the passports, and fleeing in a panic when he thought that he might be caught and killed before the end of that first day. She was astonished that Kessler had even threatened to have her executed, trying anything in his power to exert the maximum pressure on Casey.

She heard about Colorado, Arizona, the army, Germany, and the subsequent life he had built under the name "C. C. Cannon." She asked him about baseball and where he was finally able to play. He told her that he was never able to play baseball again because it would make it too easy for the Russians to find him.

"Casey," she bored in on him, "you were the best player to ever play in Aiken, and you're telling me that you never played baseball again? Why for God's sake?"

She seemed to whimper audibly as he said, "To me, the most important thing was to keep Uncle Jake, Aunt Annie Lou, and you alive and out of danger. As long as Wade Kessler did not know of my location, I felt I was safe, and as a result, the rest of you were safe. I went to a lot of trouble to ensure that I was concealed, and baseball, well, baseball just had to take a backseat." She was moved that he gave up everything that had seemed important to him back then.

"I remember when you sat in that very swing and told me how you wanted to be a major league baseball player, and it's such a tragedy that you had to abandon that dream so early. It's just a tragedy," she repeated.

"No, Arlene, the tragedy would have been the death of any one of you so that I could continue to play baseball. It was important to me, but not in the same category as life and death." He was very convincing as he said it.

At the appropriate point, she asked, "So you have your own business in Arizona . . . Now that you have the freedom to live out in the open again, what are your plans? Will you continue to use Cannon rather than Gannon? Will you ever come back to Aiken to live?"

"I really don't know what I'll do," he answered. "I've only had a few days to think about it so far. It all came at me so fast. I was convinced that the first order of business was to come to Aiken to let everybody know what had happened and try to smooth things over with them and, of course, to check on the people important to me here. You, for example, how your life is working out is important to me. How have you been, and why are you living in this beautiful house on this beautiful street all by yourself?"

She blushed uncomfortably. The last thing in the world she wanted to do at that moment was to answer that question. Finally, she said, "I know that you remember how picky I've always been about everything. This is no different. I prefer being by myself over being here with the incorrect people. Simple." She liked her own answer, and he accepted it without further comment.

While they were putting the lunch things away, Arlene made a suggestion. "Casey, this town has changed so much in your absence and I would like to show you around and point out some of the changes. A while back, I even made an Aiken must-do list for some of my out-of-town friends. I'll make a copy of it for you. And if you'll join me tomorrow, I'll drive and take you on a tour of what I'm talking about. What about it?"

"I would love to do that. It'll give us a chance to talk some more. I don't have my own car here anyway. Let's do it. Great idea!"

A few more minutes of small talk, followed by a quick, neutral hug, and he was out the door, walking back to Annie's condo. He was quite happy with the meeting of several hours and felt a slight spring in his gait.

Annie started the questions the minute she saw him. How is she? Is she still pretty? Do you still like her? Are you going to take her out to dinner? Will you see her some more while you're here, etc.

"Hold on, Annie, you're going too fast for me," he pleaded. "Will it make you happy if I just make something up? Okay, I'll do that. She's slim and trim and beautiful, and I'm mad about her. How's that? The longer, better answer is that we are going out tomorrow so that she can show Aiken to me. She seems to be very proud of our hometown and how it has developed while I was gone. She wants to be the one to show me things and explain them to me."

"Oh, that's good, a good first step," Annie said. "I've been fixing you a fine supper all day while you've been gone and looking forward to finding out more about the day you spent with her." And he debriefed his aunt about Arlene for the rest of that day.

The next morning, Annie and Casey made a quick trip to Mattie Hall to look in on Jake. He was sleeping so they just left him that way. Later, Arlene drove over to pick Casey up, parking in one of the two slots at the front of Annie's condo. He was standing on the porch when she drove up, and he asked her inside to say a brief "hello" to his aunt. Annie gushed over Arlene, having not seen her around town for several years. A short tour of the residence was also in order, when Arlene admitted to never being inside one of the condos. The neighborhood was only three years old and was ideally suited for anyone wanting to live in the downtown area.

At one point, Annie caught Casey's eye and gave him a look that told him that Arlene was met with total approval from her perspective. She also showed her genuine acceptance by the way she conducted the house tour, showing off aspects of the residence that weren't obvious to the casual eye.

As the pair was leaving for Arlene's driving tour of Aiken, Annie was effusive in inviting her back for a longer visit in the near future. Arlene assured them both that she would like to come back soon.

Once they were in the car, Arlene said, "She is a genuinely nice woman. You were so lucky to end up in her hands at age ten. I have always liked being with her. Now then, off to Whiskey Road and the South."

She drove straight to South Aiken High School, her place of employment, saying, "I'm pretty sure you haven't seen the new high school. Nothing happening in the summer, but this place is crawling with over a thousand boys and girls nine months of the year. I love teaching here, and I'm glad Margaret Bobo gave me such a strong grounding in English because that's why I love to teach it now.

"You probably noticed on the way out here just how busy Whiskey Road has gotten. That's just about the only flaw I see in Aiken right now. It has grown so vigorously toward the south—and I suppose toward SRP—that our traffic gets clogged up out here all the time. If you look at an overall map of the area, there's no simple solution. No way to construct a parallel street without somehow breaching Hitchcock Woods and Palmetto Golf Course, and those two are off limits. Aiken's leaders have their hands full trying to figure out a workable solution."

She drove over to Silver Bluff Road and out to the new Woodside community. "This development is why a lot of people from the North and elsewhere are retiring to Aiken. Besides all the nice things we know about this town, these people get to live in a protected neighborhood, surrounded by their own golf courses. Woodside has been quite a magnet for that. It's a little bit unfortunate for them that they tend to stay out here to themselves and not feel a part of old Aiken. They are missing some of the benefits that this town offers." She also drove through Gem Lakes, reminding Casey that it was already there before he left town in 1956. He had forgotten about it.

She drove the car to the Hitchcock Parkway in order to get to the Houndslake neighborhood. "This is pretty new," she announced, "and it is attracting a lot of old Aiken folks into newer and more modern houses than they had in town. And of course, you can see they have their own golf courses too."

On the way back toward downtown, Arlene mentioned Rye Patch and Hopelands Gardens. Casey admitted that he had never heard of either one, so she turned the car off Whiskey Road and explored both Berrie Road and Dupree Street, two of the Winter Resort's better known residential streets.

After that, she took them on Mead Avenue and Grace Avenue, two of the horse district's primary dirt roads and main accesses from the horse area into Hitchcock Woods. Casey asked about the pedestrian light signals he saw mounted on a utility pole at each side of each intersection. Arlene laughed and said, "Try to imagine yourself on a horse and you want to safely cross the busy Whiskey Road. Do you want to stop, dismount, just to press the button to get a green crossing light, then get back on your horse? No, you want to stay on your horse and accomplish the same thing. So the city installed two push buttons on each pole, one down low for pedestrians and one up higher for riders on horseback."

"Boy, now I've seen everything," he said. "That's a great innovation."

She showed him the Track Kitchen while they were on Mead Avenue, saying, "I eat there on Saturday mornings every so often. Good way to immerse yourself into the horse culture." And she turned off the dirt road into Whitney Field, saying, "Remember this? Polo every Sunday during parts of the year."

She wanted to show Casey "Banksia," the Winter Colony mansion that now housed Aiken County Museum, but it had also been the first location of USC Aiken back in the 1960s. They spent a few minutes inside, walking through the displays and visiting the gift shop. The clerks and attendants spoke to Arlene as if they saw her often.

As they left, she asked if he had heard of Aiken's Triple Crown. He told her that he was unfamiliar with the term as it applied to Aiken. She said, "In March of each year, Aiken has three straight weekends devoted to horse events. One is plain horse racing, the second is steeplechase racing, and the third is built around other horse events, sometimes driving, and sometimes polo. March is the peak of equestrian events for the year. For the Winter Colony folks, it's the final fling for those who have to go back to the North to resume their other lives."

At a few minutes after noon, Casey asked, "Hey, are you game for some lunch? I saw a place near the Alley called West Side Bowery that I'd like to try. I think we can eat outside in the shade."

"Great idea," Arlene said. "I go there often and know it well."

She was lucky and parked parallel on Park Avenue, just a few steps down Bee Lane from the entrance of the restaurant. A man named Sam spoke to her as they entered and seated them in the grassy patio area in the rear, which abutted the Alley itself. It was a great place for private conversation and people watching.

"Well, here we are, lady. You're quite a guide. I'm enjoying this and seeing some things I've never seen before. Aiken is something to see now."

She smiled and responded, "Oh, we have a ways to go yet. I hope to show you a lot more."

They ordered food and talked quietly like the old friends they had been long ago. At one point, he reached over and grabbed her hand to make a point, and he noticed that she responded in a noncommittal way, neither warmly returning his unexpected touch nor repelling his hand in any way. She communicated, unspoken, at that moment, "Okay, you can do that," and he noticed and translated her inaction as "she's not going to fall all over me in lavish praise. She's a perfect example of neutrality."

As they neared the end of lunch, Zach Kessler walked up to their table and sat down. He said, "I was hoping to run into both of you. Annie told me y'all were sightseeing. Arlene, it's great to see you after such a long time."

She leaned over to accept his hug of greeting. "You too. What's going on with you these days?" she asked.

Zach answered, "I have to leave town this afternoon and go back to DC. My flight's at three o'clock from Augusta. I just wanted to say goodbye to Casey."

Casey spoke, saying, "Zach old buddy, you've saved my life, at least the rest of it. I'll never be able to thank you enough for finding me and setting the record straight. I'll never forget that you persisted until you found me."

"You would do the same for me," Zach countered. "I have no doubts about that. By the way, that little item my dad left you will be on your desk when you get back to Arizona. I already sent it."

"Okay, I'll be looking for it when I get back there," Casey said.

Zach looked back and forth at both of them, saying, "One last question. Anything going on here that I ought to know about? Just being nosy."

Casey and Arlene looked at each other, smirked innocently, and said, one after the other, "Nothing that I know of."

"Okay, I'm out of here." And Zach made his exit.

The pair looked at each other, and Casey spoke first, saying, "I think we should promise to talk about that last thing before too much more time passes."

Arlene answered him immediately, "You mean that 'anything going on here?' comment? I couldn't agree with you more."

Casey paid the check and they left. At the car, he asked if she had more touring in mind, and she nodded. She drove around the immediate downtown area, pointing out the Aiken Community Playhouse on Newberry Street, the new location for AR's old business, City Billiards, and showing him that the *Aiken Standard* was no longer on Richland Avenue but had relocated to Rutland Drive, across from North Aiken Elementary School.

He spotted George Funeral Home, saying, "Some things never change."

She laughed and said, "Au contraire, my friend, the new guy in town is Shellhouse, over on Hayne Avenue, and he is giving George's a run for its money. Very competitive now."

She aimed her sedan to Chesterfield Street and the old Grammar School. "This is now the Aiken County Library, not a school any longer."

He pointed out that he still remembered all too well when Mrs. Coleman sent him barefooted out to get his shoes from the bushes.

Arlene said, "I felt so sorry for you that day. Ten years old and full of sorrow and nerves and problems."

They drove by the front of the Willcox Hotel on Colleton, and she told him that the financial health of the Willcox comes and goes and that all of Aiken prayed daily for a happy ending. Casey agreed and spoke of the elegant architecture.

She aimed the car to the west on Park Avenue. In a few blocks, Casey said, "Whoa, where is the passenger train station? Did I miss it back there?"

"No, it was torn down quite a while back. It wasn't being used anymore since Aiken had no more passenger services to offer. Progress arrives in strange ways."

"I hate that," Casey offered. "That was such a pretty little train station. It's the first thing I ever saw in Aiken."

"Our next stop is a bit out of town," Arlene said. "It's a surprise and not a very good one."

She drove out toward Columbia on Route 215, and he figured it out on the way as they motored through Couchton. "We're headed for Scott's Lake, right?" Casey was smiling at himself for remembering the way. As they got close, he noticed something different about their road. "That place where Steve Wadiak got killed while we were in high school, the place we renamed Wadiak Curve—it's gone. Not much curve now. I was bracing for it."

"You're so right," she responded. "The State rebuilt this part of the highway, eliminating as much of the sharp curve as possible. People were upset that one of the Gamecock football players died because of too sharp a curve, so it was redone as soon as they could round up the money."

After the car rounded the curve, she traveled a short distance farther, and she pulled off on the right shoulder. "Why did you stop here?" he asked.

"Because we're here," she said. "Welcome to Scott's Lake."

He looked out and saw no shimmering water, but only a swampy fen, a low marshy land with small trees and bushes growing out of where there once was a ten-acre lake, a high diving tower, a low diving tower, a sliding board into the water, and a small sandy beach. Now it was only a memory. All of those good times, all of that dancing in the building called the Pavilion, all of that flirting and chasing your friends, vanished forever. So sad to see it like this.

"Thanks for showing me. I needed to see it, I suppose." It placed a brief damper on his spirits and made him feel older than dirt.

She added another piece of information to his readjustment to being in the Aiken area. "Do you remember how we always went to Columbia this way? We would drive out Route 215 through Kitchens Mill, Wagener, and Pelion, which we always insisted pronouncing as PEE-lion? Nobody has driven to Columbia this way for years. As soon as Interstate-20 was up and running, nobody ever came this way again."

As they headed back toward town, she spoke of Aiken now being a nuclear town and a center for light industry. "You know, when we were growing up, before Dupont got here, Aiken thrived on cotton—cotton farms, cotton mills, anything to do with cotton. We even had a Cotton Festival every September to celebrate the bringing in of the cotton harvest. Now, you never hear that word spoken."

She had turned off onto the circumferential road that essentially was a bypass going all the way around the town.

She explained. "I'm doing this just to give you a flavor of the usefulness of this road and to let you see some of the light industrial businesses that Aiken has attracted since you were gone."

When they had gone all the way around, she looked at him and asked, "Any place else you want to go?"

"Yes, old Aiken High School, on Laurens."

She started in that direction and said, "You probably already know that it's no longer there, don't you?"

"Yes, I saw some other set of buildings in its place, and I don't understand why they would demolish that great high school building."

She was driving and trying to remember. "After we went to the new school on Rutland Drive in 1954, the old building became the new home for the junior high school, and it stayed that way for a number of years. Finally, the school board decided to give up on the idea of keeping it open as a school. Big estimates were made to pay for changes to the gymnasium and others to bring the auditorium up to a higher standard. In all of these educational considerations, South Aiken High, where I teach, was born and dominoes of all stripes fell all over Aiken County. When the dust settled, Aiken Junior High on Laurens was no more, and the city lost a very useful auditorium and school. Trinity Lutheran Home sits there now, and it is a very good one. My mother spent her final days there."

They parked the car on Laurens and walked to and all around the nursing home, but he could not find a single artifact or reminder of the old school that had stood there. Progress is hard on memories sometimes, and this was the proof.

Arlene had parked in front of the Stoplight Deli, and they returned there after the nursing home visit. They ducked inside for a glass of tea and a change of scenery. "I want to take you to dinner, someplace where it's not stuffy and we can get some seafood. Can you think of anything?"

"Yes," she said. "The Variety, over on York Street, toward the interstate. It used to be called Jean's. You get a lot of food for the money, and the service is good."

"Sold," he said. "Can you drop me off at my aunt's house so that I can freshen up and come back to pick me up?"

"I'll do it," she answered. And they left.

Chapter 28

She picked him up an hour later at the Sand River condos, and they were seated in the Variety Restaurant within minutes. He was starving and ordered the biggest fried seafood platter on the menu. Arlene got a small sirloin steak. While they were eating, they talked about the day they spent together, and he thanked her more than once.

"If you agree," he said, "once we are finished here, I want to go back to your house, sit on your porch, get you to make a pot of good decaf coffee, and talk some more. Can we do that?"

"I can trust you, can't I?" she asked, joking and smiling at him.

"I promise you can. I'm harmless," he said.

"Aw shucks," she said, laughing.

An hour and a half later, surrounded by darkness, they were sitting on her porch in the cushioned lounge chairs, in the half light, hidden from the street and sidewalk by the tall shrubbery, and pleasantly sipping her coffee. The fragrance of tea olive and magnolia permeated the scene.

"This has been just about a perfect visit," Casey started. "I am so impressed with Aiken and how it feels to me after so many years of not seeing it, nor thinking about it on a daily basis. It's a terrific town, and maybe it always was that and I just didn't have enough experience or maturity to appreciate it. I'm a bit overwhelmed at everything. Somebody here is really doing something right."

"Casey, you have forgotten. You always liked Aiken, and I never saw you hold back about that. You liked it from the minute you saw how it nurtured and protected you."

"I do remember some of that, of course. It seems to me that to be new in Aiken the way I was wasn't a very threatening situation. The people here actively want you to feel welcome, they want you to succeed at whatever you came here to accomplish. Nobody here feels like if he needs to win, then somebody else has to lose. People look for win-win situations and exploit them, looking for positive outcomes for everybody. Almost nobody here wants to force anything on another person."

Arlene contributed, adding, "A long time ago, we worried that the bomb plant newcomers would arrive and force their alien way of life on us and that it would change us for the worse. They did come in large numbers, but they were smart about how they handled themselves. The majority of them sensed that there was something special about Aiken, and rather than jump in with both feet with their new ideas, they waited until they understood us and how we reacted and why we reacted to things the way we did. Once they understood us, they saw the worth of Aiken's values and opted not to attack them, but to add to them and not try to replace ours with theirs. They became very willing to bend to the prevailing way of Aiken. The net effect has been that we saw our old values retained, and our Duponters slowly added their best ones to ours. Now, in 1990, the critical mass is essentially living in the 'old Aiken way,' as it has been amended, and all of us are pretty convinced it is the correct way."

"We saw examples of it today," Casey said. "There were situations in traffic where a New Yorker might have been sitting on his horn. I never heard a horn all day. And other drivers allowed you to go first, not once, but three times today alone. You were invited to cut in front of them. Then the driver waves at us, not a middle finger, but an honest, friendly wave."

Arlene spoke up again. "I'm here all the time and you're not. I listen to people and hear things. I overheard a man say, just last week, 'I quickly learned that Aiken is a very civil place.' One woman who was thinking of moving here from another nearby county asked her father, a Mr. Johnson, for his advice because he had owned businesses here for many years and was physically in Aiken several times a week. He told her this: 'Mary Jo, move to Aiken now. Don't wait any longer. You will never regret it. It's like the Garden of Eden there.' I have also heard any number of SRP wives who came here long ago from Richmond or Wilmington or Oak Ridge or Charleston, West Virginia, say very clearly, 'I don't want to live anywhere else now but here.'"

"Oh my, we sound like the Chamber of Commerce, don't we?" Casey was astounded by his own positive feelings. But he had to admit that these factors, plus the double streets and parkways, Hitchcock Woods, mature trees everywhere, horses, golf, sandy soil, a mild climate, a college town, and a lovely downtown shopping area were a unique combination. Whoever made the comment "There's only one Aiken" was totally correct.

"So what are you going to do with all this positive Aiken information, Mr. smarty-pants Arizona businessman?" She made the question have a bit of a bite in it.

He was ready. "I'm going to look at one more angle of this. The personal one." He looked at her in the dim light of the porch and added, "I think it's time for us to find out if we mean anything worthwhile to each other."

She gulped, caught her breath, and said, "I don't mind declaring myself first. You've always known that I consider you as one of my very closest friends, at least that was true years ago. Surprise, surprise, big boy! I still feel the same way today. We picked up the loose ends yesterday without skipping a beat. That felt good."

"I agree with you," he responded. "You are still the friend who means the most to me, even after all these years. I have never met anyone that I feel any closer to than I do you. So"—he paused for effect—"do we just let it stay right there, or do we try to build something more?" He realized that he was asking himself as much as her.

"Casey," she barged in courageously. "I always thought when we were younger that we would end up together somehow. Then you disappeared and I adjusted, modified, recalibrated, shifted, and adjusted some more. I probably had a number of real chances to pair off with other people, but my heart was never really in it. After the passage of a bunch of years, I have grown accustomed to being single and living by myself. Now, here you are, back in Aiken, stirring up everything and maybe me along with it. The absolute truth is that I have tried and have never met a man who I preferred more than you. You've been my ideal, my paradigm, my gold standard, the one I've always put in that special place in my head. I shouldn't have, but I did. But when I ask myself do I love you, hell, I don't know. I can admit to great admiration, but I've never had a chance to really find out, and that's God's truth."

He listened intently to her words and realized how closely her feelings were aligned with his. "Hey, it's clear that as well as we knew each other back then, our relationship never matured to a point that we could permanently make a commitment to each other. Life intervened, as well as Mr. Kessler's unfortunate secret life. We were forced to go in other directions by the circumstances. I will say to you here and now that I am impressed by the woman you have become. I find you more attractive today than I did back then. Your attitude and the way you carry yourself as an adult woman is a beautiful thing to see, and I really appreciate it. You've exceeded what I expected when I came back here. But I, just like you, cannot say that I love you or that I don't love you for the identical reason you just gave me. However, I want to suggest that we continue with our lives for a while. You come visit me in Arizona to see if you like my life there. I will come back to Aiken as often as I can to visit you, Annie, Jake, and others. Let's see what develops between us. I have a strong feeling that time and exposure to each other will be an accurate guide as to what direction our futures should take. What do you think?"

"I'll answer that, but first, let me tell you that I really like the new Casey who reentered my life yesterday too. I've enjoyed watching you for these last two days up close and with a totally fresh perspective. If it's possible, I believe you've improved with age. And, Casey, I believe you have proposed a perfect solution for both of us right now. I'm fully comfortable with it. We need to visit each other back and forth and build on the relationship we have, and see how we react to each other as adults. So I'm buying your suggestion."

She paused and smiled. "But I have one more request. This is way overdue. Would you mind kissing me right now? I don't ever remember that you and I have ever shared a single real kiss."

He laughed, stood up and took her hand, helping her get to her feet, and wrapped his arms around her as he leaned his head forward, saying, "With great pleasure. I do believe it's about time for this."

And they kissed, not a deep, invasive, passionate kiss, but one that conveyed warmth, respect, and strong and expansive emotion for the other person. After a long time, they broke contact and she looked at him with a slightly different perspective, saying, "Well, well, I admit that I always wondered. Mr. Gannon, if that's a beginning sample, it looks like the next phase of our lives could be a lot of fun. I think you really meant that."

He answered, "I think I did too."

Afterword

The story you have just read has been an attempt to merge real people with fictitious characters in an accurate portrayal of Aiken and USA history between 1948 and 1990.

Allow me to address the fictional main characters first. Casey Gannon, Jake Gannon, Annie Lou Gannon, Arlene Cushman, Wade Kessler, Zach Kessler, and Denise Slaughter were created from my imagination. The same is true of banker, James McCabe; hardware clerk, Finkelstein; and the Kesslers' maid, Katie Wilson. None of them is based in whole or in part on any real person living or deceased. The only exception to this is Casey. A few of his exploits are based on real events that happened in the author's life. Any similarities for the others are coincidental and unintended. The same is true for the traitorous acts of Wade Kessler. To my knowledge, there has never been a case of espionage connected with anyone living in Aiken or working at the Savannah River Site.

There are a few real people from Aiken or the surrounding area who were mentioned in the story. Bubba Moseley, who was killed in the 1953 Laurens Street explosion and fire, was known personally by me; and he, in fact, hired me as an eleven-year-old caddy for my first job at the Highland Park course. Ross Howard, from Augusta, worked for my father for almost thirty years in an Augusta auto supply business on Broad Street there. He is accurately portrayed as an Uncle Remus-type character. I didn't make that up. Ross was really just like he was portrayed. My brothers and sister treasured

Ross as a friend, and he doted on us as well. He died at age eighty-one in 1979. Farris Wynn was a man from Aiken who ran a car-detailing service out of his home on Kershaw Street. My father used his services many times and considered Farris to be a friend. He died at eighty-one in 1990 in Aiken. Tommy, who taught Casey how to drive a car at a young age, is Tommy Gibbs, who still resides in Aiken. I am not the only friend who learned this skill at Tommy's "driving school." If you know Tommy personally, you may be lucky enough to learn from him how he did it. Henry "Tot" Robinson was the county recreational director during the 1950s and coached many boys in football, basketball, and baseball. Tot died in 1992 and is buried in the Graniteville Cemetery. A.R. Edwards is portrayed realistically and he contributed positively to the lives of many Aiken boys. It's true that I placed a few words in each mouth of these real people, but I stuck to their true characters as to what was said and how it was said.

Teachers and administrators from the county public school system are accurately portrayed. These include Martha Coleman; Johnny Eubanks; J. O. Willis; John Wrenn; Misses Barlow, Inabinet, McLeod, and Ballard; Mrs. Bobo; and Dr. Guy.

The story about Major Joseph McCluskey in Germany and Luxembourg is a true tale in every sense. He was the S-3 in my U.S. Army Battle Group, where I was serving as an infantry platoon leader, second lieutenant. The town of Ettelbruck, Luxembourg, still considers him to be one of its local heroes.

When I was preparing to write this story, I could not recall precisely where Snake Road was and contacted Tommy Gibbs to be reminded. We drove to the site, and he refreshed my rusty memories. I will not tell you where it is here because it is now part of a private driveway leading to the home of a prominent Aiken citizen. It is still unpaved, but grass has sprouted in the ruts we created, trees overhang the road, and bushes grow close to the travel path. I would not have found it or recognized it without Tommy's assistance.

The *Augusta Herald* newspaper operated as an afternoon news source for many years, but finally ceased to operate in 1993. I delivered this paper as a young boy of eleven and twelve on the same route Casey had, on and around Hayne Avenue and Richland.

The Willcox Hotel, which was described as a hotel of sometimes good and sometimes bad circumstances, has been renovated and now operates under new young management. In 2013, it is a highly sought after place to stay, and the dining room operates one of the city's best restaurants. Conde Nast named the Willcox as one of the top fifty small hotels in the country in 2012. Travel and Leisure named it one of the top thirty-two hotels in the country in 2013.

Willcox Hotel

The passenger train station, called the passenger depot in the 1950s, at the corner of Park Avenue and Union Street, was rebuilt in 2010 and restored to its original Winter Resort condition, under the leadership of Tim Simmons. It is no longer used for train passengers, but the building is serving as a welcome center for visitors and has historical displays inside and outside. The building is evolving into a useful place for visitors and meetings.

The Sand River, located totally within Hitchcock Woods, has received renewed attention in recent years due to serious erosion of the riverbed. The water runoff from downtown Aiken heads straight for the Hitchcock Woods due to the topographical layout of downtown Aiken. Studies have revealed that increased paving in downtown, increased building "footprint" space, and the drainage of medians (parkways) in the double streets, all have increased the amount of water entering Sand River's basin, exacerbating the problem. The city is addressing the problem by changing how it discharges the runoff water. The Hitchcock Woods Foundation manages the Woods and welcomes you to join their membership. Along with the city, they are addressing erosion problems within the Woods. I am a proud member of the Foundation myself.

Hitchcock Woods, when it was initially donated to the city by Thomas Hitchcock in 1939, comprised about 1,200 acres. In 1985, another 230 acres were purchased and added. In 1991, Aiken Prep School donated another 270 acres. In later years, the Foundation was able to purchase another 200 acres. In 2013, the entire Woods adds up to approximately 2,100 acres, making it the largest park of its type within any U.S. city. Central Park in New York City would fit into the Woods two and a half times. Augusta National's beautiful golf course and grounds can be placed into the Woods five and a half times.

When I returned to the Aiken area in 1990 after years of not living here, I began to notice the little touches in the downtown area that seemed to attract visitors to come there. Shops looked spiffier than usual. Parking was free and plentiful. Restaurants were abundant. Sidewalks were populated. Street debris was nowhere to be seen. Lighting was adequate and improving. Flowers and flower pots had multiplied their numbers.

As the decade rolled on, I began to ask, "Who is behind this new look, this apparently new strategy for Aiken?" I asked the questions almost everywhere I went. At first, the answers were elusive. Slowly, a few names began to emerge. Of course, I expected to hear the name Odell Weeks, and I did. But then, I began to hear of Ambrose Schwallie, Wade Brodie, Tim Simmons, Fred Cavanaugh, and Cot Campbell. Further examination revealed that there was an early 1990s organization born out of Aiken's Greater Chamber of Commerce, named 20-20 Vision for the Future, and it was laying a plan for the long-term future of Aiken.

Wade Brodie, a highly visible Aiken banker who was acting for 20-20, along with Fred Cavanaugh, convinced Ambrose Schwallie to head up part of the 20-20 group to provide fundraising and enlightened leadership efforts for the city's future. Ambrose Schwallie was the president of Westinghouse Savannah River Site at the time, and he already had a full plate in front of him but he generously gave his time and dedication to the effort. He was able to help raise $3.5 million for downtown beautification, local education, and luring jobs into the area. This organization proved its worth by scoring large achievements, and almost every improvement to Aiken's downtown that is visible today can be traced to this organization, these men, and their efforts in the mid-1990s.

They were not the only achievers helping Aiken. Fred Cavanaugh, mayor since Odell Weeks's death in 1991, and Skipper Perry, state representative, also contributed. Clifton Weeks, Stathy Verenes, Frampton Toole, Lionel Smith, Sam Erb, Greg Ryberg, and many unnamed contributors from old and new Aiken donated huge amounts of time to secure improvements.

So what else does it take to make a good town a great one besides leadership and a good plan?

The people of Aiken have certain characteristics that gives them a recognizable DNA that can be seen by most visitors to the area. I've given it the name "gracious assistance."

It means that the majority of people who live here, as well as all over the South, are marked by a helpful kindness and courtesy, as well as a generous charm and some evidence of good manners. If your car has a flat tire in a public place, you have a great chance to receive several offers to change the tire for you by strangers who stop to help. They are not looking to be paid. In the *Aiken Standard* newspaper, you may see "thank you" letters to motorists who interrupted their day to help others in case of an accident. If this happened to you, the help you received may have come from a total stranger. It was unconditional, and you may not have discovered the helper's name before he left.

In a Lowe's or a Home Depot or a Wal-Mart or a grocery store, you may find that another customer, a total stranger to you, will stop his shopping to help you find an item in the store. He simply volunteers to do it if he believes he can help you. In traffic, you will be allowed to cut in front of other cars because another driver recognizes that if he doesn't help you, then you may be stuck in traffic for a time. If someone in your household dies, the casseroles may begin to arrive at your front door as soon as the word gets out. If the person in your home who cuts the grass becomes ill or bedridden, don't be surprised if your neighbor offers to cut your yard as well as his own until your mower is back on the job.

Many towns are essentially closed to newcomers in the welcoming sense. Not Aiken. Aiken is "open" and welcomes new residents unconditionally. In general, when you arrive in Aiken, the people of old Aiken will not probe your background in an attempt to see where you fit in our lives. The basic assumption is "yes, you fit here" until your own disqualifying behavior casts doubt on that fixed expectation.

Gracious assistance is a nice, genteel way to live, and it shows well and wears well. If Aiken does not seem to be a place where you would be comfortable around the people I have described here, please make it easy on yourself and stay where you are. We are already thirty thousand strong and do not need to crowd our citizens any more than necessary. However, if Aiken looks to be a good fit for how you want to live, this Garden of Eden is here for the taking.

APPENDIX

Arlene's Must-Do List:

1. South Boundary—see the live oaks tunnel.
2. Center for the Arts, Laurens St.
3. Go antiquing downtown.
4. Hitchcock Woods—hike in it; see Sand River.
5. Farmer's Market, Richland Avenue.
6. Plum Pudding store—browse there.
7. Drive all parkway streets, about 105 city blocks.
8. Drive the entire Beltway.
9. See Coker Springs.
10. Visit Thoroughbred Hall of Fame
11. Hopelands Gardens—see lighting at Christmas.
12. Hopelands Gardens—see a summer concert.
13. Visit Aiken County Museum (Banksia)
14. Visit Rye Patch.
15. Attend Blessing of the Hounds, Thanksgiving.
16. Visit One Table, Alley Thanksgiving feast.
17. Eat at the Track Kitchen, Mead Avenue.
18. Eat at the Variety, York Street.
19. Eat at Willcox Hotel, Colleton Avenue.
20. Eat outside at West End Bowery.
21. Eat a hot dog or two at City Billiards.
22. Eat at Carolina Barbecue, New Ellenton.
23. Have coffee at New Moon Café.
24. See a Sunday afternoon polo match.

25. Attend a Triple Crown event.

26. Aiken Community Playhouse—see a play.

27. Attend Aiken's Makin'—September.

28. Attend St. Thaddeus Home Tour.

29. Battle of Aiken—see the reenactment.

30. Attend Downtown Antique Show—February.

31. Read *Horses Don't Eat Moon Pies* by Conroy.

32. Read *Coontail Lagoon* by Louis Cassels.

James B. Osbon

This biography has been written primarily to be read by the people of Aiken, South Carolina, who plan to read or have read the book *Sand River*. Because of that, it contains more local Aiken detail than a usual author biography would.

I was born in Aiken in the spring of 1938 at a time when the Great Depression was lessening and before serious war started in Europe or Asia. The Aiken County Hospital on Richland Avenue was the place, and I was brought home in a few days to a small bungalow on Columbia Drive, now known as Columbia Avenue. In 2000, our family donated this property to the city, and it is now known as Osbon Park.

My father, Geddings Osbon, was already thirty-seven years old and my mother, Bessie Wilcher Osbon, was twenty-nine when I arrived. They had been married since 1930 and were living in the house he built for her when they married. His own parents lived a quarter of a mile away on Hampton Avenue, near Bethany Cemetery. I had three brothers—Bobby, Julian, Tony—and a sister, Carolyn, while I was growing up, with me being wedged tightly between Bobby and Julian.

Geddings had been in business with his father, Nathaniel, and his brother, Arthur, on Laurens Street in downtown Aiken. Their business was Osbon Tire Company, located in the same spot where Wells Fargo Bank is located in 2013. Shortly after I was born, my father decided to split away from his relatives and opened a similar business on Broad Street in Augusta, which he called Osbon Auto Supply Company. The year was approximately 1940. For the rest of his life (forty-five more years) he continued to live in that same house in Aiken and drove to Augusta to his businesses six days a week.

I attended the Aiken County public schools, which meant Aiken Grammar School for grades 1-6 and Aiken High School for grades 7-12. I was twelve years old when the "bomb plant" entered our lives and therefore have an excellent memory of how it affected just about everything in our town for the rest of my childhood.

My athletic life took over a larger portion of my life than I ever anticipated when it began at age ten. By the time I graduated from Aiken High, I was playing football, basketball, baseball, track (for one year), and driving a school bus during my senior year. I was fortunate to secure a full scholarship to play Division 1 basketball at the College of William and Mary, in Williamsburg, Virginia, and graduated from there in 1960 with a BA in Economics. As a college basketball player, I discovered that I was incredibly mediocre.

Since I had joined ROTC when I enrolled at William and Mary, I owed the U.S. Army up to two years of my time after graduation. I was commissioned as an officer in the Infantry and spent most of my two years in Germany during 1961-1963. Interesting duties included assisting with the filming of *The Longest Day*, a movie about the Allied D-Day landing in France in 1944, and later I became the Officer in Charge of Checkpoint Charlie in Berlin in the winter of 1963. For the curious researcher, references to these experiences are available on the Internet.

After the army, I married Beatrice McKay, a fellow W&M student from Norfolk, and began a computer career with IBM in Richmond, Virginia. We liked Virginia and stayed with IBM there for seven years, followed by seven years as cofounder of The Computer Company, also of Richmond, and another seven years as the chief officer of information technology for Blue Cross of Virginia.

In 1975-76, I wrote a book in my spare time, a reference text called the *Silver Dollar Encyclopedia*. By 1979, I had revised it completely and reissued it as the second edition of the original book.

Those two projects were extremely important in my writing development, and both were self-published successfully before self-publishing ever existed as an industry.

While I was working on the second coin book in 1979, I made a promise to myself that I would write a book of fiction before I was all finished with writing. It took me until 2008 to keep that promise. In that year, I wrote a story called *Masterplan*. It is a fictional story about the premise of there being a general plan for this life, and it specifically involved a four-year-old little girl and her grandfather being able to communicate by transmitting thoughts to each other. In their story, their abilities to perform this kind of mental magic leaked out, and the army and federal government enticed them to help with the War on Terrorism.

The cozy nature of Aiken in the 1940s and 1950s turned out to be the perfect place for the Osbon family of four boys and a girl to develop into responsible citizens of the larger world. As young teenagers, the four boys played sports and raced in the Soap Box Derby in Augusta, where two of us won (Julian in 1952, me in 1953); and when the race went dormant for several years, Tony traveled to Asheville, North Carolina, to win. In the years 1953-1957, the city of Aiken had allowed us to block off Laurens Street between Edgefield and Hampton Avenues at 6:00 a.m. several mornings per week to race each other as a way to experiment with different wheels and bearings and other competitive techniques. Aiken's cooperation helped us to become winners in this sport.

I came back to the area from Virginia in 1990, when I became president of Osbon Medical Systems in Augusta. This company had been started in the mid-1980s by my father and brother Julian. The company was sold in 1997 and I retired.

Though I love Aiken and owe it a lot, even now I don't live there full-time but share my time also in Amelia Island, Florida. We own a condominium in the downtown area of Aiken and stay there as often as we can. With one son living in the Atlanta area and the other living in the Augusta area, we have plenty of other good reasons to have replanted some of our deepest roots here.

As a writer, I have never been afraid of criticism. I am posting my e-mail address here (ozbn@aol.com) because I want readers to feel free to give me feedback about this book. Let me know if it was good, bad, or mediocre. What vital information did I leave out? I don't believe that I will be rewriting it to make a second edition out in the future. But with digital self-publishing, you never know.

One of the primary reasons I wrote *Sand River* is this: Because of digital publishing of a book's content, the book can literally be available to the public *forever.* I hope that a few Aiken citizens in the twenty-second century and beyond might be curious enough to download a copy of this book to find out what transpired in Aiken with the coming of the bomb plant in 1950. It's described right here and will forever be available.

One final thought. Originally, I had planned to solicit information from other Aiken residents so that the story would be more representative of the entire population of the town. Then I realized a basic truth. Each person has enough personal accounts about growing up in Aiken that each individual could fill a book with what they experienced in living there. I did not seek much help once I realized that. I came from a part of the twentieth century, a part of the city, was not part of the Winter Resort community, and I did not ride a horse in Hitchcock Woods and attended public schools, etc., etc., etc. Do you get the idea? Everyone's book would be almost totally different. I hope I succeeded in hitting enough of the historical high spots to make you say, "I remember that. Yeah, he's right." And I hope you enjoyed it. Now get busy writing your own book about your life in Aiken. Publishing in the twenty-first century makes it easier than it has ever been.

ACKNOWLEDGMENTS

More than a few people go into the issuing a new book. Byrd Graphic Design of Arlington, Virginia, assisted with the twenty-four photographs in this book. Eddie Byrd knows his way around in the book publishing industry.

Several current and former residents of Aiken contributed important information to the author. These include Henderson Johnson, Evelyn Hall Knight, Fred Cavanaugh, Allen Riddick, Tommy Gibbs, Doug Rabold, Bea Osbon, Sondra Shanker Katzenstein, Virginia Cumbee Summerall, Mary Jo Epps, Gary Dexter and Philip Burckhalter.

The author took the photograph of Sand River used as part of the dust jacket art, as it was made possible through cooperation by the Hitchcock Woods Foundation. Valiant attempts were made to identify and give credit to the various owners of some of the other photographs used. Most were not successful because the majority have been in the public domain for so long that the name of the originator has been lost. Apologies are in order and thus given here. Exception: The logo of the City of Aiken is owned by the city and hereby acknowledged.

Google and Google Earth are priceless tools to the author of almost any book. Research is simplified, and "visiting" a location via Google Earth is almost as good as standing on the site personally.

Made in the USA
Lexington, KY
18 October 2013